Kensington books by Daryl Wood Gerber

The Fairy Garden Mystery series

A Sprinkling of Murder

A Glimmer of a Clue

A Hint of Mischief

A Flicker of a Doubt

A Twinkle of Trouble

A Twinkle *of* Trouble

Daryl Wood Gerber

Kensington Publishing Corp.
www.kensingtonbooks.com

To Hannah Dennison, a talented author and one of my dearest friends. You have been a cheerleader for my work and a valiant sounding block as I continue my journey. Thank you. I hope I have given you the same support in return.

Acknowledgments

*A rock pile ceases to be a rock pile the moment a single man
contemplates it, bearing within him the image of a cathedral.*
—Antoine de Saint-Exupery, *The Little Prince*

I have been blessed to have the support of so many people as I
pursue my creative journey. Without them, I would have stopped
writing years ago.

Thank you to my family and friends for all your encouragement.
Thank you to my talented author friends, Krista Davis and Hannah
Dennison, for your words of wisdom. Thank you to my PlotHatcher
pals: Janet (Ginger Bolton), Kaye George, Marilyn Levinson (Allison
Brook), Peg Cochran (Margaret Loudon), Janet Koch (Laura Alden),
and Krista Davis. You are a wonderful pool of talent and a terrific
wealth of ideas, jokes, stories, and fun! I adore you. Thanks to my
Delicious Mystery author pals, Roberta Isleib (Lucy Burdette) and
Krista Davis. I treasure your creative enthusiasm via social media.

Thank you to Facebook mystery groups for giving authors a
place to share their work. I love how willing so many of you are to
reading ARCs and posting reviews. We need fans like you. Thank
you to all the bloggers who enjoy reviewing cozies and sharing these
titles with your readers.

Thanks to those who have helped make this fifth book in the
Fairy Garden Mystery series come to fruition: my publisher Kensing-
ton Books, my editor Elizabeth Trout, my production editor Carly
Sommerstein, my agent Jill Marsal, and my cover artist Elsa Kerls.
Thanks to Madeira James for maintaining constant quality on my
website. Thanks to my virtual assistant Christina Higgins for your

clever ideas. And many thanks to my stalwart supporter Kimberley Greene. You are the best!

Last but not least, thank you librarians, teachers, bookstore owners, and readers for sharing the delicious world of a fairy garden designer in Carmel-by-the-Sea with your friends. I hope you enjoy the magical world I've created. May you encounter a fairy one or more times in your life.

CAST OF CHARACTERS
(listed alphabetically by first name)

Humans

Asher Lyle, owner Lyle's General Store
Bentley Bramble, topiary gardener
Brady Cash, owner of Hideaway Café
Courtney Kelly, owner of Open Your Imagination
Daphne Flores, owner of Flower Farm
Dylan Summers, detective, Carmel Police Department
Genevieve Bellerose, social media influencer
Glinda Gill, owner of Glitz
Hattie Hopewell, Happy Diggers Garden Club chair
Hedda Hopewell, loan officer
Holly Hopewell, Courtney's landlord and neighbor
Jeremy Batcheller, owner of Batcheller Galleries
Joss Timberlake, assistant at Open Your Imagination
Kipling "Kip" Kelly, Courtney's father, landscaper
Lissa Reade, aka "Miss Reade," librarian
Meaghan Brownie, half owner of Flair Gallery
Oliver Killian, owner of Garden Delights
Petunia Fujimoto, owner of Bowers of Flowers
Redcliff Reddick, police officer
Renee Rodriguez, owner of Seize the Clay
Scarlet Lyle, product researcher
Tamara Geoffries, therapist
Tish Waterman, owner of A Peaceful Solution Spa
Twyla Waterman, daughter of Tish
Wanda Brownie, art representative, Meaghan's mother
Yolanda "Yoly" Acebo, sister of Yvanna, and part-time employee
Yvanna Acebo, employee at Sweet Treats, weekend baker for teas
Zinnia Walker, a Happy Digger

Fairies and Pets

Callie, aka Calliope, intuitive fairy
Cedric Winterbottom, nurturer fairy
Eveleen, Fiona's sister, nurturer fairy
Fiona, righteous fairy
Merryweather Rose of Song, guardian fairy
Polka Dot, Jeremy Batcheller's Dalmatian
Pixie, Courtney's Ragdoll cat
Ulra, nurturer fairy
Zephyr, nurturer fairy

Chapter 1

The fairies, it is said
Drop maple leaves into the stream
To dye their waters red.
—Kikaku, "Fairies"

Exhale, Courtney! I was holding my breath the way I did whenever I got too stressed. My father always teased me if he caught me doing it. *Take it one task at a time, kitten,* he'd say. My unease wasn't because of the tea I was drinking in my backyard, and it certainly wasn't because of the lovely twittering of birds. I adored their merry song. No, it was due to the list I was composing of all the things I needed to address in the coming week: the Summer Blooms Festival, multiple fairy garden classes, and hosting the Saturday book club tea at the shop. Sometimes I overscheduled myself. You'd think by now I'd have learned not to. *Um, yeah. No.*

Suddenly, the base of the cypress tree started to glow and sparkle, and a shimmering fairy portal about six inches wide materialized. Seconds later, Fiona tiptoed through it.

"You're here!" I exclaimed, leaping from my chair. "You're alive. You're okay." Relief washed over me as I rushed to her. My bare feet and the hem of my pajamas were getting wet from the puddles left by the recent rain, but I didn't care. "I missed you!" I squealed and scooped her into my hands. I kissed her nose. "Are you all right?"

"Yes."

Her gossamer wings were intact. Her silver dress and slippers were as clean as a whistle. I'd met my teensy fairy friend over a year ago when I'd opened my fairy garden shop in downtown Carmel-by-the-Sea. I'd believed in fairies as a girl, but I'd lost the ability to see them until that wonderful, fateful day.

"Did your mother chastise you?" I turned her in my hands, searching for what, I wasn't sure. I didn't think her mother, the queen fairy, would harm her eldest daughter. "Your hair is a different color. It's silver."

"I asked for a favor. I was getting tired of the blue. It goes nicely with my outfit, don't you think?" She grabbed the seams of her skirt and curtsied.

"It's lovely. Your wings look bigger. Have they grown?"

"Not in a month." She tittered and billowed them out.

A month. She'd been gone a whole month. Wow, time had flown! *Not.* Since she'd passed through the fairy portal in mid-May, I'd kept my nose to the grindstone, doing my best not to think about how I'd feel if she never returned from the fairy realm. To distract myself—as if the shop didn't keep me busy enough—I'd invested in a garden plot, repainted my bedroom, and added more private classes to my weekly roster of fairy garden instruction.

"How I missed the smell of the ocean!" Fiona spiraled into the air, did a pirouette, and alit on my shoulder. "Can we go for a walk on the beach?"

"Of course." It was Wednesday, but I didn't have to be at Open Your Imagination as early as usual because Joss, my stalwart assistant, said she had a surprise for me and wanted to open the store on her own.

My Ragdoll cat, Pixie, pushed through her cat door and scampered to us. She rose on her hind legs and meowed to Fiona. Like me, she'd missed her friend dearly. She'd been moping. At home. At work. Every time I tried to soothe her, she would turn heel and bat me with her tail.

Fiona flitted to Pixie's head and did a toe-heel-kick-step on the flame markings on the cat's forehead. Pixie mewled merrily and swatted at Fiona, but the little fairy was swift and sailed to a branch of the cypress. From that viewpoint, she said, "The garden looks pretty."

"Thanks." After moving in, I'd landscaped it to my liking, adding wisteria, impatiens, and herbs that grew naturally beneath the towering cypress trees. Fairy gardens stood in the four corners of the yard. I'd set a copper fountain featuring a fairy pouring water into a shell at the center near the wicker table where I was having my coffee.

"You've planted roses," she said.

"I did." Along the paths leading to each of the fairy gardens, I'd planted white floribundas. They boasted peony-shaped flowers with bright, glossy foliage and emitted a fruity aroma with a hint of champagne. "I found them at Flower Farm. The owner, Daphne Flores, sold me fully grown plants, but she's renting me a quarter-acre of the farm so I can nurture them from cuttings and transplant them, too."

There were lots of farms and ranches in Carmel-by-the-Sea, as well as wildlife trails and parks. Located on the coast of California about two hours south of San Francisco, the town was blessed with a moderate climate and populated with some of the most artistic and eco-friendly people in the world. Nearly everyone I knew loved to tinker in their gardens.

"In fact, I'm thinking of cultivating other plants on the quarter-acre, plants that we use in the fairy gardens," I said. "Hattie suggested I stop outsourcing it and do it myself." Hattie Hopewell was president of the Happy Diggers Garden Club. Every member of the club was a regular customer at Open Your Imagination. "Good idea, don't you think?"

"When will you find time to do everything?"

"You know me. I thrive when tending a garden. Besides, sleep is highly overrated."

Fiona giggled. "Well, gardening suits you. Your cheeks are rosy. You look very pretty."

"*Tà,*" I said, using her native word for thanks.

Fiona fluttered to my cheek and kissed it. "Are you and Brady still, um, happy?"

"Yes. Very."

Brady, the owner of the Hideaway Café, was now officially my boyfriend. We had a standing date on Mondays—our days off—and we got together occasionally during the week. He and I met in high school, and when we recently became reacquainted, it felt right to spend more time together. He *got* me like nobody ever had. Plus, he didn't make fun of my ability to see fairies.

Fiona said, "Has he, you know, seen her yet?"

"Her?"

"The fairy at the café."

Last month, we caught sight of a fairy in the vines on the café's patio. I didn't know her name; neither did Fiona. She was very shy.

"Not yet."

I retreated inside, threw on a pair of shorts, an I LOVE CARMEL T-shirt, and sandals, and with Fiona riding on my shoulder, strolled down Ocean Avenue to Carmel Beach, a spectacular arc of pale sand that stretched for close to a mile in length. The famous Pebble Beach Golf Links bordered the northern arc of the bay. Pixie had wanted to come along, so I'd slipped her into a cat carry pack—not her favorite thing—but I didn't want her squirming in my arms on the walk. She wasn't a full-fledged outdoor cat.

The ocean, like any other day, was lapping the sand with a steady *whoosh*. There were joggers and walkers, as well as people sitting on beach towels, drinking in the incredible view. A few brave souls in wet suits—even in summer, the water could be chilly—waited on surfboards for a wave. I always hoped to glimpse an otter at play, but this wasn't their spot. There were a number of locations nearby to see them, the best being Point Lobos State Preserve.

I kicked off my sandals, slung the straps over one finger, and traipsed barefoot through the sand. "Tell me what going back to the fairy realm was like," I said to my righteous fairy.

"It was lovely and bittersweet."

The day I met Fiona, I was surprised to learn that there were classifications of fairies. Four, to be exact—intuitive, guardian, nurturer, and righteous. Last month, I was even more shocked to learn that there was only one queen fairy and one righteous fairy. When the timing was appropriate, Fiona would become the queen fairy.

"Did you see your sisters?" I asked.

"Yes. We played and danced and rode fairy horses—"

"Hold on. You can fly fairy horses on your own in the realm?"

"Uh-huh, but not here. It's much too dangerous." She zipped off my shoulder and hovered in front of me.

"Was it all fun and games?"

She wrinkled her pert nose. "Of course not. The very first day, I had to sit through three lectures, a dinner of honey and mallow—"

"That wasn't punishment. Those are your favorite foods."

"Not when you have to eat while memorizing two dozen new fairy rules. I got a tummy ache."

"Two dozen?" I gawked. I knew a few of the rules. A righteous fairy had to help humans solve problems. A righteous fairy couldn't purposefully insert herself into harm's way. All fairies were not to be photographed, though they could pose for a painting.

"Rule number one," she said, "never lie."

"Yes, I know that one."

"Rule number six, always honor your promise. Number fourteen, keep an open mind. Number fifteen, let your emotions guide you but not dominate you."

I snuffled. "You know all these. They're your stock-in-trade."

"Yes, but we must be able to recite them backward and forward with the rule number." She crossed her arms and tapped the air with one foot. "It's exhausting."

"Well, you're back, so you must have succeeded."

"And one more thing. I have to mentor another fairy."

"You? Have to be a mentor?" Merryweather Rose of Song—who, it turned out, was Fiona's aunt—was her mentor. A guardian fairy with a lovely spirit, she could be a taskmaster. It was because of Fiona's lessons with Merryweather that Fiona had been allowed to return to the kingdom. Fiona's mother had booted her out because she had been acting like an imp and needed to learn to temper her mischievous ways. "Who's the lucky fairy? Do I know her?"

"She's not in the human world yet. Mother is sending her soon."

"Do you know her?"

"She's my younger sister, Eveleen."

A single seagull soared toward us and cawed as if approving of Fiona's new, enhanced role. Seconds later, it glided to the ocean to join the rest of its pals. Fiona dashed after the bird but quickly made a U-turn when a woman cried my name.

I spun around and spied, of all people, Hattie Hopewell, the flamboyant sixty-something leader of the Happy Diggers, striding toward me. An elegant man Hattie's age was trailing her.

"Courtney, what luck to run into you," Hattie said as she drew near.

"I was just thinking about you."

"Positive thoughts, I hope." She fluffed her ruby-red hair, a tone she changed every couple of weeks.

"Of course."

"I thought you'd be at the shop by now." Hattie often dressed like she was ready to work in the garden, today's outfit cargo shorts, colorful tee, and sandals. Her companion was clad in an Armani suit, silk tie, and expensive loafers. Clearly, he hadn't planned on taking a walk on the beach. "Why aren't you there?" Hattie asked. "Are you taking a day off?"

"A day off other than Monday?" Fiona joked. "Not on a bet."

Neither Hattie nor her companion reacted to my fairy's jesting. Occasionally, Hattie sensed Fiona's presence, but she had yet to see her.

"Joss is planning some sort of surprise," I said.

"Is it your birthday?"

"Nope."

Hattie reached out to Pixie and scrubbed her under the chin. "Yes, you're so pretty. So very pretty." Pixie chugged her thanks. Hattie adored animals. She owned a pair of brindled Scotties. Fiona alit on Hattie's shoulder and blew her a kiss. Hattie didn't react.

The man cleared his throat while smoothing his neatly shaven russet beard and mustache with his thumb and forefinger.

"Forgive my rudeness," Hattie sputtered. "Courtney, meet Oliver Killian. Oliver is the owner of Garden Delights. You know the place, don't you, dear? Not far from the precinct. Next door to Lagoon Grill and across the street from Lyle's General Store."

"Between Fourth and Fifth," I said.

"Correct."

I'd visited the police precinct more times than I cared to and had passed by all of the sites she mentioned. Brady and I had dined at Lagoon Grill, and I had stopped in to the general store. I'd never ventured into Garden Delights, but I'd meant to. "Have you always been in the flower business?"

"Yes." Oliver's intense blue eyes sparkled with pleasure. "Ever since my childhood, when I played in my grandparents' garden, I've been captivated by nature and its beauty."

"What a lovely memory," I said.

"Oliver stocks the finest seasonal garden flowers," Hattie said. "And he boasts one of the best selections of pottery in the area."

"A friend of mine used to be part owner," I said. "Genevieve Bellerose." Thanks to my weekly blog about fairy gardens, as well as the local gardeners' web forum I'd created on my website—chat rooms were passé, but forums were a great place for people with like minds to converse—I'd met a number of creative women. Genevieve had known one of the others before I came into the picture, but now we'd all become friends and regularly met in person or on the forum to catch up.

"Genevieve." Oliver's voice had an edge to it. A sharp edge.

"She's enjoying being an influencer," I said.

Oliver snorted. "Is that what she claims to be?"

"She makes good money at it."

Hattie shook her head. "How does one do that?"

"She displays advertising on her blog and podcast," I explained, "and offers affiliate marketing click-throughs. Plus, she writes sponsored posts. For example, she might do a series of posts on Instagram or send out dedicated notices on other social media sites. You should see her live chats and TikTok posts. She's really great on camera. A natural."

"A natural at taking potshots, you mean," Oliver said. "A natural for bad-mouthing products. And places. And people."

"Oliver," Hattie chided.

"I'm not kidding. When was the last time she said something nice about anyone?"

I followed Genevieve, but I didn't read all of her updates. Many I'd seen had been positive. She'd raved about Open Your Imagination. Had she vilified others? *An influencer influences,* she often joked.

"She shouldn't have quit the business," Oliver scoffed. "We had a good thing going until . . ." He didn't finish.

Until what? I hadn't known Genevieve when she'd been a partner in Garden Delights.

Hattie said, "Oliver, she sold you her half of the business for more than a fair price. I'd think you'd be happy about that."

Fiona floated in front of Oliver's face, tilting her head left and right. "He's not happy. He's miserable."

Hattie leaned toward me. "His wife wasn't pleased when Genevieve split, resulting in Oliver having to do all the heavy lifting, aka, forcing him to become a workaholic, so she left him."

"I can hear you," Oliver said.

"I'm sorry," I said.

"I'm not!" he snapped.

"That's the ticket, my friend." Hattie trilled out a hearty laugh. A former lounge singer, she enjoyed making everything sound musical. "We buck up, or we get bowled over."

Bitterness flickered in Oliver's eyes.

"Okay, enough chitchat," Hattie said. "I hailed you, Courtney, because you're taking part in the Summer Blooms Festival, and Oliver—"

"Oliver Killian!" I blurted like an idiot. "You're in charge of the festival."

"The same." He smiled, one of his better features.

I'd attended the last few festivals and had thoroughly enjoyed them. For three days, the town would close four blocks of Junipero Street, from 10th Avenue to Ocean Avenue. There would be vendors selling plants and flowers, live music, and delicious food. I couldn't wait to enjoy a blooming onion from the Awesome Blossom food truck.

"*Ooh,*" I crooned. "Lucky you."

"Lucky? Ha!" Oliver chortled. "I was hornswoggled. The mayor tagged me and said, 'You're it.'"

Hattie batted his arm. "Oliver, you know you love it. You've helmed it every year for the past few years. The town is waiting with bated breath to drink in your expertise. They'll be hanging on your every word. Oliver loves to be the center of attention, Courtney."

Oliver blew a raspberry.

"Anyway"—Hattie continued petting Pixie, who was relishing the attention—"I thought you'd like to meet Oliver, seeing as your shop is taking part."

Talk about being hornswoggled! Joss had convinced me to rent a booth, believing a presence at the event would help us win over new customers. I wasn't positive it would be worth the expense and headache, but she assured me it would. A former accountant in Silicon Valley, Joss was a whiz with numbers.

"Well, it's a pleasure to finally meet you, Oliver." I extended a hand.

When we shook, a seagull divebombed us and shrieked like a banshee.

Chapter 2

Look in the caves at the edge of the sea
If you seek the fairies of spray,
They thrive in the dampness of sea and tide,
With conch for breakfast and lobsters to ride.
—Patricia Hubbell, "Sea Fairies"

As I entered Open Your Imagination a short while later, I was still fretting over the interaction with Oliver Killian. Why had the seagull shrieked? Was it an omen? Or did it squawk because it believed that participating in the festival was a horrible idea? Not *horrible*, horrible, but exhausting for me and Joss and possibly not worth the effort. Was Fiona right? Was I overextending myself? The festival would take place Friday to Sunday, with a setup tomorrow afternoon. I would man the booth Friday and Sunday, and Joss would take Saturday so I could oversee the book club tea at the shop. In honor of the Summer Blooms Festival, the group was reading the first Flower Shop Mystery, *Mum's the Word*. Joss said she was on top of getting all our supplies delivered to the site, but was she? I was up to my ears with our regular orders, because the middle of June was the beginning of our busiest season.

"Good morning, Courtney and Pixie!" Joss Timberlake chimed

as I closed the lower half of the Dutch door. She was standing at the far end of the main showroom, looking cheery in a bright yellow T-shirt over green capris. She spread her arms wide, and the corners of her mouth turned up in the signature impish smile that under-scored her elfin appearance. "Ta-da!"

I plonked Pixie on the floor and patted her rump and, as she raced to the patio, I viewed the shop with fresh eyes. Nothing looked different. There were no balloons or cakes or, well, anything. Joss hadn't anticipated Fiona's return and planned a party to celebrate. The white display tables and shelving were still white, and the accent colors blue and slate gray, in keeping with the Cape Cod feel of the Cypress and Ivy Courtyard where our shop was located. I peeked through the plate glass windows and assessed the patio. The fountain was burbling. Sunshine was streaming through the tempered-glass, pyramid-shaped roof. The leaves of the ficus trees were clean and shiny. The wrought-iron tables were neatly arranged.

"Okay, you've stumped me," I said as I drifted toward her. "What did you do?"

"Clip-clop, clip-clop."

"Huh?"

"Look down."

I stared at my feet, not noticing anything different until it dawned on me that my footsteps weren't making a peep. Joss had laid out runners. They reflected the shop's color scheme and had a pattern that reminded me of ocean spray.

"*Ooh,* I like them!"

"The hardwood floor was really taking a beating with all the foot traffic," she said. "Rather than buff and polish and hope for the best, I thought carpets might be a good addition." She fisted her hands on her hips. "They're easily cleaned, the kinds we can throw in the wash."

"Brilliant! Thank you." I slung an arm around her shoulders. I wasn't tall, barely five-feet-five inches, but she was teensy next to me.

"Don't worry about the cost," she said, wriggling free. "Buddy knew a guy who knew a guy."

Buddy was her boyfriend of one month. I'd met him at a wine tasting last week and really liked him. He was a vintner of a small vineyard specializing in chardonnay, a favorite grape for the Central Coast. He was close to sixty, and Joss was a smidge over fifty. They looked good together. Happy.

"Well, please thank Buddy for me. And now, I have a surprise for you." Fiona had asked to remain outside so she could make a grand entrance. I'd agreed. I leaned out the Dutch door and said, "Okay."

She whizzed into view.

Joss squealed with delight. "It's you! You're back!" She raced to Fiona and opened her palm. Fiona settled on it and allowed Joss to shower her with kisses. "Have you been reading? What have you been up to? You have to tell me everything."

For years, Joss had wanted to see a fairy, but she hadn't been able to . . . until Fiona. Now, she was tutoring Fiona in literature. The two had read the complete works of Shakespeare and all of the Sherlock Holmes stories. They'd also immersed themselves in poetry and favorite children's books and had recently begun reading Agatha Christie's Hercule Poirot stories. On my "ways to improve myself" list, I'd made a vow to try to catch up to them. I wasn't sure I could slog through Shakespeare, but I'd read Agatha Christie in high school and would enjoy revisiting her stories.

Joss carried Fiona to the patio, and they settled near the fountain to chat while I went to my office to deposit my purse and shed the summer sweater I'd thrown on.

The rest of the morning went swimmingly, opening as we usually did with a steady stream of customers. At eleven, I prepped for the private fairy garden lesson I was going to give Zinnia Walker. A Happy Digger and wealthy businesswoman, Zinnia was the person who'd bid on and won a shopping spree and fairy garden lesson at the Theater Foundation Tea last month.

When Zinnia arrived at noon, she wheeled in a huge bird cage. Trim, with a silver pixie-cut, she was dwarfed by the cage. Quickly, she explained that she hoped to transform the cage into a fairy garden. Her beloved macaw, Blue, had gone to greener pastures, and she wanted to remember him with a tribute, because she'd had him since she'd graduated college, nearly forty-five years ago.

"Sure thing," I said, gulping. To be honest, I'd never turned something that large and bulky into a fairy garden, so it was going to be a challenge, but I assured her I was up to the task.

We chatted as Zinnia chose items for her garden, the first being a blue bird that was perched on a fence post, prepared to give flying lessons. Next, she selected a polymer mature-in-age fairy figurine to represent herself, after which she decided on a few miniature gardening tools. There were many choices: long and short shovels, trowels, hoes, and rakes. She wanted her older fairy to be able to prettify the area around the fence post. The story, she revealed, was going to be about the bird training the earthbound fairy how to fly once more, but the earthbound fairy was intent on teaching the bird about nature. She finished by selecting a half dozen plants and a handful of two-inch multicolored rocks to create a weir.

Zinnia assembled her items on the learning-the-craft table at the far end of the patio, and for the next half hour, she and I filled the base of the bird cage with soil, positioned the plants in place, and arranged the rocks. Fiona coasted around the Happy Digger, lighting on one shoulder and then the other. At one point, she dusted her with a lilac potion, helpful to someone who needed healing, except Zinnia appeared to be in the peak of health. Perhaps Fiona sensed that Zinnia, given the loss of her bird, needed to heal a broken heart.

As Zinnia used the miniature shovel to remove pockets of air around the plants, she began to croon the popular sixties song, "Grazing in the Grass," by The Friends of Distinction. "'Can you dig it? I can dig it, baby.'" Laughter burbled out of her. "Oh, that Hattie. Whenever a song comes into her head, she sings it, and now she's got me doing it. I'm *no* singer." She laid down the shovel. "Do you listen to podcasts, Courtney? I do. I've been listening to loads of them lately. You know what a podcast is, don't you?"

I did. I rarely had time to indulge, but there were a few I followed, most often on my morning runs.

"I'm wild about Genevieve Bellerose's podcast, *Anything Is Poddable*. Isn't that a clever name? She talks about food and restaurants and gardening and do-it-yourself projects, and well, you name it, she's an authority."

I bit back a smile. In truth, Genevieve considered herself knowledgeable on any topic under the sun. She'd once said to me that she was the Goddess of Taste. Food was her current target, but she'd also *podded*—was that a word?—complimentary things about the best bed-and-breakfasts in the area, the tastiest wines, the fun shopping meccas, and more.

"I'm going to try out every restaurant she mentions," Zinnia confided. In addition to being an astute businesswoman, she had been born into one of the richest Carmel families, so she had money to burn and then some.

When Zinnia left with her beautified cage, she said she felt lighter in spirit than she had in days. I thanked my sweet fairy for assisting and went to the table behind the sales counter that we kept stocked with beverages for customers. I poured myself a glass of water and drank half.

Joss joined me. "Don't forget your tea party today."

"Oops. I almost did." I'd offered to host a tea today for my online forum friends.

"Who's coming?"

"Daphne, Petunia, Genevieve, and Scarlet."

"I like Daphne. She has a gentle way about her."

"I like them all," I said, grinning. They each brought something different to the table. Daphne understood soil and fertilizer and was kindness personified. Petunia was an expert flower arranger who thrived on making the world a prettier place. Genevieve was business savvy and had a wicked sense of humor, but I doubt she used her humor in her podcasting endeavors. Scarlet—she and Genevieve were the two who'd known each other before I created the larger group—had an eye for design, and though she could be quite opinionated, I appreciated her honesty. I thought for our tea, seeing as we were moving into the summer months, we could all share pointers on how to improve our gardens. I wanted to pick Daphne's brain about roses. My father, a renowned landscaper in Carmel and a master gardener, could give me tips, but roses were Daphne's passion.

I glanced at my watch. "Yipes! Thirty minutes. I'd better eat something before they get here." My stomach grumbled like a freight train in response. After the encounter with Harriet and Oliver and the startling squawk of the seagull, I hadn't felt like eating breakfast. "I don't want to get a sugar rush from chocolate scones." We kept some in the freezer in the mini kitchen, at the ready for an impromptu tea.

I eyed a pair of customers browsing the main showroom. One was showing her friend a teacup fairy garden I'd created and put up for sale. The garden was fitted into a lovely Royal Vale teacup with a pink rose pattern and featured a pink princess dreaming of meeting her prince. I didn't buy into those kinds of fantasies—chancing upon the right person was fine, but making a relationship last required hard work. However, many of our customers enjoyed fairy tales.

Joss followed my gaze. "Don't worry. I'll tend to those ladies. When Yoly gets here, she'll handle the two on the patio."

"I'm here!" Yolanda Acebo—she preferred Yoly—skipped into the shop, letting the Dutch door swing shut behind her. She was working part-time for me on Wednesday afternoons and on Saturdays when we served tea on the patio. Otherwise, she helped out at Sweet Treats bakery, one of the other shops in the Cypress and Ivy Courtyard. "Nice runners," she said, instantly noticing the change to the décor.

"Thanks." Joss preened. "Courtney has invited friends to tea."

"Cool," Yoly said. She was close to my age, but that was where the similarities ended. She had long dark hair and caramel brown eyes. I leaned toward my Irish heritage, with green eyes and pale skin, and I kept my blond hair cropped short.

"Would you mind handling the customers on the patio?" Joss asked.

"Sure thing." Young and flirty, Yoly typically wore *au courant* fashions. Today was no exception. She'd donned a deep purple crossover dress that was awash with white flowers. She stowed her purse on a shelf beneath the register and trotted outside.

"Courtney, go do your thing," Joss said to me.

I slipped into the office, opened the mini refrigerator, removed a peach Greek yogurt, and sat at the chalked chestnut desk. As I was spooning a bite of the creamy goodness into my mouth, Pixie slinked into the room and nestled on her pillow at the base of the oak hat tree.

Fiona trailed her and perched on the edge of the Zen garden at the upper corner of my desk. She dipped her feet into the sand and gently kicked back and forth. Sprinkles of grit wafted into the air and fell down. "Is everything okay?"

"You bet." I polished off my yogurt, tossed the cup into the garbage, went to the kitchen, thawed a few scones, and arranged the tea cart using Royal Albert Old Country Rose-patterned plates and matching teacups. I filled a teapot with steaming hot water and placed it alongside the cream, sugar, tea bag caddy, and utensils, and wheeled the cart toward the main showroom. Pixie scampered ahead of me. Fiona winged beside me.

"Earlier, you seemed worried," she said. "After you met that man on the beach. Tell me why."

On the way home, I didn't let on that I'd gotten an eerie feeling. I hadn't wanted to alarm her. "It's nothing."

"Talk to me."

Joss was chatting up the customers. No one was looking in our direction.

I whispered, "I don't think I can trust him."

Pixie meowed, as if in agreement.

"Why?" Fiona asked.

"It's an impression." I patted my chest. "A vibe in here."

I pushed the cart through the French doors and down the ramp to the patio. I set up tea on the table beyond the fountain, closest to the ficus trees. We'd have the most privacy there. Yoly was by the green verdigris racks, laughing hysterically with a woman who was shaking a troll figurine. Pixie and Fiona hurried to them to find out what was up.

In olden days, trolls, which were prevalent in Norse mythology, were often thought of as ugly and evil. They were huge beings with large eyes, and they were rarely friendly. But Fiona changed my mind about them. She said in the fairy realm, they were rascally and comical. They liked to scare fairies because they loved to hear a fairy shriek, but they would never harm them. I'd stocked a number of troll figurines for customers who wanted to add more playfulness to their gardens.

The woman shook the troll figurine a second time. Yoly yelped. To play along, Fiona squealed at the top of her lungs. Neither Yoly nor the customer reacted.

"Courtney!" Genevieve Bellerose strolled down the ramp to the patio. "This is so lovely of you to do." Wholesome and in her forties, she had waist-length curly red hair. Her cheeks were the color of blush pink roses, and her celadon green eyes would make a cat jealous. She looked like she'd come from tending her garden, dressed in a forest green gardener's apron thrown over a neon green T-shirt and slightly dusty chinos. Her sole nod to high-end fashion was the black Michael Kors handbag she sported with its signature *MK* charm. "I promise I'm going to make a fairy garden soon. That's why you're luring us here, isn't it? To indoctrinate us?" She clasped me in a hug and air-kissed my cheek.

"I hardly indoctrinate anyone," I said. "Did our tea interrupt a gardening project?" I gestured to her outfit.

"I was doing a live chat, showing my viewers how to deadhead marigolds, and I lost track of time." She pulled a pair of shears from her pocket and *snip-snipped* the air.

"I hate deadheading," Scarlet Lyle said, joining us.

"If you don't, girlfriend, your garden won't look neat and trim," Genevieve countered, tucking the shears back into the apron and tossing her purse on a chair. She pecked Scarlet's cheek.

Scarlet was the most sophisticated of our group, with her ten-drilled updo, full lips that she always painted red, and her pouty gaze. I'd bet she'd been a model at one time. I could see her posing at the end of a runway, head cocked to one side, commanding the audience to take her seriously. Her white, sleeveless sheath highlighted her curvy frame. "I've scaled back on my garden. I'm too busy with my product-comparing business." She blogged like I did, but she also tested goods for companies for user-friendliness and chatted up the ones she liked to her twenty thousand-plus followers. I wished I had that many fans.

"How *do* you make money doing that?" Genevieve asked.

"The same way you make money being an *influencer*," Scarlet said, dragging out the word. The corners of her mouth curled up, but the resulting expression was a snarl.

"Don't," Genevieve said. "Just don't."

"Don't what?" Scarlet asked, widening her eyes, her voice rising in singsong fashion.

"Make fun of what I do."

"Oh, lighten up! You're the one who's always telling me you have a fine-tuned sense of humor."

Genevieve huffed.

"I hear you're dissing food now." Scarlet raised a dubious eyebrow. "Where do you get the nerve?"

"I'll have you know that I'm gifted in the kitchen," Genevieve said. "And where do you get your expertise, huh? You're no more a product guru than I am."

"Uh-oh." Fiona whooshed to me. "Stop them. Don't let them fight."

I fanned the air to calm her. "Ladies, ladies, enough verbal sparring." They both had strong personalities and enjoyed bantering. "I invited you today because I wanted to see some friendly faces, not to act as referee."

"I'm friendly," Daphne Flores chirped, nearly sliding down the ramp as she hustled to us. With her adorable wedge-cut hair and dressed in a skort, snug polo shirt and high-top tennis shoes, she reminded me of the famous ice skater, Dorothy Hamill. Early thirties, like me, she exuded youth and a positive spirit.

"I'm friendly, too," Petunia Fujimoto, the oldest of the group, said, following hot on Daphne's heels. She had an easy smile and downturned eyes that crinkled with good humor. Round, tortoise-shell eyeglasses bounced on the chain hanging around her neck. She owned Bowers of Flowers, the shop that was now our go-to supplier for flower arrangements whenever we threw a fairy garden party.

"I'd like to talk about gardens and such," I said. "Sit. Let's dish the dirt."

Genevieve chuckled. "*Dish the dirt*. You got that from my podcast. Love it."

"Genny," Scarlet snapped, shortening Genevieve's name, "you did not coin the phrase *dish the dirt*. Give it a rest."

Scarlet hugged Daphne and Petunia and sat down. The others took seats, as well. Pixie bounded into Daphne's lap, who seemed content to hold her, calling her *sweet kitty*.

"Um, Courtney," Petunia said sheepishly, while taming flyaway hairs. She'd recently shaped her silver hair into a cute pageboy cut with thick bangs. "Will there be any fairy sightings today?"

"Count on it." I gazed at Fiona, who was, at that very moment, blowing into Petunia's right ear.

When Petunia didn't sense the activity, Fiona soared high above and did a somersault.

"By the way, Courtney, my fairy garden is thriving." Scarlet had crafted a fairy garden with succulents. It was a reflection of her and her business, featuring a fairy who was studying an assortment of miniature books. An eclectic array of garden utensils, pots, and other odds and ends lay at her feet.

"I'm going to make one," Daphne said. "I've been saving up. Can you help me select some things today before I leave, Courtney?"

"I sure can."

"Will you make one for me, Courtney?" Petunia asked, waving her pocketbook. "I brought cash."

"It's more fun if you do it yourself," I said.

"Yes, but it's for my twin sister's birthday. I don't want to mess it up. Peony is very, um, discerning. She's a black-and-white, dollars-and-cents kind of person."

"You mean picky," Genevieve chimed.

That made everyone laugh.

"Are all the women in your family named after a flower?" I asked Petunia as I poured hot water into the four teacups.

"There's only me and my sister."

"Did she go into the flower business, too?"

"No. She does the books for a local winery." Petunia faked a yawn. "Big bore. But free wine."

More laughter ensued.

"Say, Genevieve," I said, changing the subject, "were your ears burning earlier?"

"Why would they have been?" She brushed her curls over her shoulders.

"Because I ran into Oliver Killian on my morning walk."

Genevieve grunted. "What did he blame me for this time?"

"He didn't. Not really. We were talking about Garden Delights—"

"The shop he forced me to sell?"

"That's not how he told it."

"His wife made it impossible for me to stick around, carping on me for no reason, acting like he and I were involved. Can you imagine? Me? With that blowhard?" Genevieve pursed her lips and blew.

"Petunia, is Garden Delights your competitor?" I lowered a tea bag into my cup to steep. The others brewed their teas, as well.

"Nope. Oliver is in a class unto himself," Petunia said diplomatically, meaning she didn't like him any more than Genevieve did. She lifted her teacup, pinky out, and took a sip. "If I'm truthful, his floral designs are over the top. I find them exotically bulky. They're not to everyone's liking."

"My husband knows Oliver pretty well," Scarlet offered, "which makes sense, since we're business neighbors."

Her husband owned Lyle's General Store, which carried furniture, tools, and more, as the store's slogan suggested, to make *intentional living easier.* My father had done the landscaping around the store, using a number of ornamental grasses that softened the otherwise boxy lines of the store's frame. The front door planting of fountain grass, coleus, black-eyed Susans, and trailing petunias, when in season, was particularly eye-catching.

"Did I hear there was a retail space opening up in that area?" Petunia asked nonchalantly.

"Why?" Scarlet eagle-eyed her. "Are you thinking of moving your business?"

"My lease is up. I might need a new venue. There's a lot of foot traffic up that way."

"I'll see," Scarlet said.

"*Ahem* . . . Oliver." Genevieve wiggled a hand, eager to return to the previous topic.

"Yes, Oliver," Scarlet said. "I believe he outfitted his entire home with things he purchased from our shop."

"Outfitted his bachelor pad, you mean," Genevieve said.

"Hey," I cut in, changing the subject, "will you all be coming to the festival this weekend? I'll have a booth there."

"Is Oliver running it?" Genevieve asked.

"Yes."

"Ergo, it'll be a flop." She selected a scone and cut it in half.

"C'mon," Scarlet said. "That's not fair. He's helmed it for the past few years, and it's been a success."

Petunia said, "I'll be hosting a booth, Courtney. Maybe we'll be next to each other. Has the official site map been posted yet?"

I said, "I got one in my packet." It contained a map, hours of operation, setup information, and more. "Haven't you received yours? We'll be in Section A, Booth Twelve."

Petunia donned her glasses and pulled a manila envelope from her huge tote. She rummaged through it and said, *"Aha.* Here's my assignment. I'll be in Section E, close to the other end of the festival. Oh, well."

There would be six sections to the festival, each abutting the next so attendees wouldn't get confused about navigating the event.

"I'm in Section E, too," Scarlet said.

"Why do you have a booth?" Genevieve asked.

"Because I want to show off products I've approved."

"Well, harrumph." Daphne sniffed. "No one asked me to participate. Why not? Because I'm a lowly, know-nothing gardener?"

"Ha!" I laughed. "You're hardly know-nothing. You know *everything* about gardening. If my father was twenty years younger and available, you'd be his ideal mate."

"As if!" Daphne said.

My father was currently dating the mother of my best friend. My mother passed away when I was ten, and it broke my father's heart. It had taken him twenty years to put himself out there again.

"If it's any consolation, Daphne," Genevieve said, "Oliver didn't approach me about having a booth, either. Apparently, he thought a product tester was more important than an influencer. Well, guess what? He'll find out how wrong he was. Think of all the foot traffic I could have driven his way with a few positive posts. *Ooh."* Her eyes lit up with mischievousness. "What do you think might happen if I post a few negative ones?" She let loose with a *bwa-ha-ha* laugh.

Fiona let out a high-pitched screech.

Chapter 3

The fairies hold a fair, they say,
Beyond the hills when skies are grey
And daylight things are laid away.
—Florence Harrison, "The Faerie Fair"

Fretfully, Fiona sped to the far end of the patio by the learning-the-craft corner. I could see her wings trembling. She couldn't possibly be upset by what Genevieve had said in jest, could she? On the other hand, fairies didn't have the same sense of humor as humans. They could be spirited, but they took many things seriously.

I excused myself from my friends and drew near. "What's wrong?"

"Whatever do you mean?" Fiona skipped along the table's edge, arms spread as if to balance herself. She pirouetted and stared at me.

"You *eek*ed back there." I pointed at her to spill the beans.

She worked her tongue inside her teensy mouth as she shim-mied away tension. "There's malice in your friend's heart, and it worries me."

"Who? Genevieve? She was joking." I'd recognized her playful-ness the first time I'd visited her website. It was filled with witty memes. My favorite meme consisted of black words on a white background: *I've got PMS, OCD, and ADD. I want to cry and look pretty while I kill everyone, but I can't focus on that right now. I'm cleaning.* That about summed up how every woman I knew felt at one time or another, myself included.

"She wasn't being flippant," Fiona said. "I sensed hatred."

I wagged a finger. "Uh-uh. Stop. You are not allowed to *sense* anything."

"Yes, I can. I may intuit emotions now that I've been to the realm and back. I'm not allowed to read minds, and I can't insert thoughts into peoples' heads, but I can *feel* things and prepare myself for trouble ahead." She flicked her fingers. "What's really frustrating is that I can't know why she is acting this way."

"Maybe it hurt her when Oliver drummed her out of the flower business." On one occasion, when Genevieve and I met for coffee alone, she confided that she had truly enjoyed owning Garden Delights. She'd loved making customers smile. I asked why she hadn't looked for a job with Petunia or Daphne, but she fanned the air. By then, she'd already aimed her sights on being an entrepreneur and, ultimately, an influencer.

Fiona met me eye to eye. "Should I dowse her with a forgiveness potion?"

"That's a great idea."

I rejoined my friends, and for the next half hour, we chatted about what plants were thriving in Carmel in the current climate. When Genevieve and Scarlet had to leave, I guided Petunia and Daphne to the fairy figurines and handed them baskets for their selections. Pixie, unhappy with losing her human lap, dashed after Fiona, ready for a game of tag.

"To make a fairy garden, you want to consider what story you'll be telling," I said to my friends. "When planning a story, I always start by positioning two figurines facing each other. They don't have to be fairies. They can be critters, like these." I plucked a little white kitten in a floral tutu from the shelf and wiggled it in front of them.

Daphne snatched it from me. "Mine! It looks like my Siamese cat, minus the tutu."

"Conversations don't happen when one is turned away," I continued, explaining my technique as they filled their baskets with figurines and environmental pieces.

Petunia selected a blue fairy holding flowers. Daphne chose a fairy that resembled herself in a short dress with short hair. She added a swing set to the basket. Petunia opted for a pair of slat-back chairs as well as a white picket fence that reminded her of the one surrounding her sister's house. When they'd loaded up their items, I told them to peruse our pottery as well as our selection of perennials.

Daphne picked out a small pot adorned with a flower fairy that my friend who owned Seize the Clay had crafted. Next, she made her way to the shelves filled with two-inch plants.

Petunia, however, needed more time to deliberate. After a long moment, she said, "What do you think of this one?" She lifted a blue ceramic, wide-mouthed pot. "My sister loves this color. Is it too big?"

"We'll make it work," I said.

"Petunia," a man called as he stumbled down the ramp, tripping as he reached the patio, and careening toward the fountain. He caught himself at the last second before falling into the water.

Fiona stopped gallivanting with Pixie and soared to him. She tapped his shoulder, almost like a fairy godmother granting a wish. The move helped him regain his footing. I recognized him but couldn't put a name to his face.

"Oh, sheesh!" Petunia exclaimed. "Bentley Bramble, you klutz, what are you doing here?"

Bentley. Right. He was a topiary artist who occasionally did work for my father. In fact, he reminded me of my dad. Both were in their fifties and rangy and tan. However, my father smiled easily. Bentley's smile was tight, as if it were taking all his effort to do so. Also, unlike my father, who had a thick mane of brown hair, Bentley's was thinning. It looked like he'd used an eggbeater to comb it.

"We had a d–date for lunch, Petunia," he said, covering a slight stutter.

"No, I don't think we did." She slipped her glasses over the bridge of her nose and pulled her cell phone from her crossbody purse. She swiped the screen to reveal the calendar app. "No. There's nothing written down for today. Um, how did you know I'd be here?" She removed her glasses, letting them fall on the chain, and lasered him with her steely gaze.

"Y'see, I was trimming the topiary across the street and saw you enter," he said.

"You sculpted those?" I asked, impressed. There were two standard poodle-shaped bushes in front of the Vista Inn, a bed-and-breakfast made up of a dozen cottages. Carmel was a dog-friendly town, and the owner of the inn had a pair of handsome brown poodles with the most gorgeous ears. "They're beautiful."

"Beautiful," Fiona echoed.

"Thank you," Bentley replied. Not to her. I doubted he'd detected her. If he had, he would have been following her flight as she disappeared into the ficus trees. As it was, he was staring dreamily at Petunia. "Topiary isn't for everyone. Certainly not for most gardeners. It takes a lot of patience to train perennials by clipping the foliage and twigs to maintain a shape. It's living sculpture, if you will."

When I'd worked for my father's landscaping company, I'd tried my hand at topiary. I had better luck with bonsai trees. The petite size was more to my liking.

"You weren't stalking me, Bentley?" Petunia lifted her chin, asking the question that had briefly crossed my mind. He seemed harmless, almost bumbling, but I'd been fooled by mild-mannered men before.

"N-no. I wouldn't do that. But we did have a date," he said more firmly, bordering on gruff.

Petunia blew air through her lips. "No, sir, we did not. I would remember. I have a very good mind for facts and figures. Besides, we ended our relationship months ago, so why would I have said yes to you now?"

They'd dated previously? That surprised me. They did not match in the slightest. He was a good foot taller than her, and his hesitant, coarse comportment was the antithesis of Petunia's polished demeanor.

Petunia said to me, "Bentley is an excellent topiarist, but he's not much good at keeping promises. We had a couple of dates on the calendar, but he canceled each at the last minute."

"Not true," he protested.

"He's married to his work. He rarely makes time for other things."

"Now, Petunia, that's a downright fib," he snapped.

"Oh, of course, you make time for your garden. For your pet projects. But not for me."

"I'm making time now."

"Well, I'm not interested." She turned away from him and, over her shoulder, said, "Goodbye."

Bentley's nostrils flared, and his eyes turned hard, but he accepted her pronouncement and shuffled through the main showroom and out the front door.

I pinched her on the arm. "Are you toying with him?"

"No. Of course not. I have no interest. It's too bad, because after all, he is a gifted topiarist. Oliver hired him for the festival. He'll be stationed near the fountain and showing adults how to form trees while the children sketch. There's something to be said for a man who dedicates himself to being one of the best, don't you think?" Her eyes glistened with something akin to awe. "But he can be . . ." She tapped a finger against one cheek. "He can be single-minded and lose track of time. Why, one evening when we were supposed to meet, what was he doing? Surfing the web to study images of the topiary at Disneyland."

I'd visited the acclaimed park. The whimsical animated character plant statues, in larger-than-human size, were often a subject of discussion among visitors.

"After that, I was finished with him," she went on.

"Ta-ta, Courtney! Thanks." Daphne scooted past us. "Got everything I need."

"Maybe I'll see you later tonight," I said. "I'll be stopping by the farm."

"Cool. Bye, Petunia, see you soon."

"Come to the festival, Daphne," Petunia said.

"We'll see. I'm not sure. I might stage a protest." Giving a sassy twitch of her head, Daphne darted into the main showroom to complete her purchase.

At two minutes to six, my best friend Meaghan Brownie sashayed into the shop, the skirt of her lace dress swishing with each step, her curly brown tresses bouncing on her shoulders. "Ready?" She drew near, towering over me the way I towered over Joss. She held up a ring of keys. "I'm driving, and the picnic basket is packed."

"Gee whiz, my mind is a sieve today." I turned to Joss. "I nearly forgot I promised to show my father my new garden plot. Could you—"

"Take Pixie home?" Joss winked. "You bet. I'll even feed her."

Fiona flew to me. "I'm coming with you."

Meaghan caught sight of her, and her eyes lit up. "You're back! For good?" Her gaze swung between Fiona and me. "Like forever?"

I looped my hand around my pal's elbow. "She'll explain on the drive. Do you have a change of clothes?"

"Why?"

"At least shoes. I told you we'd have a trek when we got to the farm."

"I've got tennies in the car."

"Perfect. What's for dinner?" I asked as I climbed into her Toyota RAV4, Fiona flying in behind me.

"Potato salad with mustard and chives, cucumber-dill tea sandwiches, mini ham quiches, and . . ."

"And? There's more?" I waited breathlessly.

Meaghan and I had met in our sophomore year in college. When she visited me in Carmel one summer, she fell in love with the place, gave up her pursuit of becoming a professor, and decided to devote herself to art and beauty. She now owned Flair Gallery, one of the other shops in the Cypress and Ivy Courtyard.

"Gingersnap brownies!" she chirped.

"My favorite."

Because of her surname, Meaghan had made brownies all her life. In recent years, I'd been her taste-testing guinea pig. I'd never been disappointed. The gingersnap version of fudgy goodness that she'd brought along was almost as spicy as pumpkin pie.

"Fiona, I didn't bring anything for you," Meaghan said.

"I will find plenty to enjoy at Flower Farm," she replied.

"Okay, fill me in," Meaghan said, cranking her car into gear.

Fiona recapped what she'd told me about her time in the realm, her plan to mentor her sister, and the challenges she would face ahead.

"Wow," Meaghan said. "When does your sister arrive?"

"Saturday. She's a nurturer fairy, so I'll be showing her how to bless flowers and help them grow."

"Isn't the fairy kingdom filled with flowers for her to practice on?" Meaghan asked.

"Yes, but the human world offers a tougher challenge, with climate patterns and such, so this is the skill the queen fairy wants her to master."

Meaghan looked impressed. "Was it good to be back in the kingdom, Fiona?"

"It was, but I like it here just as much." She sat cross-legged on my arm and began to hum.

I nudged her. "What's wrong?" She hummed when she was happy, but she also hummed when she was mulling something over.

"I didn't like that Bentley man."

I explained to Meaghan how he'd barged into the shop. "Don't worry about him. He won't be coming back." To Meaghan, I said, "Turn left ahead."

As the farm came into view, its hand-carved road sign a beacon, its fields of daisies, peonies, sunflowers, and zinnias in all colors made the view as pretty as a Monet painting.

One other vehicle was in the parking lot when we pulled in—
my father's Dodge Ram truck. I didn't see him in the vicinity. Most
likely, he'd proceeded to the plot, which lay beyond the acres.

"I should stop in and say hi to Daphne," I said.

Meaghan hopped out and followed me to the wood-shingled office.

I tried the front door, but it didn't open. "Huh," I mumbled,
peering through the glass window. The lights were out. A computer
sat on a desk at the rear of the room, screen-saver images of gorgeous
flowers cycling one at a time.

"Something wrong?"

"No. I thought Daphne would be here. She must have had an
appointment. Not a problem. I have twenty-four-hour access to my
garden."

A sign on the front door read: *Wholesale flowers sent directly from
the farm to you. Shipping costs included.*

"She sells directly to the consumer?" Meaghan asked.

"Yep."

"Oh, look. She's giving master classes." She pointed to another
sign. "Red and I should take one." Red was the nickname for Redcliff Reddick, a police officer Meaghan had been dating for a month.
"Wouldn't flower arranging be a fun couple thing to do?"

Brady might like it, but I wasn't so sure about Red. I didn't peg
him as a Renaissance kind of guy. However, he adored Meaghan, so
he'd probably be up for anything.

Meaghan squinted at the closing line on the sign. "What's a classic pavé?"

"An arrangement where the stems are cut fairly short and all the
flower heads clumped together, like you'd see on a wedding table.
C'mon," I said, steering my friend back to the RAV4. "You change
shoes, and I'll grab the picnic basket."

"Where are we going to eat?" she asked.

"You'll love this. The farm is like a mini sanctuary. Daphne wel-
comes the public, free of charge, to come and enjoy the view. There

are outdoor tables scattered around the property set in prime viewing spots."

"Nice."

The path to the plot was covered with gravel that crunched beneath our feet. I was wearing clogs, but they maneuvered the uneven ground perfectly fine.

When we arrived at the end of the path, I stopped and drew in a deep, cleansing breath. I'd only planted roses so far in my quarter-acre. Once I planned the design for the remaining portion, I'd get a jump on it.

My father was standing to the right, cell phone in hand. His sinewy muscles pressed at the cuffs of his polo shirt imprinted with KELLY LANDSCAPING. The hems of his jeans and work boots were sightly soiled, as if he'd come from a job.

"Hi, Dad!" I called.

He turned, his expression severe.

Uh-oh. "Why the frown?" I asked as I drew near.

"Danged phone isn't doing what it's supposed to. A text stalled."

I opened my palm. He handed his phone to me. I assessed the issue and smiled. "That's because it defaulted to the landline telephone number. You need to select the mobile phone." I fixed it for him, sent the message, and handed the phone back.

"Way to go, kitten. Make me feel like a hack." He laughed and smiled broadly, which carved deep crevices in his cheeks. "Hello, Meaghan."

"Kip," she said.

My father had been named Kipling, after Rudyard Kipling. My nana had loved literary references. Dad had hated the lofty name since forever and grew grumpy whenever anyone dared to use it. Meaghan was smart enough to know better.

"Hello-o-o," Fiona crooned as she orbited him three times, doing her best to cause a stir in the air. He didn't notice. If he'd open his heart, maybe he'd see her, but he could be stubborn.

"Tell me about your plan here." Dad motioned to the nearly barren field. "Does this mean you'll be giving up fairy gardening?"

I elbowed Meaghan. "Told you."

She guffawed. "Predictable."

My father frowned. "I am not predictable."

"Dad," I said, using the calmest tone I could muster, "I will continue to sell fairy gardens. I will continue teaching people to make fairy gardens. And I will continue to nurture people who want to see fairies. In the meantime, I'm going to grow plants here that I can sell in the shop. Cutting out the middleman will help my bottom line."

He frowned. "Keeping this much property thriving is going to take time."

"I've suggested she hire a gardener to tend it," Meaghan said.

"If I need to, I will, but for now, the Happy Diggers have offered to manage it for free if I give them fairy garden lessons. It's a win–win situation."

Dad spun in a circle. "Is your fairy here?"

"I'll never tell," I teased. "You'll have to believe to see for yourself."

He gave me the side-eye.

Giggling, Meaghan took the picnic basket to the rustic table and started unpacking it. I looped my hand around my father's elbow and guided him to a bench.

"I brought champagne!" Meaghan announced, and popped the cork. She filled three outdoor-ware flutes with the golden liquid and handed us each one. "To Courtney! To success."

We toasted and sat, and I said to my father, "Tell us about the class you taught last night."

The town of Carmel had enlisted him, as an accredited master gardener, to educate locals about the trends in gardening and climate. When he'd first told me about it, it had sounded like a yawn of a task, but he was totally into educating people about water conservation and what plants would thrive as California was forced to cut back on water use.

"Was it well attended?" I asked. "Did you know any of your students?"

"A few." For the next half hour, he regaled us with his agenda. He'd started with the basics and had finished with succulents.

"I couldn't get it all into one night," he said. "The final seminar will be Tuesday evening, if you'd like to attend. We'll be discussing tools of the trade and activism."

When we finished our delicious meal and packed up, he kissed me on the cheek and said, "I'm proud of you."

I didn't know if the compliment was because I was investing in the quarter-acre plot or a general statement—he had certainly never approved of my fairy garden shop enterprise—but I decided to let the compliment pass without a retort. He was proud of me. Good enough.

Chapter 4

Greenish frog with mottled throat,
Little imp in speckled coat,
I will teach you how to sing in a Fairy way.
Sing in drip-drop water-notes,
Lightly as a lily floats,
Softly as the rushes swing on a Summer day.
—Annie R. Rentoul, "A Singing Lesson"

By the time Fiona and I arrived home, she'd fallen asleep on my shoulder, her hand twisted around a strand of my hair. It didn't hurt. She didn't weigh more than a wisp. Pixie greeted me with a wail as I entered the kitchen.

"I did not forget you, cat." I regarded the empty can of tuna on the counter. She hadn't gone hungry. She'd licked every last morsel out of her dish. I scrubbed her under the chin, told her I loved her, and hustled her into the bedroom.

After doing my ablutions, we bundled in my bed and went fast asleep. When I awoke, I felt rested and ready to attack the next day. A quick run on the beach without bumping into anyone I knew and no squalling seagulls dive-bombing me was a good start. The weather was sublime, with a prediction that the temps would hover in the mid-seventies. I showered quickly, slipped on a red T-shirt, jumped into my favorite pair of overalls with embroidered flowers on the bib,

and warmed a breakfast taco that I'd pre-made and kept frozen for
rushed mornings. I fed Pixie and Fiona—she'd requested honey and
pansies—downed my taco in a few bites, and rushed to work.

I pushed open the Dutch door to Open Your Imagination and
put Pixie on the floor. She scampered to the patio, found the lone
spot of sunlight spilling through the tempered-glass roof, and plopped
down to warm herself. "Fiona"—I moved to the sales counter; she
fluttered behind me—"does Merryweather Rose of Song know
you're back in town?"

"She does. Mother gave her a heads-up."

Mother. Would I ever get used to Fiona calling Aurora, the queen
fairy, *Mother*? Aurora was the first fairy I'd ever laid eyes on. The only
fairy, actually, until Fiona. My mother and I had spied her in the
garden whenever we tilled the soil.

"I'm to meet with her later on today to get my instructions for
Eveleen," Fiona said.

Why was her sister coming to the human world? Had she been
acting like an imp, as Fiona had, or was this a way to test Fiona as to
her ability to replace the queen fairy at a future point in time?

"Boss," Joss said, emerging from the area down the hall. She
placed a box of tea bags and a container of sugar on the beverage
station. "What's on your agenda?"

"I want to do as much as I can in the shop before heading to the
festival venue," I said. "You've arranged for a van to take our items
over, right?"

"Already delivered." She threw me a set of keys, and I caught
them. "To open the trunks."

We were allowed to move our things into the booth today, but
none of us would unpack until tomorrow morning at six a.m. The
notion of such an early start made me yawn.

Joss brushed the front of her plaid shirt. "Mom says hello." Her
mother was in a retirement home and struggling with dementia.

"Hello to me? Specifically?"

Joss chuckled. "Okay, no, she didn't really say hello to you, but she gave me a kiss goodbye and flapped her hands like fairy wings." Joss had told her about Fiona and the fairy garden shop.

Fiona said, "Would you like me to go with you sometime when you visit her?"

Joss gazed at her. "Would you? I mean, you don't have to, but who knows? Maybe in the dream world she's living in, you exist."

"I could dowse her with a memory potion," Fiona suggested.

"Is there such a thing?" I asked.

"There must be," Fiona said. "How else would my mother have such a vibrant memory? I swear . . . I mean, I don't swear. Fairies aren't allowed to curse. But, honestly, my mother has a memory like a steel trap. That's the phrase, isn't it?"

Joss and I nodded.

"She remembers each detail of every day. There's a term for that, I think."

"Hyperthymesia," Joss said. "It's very rare."

"She said that once she became queen, it took effect."

"So perhaps you'll have the same gift," I said.

She shook her head and rolled her eyes. "If I do, I'll go cuckoo. My mind is already flooded with information that I can't sort through."

I laughed, knowing what she meant. Nowadays, with the Internet, social media, and all the other minutiae I needed to remember from day to day, my mind felt like it was constantly on overload and, like a computer, ready to crash. "Work on that potion, will you?" I joked. "I could use a dose myself."

Fiona saluted and glided to the patio to play with Pixie.

An hour later, as I was dusting the verdigris racks outside, Petunia Fujimoto rushed down the ramp to me, the flaps of her floral jacket wafting, her glasses bouncing on their chain. She reminded me of a kite prepared to take flight. "Courtney! Oh, Courtney."

"It's not ready," I blurted, referring to her sister's garden.

"That's not why I'm here. It's Daphne. Have you seen her?"

I shook my head, my heart leaping into my throat. "Why? Is something wrong?"

"Last night . . ." Petunia could barely catch her breath. "Last night, I heard her and Genevieve exchanging words. Daphne lives two doors down from me."

"On Casanova near Seventh, not far from me."

"That's right. How did you know?"

"I saw Daphne in her garden one afternoon." It never ceased to amaze me how small a community Carmel was. When out and about, I often ran into people I knew. "Why on earth would they have argued?" I asked. "They adore one another."

"That's what I thought, too, but you should have heard Genevieve. She was being downright mean"—Petunia acted out her story—"saying Daphne's roses were subpar."

I gasped. "She didn't. Why on earth? Daphne's roses at Flower Farm are exquisite."

"You're right. They're exceptional," Petunia said. "I've ordered dozens from her farm to use in our single-stem arrangements. They're tight and firm. They don't have spots or browned edges. And she uses all natural ingredients to ward off pests. Daphne ordered Genevieve to take it back, but she wouldn't. How could she be so mean? Is it possible she'd been drinking? When my boyfriend in college drank, he could be cruel."

I hadn't a clue. These women were my friends, but not close friends like Meaghan. We met for tea or coffee, not cocktails. I didn't know their proclivities or weaknesses.

"I've tried to reach Daphne to see how she's doing"—Petunia paced to the fountain and did a U-turn—"but she isn't answering her cell phone. You don't think she'd harm herself, do you?"

"Over a gardening dispute? Doubtful."

"Genevieve said she was going to post her review everywhere online."

Oh, no, that makes things worse.

Fiona alit on my shoulder. "I'll ask my friends to search for

Daphne." When I'd first met my sweet fairy, she hadn't been allowed to socialize, but now, given all the help she'd provided to me, she was permitted to reach out to others from her realm. "Bye," she said, and off she went. Fairies didn't use cell phones. They had a way of utilizing ESP.

"I'll try to reach Daphne," I said to Petunia.

"If you talk to her, text me please. I'll be at the festival site."

"Will do." Something must have provoked Genevieve. What if Daphne made the first shot across the bow? Maybe she'd said something hurtful, though I couldn't imagine her doing so. "In the meantime, if you run into Genevieve," I added, "ask her what it was all about."

"Uh-uh." Petunia shook her head. "No way. I will not take Genevieve on. I'm not that brave. She has claws."

After I finished up my chores, I dialed Daphne's number. She didn't answer. I texted her, but she didn't respond. As I tended to incoming customers and sold pots, figurines, and more, I continued to stew about Daphne. Usually, she wrote me back within an hour of a text. She once said she was chained to her cell phone.

At one p.m., with no response from her—Fiona had come back around noon, with no news of her, either—I said to Joss that I was heading to the festival site. Fiona tagged along.

Junipero Street was a two-way thoroughfare with a median of trees in the middle. On the south side were shops. On the north side were homes and commercial and non-commercial buildings.

Shy of the festival site, I spotted a number of gardeners using hoes to clear weeds from the median. Among them, to my surprise, was Daphne, her hair jammed beneath a broad-brimmed straw hat. Like me, she was dressed in overalls and a T-shirt, but hers were covered with schmutz.

I drew near and said, "Daphne, are you okay?"

She stopped hoeing and gawked at me as if I'd startled her. "I'm fine." Perspiration trickled down the sides of her face. Her cheeks were flushed with exertion. "Why do you ask?"

"I called. I texted. You haven't responded."

She pulled her cell phone from the pocket of her overalls and laughed. "Well, how do you like that? It's out of juice. Oops. Were you trying to reach me about something important?"

"You and Genevieve . . ." I paused. "I heard you had a fight."

"Oh, that!" Daphne flourished the cell phone. "Who told you? Petunia? She can be a worrywart. It was nothing."

"Genevieve verbally attacked you."

"That's because she . . . she was . . ." She rolled one lip between her teeth. "She'll have to tell you herself. It was nothing. Promise."

"What are you doing here?" I asked.

"Seeing as I don't have a booth at the festival, I thought I'd offer my services as a volunteer gardener. The city can use all the help it can get, and when called upon, the Weeders come out in force."

My father donated his time to the Weeders, too.

"Weeds are the devil," she said. "Got to get them from the root, or they keep coming back."

"What is that?" I asked, pointing to her tool. It wasn't a typical hoe. It sort of resembled an axe. I didn't have anything like it in my gardening shed.

"A hoedag. It's terrific and sturdily made. Carbon steel." She twisted the tool like a baton and tapped the irregularly shaped head, narrow on one end and wide on the other. "You use the tapered blade for precision, you know, like digging up thistle centers and crabgrass. You use the broad end for clearing large areas. And, a bonus feature, it withstands the odd whack to rock and metal." She demonstrated by clacking the head on a one-foot-round boulder. The sound reverberated through the air. "My father gave me this when I purchased the farm. He even etched my monogram on it." She tapped the handle near the tool's head. "What a housewarming gift. He sure knows how to spoil a girl." She let out a cackle.

I laughed along with her. "I hope you aren't too disappointed about not being included at the festival." I hitched my thumb at the cluster of white tents farther down the road.

"Nah. I won't cut my flowers for something like this. Too much loss, not enough reward. Festival customers are all about buying arrangements." She glanced at her watch and pocketed her cell phone. "I'd better get my portion of the median done, or I'll be late getting back to the farm. I only have one assistant. See you soon. Oh, hey—" She aimed the head of the hoedag at me. "Did you have a picnic at the farm last night, like you planned?"

"Sure did. My father loved the place. He said you have a real knack."

"That's a compliment coming from a master gardener. You made my day!"

Fiona hovered beside me as I continued on toward the festival site. "She was holding something back about Genevieve."

"I agree, but I didn't want to press."

I peeked over my shoulder. Daphne was staring after me, as if mulling over my questions. When she noticed me looking, she slung the hoedag over her shoulder and left her post.

Quickly, I texted Petunia that Daphne was fine, after which Fiona and I continued on to the festival site.

"Wow!" she exclaimed when we arrived. "It's so much bigger than I imagined."

White tents lined both sides of the street. At the near end of the corridor was Section F, even-numbered booths to the left and odd to the right. Section A had to be at the far end, I figured. The entrance was cordoned off, but when the festival officially opened, all ropes would be removed to allow easy access to attendees. There were vendors milling about, unpacking their vans.

"How do we get to our booth?" Fiona asked.

I removed a badge on a lanyard from the manila envelope I'd been sent and slipped it around my neck. Then I searched for and found the event participants' entrance.

An elderly volunteer with curly white hair and a sweet smile greeted me and un-roped the entrance. "Hi, honey—have a great time. You, too," she said to Fiona.

"You can see me?" Fiona gasped.

"One simply has to open one's heart to believe," the woman replied. "Have fun!"

I greeted vendors I knew as we passed through. There were a few I didn't recognize. The festival was open to businesses not centralized in Carmel. Earthly Pleasures, an enterprise from Silicon Valley, was hawking garden art that included metal sunflowers, colorful curved windmills, and garden gnomes taller than toddlers. The Jolly Green Gardener from Monterey was selling seed packets, seed starter kits, and glazed pots. Bare Root, an outfit based in Modesto, was peddling ready-to-plant roses and its own personalized fertilizer mix.

Luckily, the festival was populated with food and beverage vendors, too. Percolate, one of my favorite places in town to go for coffee, was offering samples of strawberry-mango smoothies to the participants. I was more than willing to take one off their hands.

Beyond them, I saw Brady and jogged to him. He was lifting a bistro table from a platform truck. I'd always admired the shape of his calf muscles—we'd shot hoops often as kids—but now, as a grown man, they were sculpted. His brawny arms strained at the sleeves of his Hideaway Café T-shirt. He spotted me and grinned. Would I ever tire of the way he drank me in with his gaze?

He slung an arm around me, kissed my forehead—his favorite spot, he said—and sneaked a look past me. "Is she here?"

"She's kissing your ear."

Fiona pecked his lobe.

"Nope. Don't feel a thing," he said. He wasn't teasing. He wanted to meet a fairy.

"Soon," I assured him.

"Did you see the fountain in the middle of the corridor?" Brady asked.

"We just arrived. We haven't made it that far."

"It's marvelous. A *pièce de résistance*. There aren't any live actors performing yet." The festival brochure shared photos of last year's event, where actors pretended to be statues in the middle of the fountain. "It will be loads of fun for kids."

The event coordinators were going to position easels and art supplies around the fountain in a circle. Only children could paint the images that the live actors created. Adults would have to be content watching Bentley Bramble sculpt bushes.

"Of course, there are already rumors that the festival will be a bust," Brady added.

"Rumors?"

"Yeah. That influencer, Genevieve Bellerose, is posting all sorts of pictures and mocking the setup. Hundreds of people are commenting on her photos."

Uh-oh.

"Do you know, she even had the gall to give me a bad review?" Brady's jaw started to twitch. He scratched it.

"She didn't."

"Yep. She said my food at the festival wouldn't be up to par with what I serve at the café. And she's right. It won't be because of the time delay to cart it over here," he admitted. "But offering a review prior to the event seems petty."

Holy moly. Genevieve didn't need to spread this much ill will. What was up with her? Granted, I wasn't her BFF and didn't know her deepest, darkest secrets, but I felt I knew her pretty well. I texted her, asking if she could meet for coffee. She didn't respond.

"What's on your menu?" I asked Brady as I viewed my cell phone, hoping to see three dots meaning Genevieve was forming a reply. "And, more importantly, do you have anything to eat right now? I'm starved."

"We'll be serving avocado toast with onion salsa."

That was one of my favorite appetizers at the café. "Continue."

"Salmon mousse bites. Teriyaki chicken-on-a-stick. Mini ham quiches."

"Oh, man. Yum." My mouth started to water.

"In the meantime, I have half of a salami, prosciutto, and Swiss cheese sandwich with pineapple that I haven't finished."

I wrinkled my nose. "Pineapple?"

"It adds a kick. Try a bite."

He fetched the sandwich from a cooler and handed it to me. I peeled back the parchment paper it was wrapped in and nibbled one end of the sub. *"Mmm.* What's the sauce?"

"Spicy mustard and basil with a dab of honey. My dad's recipe." His father owned a diner that served ridiculously delicious burgers.

"Courtney!" Hattie Hopewell waved to me from the booth two down from Brady's. Her sisters, Holly and Hedda, were with her. The three were stringing a banner with the words THE HAPPY DIGGERS HELP BUDDING GARDENERS. "Come see!"

I took another bite of Brady's sandwich, kissed him goodbye, and strolled to the trio. "What're you all doing here?" I asked.

Holly was manning a hammer. Hedda was holding a box of nails. Hattie was on the third rung of a stepladder, waiting to receive the tools.

"Putting together Hattie's fund-raising booth," Holly said.

Only Hattie was a member of the Diggers. The other two enjoyed making fairy gardens, but they weren't into full-scale gardening.

Holly, a delightful woman and exquisite artist, was my landlord and neighbor. She always exuded good vibes. Dressed in a Monet-style smock over leggings that I'd never seen before—she was a real clothes horse—she looked as youthful as her younger sister, Hedda.

"New haircut, Hedda?" I asked.

"Yes." She rarely changed her tailored look. "Like it?" She primped the bob that fell in line with the angle of her jaw.

"I do. It's flirty." I smiled and inhaled. "And new perfume?"

"Mm-hmm. Sunflowers by Elizabeth Arden."

"She bathed in it," Holly teased.

"Did not."

"To impress her boyfriend."

"Cut it out." Hedda knuckled her sister's arm.

Fiona wafted to Hedda and drew in a deep breath. Fairies tried to absorb all the healing power they could from delicious scents. Hedda, who was eager to see a fairy, turned her face in the direction of Fiona and blinked. Fiona clapped her hands, and Hedda let out a squeal of delight.

"What's wrong, Sis?" Hattie demanded. "Did you see a spider?"

"No. I . . ." Hedda covered her mouth with her hand and peeked at me. Her eyes were aglow with delight. She had spied my fairy.

Fiona circled Hedda's head before alighting on her shoulder. "Nice to meet you, Hedda," she said. "Finally."

"C'mon, ladies," Hattie said with the command of a general. "We don't have all day if we want to finalize this booth. Plus, I have to get over to the general store for some flower containers and shears. They recently got a new shipment." She explained to me, "We're filling containers with garden tools and seed packets to give our budding gardeners a head start."

I had to get a move on, too, but first I asked, "What are budding gardeners?"

"We're raising funds so the Happy Diggers can assemble a group of young folks without means who want to learn the trade," Hattie replied. "Your father, bless his soul, is going to instruct them."

"He is?"

"Yes. We were chatting with his lady love, and she offered his services and got him on board." Hattie flicked the air. "Who knew it would be so easy? Like magic. I wonder whether your fairy had something to do with it."

I eyed Fiona. She shrugged both shoulders and mouthed *Not me*.

"I'm pleased he'll be involved, no matter what made him say yes," I said. My father enjoyed kids of all ages. He hadn't pressed me to have any children yet. After the surprise breakup with my fiancé, he hadn't even questioned me about marriage. He simply wanted me to be happy and fulfilled. He liked Brady a lot.

"Don't look now," Holly said, a tinge of hostility in her tone, "but there's Asher Lyle."

"You don't like him?" I asked.

Asher was Scarlet's husband and owner of the general store Hattie mentioned. About forty years old, he had a generous head of brown hair, thick lips, and a curious gleam in his eyes, like an overgrown puppy who was always mentally asking its human questions.

"He's a bit much to take," Holly answered.

I waited, wanting to hear more. She was rarely critical.

"All that shrink talk that he spews," Holly went on. "Meh! To friends. To customers. 'Living with intention.'" She made air quotes. "Making a point to have 'values-based actions.'" More air quotes. "Hogwash."

"Now, Sis," Hedda said, "you don't mind when I say things like that. Make time a priority. Make sure you schedule your favorite activities. It's all about self-care."

"You"—Holly aimed a hammer at her—"don't make it sound like I'm as ridiculous as a skunk if I choose to follow my south star instead of my north star."

"Pfft," Hedda said. "It's entirely in the tone of delivery."

"Yeah, his delivery is pompous to the max," Holly said.

"To the max!" Hedda chimed.

Hattie said, "At least he's easy on the eyes."

"Hattie!" Holly exclaimed, gawking at her older sister.

"Well, he is well-built," Hattie countered. "And he adores that wife of his. I wish someone adored me that much."

Holly and Hedda sang in unison, "Yoo-hoo. Cliff does!"

Laughing at their sisterly banter, I continued on but jolted when something went *ka-boom!*

Chapter 5

The leaves on the tree-tops
Dance in the breeze;
Totter-grass dances
And sways like the trees—
Shaking and quaking!
While through it there goes,
Dancing, a Fairy,
On lightest of toes.
—Cecily Mary Barker, "The Song of the Totter-Grass Fairy"

People shrieked. A few cursed. I ran toward the sound and saw a booth had collapsed inward, like an umbrella in a rainstorm, its ribs sticking sideways. People were scrambling to help whoever had been pinned beneath the polyester roof. I rushed into the fray to assist.

Fiona sped past me and ducked beneath the material. She returned in seconds. "Scarlet is okay," she said.

"Scarlet? This is her booth?"

"*Mm-hmm.* She's laughing."

I sure wouldn't be laughing after such a disaster.

With volunteers following one man's command to lift on *three*, they hoisted the roof and re-propped the poles. Hedda, who had joined me, bent to give Scarlet a hand. When Scarlet was clear of the mess, those who'd stepped back to let the volunteers finalize the reconstruction, applauded.

"Are you okay?" Hedda asked.

"Yes." Scarlet, giggling, brushed herself off and took a bow. "That'll teach me to make a bet with Asher that something dire would happen today, but"—she rubbed her fingers together to mime the international symbol for money—"now I'm going to collect."

"No injuries?" I asked.

"None." Her white shirt over white capris were covered with dust. Her white sandals, too. "Next time, I'll dress more appropriately," she joked, feeling for her hair and frowning as she realized, in all probability, it was more of a messy bun than a sophisticated updo.

Fiona kissed Hedda and thanked her for helping. Hedda beamed with delight and returned to her booth.

"What happened, Scarlet?" I asked as the other helpers went their respective ways, too.

"I'm not sure. One minute, I was opening that trunk"—she pointed to a heavy vinyl laminate crate fitted with wheels—"and the next thing I know, the sky is falling." She deconstructed her hair, slipped the bobby pins into her mouth, and re-pinned the hairdo in a matter of seconds. "Better?"

"Much."

"My lipstick?" she asked.

"As perfect as always."

"Good, because I did a face-plant into that beanbag chair." She motioned to a green suede lump of a chair. "Guess I can amend my review and say it's good for pratfalls." She scanned the booth. "Do you see my cell phone? It went flying."

Fiona flitted to a far corner and said, "Here it is."

I fetched it and brought it to Scarlet.

"Thanks." She shuffled to the trunk, twisted the combination lock dial, and opened the lid. "Look at some of the other products I've approved. Face creams, clothes, earbuds." She plucked them from the trunk as she introduced them. "Nice, right?"

"Very. So, you made a bet with your husband about something dire happening?"

"Yeah, Asher and I are always making bets. Who can eat the most pancakes? Who can get to the post office the fastest on foot? That's how we met. His friend bet him I wouldn't go out with him. The same friend bet me the opposite. We are a match made in heaven." She glowed with starry-eyed love. "Today's wager was about premonitions. We both claim to have ESP. I do. He doesn't."

Fiona tittered at that. "If she had special powers, she'd see me."

Oblivious to Fiona's presence, Scarlet said, "Do you want to know his punishment for losing? He has to post an embarrassing picture of himself on Instagram. And I know the perfect one." She rubbed her hands like a miser and cackled with glee.

"Do you feel safe now that the booth is back in order?" I asked.

"Sure." She swiped the screen on her cell phone. "It's not like that roof is heavy. If it falls again, I'll survive. Say, have you seen Oliver Killian lately?"

"No, but I just arrived."

"Well, if you run into him on your way to your site, let him know he and I need to—" Scarlet screeched as she scrolled through text messages. "The nerve. How dare she!"

"Who? What?" I asked.

"Ooh!"

Fiona spiraled upward, startled.

"Ooh!" Scarlet uttered a second time and kicked the trunk. She winced from the pain. "Ow! Stupid open-toed shoes. Stupid!" She struck the trunk with her heel. The lid slammed shut with a *clack*. A spanking new shovel and rake with ornate handles wedged behind the trunk tipped sideways and fell, taking a glistening lantern and a standing Tiffany lamp with them. The lampshade shattered.

"Scarlet, calm down," I said. "Tell me what's wrong?" I righted the items that I could manage. Hopefully, she had a broom around to clean up the broken glass.

"Asher says Genevieve posted an insult about my business, claiming I'm not qualified to rate a book, let alone a whole line of products. She said that I"—she scrolled farther—"have no sense of what

people like. Where is the danged post? I have to read it for myself."
She tapped another app on her phone and browsed until she found
what she was looking for. Then she cursed. "The cow. How could
she? Look!"

I glanced at the photograph and flinched. It was a rearview picture of Scarlet, bent over in her garage, rooting in a box. The caption
read: *Take care where you share your derriere, and while you're at it, think
about what expertise you really have,* followed by a string of hashtags:
*#productresearcher #photooftheday #smile #ScarletLyleProducts #notgood-
atherjob #notaste.*

Yipes!

"The post already has three thousand likes. It's trending." Scarlet
shoved her cell phone into her trouser pocket. "Why is she singling
me out? What did I ever do to her?"

"You did make fun of her being an influencer."

"Big fat deal." She shrugged one shoulder. "She teased me, too.
It's not like—"

Fiona sprinkled Scarlet with a silver potion meant to calm the
troubled soul. I was always amazed how she could drum one up out
of thin air. It had to do with the movement of her wings. Magical.

Scarlet sat on top of the trunk, laid the cell phone beside her, and
cradled her face in her hands.

"It's just a photo." I rested a palm on her shoulder. "In an hour,
everyone will have forgotten they've seen it. It's not like it's gone
viral."

"Even so, locals . . . and my employers . . ." She heaved a sigh
and sat upright. "Go on. I know you have to set up your booth. I'm
okay."

"Poor thing," Fiona said as we veered toward Section A. "Why
would her husband send that to her? Why not act like it didn't exist?"

"He loves her," I said. "He wants her to be prepared should
someone else mention it." Joss had done that for me when the shop
had received a few subpar reviews in the month after opening. Each
of them had made me raise the bar so we could rise to our potential.

As I meandered through the cluttered staging sites, fifty percent of them flower-themed, the other half featuring jewelry, art, food, home goods, and clothing, I texted Genevieve and asked if she was all right. I knew she had a snarky side, but I didn't think she'd assail friends. She didn't respond. I slipped my cell phone into my pocket, mentally willing her to reply.

A short while later, between Sections C and D, I came upon the *pièce de résistance* Brady had mentioned, an eight-foot wide, transportable fountain, which was, indeed, beautiful. It was made of etched cement and featured a Fiore pond and one tier upon which the live actor would pose. The water was burbling and made the most soothing sound. Fiona swirled around it, humming with glee. She adored fountains and water features. There didn't seem to be a designated site for Bentley Bramble's topiary demonstration. I guessed he would cart something in and work off to one side.

I ambled past Floral Antiques, a shop that specialized in pictures, furniture, jewelry, and pottery, each item adorned with flowery designs, and I sauntered past Fine Art, a shop that featured paintings akin to Monet's *Water Lilies* and Van Gogh's *Irises* series. One, a hummingbird drinking from a lotus flower, was particularly enchanting.

By the time Fiona and I reached Section A, I was parched. Good thing I'd slipped a bottle of water into my purse. I chugged down half of it and set to work. The items our deliveryman had transported were staged behind the booth. Like Scarlet's, ours consisted of a couple of trunks on wheels and a platform truck holding tables and chairs.

As I was browsing through the contents of the largest trunk to make sure the pottery I'd packed had made the trip intact, my cell phone buzzed. I removed it from my pocket and saw a text from Genevieve.

Genevieve: **I'm fine. Why d'you ask?**
Me: **You had an argument with Daphne.**
Genevieve: **It wasn't an argument.**

Me: **You hurt her feelings.**

Genevieve: **[sad faced emoji]**

Me: **And you posted a cruel picture of Scarlet on your Insta-gram.**

Genevieve: **It was realistic.**

Me: **[frowning emoji]**

Genevieve: **Fine. It wasn't flattering. But, face it, Scarlet has no sense of humor.**

Me: **Are you lashing out because Oliver spurned you for the festival?**

Genevieve: **You sound like my shrink.**

Me: **Don't take your anger out on everyone else.**

Three little dots came into view, meaning she was typing something. I waited.

Genevieve: **I'll apologize to Scarlet.**

Me: **And Daphne?**

Genevieve: **Daphne needs to get a thicker skin.**

Me: **Meet for dinner later?**

Maybe I could talk some sense into her.

Me: **I'll invite my friend Meaghan, too.**

Genevieve: **Sure.**

When I suggested the Hideaway Café at seven-thirty, she responded with a thumbs-up symbol, and I texted Meaghan.

The rest of the afternoon went smoothly. Everything at the booth was in order. Guards would be patrolling the festival site twenty-four seven. The bright floodlights positioned every few feet would deter looters. I didn't see Scarlet or Brady as I left. Petunia wasn't around, either.

By the time I returned to the shop, Joss had put everything in shipshape. All the shelves had been restored to the way we liked them presented each morning—teacup handles to the left, wind chimes facing front, books on the book racks with titles upright. Pixie scampered to me and brushed my ankles as I finalized receipts. I lifted her and tucked her under one arm. She pawed the air, trying to bat Fiona, who vaulted out of reach.

"You two," I teased.

"Off to see Buddy," Joss said as she wended through the display tables toward the exit.

"Have a good night."

After locking up, I took Pixie home, fed her, and promised I wouldn't be late. Then I switched into a simple aqua sheath, light shawl, gold crossbody purse, and matching flat sandals, and walked to the café with Fiona sailing alongside. The night air was cool but pleasant. The aroma of delicious food stirred my senses as I entered the restaurant and headed for the rear patio.

Strands of twinkling lights arced across the expanse and glittered on the tempered-glass, pyramid-shaped roof that was identical to the one over my shop's patio. Nearly all the white wrought-iron tables were filled with patrons. The intoxicating scent from the jasmine that was climbing up the trellis at the far end of the patio wafted to me. Fiona noticed the fragrance, too. Her nostrils were twitching with pleasure.

"I'm going to search for the fairy," she said. "If I see her, I'll ask her name."

"Have fun."

Meaghan had arrived before me. She reminded me of a character out of a Jane Austen novel in her lacy white dress and cameo necklace, her hair swept into a knot at the nape of her neck. She was sipping a glass of white wine and chatting easily with Brady. I searched for Genevieve but didn't see her.

Brady rose when I approached and pecked my cheek. He whispered that I looked delicious and added that he had a special day planned for our date Monday. We would need our cameras, he said. We'd met in photography class in high school and both continued to enjoy our pastimes.

"Shorts, sunblock, and sandals," he added.

"Sounds great." I loved every minute I spent with him.

"Chardonnay?" he asked.

"Yes, please, and when Genevieve Bellerose arrives, would you bring her out?"

His gaze narrowed. "You invited her here, after what she wrote about the café?"

"Rise above, my friend," I said, drawing a fingertip along his jaw. "Rise above."

He made a small bow. "As you wish, mademoiselle."

Meaghan patted the table. "Fill me in. Why am I invited?"

"I want you to meet Genevieve."

"Yeah, but why am I really here?"

I smiled. How well my pal knew me. "She's been a bit off, and I'd like you to serve as a buffer."

"Off, how?"

I explained that she'd attacked Daphne and Scarlet. "We're all friends. It makes no sense. Why lash out with no reason?"

"My ex could be impetuous that way," Meaghan said, a tinge of sadness in her tone. Her ex-boyfriend had been murdered last month. They'd broken up before that, but his death and the truths revealed in the wake were, nonetheless, a shock. "If only he'd seen a shrink," she murmured.

Brady arrived with my wine and placed three menus on the table. He rested a hand on my back. The warmth sent a heavenly tingle down my spine.

"Has Genevieve called?" I asked.

"No."

As he moved away, I pulled my cell phone from my tote and realized I'd missed a text from her. She'd written that she had to cancel. I messaged back that I understood and asked if everything was okay. She didn't respond.

"Genevieve can't make it," I said to Meaghan. "My guess, she's doing another live chat."

Fiona shot into view, her cheeks rosy and eyes glistening. "I met the fairy. She's lovely, and she wants to meet Brady."

"He won't be able to see her," I said.

"You don't know that. May I bring her over?"

Meaghan smiled. "Who are you talking about?"

"There's a fairy in the vines." I hitched my chin in that direction. "She's shy. My bold fairy wanted to make her acquaintance."

Fiona said, "She used to have family here, but they all went back to the fairy realm, and she wanted to stay."

I sipped my wine, enjoying the notes of melon and vanilla. "Is she lonely?"

"Oh, no, not at all. She says she's busy day and night. She's a nurturer," Fiona went on. "She loves butterflies and hummingbirds."

Meaghan giggled. "Who doesn't?"

Fiona wagged her head. "No, I mean, she nurses them back to health with her love if they get hurt. She and Calliope would get along great."

Calliope was the intuitive fairy who inhabited Meaghan's garden. She didn't need or use potions as Fiona did. She could inspire life and healing using her mind. She, too, was shy, although she and another nurturer fairy, Zephyr, had bonded when they'd helped Fiona track down a missing woman.

I glanced at my cell phone again. Still no response from Genevieve. Her lack of one gnawed at me.

"Bring your new friend over," I said to Fiona.

Seconds later, she returned with a delicate fairy with pink-and-yellow hair. She wore glittery shoes and a pink tutu that sparkled in the light. "This is Ulra."

"Ulra." I held out a finger, inviting her to perch on it. She did. "It's a pleasure to meet you." She tittered but didn't speak. Her cheeks tinged as pink as her dress. "I'm Courtney, and this is Meaghan."

Meaghan studied her as if imprinting her to memory so she could paint her. When not selling art or playing the harp at our teas, she dabbled as an artist.

Brady stepped onto the patio, ushering a couple to a table. When done, he crossed to us. "What are you staring at? Why are you holding out your finger?"

"Can't you see her?" I asked.

"Who, Fiona?"

"No. Ulra, the fairy who lives in your vines."

"Ulra," he whispered, and squinted in an effort to see. After a long moment, he shook his head. "I'll never be able to." Frustrated, he turned and tended to another table of customers.

Ulra's face dropped. "But I thought . . . I thought if I revealed myself . . ." Her voice was teensy and high-pitched.

I petted her wing. "Don't worry. He'll come around." I hoped he would. "It's not you. We can see you."

Her wings folded inward, and she sobbed into her tiny hands, reminding me of Scarlet seated on the trunk, upset by Genevieve's taunt. Maybe Genevieve had decided to forego dinner so she could apologize to Scarlet and Daphne.

Except, out of nowhere, a frisson of dread spiraled down my back, making me think otherwise.

Chapter 6

They paint the flower faces,
The leaves of forest trees,
And tint the little grasses
All waving in the breeze.
—Laura Ingalls Wilder, "When Sunshine Fairies Rest"

At five a.m., my alarm blared. I switched it off, turned on the bed-side lamp, and stretched to clear the cobwebs from my head. Last night, before heading to bed, I'd been so concerned about Genevieve that I knew I wouldn't fall asleep easily, so I'd retreated to the green-house in my backyard and started the garden for Petunia's sister. It wasn't quite done. I'd finish it Saturday and deliver it to her Sunday before going to the festival.

I checked my cell phone. No reply text from Genevieve. Why had she canceled? Why not fill me in later? I told myself to simmer down. I was not her keeper. However, as I prepared to leave for the festival, a scintilla of worry wormed its way through me. Had she ghosted me because I was now on her hit list? Would she write something disparaging about Open Your Imagination?

With comfort in mind, I threw on a pair of stretch jeans, a pretty floral T-shirt, and a light summer sweater, and slipped my feet into clogs. Next, I fed Pixie and Fiona. While they dined, I poured a stiff cup of coffee into a thermos, warmed a breakfast burrito, and tossed both into my carryall. I dropped Pixie at the shop—she wouldn't want to hang around the festival all day—and with Fiona as my companion, strode to Junipero Street for the Summer Blooms Festival.

Vendors were milling about, sipping their beverages, clearly excited about the event. An instrumental version of U2's "With or Without You" was emanating through speakers. The energy was electric. Fiona and I passed Scarlet's booth, which was intact. She had laid out her wares on a variety of different height and shaped boxes, much like the arrangements I'd seen at her husband's general store. The overall display was pleasing to the eye. Scarlet, who was talking animatedly with Asher, waved to me, the billowy sleeve of her white blouse slipping up her arm.

Asher spun around and lasered me with a glare.

Scarlet said, "Friend not foe, sweetie. It's Courtney. Smile."

He rubbed his fists in his eyes, as if to help him focus, and grinned. "Sorry. I got contacts yesterday," he said. "I've never worn them before. What an adjustment."

I was grateful I didn't have to insert anything into my eyes. I could barely manage eyedrops when needed. Come to think of it, his new contacts might have been why I'd paid attention to the curious gleam in his eyes yesterday. He was no longer wearing thick-rimmed glasses.

"Good morning to you," he said, "and if your fairy is with you, good morning to her, as well."

I didn't rise to the bait. Scarlet told me last week that Asher thought my ability to see fairies was pure malarkey.

"No face-plants this morning," Scarlet joked, aiming a finger at the green suede beanbag chair. "But the day is young."

"Be vigilant," I teased. "And have a tube of lipstick around, in case."

That cracked her up. Asher didn't look nearly as amused and leaned in to her, as if he didn't understand the exchange. Hadn't she told him about her booth collapsing?

Fiona and I continued on, slowing at Bowers of Flowers.

"Ooh, pretty!" Fiona cried, flitting to a container of calendula to inhale the scent.

I peered into the booth for Petunia and saw her through a cluster of pale yellow gladiolas. Her back was to me.

"Morning, Petunia," I said.

She pivoted, which made the skirt of her daisy-print frock billow. Her outfit suggested cheeriness, but her gaze was haunted. "Oh, hi." Blinking, she swept her silver bangs to one side and slipped on her glasses.

"Not an early morning person?" I asked.

She smiled softly. "Long night," she murmured, glancing discreetly left and right. Was she on the alert for Bentley Bramble? Had he hounded her again? "Thanks for the text about Daphne," she added. "I'm glad she didn't take Genevieve's criticism to heart."

"Your displays are lovely," I said. She'd assembled long-stemmed arrangements as well as classic pavé-style ones, all in yellows and golds, leaving me to believe she'd dressed to match them. "The door wreaths are especially nice." Unlike most door wreaths, which were made of dried flowers, hers were constructed with fresh ones.

"They don't last long, but they're a wonderful way to welcome special visitors into your home," she said. "My mother taught me the art."

Fiona said, "Aren't mothers wonderful? They nurture and guide."

Nurture and guide? I gaped at her. Her mother had banished her to the human world for something as silly as acting like an imp. On the other hand, I couldn't judge how the fairy world operated, especially when it came to the education of the future queen.

Minutes later, Fiona and I reached our booth in Section A, and I started setting up the tables from the platform truck and covering them with white tablecloths. After I unfolded the chairs, I removed the fairy doors and figurines I'd pre-packed, as well as a completed fairy garden that I'd designed in a wide-mouthed terra-cotta pot. After placing the doors and figurines on a mini baker's rack, I centered the garden on a table. In it was a four-inch, Cecily Mary Barker flower fairy who was clad in a lavender dress and had golden hair. In her upraised hand, she was holding a Scottish bluebell. I'd positioned her in front of blue waterfall bellflowers, which made a dramatic backdrop. At her feet sat a darling elm tree boy fairy, dressed in a green shirt, trousers, and a green-leaf hat. He gazed at the girl dutifully, as if she were educating him about flowers. There was sheer delight in the bluebell fairy's pose. The half dozen miniature resin butterflies I'd installed in the garden added to the joyfulness.

"Morning!" The neighboring vendor, who owned Wildflower Pottery & Soap company, drew near to admire the garden. "How much?"

"It's not for sale. It's for display only."

"But you'll sell it when the festival is over, won't you? Of course you will. So I'm your buyer." He had curly hair, intriguing eyes, and an engaging smile. "My daughter will love this. It's her birthday on Tuesday. She's a flower nut. She'll be wandering through the festival, so, *shh*." He held a finger to his lips. "It's a secret. How about I pay you now and pick it up late Sunday?"

I agreed, and he pulled a credit card from his wallet. In a matter of seconds, I rang up the sale through the mobility EMV card I'd attached to my cell phone and gave him a hand-written receipt.

As he returned to his site, Oliver Killian lumbered toward me, a to-go cup in hand. His booth, Garden Delights, was cattycorner from mine. "Having fun?"

"I've made one sale already, and access to the public hasn't even started."

"Good for you." A pair of extravagant floral displays in glazed pots stood in front of his booth and were sure to lure in customers. More exotic arrangements were on display inside.

"You certainly look businesslike in your suit and silk tie," I said.

"Got to show everyone who's boss." He tweaked the knot of his tie and smoothed his mustache.

"Help!" a woman screamed at the top of her lungs.

I whirled around. "This way!" I shouted to Oliver, and bolted toward Ocean Avenue. Fiona clasped strands of my hair like the reins of a horse.

Oliver tossed his cup into a garbage can and jogged after us. A pack of vendors joined the charge. We rounded the last booth of the festival, winding up in the westernmost staging area, and came to a halt. There were clusters of unopened crates, a dumpster, and a couple of trolleys for moving boxes, but no hysterical woman.

"Hello?" I yelled.

"Oh, heavens," a woman cried. "Help!"

Fiona soared over the tops of the crates, took in the view, and did a U-turn. When she reached me, she rasped, "Courtney! Hurry. Over there. On the other side of the crates. It's Daphne."

I cut around the stacks, Oliver and the others trailing, and lurched to a stop. Daphne was bending over somebody on the ground.

I rushed to her. "Daphne, what happened?"

She peered over her shoulder at me. "Courtney. It's . . . it's Genevieve. She's . . . she's dead."

Daphne crab-walked backward and stood up, revealing Genevieve lying prone, her face turned sideways. The back of her head was bashed in, her curly hair matted with dark red goo. I rushed to her and bent down. I felt for a pulse as I presumed Daphne had. There was none. I brushed hair off her cheek. Her skin was cold to the touch, and her body looked stiff. She must have been dead for hours. She was clad in a long-sleeved black top, black leggings, and black slippers. A black fedora lay to one side. The outfit struck me as odd, because Genevieve generally preferred wearing bold, bright colors.

"Oliver!" I cried. "Call nine-one-one. Genevieve Bellerose has been murdered."

Onlookers gasped.

"Everybody back!" Oliver ordered. "Back!"

The vendors huddled together. A hush fell over them.

I rose and slung an arm around Daphne, but my gaze was drawn to the hoedag lying on the ground, off to the side. Had Daphne killed

Genevieve with that vicious-looking tool? No way. Daphne was incapable of murder. And even from afar, I could determine the sharp edges of the tool would have caused an entirely different kind of wound. The one to the back of Genevieve's head was wide and flat, as if the killer had wielded a rock or shovel or frying pan. Would the medical examiner be able to determine what had been used? Would fibers have been left in the wound? The notion made me gag.

Gently, I said, "What were you doing here, Daphne?"

"Huh?" Her eyes were glassy, with shock or in the aftermath of murder, I wasn't sure.

"Why are you here?" I asked, rephrasing the question.

"I was coming this way to do more weeding on the median. I'm supposed to start at eight."

I gestured to the hoedag. "With that?"

"Yes. Why?" Daphne sensed my concern. "Uh-uh, no! I did not kill her. She was dead when I got here."

"That hit to her skull looks pretty lethal," I said.

"Well, I didn't do it. Check my tool. There's no blood on it."

Fiona flew to the hoedag and inspected both sides of its head. "Clean as a whistle," she said.

"Besides, it couldn't have made that impression," Daphne went on. "Look at the wound. It's wide and flat. Both edges of my tool are sharp."

As I'd reasoned.

Daphne turned a ghastly shade of gray. I grabbed her elbow to steady her, studying her as I did so. There wasn't any blood on her jeans or T-shirt, and I didn't see a discarded piece of clothing or a bloody rag that she might have used to wipe off any kind of weapon in the vicinity. On the other hand, the dumpster was about twenty feet away. Had the killer discarded the weapon in there?

Oliver inched toward us. "What do you think happened?"

"Someone hit her from behind," I whispered.

A siren bleated, cutting through the pall. Two police cars pulled to a stop beyond the crates.

Detective Dylan Summers and Officer Redcliff Reddick, the lanky redhead who was dating my pal Meaghan, climbed out of the first. Two uniformed officers exited the second. Summers was a good investigator and dedicated to the law, but at times he could come across stern and off-putting, like now, with his flinty eyes and his dark brow furrowed.

He strode to me. "You found a body again?"

"Yes, but I wasn't first on the scene. She was." I pointed at Daphne.

She sputtered, "I'm Daphne Flores." She reiterated to him that she had been on her way to weed the median.

Where had she been coming from?

"I was consulting a client about a garden," she said, as if sensing my question. She hooked a thumb in the direction of the precinct.

"Pretty early for a consultation," Summers stated.

"Yes, sir, but my client is heading for the airport. She's a very busy woman."

Summers, muscular and in his fifties and tan like any other local who spent hours at the beach or on the golf course, crouched to check the victim's pulse. Over his shoulder, he ordered the uniformed officers to take care of the crowd and secure the crime scene.

"She's Genevieve Bellerose"—I swallowed hard before adding—"our friend."

"Your friend?"

"She, Daphne, and I and a couple of other women get together occasionally to talk about gardening. We met in an online forum a short while ago."

"So, she's not a lifelong friend," Summers said.

"No, sir. She's a podcaster and influencer."

"Influencer?" He squinted over his shoulder at me.

Officer Reddick said, "Sir, an influencer is a term used on the Internet for someone who, um, influences what people like and don't like. It's a form of social media marketing. Miss Bellerose's podcast is called *Anything Is Poddable*."

I was surprised that he was familiar with Genevieve's work.

"Okay." Summers waved a hand. "I get it." He rose and stepped back so Reddick could start taking pictures of the crime scene. "Miss Kelly, who are the others in your gardening group?"

"As I said, Daphne"—I pointed to her—"as well as Petunia Fujimoto and Scarlet Lyle."

His gaze narrowed as he regarded Daphne. "What did you do when you saw Miss Bellerose?"

"I bent down, sir, and felt her neck for a pulse." Daphne wrapped an arm around her torso to steady herself.

"Did you touch anything else?"

"No, sir." Her cheeks blazed pink. "I mean, yes, I made contact with the ground. For balance. And I think I brushed hair off her face."

"No, I did that," I said. "A knee-jerk reaction, sir. I'm sorry."

"Understandable since you knew her," Summers said. "Go on, Miss Kelly."

I said, "Daphne . . . Miss Flores . . . screamed, which is why all of us"—I gestured to the onlookers and Oliver—"came running. We're all participants in the Summer Blooms Festival. All except Daphne. She owns Flower Farm on the outskirts of town."

Summers pursed his lips as he pulled an old-school notebook from his back pocket. He removed the pen and the rubber band holding the two together and jotted something that I knew I wouldn't be privy to.

"I checked her pulse," I went on. "There was none."

"First impression?"

His question surprised the heck out of me. Over the course of a few investigations, he'd never deferred to me. Well, that wasn't true. A month ago, when Meaghan's ex-boyfriend was murdered and the prime suspect was killed, Summers had given me credit for my input. As a fairy garden designer and macro photographer, I paid attention to detail.

"I think Daphne is innocent, and"—I eyeballed her gardening tool—"I don't think that's the weapon."

"What is it?" Summers asked, eyebrow arched.

"A hoedag," Daphne blurted. "A hoeing and weeding tool. It's mine. But I didn't kill her."

Fiona nudged my shoulder. "Tell him there's no blood on it."

I did.

Summers shot me a look. "Did you examine it?"

"No, sir." I shifted feet. "But, um, you can see from here it's clean, not to mention, the impression on her head is flat and wide," I added, reiterating what Daphne and I had both deduced.

"Blood can be indiscernible to the naked eye," Summers said, chiding me. "And let's allow the techs to decide what weapon was used."

"I clean all my tools every night," Daphne said. "That way they don't rust. And I store them in my shed so they don't get ruined by fog and inclement weather."

"Sir." Reddick approached. "Miss Bellerose has been dead for at least eight hours. Maybe longer. Her legs are stiff."

"The coroner will determine time of death," Summers said.

"Dylan . . . I mean, Detective Summers." Oliver Killian was standing behind the crime scene tape with other onlookers. "Forgive me, but how will this affect today's festival? I know it's a tragedy, but it's not like the crime scene is inside the festival grounds. May we continue?"

I gagged. Seeing Genevieve dead was unnerving. I couldn't imagine pushing that image aside and proceeding with business as usual.

"Sir, please." Oliver fingered his mustache but quickly dropped his hand. "A lot of vendors are in attendance. Townspeople are relying on us to continue."

"Are you saying the show must go on?" Summers quipped, but his jaw was ticking.

Oliver said, "Yes, something like that."

"Move to the side, Mr. Killian," Summers said. "I'll give you an answer shortly."

"May I go to work, sir?" Daphne asked. "The Weeders are counting on me."

"The Weeders," I said in explanation to Summers, "are members of the city's volunteer group that helps maintain the landscaping."

"I know what they are," he replied, "but no, you may not leave, Miss Flores. I have a lot of questions to ask you, like where were you between, say, seven p.m. and now?"

"Last night I was home tending to my roses. I slept until five this morning. Got up. Jogged. Went to see my client. Came here."

He asked the name of her client, which she provided.

"Any witnesses as to your whereabouts otherwise?"

"My cat." Daphne's shoulders sagged. Her hopeful face deflated. "I didn't do this."

Fiona fluttered to Daphne, petted her hair, and began circling her while incanting, "*By dee prood macaw.*" Translated, that meant may God make peace upon you. I hadn't learned much fairy language, but I was catching on.

Daphne blinked. She squared her shoulders. "May I text the head volunteer that I'm not coming?" She pulled a cell phone from her pocket.

"Yes," Summers said. "And then let me see that."

"W-why?" she faltered.

Chapter 7

Faeries, come take me out of this dull world,
For I would ride with you upon the wind,
Run on the top of the dishevelled tide,
And dance upon the mountains like a flame.
—William Butler Yeats, "The Land of Heart's Desire"

"Because," Summers continued, "I'm trying to figure out why Miss Bellerose would be killed in this location. I'd like to rule out that you were the one who lured her here."

"Lured her . . . I didn't." Daphne's eyes flooded with tears. "Oh, Courtney. I didn't. You know I didn't." She turned into me, and I embraced her in a reassuring hug.

I said, "Is there anything incriminating on your phone?"

"Yes." She pressed apart. "A text telling Genevieve how much she hurt me with a comment she made, but I can't be the only person she offended."

"She's right," I said to Summers. "Miss Bellerose spared no one." I thought of how Genevieve had sparred with Scarlet about their mutual professions. How she'd left Oliver Killian to fend for himself in his flower business, possibly causing the downfall of his marriage. How she'd critiqued Hideaway Café as to its ability to provide good food at the festival.

"Except you, Courtney." Daphne created a little distance be-tween us. "She never maligned you."

"Yes, but perhaps that was a matter of time," I said. "Genevieve relished her role as the goddess of taste."

"She posted everywhere about the festival," Daphne said. "On Instagram. On her blog. She even spoke on her podcast about not being invited. I wouldn't be surprised if her comments hurt atten-dance. She could be so cruel. I'm not sure what possessed her. Possi-bly she lashed out because her father abandoned her."

"I didn't know that," I said.

"She was in therapy to talk about it." Daphne faltered. "Not *in* therapy. She didn't go in person. She spoke to her therapist on Face-Time. She told me because she said therapy was really helping her, and her doctor might help me because . . ." She paused. "Just be-cause."

I wondered why Daphne might need a therapist but pushed the thought from my mind. Not my business.

"What's the therapist's name?" Summers asked.

"Geoffries," Daphne said. "Tamara Geoffries."

I knew Tamara because of a previous murder investigation. Sum-mers did, too.

"I'm not sure I could do FaceTime with a shrink," Daphne added, removing her cell phone from her pocket. "That seems so im-personal, you know?"

"I'm sure she'd meet you in person," I said. "She—" I stopped as a realization hit me. "Detective Summers, I don't see Miss Bellerose's cell phone or purse. Was this a robbery?"

"Don't theorize, Miss Kelly," Summers said. "How many times do I have to tell you that? And did you notice her top has pockets? Her valuables might be tucked into those. We'll be doing a complete search, I assure you."

He gestured for me to move aside and beckoned Daphne to the right. Meekly, she followed him. He held out his hand. She gave him her cell phone. He tapped something on the screen—the text message app, I presumed—and began swiping his finger upward. His mouth moved, and Daphne responded, but I couldn't read her lips, because she was pressing the knuckles of her left hand to them.

I surveyed the crowd that had assembled beyond the crime scene tape and spotted Petunia and Scarlet in the mix. They were standing beside each other, Petunia's arm around Scarlet, their faces pale.

"Miss Kelly!" Summers finished with Daphne, who slinked away, head hanging low—he'd probably told her not to leave town—and gestured to me. "You're next."

"Sir," I said with respect, and stepped closer. I tried to get a peek at his notebook but failed.

His cheek ticked with tension. "You touched the victim's hair."

"And checked her pulse, as I already stated. I don't see any noticeable footprints."

He grunted, not giving me the satisfaction of corroboration.

"Genevieve and I were supposed to meet at Hideaway Café for dinner last night," I continued. "She canceled via text, but when I replied asking why, she didn't respond. Is it possible"—I fought the bile rising up my throat—"that she was killed around that time?"

"What time was that?"

"Eight, or thereabouts."

"As I told my officer," Summers said, "we'll let the coroner determine TOD. Where did you go after you left the café?"

"I went h-home," I sputtered. He couldn't possibly suspect me, could he? "Straight home."

He jotted a note. "Who do you think did this?"

I didn't want to give him the list that had cycled through my head. I wouldn't throw anyone under the bus unnecessarily. "Her podcast could be provocative," I said diplomatically. "And, as Daphne . . . Miss Flores suggested—"

"First names are fine. Continue."

"Daphne was right. Genevieve occasionally posted scathing reviews online. She might have a lot of enemies."

He questioned me about her age, where she lived. He inquired whether she had any relatives in Carmel. I told him I didn't have a clue, adding that I didn't know if she had a boyfriend or significant other, either. I didn't even know her father had abandoned her or that she'd been seeing Tamara Geoffries. How could I have been so clueless?

"May I go back to my shop now?" I asked.

"No, I'd like you to stay at the festival. I'm going to allow it to remain open," he said. "Mr. Killian is right. The murder occurred outside the confines of the tents. We'll close this exit, of course." He motioned to it.

Yet again, the idea of forcing a smile to meet and greet people throughout the day made me nauseous. All I wanted to do was return to the shop and mourn the loss of a friend. "But, sir—"

"Keep your eyes open and ears alert."

I let out the breath I'd been holding. Advising me to stay alert meant he didn't suspect me. "Are you deputizing me?"

"Not on a bet." He smirked. "But you have an acute ability to see things others don't."

Like fairies, I mused.

"Tell your father I said hello when you touch base with him."

How well he knew me. I intended to contact Dad immediately. When he heard about the murder, he would worry. Summers and he played golf occasionally. They hadn't met when my father was on the force—a knee injury had ended that career—but they were good friends now.

Summers, accompanied by Reddick, moved on to speak to Oliver Killian. Oliver smiled when he learned that the festival could remain open. I wondered if he would be forthcoming about his strained business relationship with Genevieve. He'd better be. Summers was no slouch. He would learn the truth soon enough. I thought of Oliver's estranged wife. Did she reside in Carmel? Was she harboring a grudge for Genevieve?

From the crowd, Petunia raised her hand like she had a question. Reddick crossed to her and listened to whatever it was she had to say. He advised her to stay put and made a beeline for Summers. After listening to the officer, Summers crooked a finger at Petunia. I hung back and waited as she slinked toward him. I had no doubt she was going to reveal the argument she'd witnessed between Genevieve and Daphne about the roses.

Summers asked her a question and listened. Nodding, he said to Reddick, "Get Miss Flores and bring her back."

Reddick trotted away, and my heart sank. Daphne, who was sweeter than sugar, was definitely the prime suspect in Genevieve's murder.

I returned to my booth, Fiona fluttering beside me, and resumed organizing my wares. I wasn't in the mood to sell anything, but I'd have to try. My mother had been a magician at getting me to smile when I didn't want to. I fingered her locket and found myself remembering wonderful times baking and sewing and playing make-believe. When I felt steadier, I texted my father—I didn't want to speak to him—and then I messaged Joss. She responded immediately.

Joss: **Want me to sub for you?**

Me: **No, I'll manage.**

Joss: **Poor Genevieve.**

Me: **Yes, poor G. [sad emoji face]**

Dad replied and asked if I was okay and did I need him to drop everything and zip over? I wrote back that I was fine. I'd touch base later. I didn't have the energy to write Brady, but I didn't have to. Seconds later, he appeared, his face grim.

"Is it true what everyone is saying?" he asked.

"Yes, there's been a murder. Genevieve Bellerose."

"Oh, man. How awful."

Fiona settled on his shoulder and toyed with hair at the nape of his neck. He didn't react. He didn't feel her presence. For the next few minutes, I filled him in on the basics. Daphne finding the body and screaming. The rest of us racing to the area. Genevieve clad in black clothing, as if doing reconnaissance. Summers interrogating Daphne.

"Where were the security guards?" Brady asked.

"Got me. It happened outside the festival tent border beyond the dumpster."

He drew me into a warm embrace and kissed the top of my forehead. "How are you holding up?"

"I'm shaken, but I'll be fine." I stepped away. "Do you know Oliver Killian?"

"I do." He hooked his thumbs through his belt loops. "Nice enough guy."

"I heard his wife left him."

"Yeah. He's been torn up ever since."

"Do you know if the wife lives in Carmel?"

Brady scrubbed his chin. "If I recall, she relocated to San Francisco." He kissed me one more time. "I've got to get back to work. Gates open in thirty. Reach out if you need me."

After I put out a stack of five-dollar-off coupons that customers could use in our main shop, I neatened the fairy figurines on the mini rack, turning each to face front, and thought about Summers's question. Did Genevieve have family in the area? I opened my cell phone and did a quick search for the surname Bellerose. I didn't find anyone listed in Carmel or nearby Monterey. In fact, I didn't find any Belleroses in the Bay Area. I landed upon a doctor named Bellarose, with an *A,* in Silicon Valley. I doubted he was a relation. I considered what Daphne had claimed, that Genevieve had been seeing Tamara Geoffries for therapy. Would Tamara know more about Genevieve's history and family? I hoped, if asked, she would inform Summers.

To my surprise, Meaghan showed up. She looked solemn, her burgundy boho dress somber and understated. "Hey, pal." She pulled me into a hug. "I heard."

"I figured."

She held me at arms' length and released me. "What happened?" She moseyed to a folding chair by the table with the fairy garden atop it, and sat.

Fiona winged to her and settled on her shoulder.

I perched on the chair opposite my pal and, as I had with Brady, told her everything I knew. While talking, I saw a wilted leaf in the fairy garden's waterfall bellflowers and plucked it off. I pulled the Cecily Barker fairy free—she was affixed to a stake, which aided in positioning figurines—and shifted her to the left. None of the tweaking was necessary, but I was fidgety. I couldn't help myself.

"Do you think the police will search the dumpster for clues?" Meaghan asked.

"They'd be idiots not to, and Summers isn't an idiot." I truly admired the man. We locked horns, but he was a good, thorough detective.

"Why would she have been out there?" Meaghan asked.

"Well, for one, she wasn't a participant. She'd been ostracized. I would imagine she wanted to see what was going on. What she was missing."

"Or she was lurking because someone persuaded her to meet them there."

I wrinkled my nose. Summers had suggested the same thing.

"Who would have done that?" Fiona asked, spiraling into the air and gazing between us.

"I haven't a clue," I said.

"Or"—Meaghan ran a finger along the white tablecloth—"she was riding solo, planning a nefarious scheme."

I flashed on the Garden Delights booth. Had Genevieve planned to sabotage it because Oliver hadn't invited her to participate at the festival? No way. I couldn't wrap my head around that idea. I swatted my friend's hand. "Don't say something like that. You didn't know her."

"Oh, but I did. I ran into her one time. She was *shopping*"—she made air quotes with her fingers—"for a bauble at Glitz about a year ago." Glitz was a jewelry store in our courtyard. "We chatted about this and that and who it was for. She had Glinda pull out tray after tray of earrings to look at, but she didn't buy a thing." Glinda Gill displayed some of the most beautiful high-end jewelry I'd ever seen. Her taste was impeccable. "Then, about a month later, she wrote a scathing review of Glitz, saying its jewelry was ho-hum with no imagination." She tilted her head. "Perhaps you didn't hear about it. That was before you two were buddies."

"She panned Glitz?"

"Yup. Glinda was less than thrilled. In fact, she was vowing revenge."

I gasped. "Please don't tell Detective Summers that. I don't want Glinda on his radar."

"My lips are sealed."

Chapter 8

And though you be foolish or though you be wise,
With hair of silver or gold
You could never be young as the fairies are,
And never as old.
—Rose Fyleman, "The Fairies Have Never a Penny to Spend"

For the rest of the morning, the festival chugged along. Attendees chatted happily. The vendors near me were making lots of sales.

Around noon, Brady returned to check on me and brought me a few of the appetizers that he was selling at the festival. The avocado toast was always one of my favorites. The teriyaki chicken-on-a-skewer ran a close second. I ate half of each so I could tell him Genevieve had been wrong with her assessment. They were as spectacular as they would have been hot from the café's oven.

At three, a couple of our regular customers swung by, eager to see what gardens I'd crafted and if I'd been holding back special items at the shop. Some were anxious to hear gossip about the murder, too, but I didn't reward them for their curiosity. I advised them to ask the police. Throughout the day, I sold a number of private lessons that I'd carry out at the shop. Luckily, Joss had thought to create a sign-up sheet so I could keep track. I would have two a week from Tuesday, one a week from Wednesday, and one three weeks from today. Fiona greeted everyone as they arrived. No matter how hard she tried, only one elderly customer and a tween with braces could see her.

Summers stopped at the booth around a quarter to five to ask if I'd learned anything. I hadn't and begged him for news. He smiled like he'd taken up residence in the catbird seat. I sneered at his stony response. He cackled as he sauntered away.

"Quitting time, Fiona," I said.

Foot traffic had waned. The temperature had warmed up. It wasn't hot, but heat vapors were emanating off the pavement. After turning the OPEN sign to CLOSED, I packed up all the pots and figurines and locked all the trunks, loaded the furniture onto the platform truck, secured them with the bicycle-style lock, and said goodbye to our neighboring vendors, who looked about as tired as I felt.

Fiona and I swung by the shop, where I filled Joss in on the festival as well as all I knew about the investigation—next to nothing. Then I retrieved Pixie and started for the exit. She must have sensed my discontent, because she snuggled into me, her purring pronounced. I tickled her under the neck, assured her I would be fine, and she, Fiona, and I headed home.

When we arrived, Fiona zoomed from the foyer to my bedroom and back again. I could tell she was antsy about seeing her sister the way she was circling my head.

"Light," I ordered.

"Can't." She did a few loop the loops and made another pass through the cottage.

I retreated to the kitchen but didn't prepare dinner for myself. I had no appetite. I dished up Pixie's meal of tuna, refreshed her water bowl, placed some chopped fruit with honey on a plate for Fiona, and poured myself a glass of iced tea. I sipped it and sighed.

Fiona floated over her food, looking as lackadaisical as I felt. "Are you sad?" she asked.

"Yes." I took another sip of tea. "I can't believe my friend is dead. Murdered. We weren't super close, but despite her imperious nature, I liked her. I remember the first time all of us got together, she told some great jokes. One of my favorites was, What's the difference between incomplete and finished?"

Fiona raised both shoulders in a shrug.

"A man without a wife feels incomplete. Once he's married, he's finished." I laughed jaggedly, air escaping my nose. "Oh, how Scarlet had hated that one."

Fiona shook her head, not getting it.

"Finished means done for." I paused, searching for another synonym. "Doomed. Ruined. Washed up." *And murdered,* I realized. "Let's go outside and sit in the garden."

The temperature had cooled. The birdsong was minimal. The sun was sinking toward the horizon, its waning light painting the wisps of clouds a gorgeous sherbet orange. I set my iced tea on the wicker table, eased into a chair, and drew in a deep breath. I exhaled and felt calmer.

Fiona danced along the edge of the table. She stopped suddenly and pivoted toward me, her face pinched with concern. "Do you think I should ask Merryweather to postpone my sister's arrival?"

"Why?"

"Because . . . you know . . ."

Because of the murder. Got it. "No. It's important for your sister to know that the human world isn't all sugar and spice."

"Yes, but the heartache here isn't like it is in the fairy realm."

How I wished I could go to the fairy world. Perhaps one day the queen fairy would allow me to enter through the portal.

"No, Fiona," I said. "It'll be fine for your sister to visit. The murder, the investigation, doesn't concern you, or me, for that matter. The police have it well in hand. Are you nervous about seeing her?" I asked. "Will she come through the same portal you did?" I eyed the cypress.

"She should, I would think." She plopped onto her rump, wings extended and twitching. "What if I fail her? What if I'm a terrible mentor? What if my mother . . ." She gulped in a gasp.

"What if she *what?*"

"What if she banishes me forever, and Eveleen becomes the next in line?"

I gawked. "How can she become the queen fairy? After all, you're the only righteous fairy in the kingdom."

"If the queen fairy banishes me, she could change my sister's designation."

My mouth formed an *O*, but nothing came out. This was all new terrain to me.

"*By dee mas a toil,*" she added in her native tongue.

I blinked, not understanding.

"It is God's will," she translated.

I reached out to her and stroked her wings. "I'm sure you'll do fine. You're very smart. You've tempered your impulses. You'll be a wonderful mentor."

"*Tà,*" she murmured.

"You're welcome. *Wilcuma.*"

We sat in silence for an hour, drinking in the night air. I did my best to meditate, but I couldn't erase the image of Genevieve from my mind.

While sleeping, I tossed and turned. I awoke Saturday morning feeling harried. How I wished I could wave a magic wand and wind back the hands of time. I clambered out of bed, threw on my jogging clothes, and took a run on the beach. When I got home, I checked out the cypress tree in the backyard. No portal had materialized, which disheartened Fiona. I assured her the queen fairy would send Eveleen through in the manner she felt best.

After showering and dressing in a pretty forest green sundress—with my pale complexion, I could wear darker greens, but not lime; way too yellow—I retreated to the kitchen, fed Pixie and Fiona, drank a strawberry chia seed smoothie, and slipped into a pair of cute sandals. Before leaving the house, I checked the cypress a second time. No portal.

"Maybe she'll come through a portal at the shop," I suggested as Fiona was dabbing her cheeks with silver glitter. She wanted to look pretty for her sister.

"There are no portals there."

"Oh, no? How did you come into the human world on the day I met you?"

"A portal on the beach."

"Well, don't underestimate the queen fairy. She can do anything she imagines."

Fiona brightened at the prospect and hopped on my shoulder for our walk to work.

Joss was already there when we arrived. I deposited Pixie on the floor, and off she went to play with Fiona.

"How's it going, boss?" Joss asked. "Did you get any sleep?"

"Do I look that bad?"

Joss winked. "Let's just say you might want to add some color to your cheeks before the afternoon tea."

"Good idea."

"I'm out of here in five minutes and heading to the festival. I readied the lectern for the tea and wiped down the tables, plus I added the garden-themed fairy figurines that came in this morning to the bakers' racks. Here's one of them, by the way. Isn't she cute?" She lifted a yellow fairy holding a watering can.

"Adorable." I'd installed a similar figurine in my home garden and, for a bit of whimsy, positioned her so she was watering a bunny. "How many are attending today?"

"Thirty."

I whistled. "That's a good crowd. Thanks for being so organized."

As Joss was leaving, Renee Rodriguez, the owner of Seize the Clay, pushed open the front door, carrying a large plastic bin. "Morning, Joss."

"Bye, Renee," Joss said sassily.

"Courtney." Renee weaved through the displays to the sales counter. She set the bin down. "I'm glad you're here. I wanted to give you these before I headed to the festival." She swooped her long dark hair over her shoulders and smoothed the white smock top she was wearing over leggings. At forty-something, she was a strikingly handsome woman.

"Your store doesn't have a presence at the festival. Why the rush?"

"A friend said I absolutely had to see the face cream items Scarlet Lyle was carrying before they were all gone. Most are prototypes."

Scarlet hadn't mentioned that to me when she'd shown me the creams. I'd bet it was a lot of hype—hype she'd drummed up to increase sales.

"Is your fairy here?" Renee lifted her gaze, searching for Fiona.

"Courtney!" Fiona blazed into the shop from the patio. "Come. Quickly. Come, come! A portal. I see a portal. In the ficus!"

I excused myself and dashed after her.

Renee, sensing urgency, trailed me. "What's going on? Is there a problem? I didn't hear a crash or anything."

I drew to a halt by the fountain and stared at the ficus trees. Fiona was waiting in front of, yes, indeed, a glowing portal, so tiny that I wouldn't have seen it on my own.

"What are you staring at?" Renee said. "A mouse or something? Do you have—"

"*Shh,*" I cautioned. "She's coming through."

"She, who? A fairy?" Renee tiptoed closer.

The portal glowed and widened, the leaves of the ficus shimmered and trembled, and a fairy no bigger than Fiona emerged. She sparkled like a gem, with one set of glimmering adult wings, a smaller pair of junior wings, and aqua blue hair. Her tutu was aqua blue, too, and she was wearing a pair of matching slippers.

"Eveleen, you're here!" Fiona cried, and rushed to hug her sister.

Eveleen pursed her pouty lips and kissed Fiona on the cheek, then she pushed apart and orbited the patio. She swooped to Pixie, tweaked her ear, and returned to hover in front of me. "Courtney, I presume," she said, her voice as delicate as the tinkle of chimes. "Yes, I'm right. You look exactly like Fiona described. Pleased to meet you, and you as well," she said to Renee.

"Pleased to meet you, too," Renee whispered, the delight in her eyes infectious.

"You can see her, Renee?" I asked.

"Yes. Both of them."

"Well, I'll be." I was so happy for her. "I told you it was only a matter of time!"

Eveleen giggled, her laughter much like Fiona's, and did a shimmy-type dance in front of Renee.

"You needed a frollick to occur," I said.

"A frollick?" Renee arched an eyebrow.

"A gathering of fairies—in this case, two." I wrapped an arm around her. "You have so much to learn. Welcome to the club."

"Dylan won't believe it." Renee and Detective Summers were engaged. I wasn't sure when they would set a wedding date.

"So don't tell him."

"Good idea," she said. At one time, she'd been a police officer, but the life hadn't suited her. Quitting the force and starting her own business had definitely lightened her spirit and allowed her wiggle room when it came to following rules. "I don't want him to think I'm nuts. I'm not nuts, right?"

"Far from it," I assured her.

Fiona grabbed her sister's hands, and they swirled in the air. "I'm so excited you're here. I have friends to introduce you to. And, of course, we have to visit Auntie, and—"

"Don't be bossy," Eveleen said, separating from her.

"Don't be obstinate," Fiona said. "Follow me."

When they whizzed out of the shop, Renee shook free of the enchantment, returned to the showroom, and opened the lid of the bin she'd brought. "I have more polymer fairies, and I've made some gnomes." She removed the items one by one. "I hope you like them."

I lifted an adorable gnome with a knobbed nose, his eyes obscured by a red hat, and a WELCOME sign covering half of his white beard. "You are so talented. Perfect. We have lots of customers who want gnomes."

"Great." She scanned the shop. "Are the fairies, um, gone for good?"

"For the time being." I explained how Fiona had to mentor her sister.

Renee left the shop, a lightness in her step.

Moments after I officially opened the shop, Tish Waterman, the owner of A Peaceful Solution Spa, entered with her identical black shih tzus on leashes. "Good morning," she trilled. At one time, Tish had been a dour woman who had sworn to be my lifelong enemy, but after Fiona helped find Tish's missing adult daughter, she couldn't be friendlier. "Be good, you two," she warned her dogs. The shih tzu on my left yipped. The one on the right jauntily bumped his head against the other, earning another yip.

I didn't mind dogs' noises, but I didn't want them to topple displays. "You're early," I said, moving toward her to block the dogs' progress. "The tea won't start until half past one."

"I'm not here for that." She fanned the air with a perfectly manicured hand. Dressed in a white jumpsuit, her jet-black hair a stark contrast, she looked meticulous, her way of drawing attention from the scar that ran the length of one cheek. "I've got a tidbit about the murder to impart. It's about Daphne Flores. I heard she's a suspect. I love that girl. I don't want to go to the police. I don't want to get her in trouble. However, she and I shared . . ."

She didn't finish, leaving me on tenterhooks. She and Daphne had shared what? Personal stories? The same physical trainer?

Tish continued. "I thought you, with your inside track to Detective Summers, might know what to do with my information."

"Inside track?" I snorted. "As if." On the other hand, he had asked me to keep my eyes open yesterday. He'd even praised me for my acute ability to see things others didn't. Perhaps he was warming to my natural curiosity. Doubtful. I'd guess he knew I would pay attention anyway, and he wanted to utilize that to his benefit. "What about Daphne?"

"Well, Thursday night, I was walking my little beauties. We were skirting the Summer Blooms Festival booths when I spied Daphne at the far end, toward Ocean Avenue. Standing there. Staring into space. Near the dumpster."

Uh-oh. That didn't sound good. I swallowed hard. "Did you speak to her?"

"No. She was clearly forlorn. I'm not very good at listening to people's problems."

I appreciated her honesty. Tish provided services to make people more beautiful, but she had no intention of allowing any of her staff to serve as therapists. She'd once joked that was what fairy garden shop owners were good for.

"Isn't that where they found the body?" Tish asked.

"Yes." Had Daphne been casing out the area? Or had she lured Genevieve to the site and waited to attack her? No. I couldn't wrap my head around that scenario. I said, "After hoeing weeds, she might have needed a long walk. Was she carrying a garden tool?"

"I can't remember. Is that important?"

"What time was it?"

"Around seven forty-five."

"Did you see Genevieve Bellerose in the vicinity?"

"No."

Typically, I directed people who had pertinent information about a crime to speak to the police, but not this time. I thanked Tish and said I'd give it some consideration. After all, why help the police convict Daphne if her presence near the crime scene prior to Genevieve's arrival was nothing more than coincidence?

Chapter 9

If you see a fairy ring
In a field of grass,
Very lightly step around,
Tiptoe as you pass;
Last night fairies frolicked there,
And they're sleeping somewhere near.
—John Keats, "Ode to a Nightingale"

At one p.m., Yvanna Acebo, who worked at Sweet Treats full time, arrived with a basket filled with generic bakery boxes. On her off days, she made goodies for our high teas. Her younger sister, Yoly, followed her in. Like Yoly, Yvanna had dark hair, caramel brown eyes, and an easy smile.

"What treats are we serving, Yvanna?" I asked as she wheeled her cart past me and down the hall leading to our small kitchen. Her grandmother had been a fabulous baker and had passed along the skill to her.

Over her shoulder, she said, "Apple strudel muffins, lemon raspberry delights, and banana blueberry scones that will knock your socks off."

"I prefer the muffins," Yoly said. "The strudel topping is super sugary, and the ones with walnuts have a nice crunch, I've been told. I can't eat nuts."

"You poor thing," I said. "I love nuts of all kinds, in particular cashews."

"Technically, those are not nuts," Yoly said. "They're found inside the drupe seed of a tree, so botanically, they're considered seeds."

"Okay, okay," Yvanna said, reemerging from the hall with an armful of linens. "Courtney doesn't want to hear how smart you're becoming since taking plant science at the junior college."

"Botany," Yoly said. "It's called botany."

"Whatever." Yvanna yanked her sister's ponytail and proceeded to the patio. "Help me set the tables."

Yoly went to the hall and returned with a tea cart fitted with silverware, tea caddies, and china cups and saucers.

Meaghan arrived next with her Celtic lever harp in tow. She'd learned the art of playing the instrument from my nana and enjoyed performing whenever she could for our teas. If she couldn't, Tish's daughter was adept at playing the flute. Meaghan paused, her hand on my elbow, and whispered, "Are you holding up okay?"

"I'm hanging tough," I said. She knew my mind would continue to churn out images of the murder. I was a visual learner with a distinct visceral connection to whatever I saw. "Go ahead to the patio. You know the drill." I shooed her away.

"Hello, Courtney," Lissa Reade, the seventyish librarian for Harrison Memorial Library, said as she entered the shop waving a copy of today's book club read, *Mum's the Word*. "I thoroughly enjoyed this story." She weaved through the display tables, looking as stylish as ever in a loose-knit ecru summer sweater over honey-brown cigarette pants. She would guide the book club in its discussion.

"What's not to like about the protagonist?" I quipped. "Abby is spunky and fun."

"And always finding herself embroiled in an investigation." Lissa winked. "Like you."

"I'm not—"

"Just teasing." She petted my arm fondly. "How are you doing, dear? I heard the news."

"I'm fine."

"We're here," Fiona trilled, leading a posse of fairies into the shop. "Courtney, I introduced Eveleen to my friends."

A gaggle of fairies coasted into the shop with Fiona in the lead. Calliope, directly behind Fiona, was the green intuitive fairy that resided in Meaghan's garden. Next came Zephyr, a nurturer fairy. She had lavender eyes, lavender wings, and silver hair, and she carried a flute in a bow-and-arrow style pouch. Cedric Winterbottom, a wizened fairy with silken hair, pointy ears, and green tendrilled wings, followed Zephyr. I'd met him a few months ago. He was now a full-fledged teacher in fairy science and plant psychology. Last month, his tutelage had been much appreciated.

"Good day, Courtney," he said in his English accent as he whizzed past.

I replied in kind.

Eveleen and Merryweather Rose of Song were the last of the fairies to arrive. Merryweather, Fiona's aunt and mentor, a guardian fairy, had iridescent gossamer hair that glimmered in the light. Her loose-fitting dress was a regal crimson, and her wings sported matching polka dots. She hung out at the library so she could enhance the love of the written word to readers.

"Hello, Courtney," Eveleen crooned. "We're having so much fun!" She was as giddy as a toddler at a birthday party.

"This way," Fiona said, and beckoned them to the patio. When the others disappeared into the ficus trees—for their own tea, I presumed—she zipped back to me. "I asked Ulra to join us, but she was too shy."

"She'll come around. Are you having fun with your sister?"

She bobbed her head. "Yes, but I can tell you this is going to be a challenge."

"Because she's your sister?"

"Because she's certain she's right all the time."

I giggled. "Oh, so she's just like you."

Fiona stuck her tongue between her lips and blew hard before disappearing into the ficus.

Pixie, who'd noticed the flock of fairies, bounded to the trees and pawed the leaves, but no fairies reappeared to toy with her. Frustrated, she plopped down on the patio to wait.

A half hour later, when the book club attendees were seated and the clinking of spoons on china quieted, Meaghan stopped playing the harp, and Lissa took her place behind the lectern.

"Welcome." Lissa brandished today's book. "Let's get started. Many of you are repeat book clubbers, but some of you are newbies. I ask questions. Raise your hand if you want to chime in. There are no wrong answers, and we'll have no spoilers, in case anyone hasn't finished the book. Now, what did you think of Abby's flower shop?"

Zinnia Walker, who was sitting with two of the other Happy Diggers, raised her hand. Hattie and her sisters had passed on coming to this book club so they could see to the budding gardeners' booth at the festival.

"Zinnia," Lissa said. "You have the floor."

"I'd like to own the shop."

Lissa smiled indulgently. "Dear, I think you have enough on your plate with your hotel expansion."

The audience chuckled.

Lissa asked her next question. "How would you feel if a low-cost competitor was killing your profits?"

The word *killing* caught me up short, as did the notion of a business owner being at odds with her competitor. I shuddered. Meaghan peeked at me. I waved her off, my thoughts zeroing in on Scarlet Lyle and her contentious relationship with Genevieve. I didn't want to think one of my friends could be a killer, but how well did I know Scarlet, honestly?

"Yes, a hit-and-run accident can be scary," Lissa said, in response to one attendee's comment about the brutality of an event in the story. "But as we all know, in a mystery novel, rarely is the death gentle. Now, let me ask you, if you saw a crime committed, would you report it to the police?"

The exchange of ideas went on for another hour, with Lissa guiding the Q&A. When the tea ended and the customers departed, Fiona and her friends reappeared.

"Did you have a good time?" I asked Eveleen.

She tittered and said, "I did. Everyone is so nice."

"Did you learn anything new?"

Fiona fluttered beside her, prodding her with the tip of her wing.

Eveleen scrunched up her nose. "Yes, that I daydream and must pay better attention if I hope to memorize all the blessings for the flowers."

Aha. Fiona had had her first session as a mentor. Good for her.

"I daydream, too," I said.

That eased the tension that was creasing the younger fairy's face.

Fiona beamed. "We're going out tonight. I want to show her every aspect of Carmel."

"Be safe," I said, regretting the words instantly, because they startled Eveleen. "I meant have fun."

At five o'clock, as the last of the book club participants were leaving, Joss slipped into the shop. She scooted past a few stragglers. "Good day at the festival," she said to me, handing over the proceeds. "I sold the fairy garden you had on display."

"Oh, no. I promised that to a vendor before we opened Friday. He paid cash. It's for his daughter. I forgot to tell you because—" I stopped cold. *Because of the murder.*

"Don't sweat it. It's okay. Holly was the buyer. It was for her daughter-in-law."

"Phew. I'll make her a duplicate."

Together, we tallied up the day's receipts. As I was inserting the cash pouch that we would deposit in the bank into the shop's safe, my cell phone rang.

I pulled it from the pocket of my sundress and answered. "Hi, Dad."

"Want to have dinner with me at Hideaway Café in a half hour? Just the two of us."

"Sure, but I don't need—"

"Babying. Got it."

I locked up the shop, took Pixie home, grabbed a cardigan to throw over my dress, added some rouge to my cheeks, and hoofed it back to the café. My father was already sitting on the patio, nursing a scotch—his drink of choice. He'd ordered a chardonnay for me. I pecked his cheek and sat down.

Brady was chatting up customers at a table. When he saw me, he excused himself and crossed to us. He kissed me warmly on the cheek, his hand resting on my shoulder. "You look ravishing."

"Ha! What a little bit of color will do."

He rattled off the specials.

My father said, "Give us a while to catch up."

"Sure thing," Brady said, and moved on.

Dad leaned forward on both elbows. "Is your fairy with you?"

"Don't tease."

"Wanda has me reconsidering." Wanda Brownie, Meaghan's mother, was my father's new love.

"Does she?"

He smirked. "Nah."

I harrumphed. "Yeah, that's what I thought. No, Fiona isn't here. She's out with her sister."

Dad pulled a face. "Fanciful."

"Closed-minded." I ran my finger along the stem of my wine-glass. "By the way, I heard you're going to offer your services to the Happy Diggers Budding Gardeners cause."

"Yes, Wanda talked me into it. That woman can sell freezers to ice fishermen." He sipped his drink. "Tell me how you are. Seeing another dead body can't be—"

"Easy. No, it's not. Especially when I was just getting to know her." I explained about the women I'd met because of the web forum. "Detective Summers thinks Daphne Flores did this, but there's no way she could have. She's not . . ." I let the sentence hang.

"Capable? I've told you many times that everyone has a limit. What would her motive be?"

I told him how Genevieve had dissed Daphne's roses.

He rolled his eyes. "Okay, that is weak."

I shot out a hand. "See?"

Our waitress arrived, and my father and I both ordered the Dungeness crab cakes appetizers. He asked for the crusted Monterey Bay calamari steak served in a creamy piccata sauce, and I chose salmon topped with lemon, capers, and goat cheese. When I ate at home, I rarely dressed up my fish. This indulgence would be a treat.

"Have you talked to Summers?" I asked.

Dad's gaze narrowed.

"You have." My father might have retired from the force, but he had earned their continued respect. In the past few months, he'd become a sounding board for Dylan Summers. "Did he give you details? Did he search the dumpster? Did he find the weapon? Do you know the time of death?"

"The police haven't tracked down the weapon. I don't know about the dumpster or the TOD."

Across the patio, a waiter dropped a tumbler on the brick flooring. The sound of shattering glass snagged everyone's attention. I swiveled in my seat and caught sight of Oliver Killian sitting with a man whose back was to me, but I recognized the generous head of brown hair. It was Asher Lyle. I didn't see Scarlet, and it didn't look like a place had been set for a third person.

"What're you staring at?" my father asked.

I swung back to face him. "Oliver Killian is dining with Asher Lyle."

"Oh, yes, I see them."

Asher swiveled in his chair, caught sight of us, and waved.

Dad acknowledged him and said, "Asher attended the first master class I gave."

"Really? Why?"

"He's expanding the gardening section at his general store, so he wants to stay informed."

"How will being well-versed in conservation help?" I asked, confused. The general store sold a variety of household goods, including linens, apparel, apothecary items, pottery, and, yes, some gardening ware, mostly decorative.

"He wants to know about trends in general. He's pretty hip. He asks pertinent questions. I think he wants to sound erudite when speaking to customers."

"*Ooh*, Dad. *Erudite*. Fifty-cent word. Nana would be proud."

He chuckled.

I glanced over my shoulder again at Asher and Oliver. Both were laughing. Their buoyant mood surprised me. Genevieve was dead. Surely they couldn't be amused by that. On the other hand, there had been no love lost between Oliver and Genevieve. He wasn't sharing how he'd killed her, was he?

Stop, Courtney. They could be chatting about a book they'd read or a TV show they'd watched recently.

Dinner arrived, and my father and I tucked in. Each morsel was better than the next. He let me try his calamari. The piccata sauce was excellent. My salmon was incredible. Brady stopped by, and we lauded him with praise. Blushing, he apologized because he couldn't sit and chat. Saturdays were always busy.

After paying the bill, my father offered to walk me home.

"You don't have to," I said.

"But I want to. A good brisk walk will do me good." He patted his flat belly. I doubted he'd ever need to worry about his weight, he kept so active.

Arm in arm, we strolled down 7th Avenue toward Carmelo Street. As we neared Casanova Street, I said, "Mind if we take a detour?"

He raised an eyebrow. "What now?"

"Daphne lives this way. I want—"

"To see if she's awake?"

"No. I want to peek at her garden and try to figure out why Genevieve might have dissed it."

"It's dark."

"Please."

"How can I say no to my favorite daughter?"

"Your only daughter."

Laughing, he steered me to the left. "Which house?"

"The third one. Casa Casanova. With the red picket fence." About three percent of the houses in Carmel-by-the-Sea had a name. Many were family names, but some were cute like Daphne's. My cottage was called Dream-by-the-Sea. "Our friend, Petunia Fujimoto, lives two doors down. I think you've met her. She owns Bowers of Flowers."

"I bought Wanda a bouquet there. It's a nice place. Lots of variety."

"Oh, there she is. Petunia!" I called, but she must not have heard me, because she scurried into her house and slammed the door.

At the far end of the street, I spied the silhouette of a large man. He was standing immobile, as if staring after Petunia.

"Dad, do you see that guy?" I asked.

"Where?"

"On the corner. Could it be Bentley Bramble? He accosted Petunia in my shop the other day."

"Accosted?"

"Not physically, but he was gruff." He hadn't been happy with her rebuff.

"Whoever it might be is moving on," Dad said. "Nothing to worry about. Did you need to speak to Petunia?"

"No, it's okay. I merely wanted to tell her I'd bring over the fairy garden she ordered for her sister tomorrow before heading to the festival. I'll text her in the morning."

We stopped outside Daphne's fence and peered in. Only a few lights were on in her storybook cottage. The house was not a Hugh

Comstock original, but it mimicked the famous architect's designs with heart-shaped cutout windows, flared eaves, and irregular chimney. Tulip-style lights illuminated the front yard and the cobblestone path. The garden was jam-packed with roses of all colors. I detected movement within the house, and suddenly a Siamese cat appeared in a window. It positioned itself, face forward, and sat as silent as a sphinx.

"*Hmm,*" my father said thoughtfully, eyeing the roses.

"They don't look good, do they?" I murmured.

Genevieve had been right about them. Judging by the leaves on the bushes closest to us, the plants were in need of serious love and affection. Roses were hungry feeders.

"Not enough nitrogen, I suspect," Dad said. "She could do with adding blood meal."

Nitrogen encouraged vigorous leaf growth and abundant flowers. Too little, and the result was yellow leaves and stunted trunk growth. "I wonder how she might've missed that."

"The forest for the trees syndrome," Dad said. "She's been too preoccupied with her farm to see to her own garden."

I flashed on Daphne's alibi for Thursday night. She said she'd been tending to her roses. That had to be a lie.

Chapter 10

Children born of fairy stock
Never need for shirt or frock,
Never want for food or fire,
Always get their heart's desire.
—Robert Graves, "I'd Love to Be a Fairy's Child"

Sunday morning rolled around way too fast. I awoke with muddled thoughts, but the sound of fairy laughter perked me up. Fiona and Eveleen were inside the dollhouse my grandfather had made for my mother. When I was a girl, she'd allowed me to enjoy it with her. We'd had so much fun using cartoonish voices and making up ridiculously inane stories. Each piece of handmade furniture was arranged to my mother's liking. I bit back tears, the sweet memory seared in my heart.

"Having a good time?" I asked the fairies, swinging my legs out of bed and giving Pixie a scrub on her belly.

The sisters stopped laughing and bounded out the dollhouse's front door. Their cheeks were crimson with embarrassment.

"Don't worry," I said. "You can play in it."

"It's exactly the right size for us!" Eveleen exclaimed.

After a brisk run on the beach, angst about Daphne's guilt or in-nocence plaguing my mind with every stride, I took a steaming hot shower, dressed in white capris, pretty pink floral blouse, and Crocs, and made Pixie and the fairies breakfast. I wasn't hungry—worry dampened my appetite—so I grabbed a peanut butter oatmeal protein cookie to eat later, and I retreated to my greenhouse to finalize Petunia's garden. I'd finish it, deliver it, and arrive at the festival before it opened at nine.

Slipping on an apron, I inhaled deeply, treasuring the aromas in the greenhouse. There was something soothing about the mix of earth and plants in a closed environment. I'd already filled the blue ceramic pot Petunia had selected with dirt, and I'd installed a variety of plants as well as the white fence she'd picked out. For the story, I chose a blue fairy with flowers to represent Petunia's sister, Peony. Even though Peony was a dollars-and-cents kind of woman, she loved her garden, so after positioning the slat-back chairs Petunia had chosen for the arrangement, I added a number of resin gardening tools, butterflies, and daisies to prettify the arrangement. Lastly, because Peony had two daughters, I placed a girl fairy riding on the back of a golden retriever between the chairs and another girl fairy leapfrogging a toad to the right. I wanted the story to depict how engaged the mother was with her children.

While I worked, Fiona and Eveleen appeared. Fiona showed her sister everything I used to create gardens—the fairy figurines and environmental pieces like benches and slides, the collection of miniature plants, and the homemade fertilizer I sprinkled on the vegetation to help it thrive.

Eveleen was quite impressed. "You're very talented, Courtney," she said.

"When I'm inspired," I replied.

An hour later, I was ready to deliver the garden. I texted Petunia that I was on my way. The fairies wanted to go with me to see her delight. I told Pixie I'd return soon to take her to the shop, and walked the two blocks to Petunia's house. The garden grew heavier after the first block. My arms were aching by the time I was passing Daphne's house.

"Look, there's Hedda," Fiona said, and quickly explained to her sister who Hedda was and that she'd seen Fiona for the first time at the festival.

Hedda, dressed in jogging clothes, was standing on the street with her handsome boyfriend, Jeremy, owner of Batcheller Galleries, and his adorable Dalmatian, Polka Dot. Jeremy, too, was dressed in leggings and a zippered hoodie.

Oho. What an early-morning date they'd arranged, I mused, wondering if they were taking their relationship to the next level.

As I drew near, I tensed. Jeremy had his arm around Hedda, and she was crying. Polka Dot was sitting dutifully by her master's legs.

"Is everything okay?" I asked, hoping I wasn't witnessing a breakup.

Hedda glanced at me. Tears streaked her cheeks. "No. It's . . . it's—" She broke free from Jeremy and shot a hand at Petunia's yard.

I looked where she was pointing and gasped. So did Fiona and Eveleen. Petunia was lying on the brick path, as if she'd been going toward the gate. Her head was bashed in. Her floral dress was bunched up around her thighs. A bloody hoedag was lying a few feet from her body.

"Oh, no!" I cried, my insides reeling. "Is she—"

"D-dead?" Hedda stammered. "Yes."

Eveleen burst into tears. No doubt, the young fairy hadn't seen something like this in the fairy realm. Fiona comforted her.

"No, no, no," I murmured. Not another friend. Who killed her? Why? Petunia was so kind and caring. I wrapped my arms around my torso to steady myself.

"Jeremy and I were walking the dog," Hedda continued. "Polka Dot started to whine. She must have smelled—" Her voice cracked. She couldn't go on.

Jeremy finished for her. "The blood. The dog must have smelled the blood. We called nine-one-one."

Fiona released her sister and flew to Hedda to console her.

A siren bleated. Seconds later, a police cruiser raced down the street and screeched to a halt. It was followed by a Honda SUV.

Officer Reddick, in uniform, exited the cruiser.

Detective Summers, dressed in chinos and a green polo shirt, clambered out of the Honda and strode to Hedda and Jeremy. He threw me a nasty look. "You!" he said to me.

"I didn't find the body, Detective. They did. I was delivering this." I hoisted the garden and swallowed hard. "I made it for Petunia's sister."

"Put the fairy garden on the ground, Miss Kelly," Summers said. "Away from the gate entrance, please. It looks heavy."

"It is."

Summers donned latex gloves and cloth booties over his shoes and inspected the gate. "Officer, take photographs, please."

"Yes, sir."

Summers unlatched the gate and gingerly drew it open.

Fiona ordered Eveleen to stay where she was and winged to Petunia to get a closer look.

"Wait!" I said to Fiona.

Summers said, "Why?"

I said, "Sorry. I thought you might be about to step on evidence. I don't see any footprints. Do you?"

He stared at the ground. "It looks swept clean, actually."

"With what? I don't see a broom."

"Your guess is as good as mine." He entered the crime scene and pointed to the hoedag. "Is that what I think it is?"

"Uh-huh." My head bobbed uncontrollably. There was definitely blood on the tool's blade this time.

Fiona hurried to inspect it.

Onlookers were beginning to crowd the street.

"Stay back!" Summers shouted to them, and readdressed me. "How many of those do you think we'll find in Carmel?" He wasn't expecting me to answer. His jaw was ticking with tension as he bent down, felt Petunia's pulse, and agreeing with Hedda's assessment that she was dead, turned his attention to the hoedag.

"Daphne didn't do this," I said, inadvertently glancing in the direction of her house. Out of the corner of my eye, I noticed Fiona doing a jig, not to catch my attention. She was performing the dance on top of a cell phone that was lying faceup on the ground. Was it Petunia's? The screen illuminated beneath Fiona's feet. Petunia must not have password-protected her phone.

The light caught Summers's attention. He picked up the phone and swiped the screen. Over his shoulder, Fiona seemed to be studying the display. From where I stood, I couldn't make heads nor tails of it.

"Miss Kelly, I see you texted Miss Fujimoto," he said to me, confirming it was Petunia's phone.

The killer hadn't taken it. Why not?

"Yes, sir. Saying I was on my way with—" I motioned to the fairy garden I'd set on the ground.

He browsed other messages. Who else had texted her? Had she communicated with the killer?

Seconds later, Fiona fluttered to me, her face scrunched with concern, her wings flapping like crazy. "The tool is Daphne's. Her initials are on the handle."

Daphne wouldn't have been stupid enough to leave a monogrammed tool behind. The killer must've stolen it from her shed and left it there on purpose to frame her. Who hated her that much? Or was she the convenient patsy because she was already suspected of Genevieve's murder?

My insides snagged until I remembered something else. "Detective, last night, I was walking with my father, and we saw Petunia enter her house and slam the door. Seconds later, we caught sight of a man standing at that intersection." I pointed toward 8th Avenue. "He stood there for a while before moving on."

"So she was alive at . . . what time was that?"

"Around nine p.m."

He rejoined us outside the fence and pulled his notebook from his pocket. "Do you know who the man was?"

"No, but if I made a guess, it was Bentley Bramble. He has a crush on Petunia and hounded her the other day at my shop for a date."

"Why were you on this street last night?" He held his pen poised over the notebook. "You don't live here."

"Um . . ." I didn't want to say we'd come to look at Daphne's garden. What we'd deduced might further implicate her in Genevieve's murder. But I didn't want to lie, either. "We were looking at gardens."

"In the dark?" He narrowed his gaze. "Any gardens in particular? Like Daphne Flores's garden?"

I gulped. Of course he knew where Daphne lived. He wasn't a slacker.

"To determine whether her alibi was valid?" he pressed.

"I'm not an expert."

"But your father is. I'll check with him." Summers's gaze glinted with victory. He directed his attention to Jeremy and Hedda. "Why were you two in the area?"

"We were on a stroll," Jeremy said.

"We were going to get coffee," Hedda inserted, "but now all I want to do is go home."

Jeremy grabbed hold of her hand, and his thumb began stroking gently, confirming my guess about their blossoming relationship.

"Stick around to give us your first impression," Summers said, "and then we'll release you." He faced me. "As for you, Miss Kelly, how well did you know Miss Fujimoto?"

"We'd become friendly in the past six months. She provided flowers for an event I threw, and we started chatting online. She was one of the friends in the forum I told you about." I still couldn't wrap my head around the fact that she was dead. Murdered. Like Genevieve. A chill ran through me.

"As for Bentley Bramble . . ." Summers continued. "The topiary guy. I've seen him around town. You say they were dating?"

"They did at one time, but he kept standing her up, so she lost interest. He believed he'd made another date, but Petunia said he hadn't, which irked him. I supposed she might've reconsidered the date, and they went out last night, and he walked her to the corner and waited until she was inside her house. But why did she slam the door? Did they argue?" I shrugged. "I honestly don't know enough."

"That's clear."

"Bentley knows his way around gardening tools," I added.

Summers jotted more notes. "Miss Flores knows her way around them, too," he said pointedly. "Did she have any reason to wish Miss Fujimoto dead?"

"No!" I exclaimed. "None in the world."

Not unless she blamed Petunia for making the police suspect her of murder.

When Summers released me, Fiona and her sister rushed off to convene with Merryweather Rose of Song, which sort of miffed me. I was shaken and shocked by Petunia's death and desperately wanted to know what my fairy had viewed on Petunia's cell phone other than my text. For all I knew, what she saw could help solve the case. I tried to send her a mental message to come back and fill me in but knew I would fail. ESP was not in my wheelhouse.

I touched base with Joss and told her the horrible news as I hurried to the festival. Like me, she said she was stunned. She liked Petunia as much as I did. After we consoled each other, Joss gave me a business update. People were showing up in droves with the five-dollar-off coupons, but she assured me she could handle the extra traffic. I wished her luck and entered the event at Section F. I cut a path through the attendees.

The place had only been open for a half hour, but it was crawling with people. I spied Scarlet in her booth. Asher was with her. She was dressed cheerily in a bright pink boyfriend shirt, jeans, and thick-soled boots, but she didn't look happy. She was peering at her cell phone and sobbing. Clearly, she'd heard about Petunia.

Suddenly, Asher took her cell phone from her and started scrolling through it. Scarlet reached for it. He shook his head, denying her control, and finished whatever he was doing. Erasing messages of the news, I supposed.

A few customers were browsing the wares in Scarlet's booth. I didn't see the shovel I'd seen the other day and jolted. *No way*. I didn't know for certain that a shovel was the weapon used to kill Genevieve, but if it was, did Scarlet wield it? If not, did someone else, say Oliver Killian, steal it and use it? He was constantly walking around the festival. He would have noticed it. I looked for the rake and didn't see it, either. Maybe someone had purchased them, I told myself.

Not wanting to believe Scarlet was a killer about as much as I didn't want to believe Daphne could be, I moved on. As I neared the Happy Diggers's booth, I heard Hattie call my name.

"Courtney, dear, come here!" She clasped my hand and pulled me into the shade of her booth. The rectangular display table, which hadn't been finished Thursday, was covered with a green tablecloth and decorated with complimentary flowerpots filled with shears and seed packets. "You shouldn't take too much sun with your fair skin. You'd be smart to cover your arms like I do when the sun is this bright." She was wearing a Happy Diggers long-sleeved T-shirt.

"I'll remember next time."

"I heard what happened to Petunia. Hedda said you chanced by and saw her—" She stopped and rested a hand over her heart. "What is this world coming to?"

I didn't know.

"Hedda is beside herself," Hattie went on. "I can't imagine anything worse than finding a body when you're on a stroll with your beau."

Or finding one by the dumpster. Or by the fountain in your place of business. Or slumped over a desk. Or . . .

I sighed. I had stumbled upon way too many bodies. Was I somehow responsible for drawing this kind of negative energy to Carmel? Could I do a sage cleansing to free me and everyone I cared about of bad juju?

Hattie said, "You've had experience with seeing horrific things. What would you say to Hedda?"

"To keep busy. To not dwell. And if at all possible, if there's any clue she remembers, no matter how small, to tell the police. Doing so will make her feel as if she has helped."

Hattie screwed up her mouth. "What could she possibly have seen that the police missed?"

"You never know." I wondered again what Fiona had viewed on Petunia's cell phone.

Hattie fiddled with the display of pots, raising the seed packets so passersby could read the labels: basil, chives, mint, and more. The way she was fiddling made me think of Oliver Killian and how he continually tweaked his mustache and tie as well as the arrangements in his festival booth.

"Courtney, you're clicking your tongue," Hattie said. "Is there something on your mind?"

"How well do you know Oliver Killian?"

"We've been acquainted for years. His wife was a Happy Digger until she moved away."

"He blamed Genevieve for the rift in his marriage."

"If you're asking whether he had a motive to want her dead"— she lowered her voice—"I do know she published a nasty post about his shop recently, not that a post should make anyone contemplate murder, but one never knows what makes a person snap."

"I thought you didn't know what Genevieve did."

"After our chat on the beach the other day, I thought I should check her out. She claimed in her post that Oliver was copying designs he'd found online."

"Meaning his designs were not unique."

"That was the gist."

I groaned. Why had Genevieve felt the need to go on the attack? If I went through her posts, would I stumble upon a host of suspects who wanted her dead?

"However," Hattie continued, "I happen to know that Oliver has an alibi for Thursday night. He took a friend to an AA meeting. Of course, due to the sensitive nature, he won't be able to disclose who."

"How did you find out?"

"My ex-husband, rest his soul, was an alcoholic." Hattie had been married in her heyday as a lounge singer but had never taken her husband's name, preferring to use her maiden name. They'd divorced ten years to the day after they'd married.

"I'm sorry."

"Yes, well, what's past is past. Oliver was familiar with my history, and the other day he pulled me aside and asked me how to be a good friend to someone who was troubled."

"Is he his friend's sponsor?"

"Oh, no, dear. Purely his ride. After his first drink, Oliver never touched alcohol again. He had a severe reaction to it. But the most recent AA meeting was Thursday night, so I know that's where he was. As for today's tragedy, of course, Oliver had no connection to Petunia Fujimoto at all."

Except they'd owned competitive businesses, I reflected.

"Go on now." Hattie hugged me fiercely and gave me a gentle push. "I won't keep you."

As I neared the transportable fountain, I caught the aroma of a blooming onion from Awesome Blossom and sighed. Of all the times to have no appetite. I heard the strains of a flute and guitar. A duo was serenading the crowd that had gathered to watch the Adonis in loincloth and cape-like drape pose at the top of the fountain. When he changed position and flexed his well-formed muscles, a few women in the crowd *ooh*ed. Circling the fountain were children of all ages at easels, doing their best to capture the image of the statue before he moved again.

Beyond the fountain, Bentley Bramble was working on a topiary in the shape of the Adonis. A cluster of spectators watched on, impressed. His muscles flexed against the seams of his polo shirt and cargo shorts. He squatted to trim the lower edges of the sculpture, adjusting the rim of his baseball cap for a better view.

Bentley caught sight of me and stood up abruptly. He beckoned me with the tip of his shears. I tapped a hand to my chest and mouthed *Me?* He nodded and left his audience to meet me halfway. His cheeks were streaked with dust—tear-streaked dust.

Under his breath, he said, "You were there."

"Where?"

"At Petunia's house. This morning. I heard she was murdered. I can't believe it."

"Who told you?"

"Jeremy Batcheller and I have a mutual friend. Word travels fast around this town. Who killed her? How . . . Why . . ." His shoulders rose and fell. "She and Genevieve. Both are dead. It had to be the same killer. Otherwise, it doesn't make sense."

Murder never makes sense, but that won't stop people from doing it, I mused, connecting Bentley to Petunia's death but failing to come up with a reason why he'd want Genevieve dead. I'd never heard any-one, not even Genevieve, badmouth his work. The piece that ran on him in *The Carmel Pine Cone,* our local paper, had gushed with admi-ration.

"I'm as stunned as you are," I said. "Why, I was in Petunia's neighborhood last night, walking with my father, and I saw her alive and well entering her house. You were out, too, weren't you? Tak-ing a stroll?"

"Me? No." His forehead creased with confusion. "I never walk at night. I'm always tending to my garden. I've got snails attacking my vegetables. I'm sure you, being a gardener, are aware that they come out when it's dark to eat and make slimy trails as they move around. That's when it's easiest to catch them."

"How long were you hunting?"

"Hours. My garden is huge. I sell a lot of what I grow at farmers' markets on weekends."

His alibi sounded legit, but I'd bet he could have squeezed in a trek to Petunia's house. On the other hand, how would he have known where Daphne stored her gardening tools? I supposed he might have seen her carrying the hoedag after the police released her on Friday and followed her to her house and stolen it.

He squinted, as if to fight off emotional pain. "Are the police—"

"Investigating? Yes."

"Good. Good." He removed his baseball cap, swiped his thinning hair with his palm, and replaced his hat with a grunt. "Well, I'd better get back to my work. Oliver is paying me by the hour."

At our booth, mimicking my moves on Friday, I unpacked all the items, put out the table and chairs, added more five-dollar-off coupons to the display table, and began making a fairy garden. I used one of the eight-inch fairy pots Renee had designed and installed a pair of adorable dancing fairies, hoping their joyful attitudes could infuse me with a spark of the same. As I worked, I greeted passersby.

A redheaded woman with cornrows studded with beads stopped to assess my work and smiled. "I'd like to learn to do that."

"I give classes at the shop." I handed her a business card. "Call me, and we'll arrange one."

"Do you sell fairy lights?"

"We do. I didn't think to bring any to the festival."

"My niece loves fairy lights."

"Most girls do. Adults, too. I've adorned my backyard with them."

Beaming, she pressed the card to her chest as if it was a treasure and promised to call.

My nana used to say, *If you can make one person happier each day, you will fulfill your purpose in life.*

When the woman moved on, a vision of Petunia lying dead in her garden cut into my thoughts. Who had killed her? Was it a crime of passion? I mentally reviewed the scene but couldn't find comparisons between Genevieve's place of death and Petunia's. Both had been bludgeoned from behind, making me wonder whether the sneak attack meant they had known their attackers. A hoedag had been one weapon. Was a shovel the other?

"Courtney!" Meaghan approached and drew me into her arms. "Mom told me what happened to Petunia. She heard about it at the post office." None of the homes in Carmel had mailboxes. It was a city ordinance. The post office was a good place for residents to congregate. "Everyone was huddling around Hedda, so Mom wedged her way into the knot of people to get the skinny."

Hattie would be pleased to hear her sister had found the courage to leave her house. The police, on the other hand, wouldn't be happy that Hedda was replaying what she'd witnessed.

"How are you holding up?" Meaghan released me. Swooping the skirt of her summer dress out of the way, she perched on one of the chairs. "Talk to me."

"I'm fine. I simply can't believe—" My voice cracked. I blinked back tears. I resumed making the fairy garden, twisting the fairy in the yellow dress ninety degrees to face front. "I can't believe there have been two murders."

"Do you think the same person killed both women?"

"I don't know, but what are the odds that there are two killers?"

"What did Genevieve and Petunia have in common?"

"Gardening," I murmured, as another realization came to mind. *Gardening and me.*

Chapter 11

No child but must remember laying his head in the grass,
staring into the infinitesimal forest
and seeing it grow populous with fairy armies.
—Robert Louis Stevenson, *Treasure Island*

Fiona zoomed into view. "Hello, Courtney. Hi, Meaghan."

"Where's your sister?" I asked.

"She's with Merryweather. She needs to bone up on photokinesis, and though I'm good at it, my aunt is a whiz." She fisted a hand on one hip, wings fluttering steadily. "Why did you want me to come back?"

I tilted my head.

"You sent me a mental image of you," she said.

I gasped. My ESP had worked? No way! "Um, you were dancing on Petunia's phone this morning."

"I wasn't dancing. I was opening it with magic."

"Hold on. You didn't let me finish. I grasped that's what you were up to, but then Detective Summers picked it up and started scrolling through her text messages. Did you see anything suspicious?"

"There was one from Bentley around nine thirty asking if she was okay."

Why would he send that? Had he lied about not going for a walk? Had he seen her entering her house? Did he think someone, like Daphne, had been chasing her? I recalled seeing lights on in Daphne's house, but I hadn't detected her moving about. Only the cat.

No, she did not do this, Courtney.

"Was there anything else?" I asked.

"A text to Scarlet saying they needed to talk."

"What time did she send that?"

"At eight forty-five."

Right before I'd seen Petunia go into her house and slam the door.

"She phoned Daphne ten minutes later," Fiona added.

"Oh, no."

"It didn't last long. Thirteen seconds."

"Courtney, I have to get back to Flair," Meaghan said. "Listen, I can see that brain of yours working. Try not to think about the murder, okay?"

"Murders," I corrected. "Two murders."

"The police will solve them. Don't worry. Stop by the shop later, and I'll pour you a glass of wine, and we'll talk."

"I can't. I need to swing by Flower Farm and tend to my plot."

"You're overextending yourself," she cautioned.

"Just this week because of the festival. Things will subside now that it's winding down."

Meaghan kissed my cheek and hurried away.

"She's right," Fiona said. "You've got to slow down."

"I will. Soon."

"Samples!" Yvanna Acebo called. She was in her Sweet Treats uniform, a pink scrunchie holding her hair in place, strolling toward me with a tray of cookies. "Samples," she cried a second time. "I have samples. Hungry, Courtney? Your favorite. Snickerdoodles."

I still didn't have an appetite. "No, thanks."

Fiona settled onto my shoulder and tickled the back of my neck.

Yvanna, who couldn't see fairies—neither could her sister—regarded me soberly. "Are you okay?"

"Thinking," I admitted. "It's a nasty habit."

"A very nasty habit," Fiona quipped.

Yvanna said, "I heard the news. Another body? And it was someone you knew? I'm so sorry."

"Thanks."

"I spoke to Detective Summers earlier and told him I saw that man waiting for Petunia when she left your tea party on Wednesday."

"Which man?"

"Bentley—"

"Bramble."

"Yep. He was standing outside his truck. He tried to muscle her into it, but she slapped him and shouted, 'I'm not interested. What don't you understand?'"

"Hoo-boy."

Fiona echoed my shock.

Quickly, I filled in Yvanna on seeing Bentley last night at the corner of Petunia's street. I truly believed it was him. "I ran into him over by the fountain earlier and asked him about his whereabouts. He denied being in the vicinity. He said he was removing snails from his garden."

Yvanna *tsk*ed. "That's pretty lame. I mean, sure gardeners are dutiful, but it doesn't take all night." She smiled. "Detective Summers assured me he would be talking to him."

Throughout the morning, all sorts of people stopped by the booth to say hello. Brady couldn't break free—he was slammed at the café—but he texted. I assured him I was all right.

Around lunchtime, Fiona left to check on Eveleen. A moment later, I caught sight of Scarlet slogging toward me. Her updo needed a redo. Clumps of tresses, rather than tendrils, fell from the sides. The tails of her boyfriend shirt were rumpled, too. Perhaps sorrow was making her fuss with both her hair and her clothes. She stopped suddenly, staring toward the exit, a panicked look gripping her face. Was she imagining Genevieve lying dead outside the festival's perimeter? She detoured toward me.

"Hi, Courtney." Idly, she fingered the edge of the display fairy garden. Her voice was lackluster. "I heard about Petunia. I can't believe—" She jammed her lips together, as if to keep herself from crying.

I cut around the table and chairs and rested a reassuring hand on her shoulder. "Sit." She obeyed, and I sat in the other chair.

"I'd only known her a year," she said. "I frequented her store often. She was such a gifted florist." She folded her hands in her lap and studied her cuticles. "It's tragic. Heartbreaking." She shook her head and met my gaze. "Who killed her? Why?"

"I don't know," I said helplessly. "I heard she texted you last night."

"I didn't see any message, but that's not unusual. I never look at my phone after seven. I told everyone that at our last get together, remember? On our anniversary, Asher and I made a pact to go off the grid every night."

"Could I see your phone?"

"I accidentally left it at home." She said this without guile. "By the way, Asher believes a jealous lover killed Genevieve as well as Petunia."

"Really?" I didn't buy the same lover angle. Petunia and Genevieve hadn't been close in age, plus I couldn't see them having similar taste in men.

"I think he's mistaken," Scarlet went on. "He's got jealous-lovers-on-the-brain syndrome because . . ." She mustered a tight smile. "Because he's worried that I'm having an affair. I'm not!" She held up a hand. "I haven't."

I recalled Asher commandeering her phone earlier and swiping the screen. Had he been looking for evidence of betrayal? Cheeky of him to do so in public, but shrewd, too, because Scarlet wouldn't fight him for fear of making a scene.

"I've been spending a lot of time meeting clients," she went on, "and traveling to get the product placement deals, so he worries. I understand."

When my ex-fiancé abruptly broke off our engagement, I'd wondered whether he'd fallen for someone else. He hadn't. He simply hadn't wanted to settle down with me. Luckily, I didn't think Brady's feelings for me would wane. We were a good match. I could see us growing old together.

"I'm sorry, Scarlet," I said. "That has to be tough, always proving your faithfulness to him."

"It's okay. I love him to pieces, but you know . . . *men*." She gestured with her hands. "Back to Petunia and Genevieve. Should you and I be scared? There are rumors Daphne is the killer. That sounds incomprehensible. She doesn't have a mean bone in her body. But she knew both of them, and well, we were all friends."

"No. These murders did not happen because we're acquainted." At least I hoped that wasn't the reason. If it was, the guilt would eat at me, seeing as I was the one who had encouraged all of us to meet regularly.

"They were both entrepreneurs," Scarlet said. "What if there's a misogynist running around that doesn't like women who work?"

Would Summers dismiss the theory if I mentioned it to him? Did all businesswomen in Carmel need to be on the alert?

"I heard the murderer used Daphne's weird looking hoe to kill Petunia," Scarlet said, tugging on a tress of hair.

I gawked at her.

"Like I said, the rumor mill is working overtime," she went on. "Is it true?"

I hadn't mentioned the hoedag to anyone, and I doubted the police had, which meant either Hedda or Jeremy must have released that tidbit. "I don't know," I lied.

"What about the weapon used to kill Genevieve?" Scarlet asked. "Did the police find it?"

"I don't know that, either." How I wished my father had been able to fill in some blanks on the police investigation.

She started fiddling with the fairy garden, touching the tips of the leaves, fingering the bluebell the fairy was holding.

I reached across the table and steadied her arm. "You seem distracted. Why don't you head home?"

"I was going to but stopped when I realized I couldn't pass by the spot where . . . where Genevieve was killed." She sighed. "I wish I could have been there to help her."

Did she really? The two had been at odds. She'd even cursed when she'd viewed the offensive post Asher had brought to her attention.

"If only I hadn't gone for a walk on the beach that night," she said.

"You weren't with Asher?"

"No, I needed to be alone. It was the anniversary of my mother's death." Her voice caught ever so slightly. "She had a stroke when I was in high school, and I still have trouble wrapping my head around it. She was always as fit as a yoga instructor. Listening to the ocean calms me like nothing else. Asher tries to console me, but he knows being coddled makes me more upset, so he went to play tennis with a friend on the friend's court. They have a regular game on Thursdays and play until midnight. When I got home around ten-thirty"— she rose to her feet and smoothed the front of her shirt, frowning as if just now realizing how rumpled it was—"I took a sleeping pill and was out like a light."

I didn't know what the police had determined regarding time of death, but if Genevieve had been killed closer to midnight, then being in bed by ten-thirty might clear Scarlet.

"Hey, are you okay?" Scarlet asked, lifting her gaze. "I mean, you saw her as well as Petunia. I know you've seen dead bodies before, but ugh."

"I'm sad, and I'm angry that someone feels he or she can do this and get away with it."

"They won't, will they?" Scarlet asked, eyes wide.

"They'd better not."

⋆ ⋆ ⋆

The afternoon passed quickly. I scored five new clients for private fairy garden lessons and sold the entire allotment of fairy doors to a tour group that arrived *en masse*. By three p.m. I was down to ten fairy figurines, a red spiral slide, a few red-and-white mushroom stickers, and a slew of pots and plants. Many who'd bought figurines told me they had purchased them as surprise gifts. Most promised to come to Open Your Imagination with the recipient to finalize the gardens.

At four-thirty, Fiona and Eveleen rejoined me. Eveleen was excited and spoke so quickly about what she'd learned, I could barely understand a word. It wasn't until Fiona pinched her sister's wing that she grew silent. From what I'd gathered, she had loved, loved, loved photokinesis, even though all fairies learned some form of that from birth, and she couldn't wait to learn plant psychology, an art Fiona had mastered, thanks to Cedric Winterbottom's counsel.

"Are you going home?" Fiona asked.

"I have to pack up and contact the deliveryman so he'll bring everything back to the shop. After that, I'm off to Flower Farm. My plants won't feed themselves." I thought of Bentley Bramble and his dedication to his vegetable garden. Had the police spoken with him yet? Had anyone been able to verify his alibi?

"Do you want us to come with you to Flower Farm?" Fiona asked.

"You don't have to. Go have fun."

The vendor for Wildflower Pottery & Soap company stopped by to pick up the display garden he'd purchased for his daughter's birthday. He gushed about how happy she was going to be. I made sure he took a coupon and reminded him that I gave classes at Open Your Imagination. He and she were welcome any time.

An hour later, as I was finalizing things with the deliveryman, Oliver strolled to me, smiling broadly.

"Did you have a successful festival?" he asked.

I frowned. Had he sported this genial a face throughout the

weekend? Hadn't the fact that Genevieve died outside the perimeter fazed him? And what about Petunia, one of the vendors, being murdered this very morning? His eyes were placid, his attire pristine. He hadn't sweated an iota. Did guilty men lack pores? I considered his motive to want Genevieve dead. He'd been upset with her. He might have lost his marriage because of her. As for Petunia, the two of them were in the same business. Had he killed her to get rid of the competition?

"Courtney," he said, jolting me to the present.

"Yes. Very successful. We sold almost everything, and we introduced a number of people to the shop."

"Excellent. The festival has always been about goodwill." He had the decency to balk. "I didn't mean . . . That was insensitive of me, given the . . ." He rotated a hand. "It's certainly not goodwill to have a murder occur so close to the premises."

"Or to have one of the vendors killed."

"Yes. So true." He swiped a hand down the back of his neck. "I spoke with Detective Summers about Petunia a bit ago. He asked if I was worried about the killer going after florists. I scoffed. Garden Delights is hardly considered a florist, I told him. I peddle dramatic pieces of art."

I thought of Genevieve's post claiming he'd stolen the ideas for his arrangements, and I recalled Petunia saying that his works were overdone and not to everyone's liking. I had to agree with her assessment, given what he was selling at the festival. One display that he'd dubbed "Heart of the Jungle" included a wealth of amaranths, coxcomb, and protea, surrounded by banana leaves and ferns, all tucked into a dark green vase for the bargain price of five hundred dollars.

Had Petunia and Genevieve's critiques harmed his business? Had that miffed him so much he'd killed them both?

Stop, Courtney. Just because you don't like the man doesn't mean he had a reason to off your friends. Besides, spite seemed a paltry motive.

"I must go." He straightened his tie, wiggling his neck as he did. "Thanks for running a smooth festival."

Smooth, except for the murders, of course.

On my way to fetch Pixie at the shop, I couldn't shake the notion that the same person had killed both women. I didn't have any evidence to support my theory, except both had been struck from behind. Were each of the weapons gardening tools? If they were, would that convince the police there was only one culprit?

As I was rounding the corner on 8th, I spotted Detective Summers entering Seize the Clay, the pottery store across the street from Open Your Imagination. Eager to test my theory, I trotted to the shop and hurried inside. The shelves were filled with handmade bowls, plates, goblets, and more. I drew in a deep breath and exhaled. Something about the aroma of freshly baked pottery, wet clay, and burning sage soothed me. I had yet to take the pottery lesson I'd promised myself and decided arranging the class would be my excuse for stopping in. One of Renee's assistants was showing a gawky man a trio of vases. Another clerk was showing an elderly woman a flyer of events. I didn't see Renee, but I heard the whirr of a pottery wheel coming from beyond the drapes that led to her office, teaching space, and kilns.

Summers pivoted and frowned. "What are you doing here?"

"I want to sign up for a pottery lesson."

"Uh-huh," he said skeptically.

"Meaghan and Glinda, too," I said, hoping that would add weight to my pretense. I drank in the calm of the melodious music playing through speakers, unwilling to let his snarky attitude unnerve me.

Renee emerged through the drapes while brushing stray hairs off her face. She rounded the counter and kissed Summers on the cheek. "Hi, sweetie. What brings you this way? And Courtney." She wiped her clay-stained hands on her apron. "Did you two come together?"

"I want to sign up for a pottery class," I said, continuing my ruse.

"And I'd like to escort you to dinner," Summers said.

"I'll be free in an hour," she replied.

"Swell." Summers turned to leave.

I said, "Detective, wait. Have you learned anything new about this morning's murder?"

He threw me a snide look. "I knew it. You came in here to pump me for details."

"The other day you told me to keep my eyes open and my ears alert."

"Do you have something to share?"

Dang, he was good. I swallowed hard. "No, but I was wondering, did the coroner pin down the time of death for Petunia's murder?"

"Between nine and midnight."

"And for Genevieve's?"

"About eight and midnight. A wide window for both. Goodbye."

"Wait. Did you find the murder weapon that was used to kill Genevieve?"

He squinted at me, malice in his gaze.

"I'll take that as a no," I stated. "Have you figured out whether there are one or two killers in Carmel?"

He worked his tongue against the inside of his mouth, clearly trying not to snap at me.

"Is it possible—"

"Don't!" he barked. So much for not snapping. "Do. Not. Theorize. Any. More."

"Dylan, let her speak," Renee said. "You know you admire her mind almost as much as you admire mine."

He grunted.

"Is what possible, Courtney?" Renee coaxed.

"That Petunia figured out who murdered Genevieve and confronted the killer."

Summers coughed out a laugh. "She would have told the police."

"Okay, perhaps," I said, "but if she figured it out and planned to go to the precinct Sunday, she might have mentioned it to someone on Saturday, perhaps a confidante, and that person accidentally let the killer know."

Summers fanned the air with a hand. "How does one *accidentally* tell a killer she knows what happened without expecting consequences?"

When he said the theory aloud, it did sound ludicrous.

I said, "What if, before coming to you, Petunia was snooping around to confirm what she thought had happened, but the killer caught sight of her and followed her home?"

Summers considered that.

"In that case," I continued, "you need to pin down where she might have been before I saw her entering her house."

"Unless she went out after that, and she was killed at the end of the time of death window. Thank you, Miss Kelly. You've been heard." He waved a hand. "Now, make an appointment for your class and scat."

"Did you learn anything when you scanned Petunia's cell phone?" I asked, pressing my luck.

Summers shot a hand at Renee as if to say *See? She's a pain in the butt.*

"I mean, you know I texted her Sunday morning," I continued. "Did anyone else reach out to her recently?" I would not reveal what Fiona had shared with me. "Or did she write or call anyone in particular?"

"Interesting that you would ask. Saturday night, she texted Scarlet Lyle saying she needed to talk. Ten minutes later, she dialed Daphne Flores. That call lasted thirteen seconds."

"Thirteen seconds isn't long enough to have a conversation."

"Oh, no? What if, going with your theory, she said, 'I know what you did,' and hung up?"

"Have you asked Miss Flores?"

"As a matter of fact, she and I had a lengthy conversation earlier today."

Renee was pressing her lips together, as if forcing herself to keep quiet so our exchange could play out.

"What did she say?" I asked.

"That Miss Fujimoto left her a message she couldn't understand."

"As in it was garbled?"

"As in she said, 'Never mind, ask her.'"

"Ask who what?"

"Miss Flores didn't have a clue. She assumed Miss Fujimoto meant she would ask her sister something. Unfortunately, Miss Flores erased the message, which I have to admit sounds dodgy to me," Summers said. "My bet is she's the killer."

"Are you going to arrest her?"

"I will if I gather more evidence. In the meantime, she has secured legal representation."

"C'mon, Detective Summers, why would she leave a tool with her initials on it at the crime scene? That's plain stupid. I think someone's framing her."

"How do you know about the ownership of the hoedag?"

I gulped. He was right. I couldn't have seen the initials from where I'd stood, but I sure as shooting couldn't tell him my fairy told me. "Um, Daphne's father gave her monogrammed gardening tools when she started her business, and I could see something was etched into the handle. Plus, I can't imagine there are a lot of people who own hoedags," I added, "though I could be wrong about that. There are lots of gardeners in Carmel."

"Don't go making assumptions or spreading rumors out of hand."

"I won't. I haven't. But, just so you know, someone *is* spreading rumors. At the festival, I—" I hesitated, not willing to let on that it was Scarlet. "This particular someone said Daphne is the likeliest suspect because she knew both women."

"Who is this certain someone?"

"I can't say, but she was concerned that she and I might be targets, because we knew Genevieve and Petunia, too."

"*Ah.* Your forum buddy, Scarlet Lyle," he said. "We've spoken."

"She thought the killer might have a thing against women who own their own businesses."

Summers didn't respond. He kissed Renee on the cheek before heading for the front door. Renee moved away to help an incoming customer.

I followed the detective. "Did you find Genevieve's cell phone and her purse?"

He heaved a sigh. "For a second time, no. Now leave me alone and butt out."

I saluted, arranged for a class for me, Meaghan, and Glinda on Thursday afternoon, and returned to the shop to fetch my cat. To-gether, we raced home. I fed her—my appetite was still nil—and changed into gardening clothes. I promised I'd return soon and drove to Flower Farm.

Chapter 12

I never make the littles sound
I never sing or coo-ee,
Nor touch the Fairies' dancing-ground
Among the grasses dewy.
—Annie R. Rentoul, "In the Gully Green"

The sun hung low in the sky as the farm came into view, its waning light gracing the fields of flowers. I parked next to Daphne's Ford pickup and made a beeline for the office to let her know I was there. Unlike Scarlet, I didn't want to believe Daphne was the killer. On the other hand, why had Petunia called her and said, *Never mind, ask her.* Could Summers be right? Was Daphne lying about the message? Did Petunia say, *I know what you did?*

The lights were on inside the office, but as before, the door was locked, and the computer was in screensaver mode. I knocked and called her name. She didn't respond.

I turned and raised a hand to block the last remnants of sunlight from my eyes and searched the expanse. Off at a distance, Daphne was bent over, her sunhat bobbing up and down. She was checking beneath the leaves of a plant. I didn't yell to her. By taking the path to my plot of land, I'd pass right by her.

"Courtney!" Fiona chirped as she flew into view. Eveleen followed in her wake. "My sister grew weary of reading at the library, so we decided to join you."

"What were you reading? Plant psychology?" I asked. Were there books on that? I'd never thought to check.

"I was trying to get her interested in Agatha Christie novels," Fiona said.

"Oh, Eveleen, I love those," I said. "Particularly the ones featuring Hercule Poirot. I appreciate the way he deduces things. 'Use your little gray cells, *mon ami,*'" I said in a bad French accent.

"She's not a reader like us," Fiona said, "but we'll convert her."

Eveleen spun in a circle, her eyes wide. "It's beautiful here. May I bless some of these flowers?"

"Feel free," I said, and signaled them to fly at will.

I strolled along the path, inhaling the fragrant air. As I neared Daphne, I said, "Don't let me scare you."

But she did startle. Her gloved hand went to her throat. "Courtney!" She brushed leaves off the apron she was wearing over her clothes and smiled warmly.

"I called for you back at the office, but you didn't hear me." I hooked a thumb over my shoulder.

"What're you doing here?"

"I need to tend my plot."

"Me, too. I'm snail, grub, and aphid hunting."

I thought of Bentley Bramble and his alibi for Saturday night. "How long do you search?"

"Every other night for an hour or two." She brandished a hand at the acreage. "It's a never-ending process. It's so sad about Petunia," she said, sobering. "When I woke up this morning to the sound of sirens . . ." She shook her head. "I really liked her. We often talked about our gardens."

"Speaking of which, my father and I were strolling by your house last night. We noticed your roses look undernourished and in need of nitrogen."

"Why were you walking by?"

"I live two blocks away. On Carmelo Street."

"That's right. I remember you telling me."

"We were checking out the neighborhoods after a nice dinner at Hideaway Café."

"I love that place," she said. "They make a mean Monte Cristo sandwich for their brunches."

I'd been intending to order one of those and mentally added it to my to-do list.

"As for my roses"—she removed her hat and mopped her brow with a handkerchief she pulled from her apron—"I've been meaning to feed them, but I've gotten behind on the basics."

"Was that why Genevieve harangued you?" I asked.

Daphne's eyes widened. "She didn't harangue me. That's too strong a word. She belittled me, but I didn't kill her."

"I know you didn't." At least I hoped she hadn't. "Daphne, this is a delicate topic, but I have to ask. Someone says they spotted you by the dumpster near Section A that night, close to eight. Were you there?"

She gasped. "Who?"

Uh-oh. She didn't deny being there. "That doesn't matter."

"It does."

"Why were you in the area? The person said you were staring into space."

"Who was it?" she demanded.

I fanned the air. "I won't reveal the name."

"It's not like it sounds. I was in a rush to get home before . . . before I had a *thing* to attend to, and I'd been running, and I was out of breath. I needed to pause for a moment. So I stopped. That's all."

"And you didn't see Genevieve?"

"No! She wasn't there. She wasn't dead yet. Courtney, I didn't kill her. I didn't! And I didn't hurt Petunia, either." She clicked her tongue. "But why would you believe me? You were there this morning with the police and the others. You must have seen that the killer used my hoedag."

"Daphne, I don't think you'd be stupid enough to leave a tool with your initials on it at a crime scene. I think you're being framed. I told the police that."

"Exactly." She spanked one hand against the other. "That's what I said to Detective Summers when he interrogated me, but he was skeptical."

"He said you've retained council."

"Yes. Victoria Judge. She represented you at one time, didn't she?"

"She did." And Meaghan's mother and Meaghan's business partner. "She's an ace when it comes to defense."

Daphne pulled her gardening gloves off and shoved them in the pocket of her apron along with the handkerchief. "I told the detective I brought the hoedag home Friday after weeding the median. I cleaned it and stored it in the shed in my backyard, as I always do. And then I saw it again when I put another tool in the shed on Saturday around seven. Unfortunately, the lock is broken. Anyone could have gotten in." Her shoulders slumped. "I've been meaning to replace it . . ." She didn't finish.

I presumed she'd meant to add that, like nurturing her plants, she hadn't gotten around to it. Was she in over her head at Flower Farm? Was that why she'd leased me an acre? An expansive business such as hers had to be a lot for one person to handle. She only had one employee, she'd told me.

"I don't have security cameras at my home, though, like I do here, so I can't prove it." She motioned to the office and to the barn. "I've got mowers and rototillers in there, and I can't very well tote those home every night."

"Why do you store tools at your house?" I asked.

"My father was adamant that all my personalized tools went home with me. He was a dutiful gardener. Everything I learned about tilling the land, I learned from him."

"My father taught me, too," I said.

She whistled. "Dad aspired to be a master gardener but didn't achieve it."

A silence fell between us. Fiona and Eveleen came into view.

Fiona flew to Daphne, settled atop her head, and patted Daphne's hair, beckoning her sister to join her. Eveleen was hesitant to sit, but Fiona insisted. Eveleen alit and, like Fiona, crossed her legs. Their wings fluttered at the same tempo. Daphne didn't appear to detect them.

"What were you doing last night?" I asked. "You weren't home. The lights were off."

Daphne pursed her lips. Her gaze narrowed.

"Did Petunia call you?"

"It's none of your business."

Fiona bounded off Daphne's head and stared directly into her eyes. After a brief second, she soared above Daphne and ordered her sister out of the way. Eveleen obeyed, and Fiona dashed Daphne with a shimmering green potion designed to help someone trust another person. Daphne stiffened, as if she'd felt the dust descend upon her. Eveleen squeaked and inspected Fiona's wings, trying to understand, as I did, how she created potions.

"Have fun working your plot," Daphne said flatly. "I have to go. I've got an appointment." She strode through the garden toward the office.

"Well, that was interesting," I said to my fairy companions. "Her appointments and dates sound nebulous. Manufactured, even."

"She's hiding something," Fiona stated.

As Hercule Poirot would say, *Everyone has something to hide*. Daphne mentioned that Genevieve suggested she seek the counsel of a psychiatrist. Had she finally knuckled under and made an appointment with one but was embarrassed to say so?

I tended my plot for an hour, mulling over Daphne's behavior. When I got home, I wasn't hungry but knew I should eat. I fed Pixie some tuna and threw together a plate of sharp cheddar cheese and fruit for myself. I chopped apples into teensy bits for Fiona and Eveleen—fairies loved sweet things. After I poured myself a glass of sauvignon blanc, I set my mini meal on a tray, donned a jacket, and

Pixie, the fairies, and I retired to the backyard. I sat at the wicker table with Pixie nestled in my lap. Her steady purring should've brought me comfort, but it didn't.

Oblivious to my angst, Fiona and Eveleen dined on their fruit before taking off for a game of chase through the cypress trees. They didn't illuminate like fireflies—I couldn't see them whizzing between branches—but I could hear them giggling hysterically.

As I sipped the wine and listened to the burbling fountain, I wondered why Daphne had been so circumspect about her where-abouts. She hadn't killed anyone—I would bet my life on it—but something was amiss. My mind jumped ahead to the notion of funerals for Genevieve and Petunia. Would they occur soon? Cause of death was pretty obvious. The coroner wouldn't hang onto the bodies. Who would handle the arrangements?

"Courtney," Fiona said, tiptoeing along the edge of the table. "You look stressed. Do you want to talk about it?"

Eveleen alit on the table, as her sister had, and followed Fiona like a shadow.

"My sister could learn a thing or two about how you process a mystery," Fiona added. "When you're finished here, we could go to the living room. You could work through your thoughts on the whiteboard."

I'd purchased a second whiteboard a week ago, because the one at work was helpful when I wanted to plot out new fairy garden ideas, so I thought an additional one at home might stir my imagina-tion. "I don't need to. The police are investigating the murders."

She said to her sister, "Courtney told me that writing things down can help us learn things faster, and it's true. That's how I mem-orized all the rules." To me, she added, "I know you're wondering who killed both of your friends."

I wagged a finger. "Don't go reading my mind."

"I'm not, but you're sending me signals, whether you like it or not."

I gawked, astonished that Fiona and I were connecting on an ex-trasensory level. Was that normal? Others who had a strong connection to the fairy world hadn't mentioned that ability. I'd have to ask Lissa Reade about it.

"Will you get in trouble?" I asked, suddenly worried for Fiona.

"If I don't instigate it, no. This is all on you because you're using your little gray cells." Saying the Poirot phrase made her laugh. "C'mon. Let's go inside."

I gathered the tray of food, took it to the kitchen, and followed Fiona and her sister to the living room, which was also my home office. Pixie leaped onto the ocean-blue love seat and curled into a ball. Eveleen soared to the top of the reading chair and, using it like a slide, slid down to the cushion.

"Stop!" Fiona said. "No playing. We're here to help."

"You're no fun," Eveleen said, sticking out her tongue.

I retreated to the antique desk by the window and pulled a dry-erase marker from the center drawer. I'd rested the whiteboard on an easel next to the desk. My laptop computer stirred when I closed the drawer. I tapped the space bar on the keyboard and, placing my finger on the upper rightmost key, opened the screen with my fingerprint. My website surfaced. The last thing I'd been doing on the computer had been sprucing up the header. I noticed the local gardeners' web forum had a couple of messages. I clicked on it and saw a note from Petunia asking about the garden for her sister. Tears pressed at the corners of my eyes. Petunia said Peony did the books for a local winery. To honor Petunia's memory, the least I could do was take her sister the garden I'd made.

"Courtney," Fiona said.

I swiped away the tears, closed the forum, and addressing the whiteboard, created a grid with two columns. I wrote down Genevieve's name in the left one and Petunia's name in the right. I drew a line beneath their names. "First, I want to know if the same person killed both of them."

In Genevieve's column, I jotted down the word *Weapon* and wrote a question mark plus the few items I'd considered: *shovel, frying pan, rock*. I flashed on making the garden with Zinnia when she'd fussed over which shovel to include. It had no bearing, but it resonated in my head.

Under Petunia's name, I wrote *Weapon: hoedag.*

Beneath the word *Weapon* in each column, I wrote *Crime Scene: similar.* Both women had been found in the morning, their heads smashed in, no witnesses. I added *no phone or purse* under Genevieve's name and *phone with text messages and 13-second call to Daphne* under Petunia's.

Then I wrote the word *Suspects.*

For Genevieve, I started with *Oliver Killian.* Motive: *resentment for losing business partner; anger because wife walked out.* Beneath that, I wrote his alibi: *taking friend to AA but won't divulge name. Do police know?* Under that, I added, *Is his estranged wife living in San Francisco as Brady thinks? Could she have killed Petunia?*

Next came *Scarlet Lyle.* Motive: *antagonistic friendship plus upset by rude post by Genevieve.* I scribbled her alibi: *Went on long walk on beach because anniversary of mother's death.* I added: *From what time to what time? Home by ten-thirty really?* Her husband wouldn't be able to corroborate any of it, because he was out for the evening. I added *new shovel not seen in festival booth* and wondered whether I should text Detective Summers about that. If a shovel wasn't the weapon, that theory wouldn't matter.

I wrote *Daphne.* Motive: *G taunted her about her gardening skills.* She said her alibi was tending to her roses that night, but if she'd meant the ones at her house, her alibi was sadly lacking.

Lastly, I added *Additional Suspects* but couldn't fathom who else to include. Genevieve had insulted Brady and Glinda, and she'd posted that Oliver Killian had stolen someone's ideas for his floral arrangements. Had she attacked other restaurateurs and shop owners?

In Petunia's column, I scrawled *Bentley Bramble.* Motive: *jilted lover.* He said he was hunting for snails that night. That alibi sounded as flimsy as Daphne's. How long could he have been searching? I tapped the pen on my chin and studied Genevieve's column. I couldn't come up with a reason for Bentley to want her dead, too.

I wrote Daphne's name beneath Bentley's, but I couldn't visualize a reason for her to want Petunia dead. I wished she hadn't refused to tell me her alibi for Saturday night. She'd acted as if I'd overstepped, and honestly, I might have. *Don't be so dogged* was a directive I'd added to my "ways to improve myself" list. On the other hand, doggedness was what was driving me to figure out who had killed two of my friends.

I thought about what I'd told Summers—that Petunia figured out who murdered Genevieve. Was I correct? Did she have proof? Did she call Daphne to confide in her but changed her mind, deciding to touch base with her sister instead, but the killer murdered her before she could?

A dreadful thought occurred to me. What if Petunia texted Scarlet because she'd seen the shovel in Scarlet's booth and, theorizing like I had that a shovel was the weapon used to kill Genevieve, believed Scarlet was the murderer? Could Scarlet have deduced that from Petunia's cryptic text?

I wrote Scarlet's name in Petunia's column, added that hypothesis, and continued.

Oliver Killian. Motive: *competitive business.* Petunia mentioned that she was searching for a new venue for her flower shop. Did that outrage Oliver? Was he that territorial? Perhaps his business was struggling. What was his alibi for Saturday night?

I yawned and placed the dry-erase marker on the board's aluminum marker tray.

Fiona sailed over to study what I'd written. "Eveleen, come here. Take a look."

Eveleen stretched her arms wide. "Why? I'm not a righteous fairy, and I never will be."

"Maybe not, but you're not allowed to be lazy," Fiona said imperiously. "Come here."

Eveleen, acting like a pouty younger sister, hissed, "Fine," and winged to the board.

They chatted in their native tongue about what I'd written.

"English, please," I said.

"Sorry, Courtney." Fiona tittered. "I was telling her how organized you are, and I explained that you're trying to see parallels between the two women's deaths."

"I wish we knew what weapon was used in Genevieve's murder," I said.

"A shovel is a gardening tool," she suggested. "If the same person killed both women, he might have used the hoedag for one and a shovel for the other."

"Good analysis."

Eveleen said, "Um, hello, *he* might have been a *she*."

Fiona clapped her sister on the wing. "Right you are!"

I eyed the board again. "Why did the killer take Genevieve's cell phone but not Petunia's?"

Eveleen said, "Because the killer didn't have time. Someone was coming."

"Brilliant!" Fiona grabbed her sister's hands, and the two twirled gleefully.

My gaze was drawn back to the screensaver on my computer screen, which was now a flurry of dancing swirls. Something niggled at the edges of my mind. Curious, I reengaged the computer, opened an Internet search page, and typed in Genevieve's Instagram account name. I scrolled through her most recent posts. There was a negative post about a jewelry store as well as an art gallery, both entered on Wednesday, but there were plenty of positive posts on that day, too.

I halted when I realized there weren't any posts for Thursday. I flashed on Genevieve's getup when she was killed. She had been wearing all black. Had she been doing reconnaissance, as I'd speculated? If so, given her fondness for attacking everyone, why hadn't she posted anything that night? Daphne said Genevieve had publicized all sorts of negative things about the festival. I juddered when it dawned on me that even the nasty one she'd written about Scarlet on Thursday was missing. Had the killer erased them, or had Genevieve?

"Maybe she was taking pictures of someone in particular," I mused aloud.

Fiona flew to my shoulder. "She, who?"

"Genevieve. On the night she was killed, what if she saw some-one doing something illegal and decided to document it?"

"Something illegal or naughty," Fiona said.

I thought of Scarlet and how her husband suspected she was step-ping out on him. Was he correct? Did Genevieve catch Scarlet in the act? Did Scarlet see Genevieve taking incriminating photos and kill her and steal her cell phone to get rid of the evidence?

I wished I could figure out what Genevieve had been up to that night. I recalled the name of her podcast, *Anything Is Poddable*. Did she have a second Instagram account using that name? I typed Instagram.com plus the podcast name into the search engine. It landed on a site, and my eyes widened. "Yes!" I cried. Genevieve had created another account, and on it, she'd posted tons of photos with myriad hashtags. The photos weren't proving someone was having an affair, but there were dozens of additional slams against restaurants, gyms, and local vendors. Included in the mix was a scathing post about Bentley Bramble's topiary artistry. Genevieve had called his work mundane and lacking inspiration.

"What did you find?" Fiona asked, soaring to me.

I outlined my thinking to her and her sister as I jotted Bentley's name in Genevieve's column. Suddenly, I got an itch to swing by his house and peek at his yard, but I didn't have his address. On the off chance my father did—after all, he'd employed Bentley—I texted him. He responded immediately, asking why I wanted it. I explained. Three dots appeared, as if Dad were mulling over my unusual re-quest. Finally, he wrote, *On Monte Verde Street, three houses south of 9th Avenue, east side. Want me to join you?* I texted back that I was good to go. It wasn't like I intended to stand around making myself a target. Besides, I had two plucky fairies to accompany me.

To disguise myself, I threw on a black jacket and hat, as Gene-vieve had, and headed out with Fiona and Eveleen.

Bentley's house was a mission-style home with red-tile roof and stucco walls. Stained-glass sidelight windows flanked the front door. The shadow of a large person obscured by the drapes drifted past the plate-glass window. If it was Bentley, he didn't appear to have seen me. He didn't peek out.

"His garden is magnificent," Fiona said.

He hadn't been lying about the scope of it. The garden, which encompassed the entire front yard, was planted with tomatoes, peppers, beans, zucchini, cabbage, corn, and pumpkins, all rooted in raised, natural cedar beds. Poles and stakes held the tomatoes and beans in place. I noted the pungent scent of blood meal.

Fiona dashed away, Eveleen following. In seconds, they reappeared, and Fiona said, "I don't see any snails."

Meaning Bentley might have been telling the truth. However, even as large as his garden was, I still couldn't imagine it taking him hours to de-snail it.

"The plants by the front door are pretty," Fiona added. A pair of topiaries in the shape of flamingos flanked the sidelights.

"Why would Genevieve criticize his talent?" Eveleen asked.

"Good question, and one the police should ask," I said. Had Genevieve been snarky because Petunia had paid her to be?

In the quiet, I heard a bolt being flipped on the front door. My heart leaped into my throat, and I galloped away before Bentley could catch me spying.

When I got home, I did my ablutions and quickly climbed into bed. Pixie was more than happy to join me as I snuggled beneath the comforter, yawns overcoming me. Fiona and her sister, on the other hand, weren't remotely fatigued. Oh, to have their energy.

To my surprise, however, I didn't fall asleep, and at two a.m., my mind was whirling with theories, so I sat up, turned on the lamp on the bedstand, and opened my copy of *The Mysterious Affair at Styles*. Ever since thinking of Hercule Poirot, I'd been fixated on re-reading the book. I skimmed a chapter of the mystery and realized that stirring my little gray cells was probably not the best idea. An active mind would keep me awake all night. So I swapped the mystery for a primer about fertilizing plants—a real snooze fest—and finally, with Fiona and Eveleen singing me lullabies, I drifted off.

At dawn on Monday, to refresh myself, I took a brisk run on the beach. The air was cool and damp, and I was glad I'd thrown on a hoodie. Seagulls cawed overhead, but none, thank heavens, dive-bombed me. When I got home, I felt better. I fed Pixie, Fiona, and Eveleen, who said the bits of apple I'd given her were the best she'd ever eaten. I thanked her and put on a pot of coffee.

As I was finishing my first cup, Brady texted me.

Brady: **Ready for a fun day?**

Me: **Can't wait.**

I threw on jeans and a red long-sleeved shirt—whenever I wore red, I felt energized—slipped on my favorite tennis shoes, and lathered any exposed skin with sunblock. Next, I checked my camera equipment, tossed together a backpack of power bars and bottled water, drank another cup of coffee, and began to type a text to Detective Summers as to my discovery about Bentley Bramble. Engrossed in choosing exactly the right words for my message, I startled when someone knocked on the front door.

Chapter 13

The little shoes of fairies are
So light and soft and small
That though a million pass you by
You would not hear at all.
—Annette Wynne, "Fairy Shoes"

I peeked through the peephole. It was Brady looking as handsome as ever in cargo shorts and a white polo shirt, a backpack slung over both shoulders. I stopped writing the text message and opened the door.

"Good morning," he said. His hair was slightly windblown. He leaned in for a kiss, and I melted into him, inhaling his musky scent. He stroked my cheek and whispered, "I've missed you. How are you doing?"

"I didn't sleep well. Thoughts of sugarplums did not dance in my head."

"Are you sure you're up for an adventure?"

"Absolutely. Fresh air will do me good. I've packed a few snacks and water."

"And I've brought prosciutto-and-cheddar scones, deviled eggs, and fruit salad."

Out of nowhere, my appetite returned. Phew.

"A man after my heart," I murmured, and promised Pixie I'd be home soon. She didn't understand time. *Soon* was relative. She meowed happily and retreated to the bedroom for a nap. Next, I told Fiona and Eveleen I was off. They were going to the library to study with Merryweather and Cedric.

"Ready," I said, slinging on my backpack, and Brady and I walked the two blocks to the ocean.

On weekdays, fewer people visited the strand than on weekends. I spotted Jeremy Batcheller playing Frisbee with Polka Dot. A man and woman were standing in front of easels, their backs to us. I was pretty sure the woman was Holly Hopewell. She was wearing a wildly colorful smock over knee-length leggings. Farther away, a young couple in rolled-up jeans and tank tops were wandering at the water's edge the way lovers would, hand in hand, kicking up foam to lightheartedly splash the other. Way, way down the beach, toward the Clinton Walker House, a passel of children were playing tag. A single adult watched on. Homeschooled kids, I decided.

We settled mid-beach, spread out the blanket Brady had brought along, and laid our breakfast on top. Then I pulled my Nikon and close-up lens from my pack. The blue sky was rife with white clouds. I felt like I could soak in the beauty for ages.

"Today, I thought you'd show me how to take photos of seashells," Brady said as he set two halves of deviled eggs and a warm scone on paper plates and doled out forks and napkins. "But first . . ." He popped open a Tupperware filled with fruit salad. "We dine. After you, milady."

I scooped the fruit salad onto my plate and forked a piece of pineapple. I popped it into my mouth and hummed. "Perfect!" I ate a strawberry and said, "So, why seashells? What's the fascination?"

"I've collected them over the years."

I squinted at him and smiled. "You have not."

"Okay, you know me too well." He chuckled. "My mother collects sand dollars. I want to surprise her with some framed photographs for her birthday, because what do you get a woman who has everything?"

His mother was a famous historical romance author.

"Another sand dollar," I joked. "Perfect for right now as Carmel continues to urge everyone in town to embrace solidarity." As a response to the pandemic, the library had suggested the townsfolk hang seashells on their porches and in their windows as they *shell-tered* in place. It had subsequently become a tradition.

I said, "Where's your camera?"

He removed his Nikon from his pack.

"Did you buy the macro lens I suggested?" I asked.

"I did. I follow orders." He took the lens from the pack and removed it from its protective case.

"Make sure you don't get sand anywhere," I cautioned.

"Aye, captain." He winked.

We finished dining—the prosciutto-and-cheddar scones were as yummy and flaky as any I'd ever had—after which we stowed our dishes so birds wouldn't come hunting for scraps, and we scrambled to our feet.

I slipped the strap of my camera around my neck, and Brady attached his new lens.

When he was ready, I said, "Let's go." I tiptoed closer to the ocean until the waves were licking my ankles. I dug into the sand with my toes, searching for seashells, keeping the camera well away from the water. We found broken remnants of sand dollars. It was rare to find any perfectly formed ones.

Squatting down, balancing my elbows on my thighs to make myself the tripod, I snapped a few shots. Brady mimicked me, readily getting the hang of it. I checked my photos. He reviewed his.

"Good," he said, "but not good enough."

"We've got plenty of time," I assured him.

About an hour later, as I was wading through the water, salt started tickling my calves. When I went to brush it off, I spotted something round. Perfectly round. It was a half-buried sand dollar, wedged on its side. Something about it gave me hope. I bent down, braced my elbows, and snapped a picture. "Brady, look."

He came over, but I warned him to stay a decent distance back. Heaven forbid he step on it.

"A sand dollar," I said.

"Are you whispering because you're afraid you'll wake it up?" he teased.

"Ha-ha."

"Is it—"

"I think so." Gingerly, I lifted it out of the sand. It came loose with a sucking noise. "Wow."

"Double wow."

It was round and one of the prettiest shells I'd ever seen. Its body was purple with shades of its former life. A barnacle was attached to it.

I laid it on dry sand and said, "Shoot away."

Getting the hang of positioning himself, he took his time taking photographs. When he was done, I picked up the sand dollar and said, "Your mother should add this to her collection."

"But you found it."

"No. This whole expedition was for you to impress her with your marvelousness."

He wrapped an arm around my waist and hugged me. "I love you," he murmured.

I stiffened. That was the first time he'd ever said the words.

As if to assure me I'd heard right, he repeated himself. "I love you. I hope you feel the same."

"I—"

"Courtney! Brady!" Holly was trudging toward us, her legs straining against the sand to gain purchase. With her was her artist-slash-carpenter boyfriend. He was carrying all their painting paraphernalia. "Hello! Isn't it a glorious day?" she crooned and then blanched. "Oh, heavens, that's horrible of me. It's not glorious, on the heels of another murder." She shook her head. "My apologies."

Her boyfriend said, "Don't be hard on yourself, sweetheart. We all do it. Life goes on."

"For the rest of us, perhaps," she said. "Are you all right, Courtney? I heard both women were your friends."

A lump formed in my throat as images of Petunia and Genevieve swirled in my mind.

"You know, dear"—Holly leaned forward to impart a secret—"I saw Petunia with Scarlet Lyle the other day. They were at Percolate. They were using their inside voices, but I have the ears of an elephant, my son says. Scarlet was upset that her husband had accused her of having an affair." Holly pressed a hand to her chest. "She swore she wasn't, so Petunia asked if he suspected her because he was guilty himself, which made me wonder whether Asher was having an affair with Genevieve. I mean, she and Scarlet were sworn enemies, weren't they?"

"No, they were friends," I said.

"Yes, but I heard somewhere that Genevieve hadn't been keen on Scarlet's new business. What if Scarlet killed Genevieve to remove her from the picture?"

"Oh, darling, your overly active mind," Holly's beau said. "Remove her from the picture? How many noir mysteries have you been reading?"

I peeped at Brady, who was tamping down a smile. To avoid making eye contact with me for fear of bursting out laughing, he inspected his camera lens.

I said, "Scarlet might be innocent. She has an alibi for that night. She was here on the beach. It was the anniversary of her mother's death." I paused. If I really didn't believe Scarlet was guilty, why had I written her name on the whiteboard, not only in Genevieve's column but also in Petunia's?

"Can her husband corroborate that?" Brady asked.

"Asher was playing tennis with a buddy, so she took the time for herself," I replied.

"Oh, my, you know . . ." Holly wiggled her fingers. "She might be telling the truth. We were strolling that night, too, and we saw a woman. She was sitting on a blanket right there. Remember, sweetheart?"

Her beau nodded.

"Her hair was coiled, like so." Holly motioned to the back of her head. "She wasn't warmly dressed. She had on a thinnish jogging suit and was clutching herself as if to fight off the chill. It was around ten. I remembered having seen her earlier when we'd first passed by around eight-thirty."

"Sounds like Scarlet," I said.

"*Pshaw.*" Holly blew air between her lips. "Discard everything I said about her killing Genevieve, Courtney. Have a good day."

When they walked on, the clouds that had been so beautiful earlier started to amass. A storm wasn't coming, but the day would turn cold fast. I shivered.

"I've got my photos and a treasure," Brady said, holding up the sand dollar. "How about I treat you to a latte to warm up?"

"Sounds delicious."

On the way, I said, "You know, even though Holly could place Scarlet on the beach between eight-thirty and ten, the time of death is a broader window, possibly eight to midnight, so who's to say Scarlet didn't leave the beach and return?"

"Meaning she's not off your suspect list."

"Not yet."

We strolled to Cypress and Ivy Courtyard and turned in. I peeked in Open Your Imagination as we passed by. The lights were out, the CLOSED sign in place.

"Need to go inside?" Brady asked.

I slipped my hand around his elbow. "Nope. It's my day off."

As we were climbing the stairs to Sweet Treats, I spotted Detective Summers talking with Asher Lyle. Both men were holding bakery bags and to-go cups. Glinda Gill was outside of Glitz cleaning the window on the entry door, but her movements were clumsy, as if she were trying to hide that she was eavesdropping.

"Thank you, Asher," Summers said. "Have fun shopping for your wife."

The fact that the detective had used Asher's first name didn't surprise me. The general store was next to the precinct. They probably knew each other. Summers headed toward Dolores Street while sipping from his cup, and Asher made a detour into Flair Gallery.

Before Brady and I entered the bakery, Glinda rushed to me. "Courtney, hold up. I think there's activity in Genevieve's murder investigation." She aimed her cleaning rag toward Flair Gallery. "Asher Lyle . . . do you know him?"

I said, "Of course. He owns Lyle's General Store. He's Scarlet's husband."

"Yes. They're steady customers of mine. Well, Asher said he saw Oliver Killian buying new garden tools at a shop out of town."

"Any specific tools?" I asked.

"A hoe and a shovel."

Brady whistled.

Glinda went on. "He said Oliver was acting suspicious, checking over his shoulder and such."

"What was Asher doing there?" I asked.

"He didn't say. Comparative pricing would be my guess. He added that he thought it was weird for Oliver to buy stuff out of town, because after his wife left and took the whole kit and kaboodle—she even took his mother's china, can you imagine—Oliver purchased everything, and Asher stressed *everything*, at Lyle's General Store."

"Perhaps Oliver was being frugal," I suggested. "I mean, why pay general store kind of prices for garden tools? Lyle's collection is high-end with pretty handles and such, but I'd be afraid to get them dirty." I knew the prices for a lot of the inventory. I'd bought a wedding gift there last year.

"Exactly," Glinda said, "but Oliver prides himself on everything he owns being top-notch quality. He's sort of smug that way."

"Why do you think this helps the investigation?" Brady asked.

"Don't you see?" Glinda blinked rapidly. "Garden tools must have been used in both murders."

"I only know about the hoedag," I said. "And that was Daphne's. It wasn't a new one purchased at a store."

Glinda rested her fingertips on her chin. "I'd forgotten about that."

"And we don't know a shovel was used to kill Genevieve," I said. "Unless Summers confirmed it."

"He didn't, but back to Oliver." Glinda flicked her towel. "Asher theorized that Oliver held Genevieve responsible for his wife walking out on him."

"But why kill Petunia?" I asked.

"Summers raised the same point. Asher said he didn't have an inkling, adding that he'd asked Scarlet, and she was clueless, too." Glinda glanced right and left, as if ensuring no one was listening in. "Also, get this, Summers said he heard that Scarlet and Genevieve had locked horns, but Asher quickly dismissed that, claiming his beautiful wife adored Genevieve. *Adored* her. She loved their sparring because it challenged her to be bolder."

"Most likely, Scarlet didn't kill Genevieve," I said. "We ran into Holly Hopewell a bit ago, and she saw Scarlet on the beach that night."

"Oh." Glinda screwed up her mouth. "Well, I suppose that leaves Oliver or Daphne as the main suspects, doesn't it?"

I flashed on Oliver and Asher having lunch at Hideaway Café, both men laughing. I'd thought they were friends. Did they have a falling out? Was that why Asher was turning on him?

Brady and I purchased two lattes and two slices of chocolate mousse pie, a Sweet Treats specialty. After we polished off our snacks, I asked him if he wanted to come to my house for a cocktail and try his hand at making a fairy garden. He leaped at the chance. He was adept at making fairy doors—long story—but he hadn't ever made a garden in a pot.

Fiona and Eveleen were at the house, whizzing through the trees when we returned. While Brady poured a glass of wine for me and fetched a pale ale for himself, I asked Fiona how her class went.

She brushed my nose with her wing. "As well as can be expected."

"What does that mean?"

"My sister struggled."

Eveleen sneered at her. "I didn't understand what Cedric was telling us. I had to ask lots of questions."

"He grew weary of them," Fiona added, "and ended the class."

"Oh, my," I said. "That doesn't sound very gracious of him."

"He's going through something." Fiona wriggled her fingers next to her head. "He's pondering whether he belongs in the human realm any longer."

"I see." That could be a daunting question. "He'll come around."

Fiona tweaked her sister's wing.

"She blames me!" Eveleen cried.

"Now, now," I said. "Don't fret. It's his issue."

"That's what I told her, but . . . *ooh!*" With an explosive huff, Eveleen darted into the cypress to sulk.

"Courtney!" Brady called as he passed through the door to the backyard. "Guess who has become my shadow?"

Pixie pranced after him, looking for all intents and purposes like a show cat, her head held high, tail pointing at the sky.

I laughed. "She treasures you."

He handed me my glass of wine and clinked his beer bottle with it. "What's not to treasure?" He scanned the area. "Is Fiona here?"

"By your ear."

He turned left.

"The other ear."

He pivoted, but she scooted away, giggling hysterically. Mock-grumbling, he slogged to the greenhouse and swung open the door. "I'm ready if you are." He stepped inside and let the door swing shut.

I threw Fiona an exasperated look.

She hitched up her shoulders and let them fall. "I can't help myself."

"You're not being a good role model for your sister," I whispered. "Go make amends with her, or your mother will be upset."

With a cry of disgust, she tore to the cypress and disappeared.

At the same time, Eveleen zipped out, cackling mercilessly.

I glowered at her. "You're being an imp. Go back in there and tell Fiona I was kidding about the queen fairy being mad at her."

"But she will be," Eveleen said.

"Not if we don't tell her. You won't, will you?"

The young fairy wagged her head vehemently. "No, of course not. I was emoting. Fairies love to emote."

"Coming?" Brady poked his head out.

"On my way." I worried about Fiona, but I knew she would be able to deal with her frustration in time. I stepped into the greenhouse and said, "Well, well, look at you." He'd set his beer on a shelf and had already selected two fairy figurines, a boy hugging a puppy and a girl with a white cat.

"You told me making fairy gardens is all about the conversation or setting the scene," he said, wiggling the boy figurine.

"What will yours be chatting about?"

"His friend thinks he should adopt a pet."

My mouth fell open. "But you've said you don't have time for a dog. They're a lot of work. They need to be walked every day. They need to go outside every few hours. They're not like cats, who are independent and can survive days at a time without seeing a human." Other cats. Not Pixie. She was quite addicted to humans.

"Oh, I don't want a dog," he said. "I want a macaw, but I don't see a boy figurine with a bird anywhere."

A laugh burst out of me. "A macaw? They're loud and noisy."

"Like this?" He made raucous cawing sounds.

"Yeah, right, your neighbors would crucify you," I said.

"I've heard they can be wonderful pets. They're playful and active and communicative. Zinnia Walker was dining at the café the other day and raving about how special her Blue was."

"Zinnia lives acres away from anyone who could hear that bird," I argued. She resided on 17-Mile Drive, a scenic loop circling Pacific Grove, Pebble Beach, and Carmel, populated with some of the most gorgeous high-end homes in California. "Your house is wedged between other houses."

Picturing where his house was situated made me think of the murders. How rare that no one was around when either woman was killed. Carmel citizens roamed the town at all hours of the night on foot. Why hadn't anyone heard the fracas between Genevieve and her killer? She must have screamed. Petunia, too. Unless the killer or killers had lain in wait for exactly the right moment. One swing of an implement, and *thud*. No screams. No protests. Each nasty deed would've been over and done in a nanosecond. I pictured Petunia's prone body, her head closest to the front gate. Had the killer sneaked into her house and surprised her? Had she fled out the front, too panicked to scream, and was struck from behind? Genevieve had been facing the festival tents. Had she been so preoccupied taking photographs that her killer had the opportunity to creep up on her unobserved?

"Okay, okay, you've convinced me," Brady said. "No pets. I'm too busy at the restaurant to devote enough attention. How about . . ." He replaced the boy figurine on the shelf and viewed the other ones. "How about I make the story about a boy seeing his first fairy? They could be playing hide-and-seek."

"You will see one soon. I know you will."

He encircled me with his arms and kissed my forehead. "At least I should be able to see the one who is residing in the café's vines."

"She's shy."

"So am I. We have something in common." He kissed me on the lips.

I pressed apart and swatted him playfully. "You are the farthest thing from shy, Brady Cash."

He chortled.

For the next hour, I guided him in making a fairy garden. When he selected a daydreaming boy fairy figurine leaning on a shovel, I jolted. Were Glinda and I right? Had the killer used a shovel to kill Genevieve? Was Asher Lyle telling the truth about Oliver having purchased one recently?

"What are you thinking about?" Brady asked.

"Nothing," I said, feeling like I was grasping at straws.

"Liar."

I pecked his cheek.

After installing the boy into his garden of baby's breath, Brady landed on a teensy fairy with purple wings hiding behind a red-and-white toadstool. She was impish and perfect for his design. I suggested he plant a tall fern at the center of his garden and place her behind it, to draw the viewer's eye to it. When that was complete, he chose a preformed path that wound its way from the tree to the boy, urging him to go in search.

Garden complete, he stepped back to admire his handiwork. He slipped an arm around my waist. "This was a fun day. I loved every minute of it."

"I did, too."

If only I hadn't thought about murder throughout most of it.

Chapter 14

❧

But a sunbeam entered softly
And touched her hair, as she lay.
Whispering that 'twas morning
And fairies must away.
—Laura Ingalls Wilder, "When Sunshine Fairies Rest"

Brady and I ate a simple meal of stir-fried chicken, snow peas, green onions, and mushrooms on rice. My father, who was a good cook, had always added mustard to the sauce, and I carried on the tradition. Brady raved about my culinary expertise—that made me snort wine out my nose; I liked to eat, but I was no chef—and at ten, after a tender kiss good night and me admitting out loud that I loved him, too, he left.

When I retired to the bedroom, I saw Fiona and Eveleen skipping through the dollhouse, which made me smile. They had resolved their issues for the time being.

Tuesday morning arrived fast. I stretched, ran on the beach, fed the fairies and Pixie, made a peach protein smoothie for myself, and headed to the shop. After dusting and rearranging items that were slightly askew on the shelves, I completed the text I'd started yesterday to Detective Summers regarding the dismissive post by Genevieve about Bentley Bramble. Three dots appeared, followed by the words *Thank you.* I wasn't miffed that he wouldn't elaborate, but I would have appreciated a tad more, like *I'll check it out* or *You're the best* or *What would I do without you?* I considered asking him whether Oliver Killian's wife had an alibi for Thursday night, but let it go, knowing he wouldn't tell me. Certainly not in a text.

"Morning, boss," Joss said, as she entered carrying a tower of packages so tall that I couldn't see her face behind them.

"What are those?" I asked, hurrying to help her before any fell. "I didn't see any standing outside when I got here."

"The UPS guy swung by as I arrived. I think they're the fairy solar globes you ordered."

Fairy solar globes were about eight to ten inches in diameter and made of durable resin that resembled crushed stone. The ones I'd ordered had a bronze fairy sitting atop and after a day of sunlight would glow into the night. Like many people, I loved stringing LED fairy lights in my garden, but a solar globe would add one more touch of whimsy. I believed my customers would feel the same. I set the stack on the sales counter, unpacked one box, and positioned the globe beside the array of wind chimes. I placed another on the patio, where it could absorb sunlight. We closed too early for our customers to really experience the beauty of the globes in the dark, but they would get the general idea. Pixie, who was nestled in a spot of sunlight, peered up at me.

I said, "Go to sleep, girl." I didn't have to tell her twice. When I went back inside, I said, "Joss, how's your mom?"

"Not bad." She smoothed the front of her moss-green, fairy-grunge T-shirt. The fairy was pale blue and stepping through a portal. "But she's sort of falling into gibberish now. It's very sad."

Fiona flew to Joss and kissed her cheek. Eveleen alit on Joss's shoulder and stroked Joss's earlobe. Joss giggled.

"I took Buddy with me this morning," Joss went on. "Mom wasn't frightened of him, even though she didn't know him. I think it was because he sang songs that she remembered from her teenage years. She let him hold her hand."

"Sweet," I said.

"And she kept calling him a nice young man. He's sixty, but to her, that's young."

I strolled to the shop entrance and opened the top half of the Dutch door. I spied Tamara Geoffries carrying a gray cat into the pet grooming store across the courtyard. Not her Angora. And not just any gray cat. The ghostly gray one that belonged to a woman who lived near the Meeting House. Was Tamara cat-sitting? I was surprised to see her wearing a shabby-chic, multicolored smock dress. Usually she wore somber clothes, as if in mourning. The soft green tones complimented her beautiful olive-toned skin. With her long hair braided loosely, she came across as relaxed yet focused.

"What's caught your attention?" Joss asked, joining me.

I told her about Tamara being Genevieve's therapist. "I know she can't reveal anything about their exchanges, but perhaps she could shed light on why Genevieve was so dismissive of people."

"Ask her to lunch."

"She won't go. She barely knows me. And, given our history . . ." At one point, I'd wondered if she had murdered the town's pickleball champ. I'd apologized since then for my error, and she'd forgiven me, but . . .

"Isn't she Meaghan's friend?"

"They have mutual customers." In addition to being a therapist, Tamara sold antiques. Actually, she was the person who'd suggested Meaghan find a therapist to sort out her feelings about her ex-boyfriend.

"Have Meaghan ask her to lunch," Joss said, "and you happen into the café at the same time."

I aimed a finger at her. "You're sly."

She grinned. "I get that from my mother."

I touched base with Meaghan and proposed the idea. Although she wasn't happy that I'd found myself enmeshed in not one but two murder investigations, she was always eager to get the inside scoop and agreed. Minutes later, she texted that she was meeting Tamara at Hideaway Café at twelve-thirty.

I sauntered in shortly after and lingered close to Meaghan and Tamara's table, acting as though I was supposed to meet a friend who hadn't shown up. Brady, catching on to my scheme, said my *date* had called and apologized for canceling, adding that he'd already planned on serving us Monte Cristo sandwiches—last night, I'd told him about my craving for one—so he suggested I stay.

Meaghan overheard and said, "I'd like a Monte Cristo, too, Brady. How about you, Tamara? They're a specialty of the house."

"Sure. Sounds terrific." Tamara had a resonant, radio announcer-type voice.

Meaghan asked Tamara if she'd mind if I joined them.

"Why not?" Tamara said. "The more, the merrier. I haven't seen you in ages, Courtney."

I sat down, and Brady brought another place setting. I unfurled my napkin and laid it on my lap.

"I've been meaning to come into the shop," Tamara went on, which I was pretty certain was a fib. "Have you made a fairy garden?" she asked Meaghan.

"Two so far, one for my mother and another to honor the fairy that lives in my garden."

Tamara raised an eyebrow. "Oh, no. You believe in fairies, too?"

"I don't simply believe in them," Meaghan said. "I know a few."

Fiona coasted into the café and alit on my shoulder. Breathless, she said, "Eveleen is off with Merryweather trying to coax Cedric to teach. I'm on my own. What did I miss?"

"In fact," Meaghan said to Tamara, "there's a fairy on Courtney's shoulder right now."

Tamara glanced in my direction, a smile tugging at the corners of her mouth. "Okay, I can't see her, but I won't be a spoilsport. Why should I be? I'm crazy enough to believe my cat might be, um, possessed."

"Fairies don't possess," Fiona said.

I tapped her foot to quiet her. "Why do you think your Angora might be possessed?" I asked Tamara.

"Not my Angora. My gray cat. You've met him. He has a white muzzle." She stroked the hollow of her neck.

"He's yours now? I thought he belonged to the woman who lives next to the Meeting House. Did she pass away? Did she bequeath you the cat?"

"No. She's fine. A few months ago, Ghost—that's what she called him—refused to go back to her house, adamant about staying at mine, so I adopted him. But lately, he's been acting weird, doing flips at all times of the night, like he's chasing something, and he yowls at things humans can't see."

Like fairies? I wondered.

Our waitress brought each of us iced tea.

Tamara dumped a sweetener into her tea and took a sip. "Courtney, I'm sorry to hear you knew both of the murder victims."

Happy for an opening, I said, "Yes. They were members of my gardening forum. You were Genevieve Bellerose's therapist, weren't you? Daphne Flores divulged that."

"*Aha.* So that's how it became public knowledge," Tamara said. "I've spoken to the police," she said as a non sequitur.

Meaghan leaned in. "What did you tell them?"

Tamara clicked her tongue. "You know I can't answer that."

"Actually, I can," I cut in. "Daphne said Genevieve was working through the issue of her father abandoning her. I got the feeling they'd shared a lot of personal stories." Stories I hadn't been privy to. "Genevieve referred Daphne to you."

"Has she reached out?" Meaghan asked.

Tamara took another swig of her iced tea.

I said, "I suppose Genevieve's father issue might explain why she was so hard on everyone she reviewed. She did it to bolster her self-esteem."

Tamara was superb at remaining stoic. After a long moment, she ran her tongue along her teeth, a move that made a squeaky sound. "You didn't really have a lunch appointment, did you, Courtney?

And you, Meaghan"—she scowled at her—"invited me to lunch so Courtney could grill me, didn't you?"

Meaghan sputtered. "Gr-grill you? No. I—"

Tamara raised a hand. "I like both of you, but I will not breach my vow to protect a client's privacy. However, I can tell you that if either of you are in need of a therapist, I'll be glad to be of service. Seeing fairies could be an issue. Talking to them, quite another thing."

"Oh, yeah?" Ulra hooted as she swooped out of a nearby tree and soared in front of Tamara's face. Using her wings, she flapped hard to create a breeze. Tamara swatted the air, as if trying to get rid of a pesky fly.

Fiona giggled and joined Ulra in the invasion. I bit back a smile. Meaghan did, too. When the pair had had their fun, they clasped hands—best buds—and sailed into the tree.

"I found a therapist, Tamara," Meaghan said, "so I must admit I appreciate your confidentiality. I would hope my therapist would be equally discreet."

"I admire you, too, Tamara," I murmured. "I'm sorry for even thinking I could persuade you to . . ." Embarrassment coursed through me. I rose to my feet and rested a hand on her shoulder. "Enjoy your lunch."

"Courtney," Tamara said. "I'm not upset."

"I overstepped."

"I get it. Your reputation precedes you. You care about your friends, and you'll do practically anything you can to help solve the crimes." She smiled warmly. "Sit."

As I resumed my seat, our waitress arrived with our meals as well as a pitcher of warm syrup and a pot of strawberry jam.

I didn't need either of the accoutrements. I tucked in immediately and cut off a corner of my Monte Cristo sandwich. The crispy fried bread resisted, as I'd heard it should. I popped the bite into my mouth. "Oh, man." I hummed. "This is everything I'd hoped it would be. The cheese is oozing out perfectly, and the turkey and ham have just the right saltiness."

Tamara drizzled syrup on her sandwich, taking pains not to overdo. Meaghan added a dollop of the jam to hers and downed a bite.

I said, "Tamara, I hope Ghost is all right."

"I'm sure he's just acting out. Or he really is my husband, and he's showing off." She'd lost her husband in a car accident a number of years ago.

"Do they have cat whisperers at Wizard of Paws?" I asked.

Tamara puckered her brow until realization hit her. *"Ah,* seeing me outside the shop is what made you concoct this scheme." She nudged her iced tea away. "For your information, no, there are no cat whisperers at the groomers. Ghost needed to get a bath. He rolled in stinkweed yesterday. I could kill my gardener for—" She halted, her face flaming red with mortification. "I didn't mean to say . . . that was thoughtless of me."

I said, "It's okay. Meaghan and I have both made blunders when it comes to discussing murder."

For the remainder of lunch, we talked about art and antiques, and I mentioned to Meaghan that I'd signed her and Glinda up for a pottery class on Thursday at three. Tamara asked if she could join us. I said absolutely.

As I was paying the check—I offered to do so, seeing as I was the one who'd created the ruse—Tamara said, "To bring you up to speed, Courtney, all I told the police is that I knew nothing that might help them, and what I'm about to tell you is not privileged."

Meaghan and I waited with bated breath.

"Genevieve did not have a violent boyfriend or significant other." Tamara eyed Meaghan pointedly. "She never mentioned anyone wishing her ill. She was very self-aware, and she knew she was throwing shade on a lot of people, but in her mind, she was doing so in fun."

In fun? C'mon. I didn't believe that for a second.

Tamara sighed. "I'm sorry it ended badly for her and for the other victim. I didn't know her, but my guess is the two murders are related. I think the police believe that, as well."

"Why?" I asked.

"Detective Summers happened to be reviewing the coroner's report on Genevieve when I arrived. He pushed it aside, but I can read upside down. It seems a garden tool was used to kill her."

"What kind of tool?" I asked.

"A shovel."

Back at Open Your Imagination, I asked Fiona about her new BFF, Ulra. "She seems to be less shy."

"I think she's comfortable around me now."

"She was acting a bit impish."

Fiona giggled. "All fairies are allowed some impishness, but not as much as I was displaying before I was expelled from the realm."

I didn't press her for details. She'd already shared that her go-to pranks had involved toying with plants and with other fairy creatures' living quarters. I presumed she'd done something akin to short-sheeting beds and applying honey where it might attract unwanted critters—child's play—but unthinkable for the future queen of the realm.

"Courtney, hello!" Zinnia Walker called as she weaved through the display tables. "I hope you don't mind. I scheduled another class. I had such a good time the other day. I want to create one more garden, this one in honor of my dearly departed father. He taught me everything I know about hotel construction."

"Sure thing."

As she had before, she chose one of the elderly polymer fairy figurines that Renee had created and caught sight of the adorable gnome with a knobbed nose, its eyes obscured by a red hat.

"I love this one!" she exclaimed, snatching it up. "My father had the hardest time keeping a hat above his eyes. It had something to do with the odd shape of his head. He fell when he was a kid and flattened half of it."

I winced, thinking of poor Genevieve and Petunia, their heads bashed in.

"The *Welcome* sign is a nice touch," Zinnia said. "And Dad had a white beard. It's perfect." Like a kid with a precious toy, she cradled the gnome and bustled to the learning-the-craft table. "You pick the plants, Courtney."

For the next half hour, we created her celebratory garden. When she left, I joined Joss to handle sales. A busload of tourists had arrived in town. The tour guide loved Open Your Imagination and had touted it to all on board. We nearly sold out of teacups, saucers, and wind chimes.

After they departed, Joss said, "By the way, boss, the coupons we handed out at the festival were a hit. I'll have to reorder half of our stock."

"That's great." I'd be excited if two murders weren't putting a pall over the whole affair. "Tea?"

"Yes, please, and brownies. Yvanna brought some by when you went to lunch. Chocolate ones made with cacao nibs."

I wasn't sure I could eat another bite until Joss showed me the brownies. They looked rich and luscious, and my mouth started to salivate.

Over tea and a small brownie, very small, I filled her in on the minimal information I'd gleaned from Tamara Geoffries.

She whistled. "And you think Oliver Killian might be the best suspect?"

"If Asher is right, and Oliver bought a new shovel for no apparent reason . . ." I let the rest hang. Oliver's motive was solid. "Most likely, Detective Summers has followed up already. If Oliver killed both women, the case is closed."

"Here's hoping." Joss crossed her fingers. "What's his alibi for Thursday night?"

"Taking a friend to an AA meeting."

"Sounds legit. And for Saturday?"

"I don't know." Would it be as tenuous as the other?

"Is Fiona enjoying mentoring her sister?" Joss asked.

"She's not telling me much about it, but they seem to be getting along, although Eveleen needs to pay better attention. Fiona really wants to go with you tomorrow to see your mom."

"Tell her to meet me at Flower Farm at dawn. Daphne said she'd make an arrangement of peonies that I could take her. Those are Mom's favorites."

"Will do." I snapped my fingers. "That reminds me. I've been meaning to track down Petunia's sister. Her name is Peony. She does the books for a local winery. I want to take her the garden Petunia ordered for her and give her my condolences. Do you think Buddy might be able to help me locate her?"

"He'd be happy to. What's her last name?"

"I'm hoping it's Fujimoto. If not, I haven't a clue."

An hour later, after I'd concluded a reorder with our supplier, putting a rush on a few items like wind chimes, Joss slipped into the office, grinning. She wagged a Post-it note. "Got it. Peony Fujimoto's number." She rattled off the name of the winery and said the woman who'd answered was more than happy to give out Peony's cell phone. Many people were calling with condolences.

I thanked her, closed out the register, nabbed Pixie, and headed home. Once there, I reached out to Peony. She didn't answer, so I left a message explaining who I was and that I had a gift for her. Afterward, I changed into a simple blue sheath and ballet slippers, grabbed a matching silk cardigan, and hurried to the library for part two of my father's master gardening class.

Chapter 15

~~~~~

Harrison Memorial Library was located at the corner of Ocean Avenue and Lincoln Street. One of my favorite aspects of the place was its drought-resistant garden. Every time I visited, I paused for a moment to appreciate the artistry of the plantings.

My father was conducting his seminar in the Barnet Segal Reading Room, an expansive, light-filled space fitted with a fireplace, tables, and easy chairs. He was standing at the lectern looking relaxed in a white polo and jeans. A tall, draped object stood beyond him. At least twenty people were attentively waiting for him to begin. Folding chairs had been set out for the occasion. I spotted Asher and Scarlet Lyle in the crowd. Dad hadn't mentioned Scarlet attending the first class. Perhaps she was with Asher tonight because she didn't want to be alone in her house after two murders had occurred—two murders of people she knew. She and her husband seemed a mismatched pair. She was overdressed for a gardening class, in a white silk dress, her hair artfully arranged in a French twist. He was wearing tennis shorts and a striped gray polo. A red-and-black Head tennis bag rested on the floor to his right. I guessed that he had come from a match, and she had come from meeting a client.

On a portable table to the right of my father stood a slide projector. Dad was sorting through his carousel of slides, I assumed to make sure each was inserted right-side up.

I sneaked up and whispered, "Hello, Father."

"Hello, kitten," he said. "Let me know if I bore you."

"You never could. What's under the drape?"

"My secret."

I screwed up my mouth. He mimicked me. Had he brought a statue or one of Bentley Bramble's topiaries?

"Sit." He shooed me away.

I pecked his cheek and took a seat at the back of the room. Scarlet peeked over her shoulder at me and waved. I responded in kind. Asher cut a look in my direction, too. He frowned. Scarlet elbowed him and said what she'd said the other day, I presumed. *Friend not foe.* His mouth turned up at the corners in greeting.

"Courtney!" Fiona flew in front of me, her sister trailing her. "Sister and Auntie finished up with Cedric."

"I learned so much," Eveleen chirped, clearly delighted. "Plant psychology is all I dreamed it would be."

"May we stay and watch your father teach?" Fiona asked. "I've told Eveleen so much about him."

I nodded, unwilling to speak aloud lest my father catch me conversing with fairies.

"I'm going to say hello to him," Fiona said.

Before I could stop her, she glided to him and did pirouettes to his right. As always, he didn't notice a thing.

"Someday," she said when she returned to me. "Someday."

I whispered, "Sit."

She and her sister settled on each of my shoulders.

At exactly seven-thirty, my father began by welcoming everyone, adding that he recognized a few faces in the crowd, after which he launched into his spiel. When he'd told me the other day that his chat would be about *tools of the trade*, I'd thought he'd meant PR tools, like how he found and managed clients. But he'd literally meant tools, I realized, when he removed the drape from the object to his left to reveal a free-standing tool holder. It was constructed of aluminum bars with moveable racks so the owner could adjust it to his or her personal needs. I'd erected a similar tool holder outside my greenhouse. On this one, Dad had hung a broom, shovel, sprayer, lawn edger, and a couple of hoes.

A few in the audience *ooh*ed.

"Tools," my father said. "How many of you own a set?"

Ninety percent of the attendees raised their hands.

"Organization is the name of the game," he went on. "It's important to own the tool that will do the right job. For someone in my line of business, with a full crew to outfit, that means I need lots and lots of tools, plus replacements in case one breaks."

He lifted the shovel, and my stomach lurched. Wielding it as he was, with two hands on the grip, I could easily see it as a murder weapon. He replaced the shovel and pointed to another tool. "What's this one?"

"A broom," a man said, chuckling.

"And this?"

"A weed hacker?" a tentative woman asked, her voice rising unsurely at the end.

"A lawn edger," Dad corrected. "Vital for grass, but it will destroy a mesh pool fence. Beware. And this?"

"A hoe," the tentative woman tried.

"No," my father said.

"A hoedag," Asher offered.

I gulped. Fiona inhaled sharply.

"We carry them in the shop," Asher explained to the audience. "Stop by Lyle's General Store and take a tour of all the tools we have in stock. We care about your gardens."

"Okay, okay, Asher." My father flapped both hands. "No advertisements during the class."

That elicited chuckles from the crowd.

"But he's right," my father said, lifting the tool from its hook. "Its official name is a hoedag. It's good for hoeing and weeding, and—" Suddenly, as if realizing that the tool might remind many in the audience about Petunia's murder, he had the civility to blanch, and return the tool to its place. His gaze locked on mine. He mouthed *Sorry*.

I hadn't heard anyone gasp. Conceivably, the weapon hadn't been mentioned on any news programs. I offered a sickly smile and rotated a hand. *Continue.*

"Moving on," he said, turning to the importance of well-made tools. Cheap ones were a waste of money, he warned, and cautioned the crowd not to look for bargains. Tools could break easily. Bully Tools, he said, were made entirely in America. Fisher Blacksmithing made artistic tools with walnut handles, perfect for the discerning gardener. He handed out a list of his other favorite manufacturers.

A half hour later, he suggested everyone take a fifteen-minute recess. Afterward, he would have a slideshow touting environmental activism. I'd seen the slideshow many times—over the years, I'd been his guinea pig for honing his chat—so I wouldn't be sticking around.

With Fiona and Eveleen trailing me, I pushed through the front door and slipped my arms into my silk cardigan. The evening air had turned chilly. I caught the hint of cigarette smoke and spied a knot of audience members near the street corner. Asher and Scarlet were among them. Neither was smoking. Asher seemed to be inspecting Scarlet's left hand. Specifically, her ring finger. She pulled free. Where was her wedding ring?

"Kitten." Dad caught up to me along the walkway. "I'm sorry about—"

"No worries, Dad." I rested a hand on his shoulder. "I don't think anyone other than me picked up on the gaffe."

"Your father seems upset," Fiona said, and circled his head to dash him with silver dust. She added an extra flick of her wings to make sure all of it descended on him.

I remained focused on my father. "But why *did* you bring that tool of all tools?"

"Late Sunday, I was talking to Dylan. He asked me for my expert opinion on hoedags, letting me in on the fact that it was the weapon used in the Fujimoto murder. He was wondering how many people might own them and were they typical in a home assortment of tools. I suppose it's been preying on my mind."

"Where did you see Detective Summers?"

"Outside the precinct. I'd gone to the general store to pick up some linens Wanda ordered. Nice place, though I think the prices are a bit steep."

"Now, now, Kip, is that a nice thing to say?" Asher joked as he approached with his wife. They were holding hands. "After all, the cost of hiring you to do the landscaping outside the shop was no drop in the bucket."

"I gave you options," Dad said. "You happened to pick the highest-priced design."

"Yeah, you're right." Asher smirked. "It looks terrific."

"When I was there, I was noticing the signs you have throughout the store about living intentionally," Dad said. "'Make sure your favorite activities are on your schedule.' 'Take a long walk with your loved one because quality time should be a priority.' All good advice." Now that they were a couple, my father and Wanda took strolls almost every night.

"Were you a therapist at one time, Asher?" I asked.

"Him? Ha! Not a chance." Scarlet twirled her left hand by her head. "He was in a cult."

Fiona startled. She hovered in front of Asher and studied his eyes. "Cults are bad," she said to her sister.

"It wasn't a cult," Asher countered. "It was a group, a faction if you will, intent on altering one's mental belief systems."

"Cult." Scarlet snickered.

Asher mock-frowned at her. They were joking, but Fiona looked grave, doubtless because she'd helped rescue Tish Waterman's adult daughter from a cult soon after we met.

Switching subjects to ease the tension, I said, "What kind of tennis racket do you use, Asher?"

"Depends on the day."

"Your bag looks like it holds quite an assortment."

"I've got a Wilson Ultra, Babolat Aero, and a Head Microgel in here."

"He has more at home," Scarlet said.

"I'm a Wilson guy," my father said. He not only played golf, but he also played tennis every few weeks and biked ten miles on weekends.

I said, "Asher, Scarlet told me you have a regular tennis game at a friend's house."

"His name's Fritz Bomer," Scarlet offered.

Asher grinned. "Fritz is a do-gooder to beat all do-gooders, isn't he, honey?"

"I know Fritz," Fiona said. "A fairy friend of Cedric's lives in his garden. We held a class there a week ago."

"He's off in Guatemala now," Asher said.

"Saving the trees," Scarlet chimed, her nose crinkling with humor, as if saving a tree was a ridiculous pursuit.

"Trees, my darling bride, provide shade for the coffee plants," Asher added.

"You played tennis with Fritz Thursday night, didn't you?" I asked.

"Yes, I did. I—" He balked, and his face grew grim. Was he just now realizing that by being out that night, he'd left his wife without an alibi?

"By the way, Scarlet," I said, "I'm happy to say someone saw you on the beach Thursday night. My neighbor, Holly Hopewell."

"Why does that make you happy?" she asked innocently. "Why would it matter whether I was seen or not? I was there."

I swallowed hard. Didn't she grasp that she might be a suspect in

Genevieve's murder, given all the negative social media posts Genevieve had written about her? "Um, I think the police are considering any of us who knew Genevieve and Petunia persons of interest."

Her mouth formed a shocked O. "Well, I was home the night Petunia was killed." Scarlet eyed her husband. Was she worried he wouldn't believe her?

"Can't help you there, either, hon," Asher said, missing her eye movement. "I was doing inventory all night."

"Help me?" she asked. "Why would I need your help?"

Is she that naïve? I wondered. Clearly, Asher understood the significance of having a verifiable alibi.

"FYI," Scarlet went on, "you do not want to be in the vicinity of the General Store when my husband does inventory. He turns up the music and sings really loud. He's not a singer."

He knuckled her arm fondly.

"I can fix his singing voice," Eveleen said. "Mother taught me a spell."

Fiona held up a finger. "Do. Not. Do. A. Spell. Not here. Not in the human world."

"But—"

"No."

Eveleen, feelings hurt, soared toward the library. Fiona cruised after her, apologizing.

Scarlet glanced at her watch. "Sweetheart, we'd better get inside." She started for the front door. "The class will be continuing soon."

"Not unless I'm there," my father said, a playful gleam in his gaze.

When Asher and Scarlet disappeared into the building, my father turned to me. "Are you a suspect?"

"Heavens, no."

"So, why are you asking about alibis?"

"Because Detective Summers told me to keep my eyes open and my ears alert."

Chapter 16

There are fairies at the bottom of our garden!
It's not so very, very far away;
You pass the gardener's shed and you just keep straight ahead—
I do so hope they've really come to stay.
—Rose Fyleman, "Fairies"

Wednesday morning, after Fiona and Eveleen left to meet Joss at Flower Farm, I decided to relocate the whiteboard from home to the office. Thoughts were swirling around in my head about the murders, and having my ideas written on a board that was sitting in my living room was doing me no favors. I draped the whiteboard with a cloth and inserted Pixie into her cat carry pack, and we walked to work.

When I arrived at the shop, Yoly was there to assist. "Morning, Yoly!"

"Hi, Courtney."

I took the whiteboard to the office, positioned it beside the one I kept in the office to plan my gardens, removed Pixie from her prison, stowed my purse, and returned to the main showroom. Pixie scampered to the patio, and I crossed to the Dutch door and opened the top half.

"I hope we're flocked with customers today," Yoly said. "I like when we're busy." Today, she'd swooped her hair into a fashionably messy bun. The fluid skirt she was wearing swished with every step she took as she dusted the fairy orbs. "Don't forget. Meaghan and her mother are due at nine for their fairy garden session."

"On it."

Wanda had never made a garden. Meaghan told me she was super excited. Quickly, I tended the till and checked items on the patio.

At a quarter to nine, I heard a shrub-shearing tool kick into high gear. The noise was infuriating. I peeked out the front door and saw Bentley across the street in front of Acosta Artworks, tending to two new gigantic boxwood bushes in red-glazed pots. He was wearing cargo shorts and an olive-green T-shirt. Goggles protected his eyes. Leaves were flying helter-skelter.

A few feet from him, Twyla Waterman was watching with rapt attention. Once a broken woman because of the cult experience, she was now poised and at peace with her life.

"Could that racket be any louder?" I asked Yoly.

She joined me and peered out. "Why isn't he wielding clippers? Doesn't he usually use those?"

"The bushes are huge. I guess he starts with the cordless shearer and fine-tunes with the clippers. Sheesh." I closed the top half of the door and locked it into place.

"So much for fresh air circulating through the shop," Yoly quipped.

"Hopefully, he'll be done soon." The people and tenants at Village Shops had to be unhappy with the noise pollution, too.

I proceeded to the sales counter, wondering whether Detective Summers had questioned Bentley about the scathing post that Genevieve had written regarding his work. Would it hurt to casually ask Bentley? He wouldn't lash out at me, not with people milling about.

"Do you think Say Cheese is open?" I asked Yoly. The gourmet shop was located in the Village Shops. "I have a craving."

"Go. I'll take care of Meaghan and her mother when they get here."

Similar to Cypress and Ivy Courtyard, the Village Shops were tiered, and a staircase wound through the center. Unlike our courtyard, there were a lot more units. Three of them boasted two stories. An attorney, a dentist, and a hot yoga studio occupied the upper floors. Hideaway Café, Seize the Clay, Acosta Artworks, Say Cheese, and a few other shops were housed in the lower units.

Bentley stopped shearing when he saw me approaching and lowered the cordless tool. He leaned it against the side of his leg and pushed his goggles to the top of his head. His BRAMBLE TOPIARY T-shirt was covered with leaf debris.

"Hi, Courtney," Twyla said. Her dark hair graced her shoulders, and the pink sheath she had on complimented her beautiful skin. A pink flute case hung over one shoulder.

"Morning, Twyla."

"Lovely day, isn't it? Perfect for a tootle on the beach." Twyla enjoyed practicing near the ocean.

"Coming to see me, Courtney?" Bentley asked, his gaze wary.

"No. I'm going to Say Cheese to grab some sandwiches."

"Uh-huh. Why don't I believe you?"

I had to admit, it did sound lame this early in the day. "What are you sculpting?"

"Miss Acosta wants something Picassoesque," he said.

Twyla snickered. "That should be a challenge."

Bentley cocked a hip, studying me. "I suppose you're the one who told the police about what happened between me and Petunia outside my truck."

"No, that wasn't me."

"What happened?" Twyla asked.

"She slapped me. I . . ." He lowered his chin. "She'd gone to Open Your Imagination for tea, and afterward, I wanted her to take a ride so we could talk things out, but she didn't want to get in, so she—"

"Bennie, Bennie, Bennie," Twyla said. "That's exactly the kind of thing I've been telling you not to do."

"I know. I know." He lifted his shoulders and let them fall, sufficiently chastised. "Well then, Courtney, I guess you're here to hound me about what Genevieve did."

"What did she do?" Twyla asked.

"She mocked my work. Courtney saw the post and told the police."

I didn't deny it, but I was surprised that Summers would reveal his source.

"What she wrote meant nothing to me," Bentley said. "I don't have thin skin."

Oh no? He had been quite sensitive about Petunia's disregard for him. On the other hand, that was personal, not business.

"What upset me most about it," he went on, "was the dig lost me a huge hotel job in Silicon Valley. Forty topiaries. That's big bucks."

And big motive, I thought.

"I told the police my alibi for Thursday night," he said, "in case you were wondering."

"I wasn't," I replied, lying through my teeth.

"I was treating pumpkins with hot pepper spray to keep squirrels at bay."

Okay, spraying pumpkins was a nighttime activity, and given the size of his garden, I supposed it could take a while, but like his snail hunting alibi, it sounded weak.

"He's telling the truth," Twyla said. "I saw him, and believe me, I have no reason to lie."

"Are you two an item?" I asked.

Twyla tittered. "Not on a bet."

Bentley grunted.

"He and I dated for a nanosecond."

"For a week," he groused.

"I knew instantly he wasn't the man for me. He's prickly and sensitive and overly protective." She threw him a look. "I do not need a keeper."

Abashed, he lowered his head. "I care. Sue me."

"Why are you watching him trim the bushes then, Twyla?" I asked.

"I find it fascinating. That's what intrigued me about him in the first place." She beamed. "It's Zen-like, and he's so talented."

"Twyla," he began.

She held up a palm. "Uh-uh, I will not reconsider going on another date. We're friends, Bentley." She shifted her focus to me. "But not good enough friends that I would lie."

I believed her. "When did you see him spraying the garden, Twyla?"

"On each of my loops around the neighborhood." She was an avid walker. It was a way for her to relish the freedom she had, post-cult. "I think I walked for two hours that night."

Two hours wasn't long enough to fully exonerate Bentley, but there was something honest and vulnerable about him right now that made me want to remove him from the suspect list.

I wished them both a good day and headed to Say Cheese. While I waited for the server to prepare my Italian hero sandwich decked out with salami, prosciutto, provolone, red onions, and diced pepperoncini, I continued to mull over the murders. If Bentley didn't kill Genevieve and Petunia, who did? I tried to mentally review what I'd written on the whiteboard but couldn't picture everything.

Exiting the shop, I ran into Detective Summers and Renee, who were entering, both dressed for the beach.

"Day off?" I asked.

"Can you believe it?" Renee bumped Summers's hip with her own. "He's actually taking me on a picnic. What did you get?" She gestured to my takeout bag.

I told her. "Detective, you got my text message about Bentley

Bramble. Did he tell you that the post Genevieve published lost him a huge account?"

"He did not."

I explained that I saw him on my way to the cheese shop, and he offered up the information on his own.

"You were prying," Summers said.

"I wasn't prying. By the way, he mentioned that you'd received that tidbit about the negative post from me, which leads me to ask, how did he learn that?"

"By accident. Sorry." Summers screwed up one side of his mouth. "He viewed a memo on my desk."

I tamped down a laugh. Was Summers getting careless, or had he intended for Bentley and Tamara to catch a glimpse of the documents they'd seen?

"What's so funny?" he demanded.

"Someone else . . ." I paused. "I won't name names, but this other person got a peek of something in your office, too, which stated a shovel was the weapon used to kill Genevieve."

Renee moaned. "Do we have to talk about this right now?"

"No, we don't," Summers said. "In fact, let me ask you, Miss Kelly, have you joined the police force?"

I glowered at him for using his standard go-to snub.

"Because I don't remember you taking the exam and doing training, and let's face it"—he slung an arm around Renee's shoulders—"you know how unhappy my intended was as a police officer, so what makes you think you could stomach it?"

I sniffed. "Are you trying to say women aren't cut out for the job?"

Renee unpeeled his arm and gave him the stink eye.

Summers faltered. "No. Of course not."

"Look, what I've got to say will merely take a sec," I said. "Please. This is driving me nuts. Do you think it's the same killer, given both murders were committed with gardening tools?"

"Possibly," Summers admitted.

"I can't see Daphne Flores murdering either woman. She certainly had no reason to want Petunia dead."

"Unless, as I speculated, Miss Fujimoto realized Miss Flores was the killer and telephoned her to say she knew what she did," Summers reasoned.

"But that's not what she said. 'Never mind, ask her,' was what Daphne told you."

"Unless she was lying."

It was an odd phrase to pull out of thin air, I thought, but kept my opinion to myself. "My money is on Oliver Killian," I said, outlining his dual motives for murdering two women. "If he learned Petunia planned to rent space near Garden Delights—"

"Mr. Killian has a verifiable alibi for Thursday night."

"I know. He says he took a friend to an AA meeting, but that's hard to confirm."

"Yet his friend has come in and sworn under oath."

"But Oliver wouldn't have been allowed inside the AA meeting. That's why they're anonymous. So, couldn't he have dropped off his friend, gone to the festival site, killed Genevieve, and driven back?"

Summers chewed on that.

"And don't rule out Scarlet Lyle." I hated bringing her into the equation, but she didn't have a solid alibi for either night. Not really. I told him how Holly had seen Scarlet on the beach Thursday night, but added that Scarlet could have left and returned. Plus, Scarlet's claim to have taken a sleeping pill when she got home sounded weak. "Her husband can't confirm where she was, either. He was playing tennis until midnight. By the way, I saw her last night at my father's seminar, and she blurted out her alibi for Saturday night." I told him how cagey she was acting, saying she was home alone when her husband was doing inventory. "A source tells me Asher is worried his wife is having an affair." I didn't mention that my source was actually Scarlet. "I can't figure out why she'd kill Petunia, but if Petunia touched base with the killer like we theorized before—"

"*We* didn't. *You* did."

"Say, what if Petunia caught sight of Scarlet's shovel in her festival booth and thought it might be the murder weapon like I did?"

"What shovel?"

"The one she was reviewing as a new product."

"A shovel can be a new product?" Summers scoffed.

"It had an ornate handle."

"I doubt—"

"Dylan." Renee cleared her throat. "Please. Cut the shop talk."

"Yes, darling. You're right." He glowered at me. "Miss Kelly, if you have anything further to report, reach out to Officer Reddick. But not with suppositions. We want hard facts and only hard facts."

Chapter 17

I often see the Fairy rings
With dew-drops all aglisten,
And hear the noise of Fairy wings
So tiny,—if I listen.
—Annie R. Rentoul, "In the Gully Green"

When I returned to Open Your Imagination, I ate one portion of the sandwich—the server had graciously cut it into six pieces—and offered the others to Yoly, Meaghan, and Wanda.

"It's a little early for lunch," Meaghan joked, "but I skipped breakfast, so this is perfect."

"I never turn down food," Yoly said.

They helped themselves, and I moved to the verdigris bakers' racks to help Wanda pick her items. She resembled her daughter right down to her towering height and curly brown tresses, though she preferred more form-fitting clothing than her daughter, like the peach-toned jumpsuit she was wearing, which made her appear years younger. Meaghan, as she was in the habit of, had donned a boho, mid-calf knit dress, a perfect look for someone who sold art for a living.

"I'm so excited," Wanda said, inspecting one figurine after another. "I've envisioned the ideal garden. I'll create a fairy portal like the one I painted." Wanda continued to serve as an artist's representative and had numerous well-known clients, but she was an artist in her own right and recently had been obsessed with painting portals. "We can do that, can't we?"

"To create a portal," I said, "we'll have to fashion that ourselves."

Fairy portals, for the fairy world novice, were magical entrances that could lead into the fairy realm.

"How will we do that?"

"We could dress up a bowl, place it at the far end of your garden, and fill it with fairy kingdom flowers and purple mushrooms. We'll add glitter to create a glow."

"It sounds wonderful."

Meaghan, with sandwich in hand, joined us. "I want to do the same thing."

"No copycatting," her mother said. "Now for the figurines. I want an artist and a magician. Do you have something like that?"

I smiled, impressed by how much she had been planning her garden in her head.

"How about this polyresin magician holding an orb?" I lifted the piece. "He's pretty large, though. Nearly ten inches high."

"Magicians should be giants," Wanda said, removing him from my hand. "He's magnificent. I love the tilted hat and his staff."

"For the artist fairy, we could try this one." I picked up a little redheaded girl fairy holding a paintbrush and palette, as if ready to add color to a flower.

"Oh!" Wanda snatched her from me. "She's adorable. Did you know Meaghan's hair was this color when she was a baby?"

I gazed at my pal.

"No more childhood secrets, Mom."

"I can't tell her about the time you—"

"No!" Meaghan threw her mother a warning look, and Wanda cackled.

"What are you making?" I asked Meaghan.

"Guess." She chose a couple of figurines for herself, which came as a pair—an adorable fairy and a small frog. The fairy was kissing the frog.

"Is that a depiction of you and Officer Reddick? He is a prince." I waggled my eyebrows at her.

Her cheeks tinged pink, something that rarely happened. In fact, she was probably the hardest person in the world to embarrass.

Wanda placed her figurines on the craft table and revisited the racks. "I think mine should be set in the wilderness, don't you?" She selected a fairy log cabin, nodding as she did, and picked up a garden shed complete with a shovel, broom, and sunhat hanging on the opened doors. Within stood a watering can and a stack of clay pots. The shed was a fairly new item that we'd ordered, and we couldn't keep them in stock. "This is perfect," she cooed, and went about collecting a handful of miniature wood slices for stepping-stones, a pair of wood fences made with durable resin, and a birdbath. "How big a pot will I need?" she asked.

I grinned. "With two sizeable environmental pieces, a portal, and all the other items you intend to add, you'll need a wide-mouthed pot." I led her to the pottery, and she chose a dark green one about twenty inches wide.

Meaghan followed and selected an eight-inch pot that was etched with vines.

"I want this to look as natural as possible," Wanda said. "It's going on my front porch."

Customers wandered onto the patio to peer at the fairy figurines. Pixie stirred briefly and nestled down. She knew when customers weren't interested in socializing.

At the same time, Yoly dashed to me and whispered, "Those coupons you gave at the festival are a hit! We should hand them out more often. You could do so at Sweet Treats and other shops in the courtyard. In fact, we could do a coupon swap with other places in town, too."

"Great idea."

While Wanda and Meaghan filled their pots with dirt, Wanda said, "Why did you go to Say Cheese, Courtney?"

"Yeah, why?" Meaghan asked suspiciously. "Were you investigating?"

I felt heat rise into my cheeks. *"Moi?"*

"Spill." She tamped down the dirt.

I started creating the portal by coating the exterior of a three-inch bowl with hot glue. I pressed moss into it, following which I drizzled more glue on the interior of the bowl and sprinkled it with gold glitter. As I proceeded, I told them about confronting Bentley and how Twyla corroborated his alibi for Saturday night.

"Bentley is a dear," Wanda said. "He's harmless. I doubt he's lying. I often hear him rooting around his garden at night."

"You do?" I tried to picture where Wanda lived and realized her home was near Bentley's.

"He snorts and he whistles," Wanda went on. "Like he's trying to coax bugs and predators into view."

Meaghan spit out a laugh.

"Did you hear him Saturday night?" I asked. I told them about the post Genevieve had published, vilifying Bentley's artistry. "He swears he was snail hunting."

"He was." Wanda made a well in the dirt and inserted a fern into her garden. "I saw him. You were having dinner with your father, so I went for a stroll. Bentley was in his garden when I left the house and still there when I came home."

The fact that he had similar accounts for the nights of both murders led me to believe him.

"Okay," I said, "he's officially off my list."

I showed them the portal I'd created thus far. Both *ooh*ed. Next, I balanced the bowl on its side and glued small stones and moss to the lower rim. For a bit of whimsy, I inserted some speckled glazed toadstool stakes that were delivered last week. I finished off the portal with a jutting of white quartz fixed to the rear of the bowl, giving it a fantastical focal point.

"Voilà!" Meaghan finished up her garden and took a few pictures

of it as well as snapshots of her mother's work-in-progress. When done, she scrolled through messages on her cell phone.

Wanda, who seemed transported by the story she was creating, said, "Should these go here and here, Courtney?" She positioned the log cabin and the shed on opposite sides of the garden.

"Move them a little closer, at an angle."

She did so.

When I was done with the portal, I positioned it at the rear center of Wanda's garden, between the cabin and shed, and said, "Ta-da!"

She applauded.

Meaghan took another picture. "It's looking great, Mom."

Fiona and Eveleen soared onto the patio. Pixie, instantly alert to their arrival, darted to them and rose on her hind legs to play her fa-vorite bat-the-fairy game. Fiona and Eveleen orbited her, giggling.

Joss trotted to the patio, waving. "Hi, boss. We're back!" She was wearing a pretty floral camp shirt over shorts.

"We?" Wanda said, an eyebrow raised. "Oh, is your fairy with her?"

"She is," I said, "and so is her sister."

Wanda's mouth dropped open as she searched overhead and be-hind her. She turned back to me. "She has a sister? Pooh. Why can't I see her . . . *them?*"

Fiona gave up playing with the cat and cruised to Wanda. She stroked her hair. Eveleen, taking her cue from her sister, did the same.

"How's your mother, Joss?" I asked.

"She loved seeing Fiona."

"She could see her?" I hooted. "That's great!"

"Yeah, she's a believer now." Joss threw a sideways glance at Fiona and her sister. "They were on their best behavior. Eveleen blessed the peonies before I gave them to Mom, who was remarkably clear-headed. She talked about Dad. And music. And, well, it was a truly special visit." She placed a hand over her heart. "I wish they could all be that magical."

Fiona kissed Joss on the cheek before flitting to Wanda's fairy garden to inspect it. She stopped at one point, peeked over her shoulder at me, and returned her gaze to something. *"Psst.* Courtney."

"What's up?" I asked, joining her.

"The broom," she said. "Remember the broom?"

I frowned, not having an inkling as to what she was referring. The broom my father had brought to his demonstration?

"The broom!" She jutted a hand.

"The broom."

When I said the word out loud, it came to me. On Sunday at Petunia's house, Summers had suggested that the crime scene had been swept. I asked with what, a broom? He didn't know, but it mattered to him that someone had tampered with the area. What had the killer hoped to hide? I imagine footprints would have been telltale. Daphne had small feet. Scarlet's were larger and her wardrobe was unique. Something like her thick-soled ankle boots would leave a specific imprint. Oliver Killian's shoeprint would be much larger than both women's. I paused as I considered him. He had a verifiable alibi for the night Genevieve was murdered. Did he have one for the night Petunia died?

Remembering the whiteboard I'd brought from home, I excused myself from Wanda and Meaghan, directed Joss to handle any questions they might have, and made a beeline to my office. Fiona and Eveleen trailed me.

I removed the cloth I'd used to cover the board and studied what I'd created—two columns for two similar murders and a left-hand column for organizing clues. To be honest, it was a muddled mess with Oliver, Scarlet, and Daphne in Genevieve's column, and Bentley starting off Petunia's column. It required more order. I needed to see the names match on both sides.

With my cell phone camera, I took a picture in case I didn't remember all I'd written and began erasing everything in Petunia's column except the weapon, method, and note about the use of her cell phone.

"Wait!" Fiona cried. "What are you doing?"

"Starting over."

I wrote Oliver's name in Petunia's column, exactly opposite his name in Genevieve's column. I added his motive: *competitive business.* Granted, Summers had all but exonerated him of Genevieve's murder, but I'd tossed a wrench into his theory when I'd suggested that Oliver could have left his post outside the AA meeting, committed the crime, and driven back before his friend emerged from the building. Gaps in alibis were always a challenge to prove.

The next name in the leftmost column was Scarlet Lyle. Last night, she'd acted sketchy. She had a secret. I was sure of it. Petunia had texted her before she was killed. Why? Scarlet claimed not to have received the message, but she could be lying. When not reaching Scarlet via text, did Petunia call her using her landline phone? Did she, like Summers and I speculated, say, *I know what you did.* Scarlet's alibi about being home alone when her husband was doing inventory couldn't be proven.

In the column beneath Genevieve's name, I jotted that Holly had placed Scarlet on the beach Thursday night.

"She did?" Fiona asked.

"Yes," I said, and added that, like Oliver's alibi for that evening, however, the sighting confirmed her whereabouts for the entire two-hour window, and because her husband was out with his buddy, he couldn't corroborate where she was or when she arrived home.

The next person listed on the left was Daphne. I wrote her name beneath Scarlet's in the right-hand column.

"I like Daphne," Eveleen said.

"So do I." I didn't want her to be guilty, but the murderer had used her hoedag to kill Petunia, and Petunia had made a thirteen-second phone call to her.

Due to the proximity of their houses, Daphne would have had an easy job of getting away without being seen. When my father and I'd passed her house, she hadn't been home. If she'd sneaked into Petunia's cottage and waited for her to arrive, she could have struck her down after we'd left the neighborhood and disappeared into her own house in minutes.

Lastly, I wrote Bentley's name in both columns. His alibi for Thursday: pumpkin spraying. His alibi for Saturday: snail hunting. Wanda could corroborate that he was in his garden the first night, and Twyla supported his whereabouts for Saturday, but like the other suspects, neither of his alibis were strong enough. He would have had the freedom to leave and return. Motive for the first murder? Genevieve's scathing post had cost him a sizeable job. Motive for the second? Anger that Petunia refused to date him. Twyla hinted that he had a predilection for being overly protective. Petunia had mockingly called it *stalking*.

I added the other things I'd learned in the past few days. A shovel was indeed the weapon used to kill Genevieve. Oliver Killian purchased a new shovel out of town, Scarlet's shovel was missing from her festival booth, and Daphne's toolshed lock was broken, giving a killer access to her tools.

My hand started to cramp. I put down the dry-erase marker and took a step away from the board. "This is insane," I muttered, throwing the cloth over the board.

Fiona said, "*Ah,* yes, as Agatha Christie says, 'There is nothing more amazing than the extraordinary sanity of the insane.'"

I smiled and finished the quote. "'Unless it is the extraordinary eccentricity of the sane.'"

Chapter 18

A fairy went a-marketing—
She bought a little fish;
She put it in a crystal bowl
Upon a golden dish.
—Rose Fyleman, "A Fairy Went A-Marketing"

The day progressed without event. I continued to reflect on the whiteboard notes while selling fairy figurines, pottery, teacups, and books. As instructed, I didn't text Summers with my theories, and I didn't feel the urgent need to reach out to Reddick because I didn't have any concrete answers.

Around three in the afternoon, while I was on the patio rearranging environmental pieces on the bakers' racks, Hedda Hopewell showed up. The linen A-line skirt and silk blouse she was wearing were very appropriate for someone who worked in a bank, although she did have a penchant for unique eyewear. Her glasses were cat-eye frames in a colorful blend of pinks.

"On a coffee break?" I asked.

"On a walk-around," she said. "I was feeling stifled at my desk. Please tell me you have that adorable garden shed in stock."

"I'm sorry. Wanda Brownie purchased it this morning. I can order one for you and have it by next week."

"Wonderful. I've been so inspired by the Summer Blooms Festival that I have gardening on the brain."

"Did you and your sisters meet a lot of budding gardeners there?" I asked.

Hedda frowned. "Um, I don't really know the final numbers. I didn't go on Sunday."

"Of course you didn't," I said hurriedly, sorry to have raised the subject. "You had quite a shock that morning."

"We all did."

Fiona flew into view and hovered in front of Hedda. "Breathe," she coached.

Hedda inhaled and exhaled. Her mouth turned up at the corners. "It's so lovely to see you, Miss Fiona."

"*Tà.*" Fiona curtsied, and said to me, "Off to mentoring, and after that, to the library."

"Who will be there?" I held out my hand for her to light on.

"The whole gang. Callie, Zephyr, Cedric."

"And Ulra?"

"I'm working on it." She spiraled into the air.

"Is Eveleen allowed to socialize?" I asked.

"Oh, yes. Very much so. Bye!"

Hedda watched her fly away with rapt attention. When Fiona was out of sight, she said, "Courtney, there's another reason I came in today. I was talking with Hattie, and she said if there was any clue I recalled from Sunday morning, no matter how small, I should tell the police."

"Have you remembered something?"

Hedda screwed up her mouth. "Possibly. As Jeremy and I were leaving the scene, I noticed a broken branch lying in the neighbor's yard."

"Not unusual."

"True, but today I remembered the branch was from a bay tree, but there wasn't a bay tree growing in that garden. However, there was one in Petunia's yard. What if Detective Summers was right? The killer swept away footprints . . ."

"With a branch and discarded the branch elsewhere," I finished.

"Exactly. Would there be fingerprints on it?"

"Maybe," I said, doubtful that a DNA technician would pick up prints on wood. On the other hand, I could be wrong. As Summers was inclined to remind me, I wasn't an evidence expert. "Is the branch still there?"

"I don't know. I suppose by now the neighbor has removed it, thinking it blew in with the wind."

Except there hadn't been a stiff breeze for weeks.

"The police might have seen it," Hedda said. "I'm sure they canvassed the neighborhood."

"Yes, but they might have overlooked something as natural as that. How big was it?"

"About five feet long." She spread her arms to show me. "At least three inches thick."

"Was it living or dead?"

"It was green."

"*Hmm*, a branch that size would be hard to tear off a tree," I said. "Whoever did so would've needed a good amount of strength or a saw of some sort. Have you told the police?"

"Um, no. Would you do it?" Hedda asked. "I . . . I get really nervous around them."

"Why?" I was surprised. She was one of the most assured women I knew.

She lowered her voice. "When I was a teenager, I attended a wild party. I mean *wild*."

I tried to imagine Hedda ever doing something wild but couldn't picture it.

"The police busted it up, and I spent a night in jail, waiting for my parents to bail me out." She wriggled her nose. "They left me there on purpose. It was their way of making sure I never did something like that again. The ploy worked." She laughed softly. "I have toed the straight and narrow ever since, but I get the willies whenever I near the precinct."

"I'll be glad to convey your message. Why don't you take this little token of thanks?" I handed her a set of miniature wind chimes hanging from a wreath of yellow flowers. "You can add it to your garden when you're ready to design it. It'll look perfect next to the shed I'm ordering for you."

She gushed her thanks and accepted it readily.

When she left, I mulled over her account. Daphne or Scarlet might have the strength to pull a big branch off a living tree. Both were gardeners. Both worked out. And I supposed either might have a handsaw in their tool collections. But Oliver Killian and Bentley Bramble seemed the likelier culprits.

I dialed the precinct and asked for Officer Reddick. He was out handling a fracas at a restaurant. I left a message for him to call me. I didn't disturb Summers on the off chance his date had turned into a full day's affair.

At four, a regular customer with her two pigtailed daughters popped into the shop. Each girl was waving a festival coupon. The mother crooned *Hello*, and the girls begged me to accompany them to the patio. They made fairy gardens every month. Joss said she was perfectly able to handle the three customers in the main showroom, so I guided the trio to the patio.

"That one, Mommy," the youngest girl cried. She hopped on the short stool I'd parked on the patio to help customers reach items that were higher up. "The one with the blue wings. She looks like Fiona."

The mother smiled indulgently. She couldn't see Fiona, but her daughters could.

"Where is she?" the older girl asked.

"Mentoring her sister," I said, wondering what she'd be teaching Eveleen today. Last night, she'd said her sister needed to learn to focus, which had made me smile. Fiona was maturing into a wonderful adult fairy. I hoped she would be prepared when the time came to take the helm as the queen.

The mother allowed her daughters to choose two figurines and one environmental piece but warned that they could not buy any more toadstools. They were overrun with them.

While they mulled over their options, Joss beckoned me from the entrance to the patio.

"I'll be right back," I said to the mother, and crossed to my plucky assistant. "What's up?"

She hitched her chin toward the book rack, where Twyla was standing with Bentley. "They want to speak with you."

Twyla's hand was wrapped around Bentley's elbow. He had anchored his goggles on his arm and was twisting his cap in his hands.

I weaved through the display tables to them. "What's up?"

Bentley wouldn't meet my gaze. His jaw was ticking with tension.

"May we go to your office?" Twyla asked.

"Sure," I said, relieved I'd thought to cover the whiteboard with the cloth.

I led the way through the showroom and down the hall to the office. I apologized for not having guest seating for two, merely the one Queen Anne chair.

"We'll stand," Twyla said, and nudged Bentley. "Tell her."

Tell me what? I held my breath.

Bentley chewed his lower lip.

"Look, Bennie," she said, "I agreed to have coffee with you if you'd tell all."

If she'd agreed to coffee in exchange for whatever secret he was harboring, he wasn't about to confess to murder.

"Y'see . . ." Bentley hesitated.

Twyla offered a supportive smile. "You're a good guy, Bennie. A little screwy but a good guy. Now spill!"

I couldn't believe how forthright she'd become. Perhaps being considered a murder suspect last winter had strengthened her backbone and given her the courage to face any challenge.

"I don't bite," I said to Bentley.

"I was there," he said.

"Where?"

"At the corner. You did see me. Saturday night. I lied." He spoke haltingly. "I saw Petunia running, but I didn't follow her because I didn't want to scare her. I intended to convince her to date me, so I went home. I texted her a little later asking if she was okay. She didn't respond."

Summers hadn't mentioned that text to me.

"I didn't tell you the truth because . . ." Bentley didn't finish.

"Because you didn't want me to think you were keeping tabs on her," I said.

"Around eleven, I got to wondering whether she'd been running because she was frightened, and I thought I should . . ." He paused, searching for the words.

"Check on her," Twyla finished for him.

"And?" I asked. He was so jittery, I wished I had Fiona's magical calming potion in my fingertips so I could dowse him with it.

Twyla poked his arm.

He continued. "And, y'see, I went to her house. The lights were out, but I was worried. So I opened the gate and started down the path. I planned to listen at the door, and if I heard her moving around inside, I'd knock. But then . . ." Tears pooled in the corners of his eyes. "I saw her. Lying there. She was dead." He blinked, and the tears leaked down his dusty cheeks. "I couldn't believe it. Who would do that? She was so sweet. So . . ." He smacked his hat against his thigh. "I panicked. I'm not proud of that. But I thought the police might suspect me of killing her because, well, I haven't been shy about letting her know I wanted to date her."

"Stalk her," Twyla said.

He growled. "I freaked out, because I figured if the police discovered my footprints, they'd arrest me, so I—"

"Tore a branch off the bay tree in her yard to use as a broom!" I blurted.

"Yes." His eyes widened. "How did you know?"

"Someone thought it was odd to see a green bay tree branch in a neighbor's yard where there was no bay tree. Go on."

"I swept away my footprints, and I ran home." His voice trembled. "I was so shaken. I didn't know what to do."

Twyla sighed. "He didn't want to call the police then, either, because they would question him about why he knew so much."

"She was dead." He splayed his hands. "Anything I could do wasn't going to change that."

I thought of Eveleen's theory about Petunia's cell phone. Perhaps Bentley's arrival was the reason the killer hadn't been able to abscond with it. "Did you glimpse anyone running away, Bentley?" I asked.

"No one."

"Did you sense the killer might be hiding?"

"I . . . I didn't think about that." He gulped so hard his Adam's apple wobbled.

"You were selfish," Twyla said. "Admit it."

"I wasn't. I—" His voice cracked with a sob. "I was scared."

"It's okay, Bentley." I rounded the desk and rested a hand on his arm. "I get it. Let's fix this. Let's contact the police. You have an alibi. It's not exactly airtight, but you are a responsible man who maintains schedules. Your neighbors know that you work in your garden every night. Twyla confirms you were doing so Saturday." I didn't add that Wanda could do the same for Thursday. He didn't need to know I'd been speculating about his guilt.

I reached out to Reddick again, and this time, he was in. Within minutes, he arrived at Open Your Imagination. An hour later, after Bentley gave his statement to Officer Reddick, he was released on his own recognizance. Twyla looked pleased to have helped. I knew Hedda Hopewell would be relieved that I'd intervened on her behalf, too. Reddick said he wouldn't need her testimony, since Bentley had owned up to the evidence tampering.

As Joss and I were closing up shop, I filled her in on the situation.

"Wow," she said. "That Bentley guy is quirky, isn't he? Do you think Twyla will be safe around him?"

"I think she clearly understands setting boundaries."

"By the way, I meant to tell you Meaghan dropped by. Her mother is so thrilled with her new garden."

"Cool."

"She asked if you'd meet them at Hideaway Café for dinner. Their treat. I'll close up."

I didn't have plans, and seeing friendly faces with no ties to a murder sounded like a perfect idea to round out my evening. I blew her a kiss, took Pixie home, and dressed in a cream-colored halter dress, sandals, and crossbody purse. I grabbed a floral shawl for later, when the evening cooled down, and walked back toward the café.

As I neared Lincoln, I spotted Oliver Killian and Asher Lyle facing off in front of Open Your Imagination. Oliver said something I couldn't make out and shoved Asher, who reeled into the shop's front door.

Uh-oh. Worried I might have to protect my business property, I picked up my pace.

Chapter 19

We dance on hills above the wind,
And leave our footsteps there behind;
Which shall to after ages last,
When all our dancing days are past.
—Anonymous, "The Fairies' Song"

Asher quickly found his footing and offered a retort. Oliver shot a finger at him. From the way he was scowling, I presumed he'd learned that Asher ratted him out to the police about the shovel he'd purchased. A few passersby stopped and stared.

"Don't worry," Asher said loudly enough for anyone in the vicinity to hear. "You're not on the police radar any longer. They're focusing on Daphne Flores. I'm sure of it."

Why was he so certain? Had he said something to Detective Summers to divert suspicion from his wife?

Oliver shook his fist. "Don't expect me to throw any business your way ever."

"Yeah, fine, whatever."

Oliver turned to the left and raced toward the north entrance to our courtyard, taking the steps two at a time.

Asher didn't budge, preoccupied with smoothing the front of his button-down shirt. When he caught sight of me and everyone else, he gave a curt nod. "Sorry you had to witness that, folks. Show's over."

I lingered, concerned about my shop if Oliver was to make a U-turn. I breathed easier when he entered Sweet Treats.

Asher smiled, noticing my gaze. "Don't worry. He won't be back, and I assure you, if we'd broken anything, I would have covered the damage."

"Are you okay?" I asked.

"Oliver's a hothead."

"You don't happen to know where he was Saturday night, do you?"

"Why?" Asher tamed his unruly hair with both hands. "Do you think he might have killed Petunia Fujimoto?"

"She was looking into finding a new site for her shop in your neck of the woods. That could have angered him."

Asher rubbed his jaw. "Nah, I think Daphne is the killer."

"Why do you suspect her?"

"Genevieve insulted her."

"She slighted Scarlet, too."

"Yes, but Scarlet wouldn't hurt a flea. Daphne, on the other hand, has a history of violence." He glanced over his shoulder and back at me. "Between us, and this is only because Scarlet confided in me, Daphne beat up a girl in high school."

Yipes! I didn't know Daphne well enough to know whether that was true. "Beat her up how?" I asked.

"Clocked her with a rake for homing in on her boyfriend." Asher frowned. "Why she's running around town as free as a bird when the police know this about her is beyond me."

"They know?"

"I brought it to their attention."

Of course he did. To divert suspicion from his beloved wife.

"They're dragging their feet, like always," he went on. "My shop was burgled last year. Do you think they came running? Ha! Not a chance. It took them an hour to show up, and they never did catch the thief." He regarded his watch. "Gotta go. I'm meeting my bride for dinner." He hooked his thumb at Hideaway Café.

"I'm headed there myself."

We walked across the street together. He held the door open for me. When my eyes adjusted to the dim light in the restaurant, I spied Scarlet seated in a corner booth. She gazed at her husband adoringly. I wished him good night and proceeded to the patio.

Meaghan and Wanda were sitting at a table in the far corner. Ulra was perched above them on a tree branch, her legs dangling. I crooked a finger in *hello*. The sweet fairy smiled and bowed her head in greeting.

Brady appeared as I was sitting down. "Chardonnay?" He pecked me on the cheek.

"Yes, please."

When he moved away, Wanda muttered, "Harrumph. He didn't kiss me on the cheek."

Meaghan thwacked her mother's arm. Both of them giggled.

"He is such a catch, Courtney," Wanda said.

"Yes, he is. Your daughter is dating a wonderful guy, too."

"Officer Reddick is nice enough," Wanda agreed, "but—"

"No one will ever be good enough in your eyes, Mother." Meaghan huffed while plumping the lacy sleeves of her blouse.

"Honey, I'm not sure I want you involved with someone who faces danger every day." Wanda sipped her wine.

"The world is a perilous place," Meaghan said philosophically. "Therefore, everyone I meet will face danger."

Wanda leveled her daughter with a glower. Meaghan countered by raising her chin defiantly.

I viewed the menu and landed on a crab and shrimp salad with a zesty Thousand Island dressing—the café made it from scratch, and the zing was incredible—and then I launched into my account of Asher and Oliver's altercation and Asher's revelation about Daphne's past.

"Daphne clobbered another woman?" Meaghan whistled.

Brady brought my wine and said they were so slammed tonight, he would be taking our orders.

"Are you offering a two-fer?" I asked.

"Nope. But Wednesday is our busiest night, other than Saturday. I think people like to get out midweek."

We told him what we wanted to eat, and as he walked away, I scanned the patio. Every table was filled. To my surprise, Renee and Summers were sitting at a table for two. He was gazing in my direction and didn't look pleased. Renee peeked over her shoulder and pursed her lips. She put a hand on his arm, but that didn't seem to deter him. He wadded his napkin on the table and rose to his feet. Like a man on a mission, he strode to me, his face grim.

Uh-oh. I sat taller. "Did you have a nice picnic?" I asked, forcing a lilt into my tone.

"Swell." He greeted Meaghan and Wanda. "Now, Miss Kelly . . ."

I cringed. He'd used my surname. This was not a social call.

"I hear you couldn't help yourself, yet again," he said.

"I don't know what you mean."

"You sought out Bentley Bramble after I specifically told you I'd handle the issue, and you wrangled information out of him."

"No, sir," I said. "I did not seek him out. He came to me. Twyla Waterman made him. She did the wrangling." I explained how Bentley was sweet on Twyla, but she wanted nothing to do with him. "However, after I questioned him about Saturday night outside Acosta Artworks, Twyla sensed he was holding something back, so when I left, she needled and wheedled and promised to go to coffee with him if he'd come clean. Getting him to admit what he'd done with the branch wasn't my doing, but aren't you pleased with the information? Now you know why the area was swept and there were no footprints."

Summers growled under his breath.

I said, "Did your people find the branch?"

"No."

"Might I ask"—I rearranged my silverware—"did Asher Lyle reach out to you about Daphne Flores's past?"

Summers worked his tongue inside his cheek. "Have a good evening, Miss Kelly." He strode to Renee, who leaned in to assuage him.

Wanda patted my arm. "You handled yourself valiantly, dear. Dylan can be quite intimidating." She would know. They'd attended the same college. He'd been into sports, and she had been into art, but they'd gone to many of the same parties. "Don't let him goad you."

"I won't." I was lying. I felt chastised. On the other hand, could I help it if people came to me with information because they trusted me to convey it to the police? Sheesh.

We tabled any discussion of the murders and, as we dined, turned the conversation to the wonderful time Wanda and Meaghan had making fairy gardens.

Toward the end of dinner, Brady came by, kissed me softly on the forehead, and whispered, "Did Dylan give you guff?"

"No worse than ever."

"I still haven't seen the fairy who resides here."

"Well, she's keeping an eye on you." I wiggled a finger at Ulra. She soared to us, did a hop, skip, and jump across the top of Brady's head, and whizzed back to her perch. I laughed at her antics. He scowled.

Minutes later, I said goodbye to Meaghan and Wanda outside the café, and I headed home. As I neared Casanova Street, I heard Fiona and Eveleen trill *hello*.

I halted, allowing them to catch up. At the same time, movement to my left caught my eye. Daphne was racing from her car into her house. She was dressed in a shimmery caftan and turban, an odd outfit for someone who preferred jeans or coveralls. If it had been October, I might have thought she'd attended a costume party.

Curious about what Asher Lyle had revealed, and hopeful that Scarlet had been wrong about Daphne attacking a rival in high school, I strode toward her house. I stopped when I spied a woman in a black hoodie and leggings coming from the opposite direction down the street. I recognized the woman's bearing. It was Tish Waterman. She opened Daphne's gate and clandestinely sneaked around the side of the house.

My interest aroused, I followed her.

"Where are we going?" Fiona asked.

"*Shh.*" I tiptoed along the side of the house toward the backyard, keeping to the path to avoid snagging my clothes on the thorns of the myriad rose bushes. I paused at the corner and peeked around. The heady scent of roses wafted to me. Like in front, the backyard was planted with rose bushes and trellises. A toolshed was positioned against the fence. Beyond it, at the far corner of the yard, stood a small cabana. Flickering light from a candle shone through the cabana's window. Tish opened the door and slipped inside.

What was going on? Why the secrecy? The cabana, which was about the size of my greenhouse, wasn't large enough for more than two people, so it wasn't like Daphne was holding a meeting for a group of conspirators.

"*Psst,* Fiona," I said. "Fly over there and peek in the window and tell me what's up."

She zipped away, Eveleen trailing her, and they returned in a flash. "There's a crystal ball on a table," Fiona said, "and Daphne is waving her hands over it. Spooky music is playing."

Oho! Was Daphne a part-time fortune teller?

Deciding to wait it out so I could learn more, I crouched down and scurried to the other corner of the house. That way, Tish wouldn't see me when she left. Fifteen minutes later, the door to the cabana opened. I recognized the spooky music. It was *Danse Macabre* by Camille Saint-Saëns. In high school, a couple of girlfriends had talked me into doing a modern dance performance to that piece for a talent show.

Tish exited, whispered, "Thank you, Madame Flor," and sneaked off in the same direction she'd arrived.

In seconds, I raced to the cabana and knocked on the door.

Daphne yanked it open as if expecting Tish. Seeing me, she blanched. "Wh-what are you doing here?"

"Why are you dressed like a medium? Why did Tish call you Madame Flor?"

Daphne sagged. She whisked off the turban and smoothed her hair. "Would you like some tea?"

I mulled over the offer. Trusting my gut instinct that Daphne was not guilty of murder, I said, "Sure."

She led the way to her house and into the kitchen. Fiona and Eveleen followed us. Daphne placed her turban on the counter and turned the burner beneath the teakettle to high.

The Siamese cat I'd seen in the window the other night yowled and pawed at Fiona. He wasn't playing like Pixie. He wanted the fairies to leave. Fiona instructed Eveleen to join her atop the kitchen cabinets. The cat remained on the floor, its gaze fixed on them.

"What a nice space," I said.

Daphne's kitchen wasn't large, but it was tastefully appointed with white furniture, white appliances, white tiles hand-painted with herbs, and pots of herbs in the bay window over the sink.

"Thanks." She pulled two teacups from a cupboard. "Earl Grey or chamomile?"

"Earl Grey."

"Sugar cookies?"

"No thanks. I just ate."

Her caftan swished as she prepared the tea. After filling our teacups with hot water, she put the cups, a sugar bowl, and two spoons on the table and settled in a chair. I sat on the other one.

"To explain . . . my farm is struggling. I was hoping more people like you would rent acreage, but that didn't come to pass. I'm afraid I'll have to sell it."

If she sold the farm, I'd be back to square one. Oh, well. *Such is life,* as my nana would say.

"To make ends meet," she continued, "I started working a second job." She gripped the seam of her skirt and let it fall. "*This job*, posing as Madame Flor," she added with dramatic flourish.

"Why wouldn't you tell me the other day? There's no need to be embarrassed. Lots of businesses need a boost," I said. If I hadn't had a nice inheritance from my nana, I couldn't have invested in Open Your Imagination.

"I'm not embarrassed. I simply can't let anyone discover what I do, because it could get back to my mother."

"Mothers," Eveleen huffed from above. "They can be so judgmental."

Fiona shot her a sharp look. Eveleen cringed.

I said, "Would your mother be ashamed, Daphne?"

"Worse. She'd be livid. She thinks communing with the other world is wickedness."

"I won't tell." The moment the words came out of my mouth, I thought of Genevieve. Had she found out Daphne's secret? Had she threatened to post about her *evil* ways? "Did Genevieve know?"

"About this? Yes."

I inhaled.

"Uh-uh, don't get the wrong idea." Daphne added sugar to her tea and stirred. "She wouldn't have told anyone. In fact, she asked if she could join me. She wasn't making enough money as an influencer, no matter how much she proclaimed that she was. In fact, this was what I was doing the night she died. I had three clients. Three appointments. From seven until nearly eleven thirty. They are all sworn to secrecy. I had appointments Friday and Saturday night, as well."

"Was your failing business why Genevieve suggested you consult a therapist?"

"No." Daphne shook her head. "That has to do with something . . . from my past. Something I can't seem to get over."

"Like when you beat up a girl in high school?"

Her eyes widened. "How could you know? I've never told—" She stopped abruptly. "Scarlet. Dang her!"

"Scarlet didn't tell me. Asher did."

"She swore she'd never blab. What a liar!" Daphne scrubbed her hair in frustration. "Want to know everything?"

I did with a passion, but I kept mute.

"One night, Scarlet and I had too much wine, and we were talking about our mothers. Her mother was emotionally cruel to her, telling her she was a loser all the time. Scarlet said she was lucky when her mother suffered a surprise stroke and died, releasing her from her mother's cruelty. Scarlet was eighteen."

"Hold on. Scarlet hated her mother?"

"Yes."

Whoa! That didn't jibe with what Scarlet said about going to the beach to find solace on the anniversary of her mother's death.

"Go on," I said.

"Scarlet said she wanted to be supportive of me and encouraged me to unburden myself, and, well, the story slipped out. I told her my mother, the fine upstanding religious woman that she was, whooped me within an inch of my life when she learned I hurt another girl."

"I'm so sorry."

"I'm over it, but I don't want my mother to know anything about my current life, where I am, or what I do. If anything gets in the news . . ." She groaned. "I didn't kill Genevieve. I didn't murder Petunia. And the girl in high school forgave me."

"Why did you beat her up? You had to have a good reason."

Daphne shuddered.

Fiona swooped from the cabinet and circled Daphne's head. A silver calming dust drifted from beneath her wings. Daphne inhaled and exhaled. She wasn't in a trance, but the potion was definitely having an effect. The cat reared up on its hind legs. Fiona stuck her tongue out and resumed her position at the top of the cabinets. The cat hissed and sat on its haunches at the ready if either fairy dared to fly within paw's reach.

After a long moment, Daphne said, "I was outside in the garden, cleaning up leaves. The girl—you don't need to know her name—came to my house one night, gloating about winning over my boyfriend. I knew she'd used sex to lure him, so I called her a tramp. She grabbed the rake I'd been using and lashed out at me. I was stronger. I wrenched it away and hit her hard. The tines scratched her face." Daphne sucked back a sob. "I dropped the rake and apologized immediately, but friends of hers were nearby, watching so they could report back what went down. The next day, her parents came to confront me. Afterward, my mother shaved my head and lashed my legs with a briar rod. Two years later . . ." Daphne heaved a sigh, as if telling the story was releasing years of pent-up torment. "Two years later, the girl took responsibility for what happened. She asked my forgiveness and has since relocated to New York to become a Krishna devotee. But I still haven't absolved myself for having such a short fuse. I'm not sure I ever will."

"And your mother?" I asked.

"Is alive and well in North Carolina, the last I knew. We haven't spoken in ten years."

Chapter 20

Buds that open to disclose
Fold on fold of purest white,
Lovely pink, or red that glows
Deep, sweet-scented. What delight
To be Fairy of the Rose!
—Cecily Mary Barker, "The Song of the Rose Fairy"

I promised Daphne I wouldn't betray her. What she did in her spare time to make ends meet was her business, and what happened in the past was in the past, but I cautioned her to get ahead of the story and talk to the police in the morning. Her clients needed to provide her with a verifiable alibi. She agreed, but she seemed so reluctant to follow through that I felt compelled to continue thinking outside the box on her behalf.

Pulling my shawl around my shoulders, I stepped into the dark night with Fiona and Eveleen trailing me. We made it as far as Daphne's gate when I saw someone entering Petunia's house two doors down—a woman who looked identical to Petunia. It had to be her twin sister Peony. Same body shape, her silver hair styled in a pageboy. She hadn't returned my phone call yet. My watch read eight-thirty. It wasn't too late to approach someone.

I called out, "Peony!"

She turned and shaded her eyes with a hand to get a better look at me. Landscaping lights in the neighbor's yard were creating a glare.

"It's Courtney Kelly! I'm the fairy garden person." My heart snagged as I hustled toward her. I was sad to have lost a friend, but Peony had to be grief-stricken to have lost her sister. "I apologize for touching base so late in the evening. I was visiting a friend." I pointed at Daphne's house, hoping she wouldn't make the connection between Daphne and the garden tool used to kill her sister.

"Courtney, hello. I got your message. I haven't had time to return your call."

"I'm sorry for your loss."

"Thank you. That's very kind." Her smile was thin and tight. "I've been going through Petunia's things. She was a bit of a pack rat. There's so much stuff, I had to get a jump on it. The Realtor has already found an all-cash buyer, and they want to move as quickly as possible. No restrictions."

I knew property was dear in Carmel, but I had no idea it was that dear. An all-cash sale in a matter of days? Yipes! Most likely, she would have to deal with the sale of Petunia's business, too. Poor thing. What a daunting task.

"Would you like to come in?" Peony asked. "I . . ." Tears pooled in her eyes.

I reached to console her, but she waved me off.

"The crying will stop at some point," she said. "When our parents died, the waterworks lasted for days. Tea?"

I wasn't sure I could consume anything else, but I nodded. "That would be lovely." I followed her into Petunia's house. So did Fiona and Eveleen.

"Whew! That's a lot of reading material!" Fiona exclaimed.

She wasn't kidding. There were piles of books and magazines stacked against the walls in the foyer and on all the furniture in the modest living room.

"When my sister wasn't designing floral arrangements, she devoured nonfiction history," Peony said in explanation, though I doubted she'd heard Fiona. "Petunia knew everything there was to know about ancient Japan. She also read fiction like *Memoirs of a Geisha* and *Shōgun*. Me? I'm not much of a reader. After work, I like to come home and watch television."

"She had lots of photos, too," I noted. There were images of single flowers or floral arrangements everywhere. Small ones, large ones. The framing alone must have cost Petunia a pretty penny.

"Yes. She loved her flowers." Peony walked into her sister's kitchen, which was similar in layout to Daphne's, but it was decorated in pinks and greens. Vintage light-green vases filled with fresh languishing flowers cluttered the windowsill and square country table as well as many of the shelves of the light-green hutch. The lower half of the hutch was designed to be a desk. On it sat a container of pens, an illuminated dichroic orb on a pedestal, piles of drawing tablets—for sketching arrangements, I supposed—and a stack of books that included a gardener's almanac; *The Well-Tempered Garden*; *Planting: A New Perspective; Tarot for Beginners;* Agatha Christie's *How Does Your Garden Grow?*, which was a collection of unabridged short stories—I'd read a few—and myriad flower arranging books.

Fiona and Eveleen darted to the far end of the room to inspect a pink-and-green-checkered cat bed. "Courtney, where's the cat?"

Good question. I didn't see a litter box or dishes for the cat's food and water. "Um, Peony, where's Petunia's cat?" Hopefully, she'd been feeding it.

"Poor Hyacinth died last year."

"Hyacinth. What a pretty name."

"Like our mother, Petunia named all the things she loved after flowers. She was heartbroken when that cat passed on. She couldn't bring herself to get rid of the cat bed. She always planned on adopting another kitten, but she hadn't gotten around to it." Peony placed the teakettle on the stove and switched on the burner. "Do you think I can donate all of my sister's books to the library?"

"If they can't find space for them, they'll gladly sell them at a used-book fundraiser."

"Excellent."

"I'll hook you up with Lissa Reade. She's the head librarian. She has a staff devoted to helping people find good homes for books."

Peony said, "That makes them sound like they're alive."

Fiona said, "To some readers, they are." She darted away to explore the house.

Eveleen followed in her wake.

Peony put tea bags into two mugs with floral designs, and set the mugs, a bowl of sugar, and spoons on a floral tray.

"As I said in my message to you"—I sat at the table and slid two vases of flowers to the right—"Petunia commissioned me to make you a fairy garden for your birthday."

"That's so sweet." A sob escaped her lips. She pressed her knuckles to her mouth to contain herself. She was probably contemplating how she'd get through another birthday without her twin. The notion made me ache.

"I'd like to deliver it to your house if you'll give me the address."

"Sure." Peony lifted a silver cell phone from the counter and quickly dropped it, as if it were hot.

"What's wrong?" I asked.

"This . . . is Petunia's. Not mine."

"I thought the police took all the items found at the crime scene."

"Their forensic person, whatever he's called, went through her phone and decided he didn't need it any longer." She retrieved hers, which was also silver but different in size. "What's your mobile number? I'll text you my contact card."

I rattled it off. She typed in the message, and I felt my phone vibrate in my crossbody purse.

"Why did someone do this, Courtney?"

I'd anticipated her question but didn't know how to answer it.

"Two women . . . two friends dead in the same week," she whispered. "I heard you might be trying to find out."

"Who told you that?"

"A friend at the winery. She says you and your . . ." She gazed into the air but didn't finish the statement, *you and your fairy.* "She says you've solved other crimes."

Fiona and Eveleen alit on the table near my teacup.

"*Solved* is a stretch." I sighed. "Rest assured that the police are investigating, and they're good at their jobs." *Just not very fast,* I groused. Summers once told me that he'd worked a case for four months without resolution. Four! I flashed on the message Daphne claimed Petunia left her. "Peony, did your sister reach out to you that night, by phone or otherwise, to ask you something?"

"No."

So Peony wasn't the *ask her* Petunia had mentioned in her message to Daphne.

"I wish she had. I wish . . ." Fondly, Peony ran a finger along her sister's mobile. "I wish I could open this, but I don't have her passcode."

"Why do you want to open it?"

"I'd like to see the photos she took before . . ." She sniffed. "Every day, she would snap pictures of her flower arrangements and text them to me, and I'd send her pictures of the vineyard. Our parents were amateur photographers. Our father even sold a few of his pieces to *National Geographic.*"

"That's quite an honor."

"I suppose I could go to a computer store, and someone there could help me."

The teakettle whistled, which startled Eveleen. It hadn't tootled at Daphne's house. The little fairy reeled backward, nearly falling off the table. Fiona nabbed her by the tip of her wing to steady her. When Eveleen quietened, Fiona suggested she tour the kitchen and stimulate the languishing flowers.

With her tongue braced between her teeth, Eveleen flitted from flower vase to flower vase. She chanted as she went, and some of the flowers rejuvenated. I kept my astonishment to myself. I didn't want to spook Peony.

"Here we are." Peony brought the tray to the table and sat with a *thwump* in her chair.

I added sugar to my tea and stirred, but I didn't take a sip. My gaze was fixed on Petunia's cell phone. Would the police have wiped it clean? If they hadn't, and I could access it, without asking Fiona to dance on it, would I be able to see who else she might have texted or called on Saturday, in addition to Scarlet and Daphne? "Let me see if I can open your sister's phone for you."

"Thank you." Peony pressed a heartfelt hand to her chest.

I fetched the phone, brought it back to the table, and swiped the screen. "Maybe her passcode matches another number she'd remember. Does she have an alarm system on the house? Something with four digits?" I asked, although I doubted she did if the killer had sneaked in and lay in wait to surprise her. I hadn't seen an alarm company placard outside.

"No."

"How about her birthdate?" *Your birthdate, too,* I thought.

"July tenth."

I typed in *0710,* but that didn't open the phone.

"Your parents' birthdays?" I asked, and repeated the action as she relayed them. Neither worked. "How about the last four digits of her social security number?"

She recited them, but they didn't open the phone, either.

Frustrated, I glanced around the kitchen. My gaze landed on the cat bed. "Did she have other cats beside Hyacinth?" That name contained way too many letters.

Peony smiled. "Oh, yes. She had dozens over the years. Her ginger cat was Tulip. Her tabby was Freesia. She called the tuxedo cat Poppy, which truly didn't fit, but no one could dissuade her. Black Dahlia would have been more appropriate. She was a rascal." The memory made her smile.

"Any cats with four letters, like Rose or Iris?"

Peony tapped the rim of her saucer as she thought. "Lily! Of course. Lily. How could I forget her? She was a beautiful Persian, the first cat Petunia owned after she moved out of our childhood home. That cat hated me, but she doted on Petunia. I think the cat thought I was toying with her because I looked like her human."

I typed in Lily's name using the keypad alphabet: *5459*. The phone opened. All the typical apps were visible: messages, mail, phone, contacts. I clicked on the pictures app. A grid of photos appeared. I turned the phone toward Peony and handed it to her. "Here you go."

Tears flowed freely as she scrolled through photos, dragging from the top down. "Oh," escaped her lips. "Oh, oh, oh. They're so pretty. She was so talented. A little obsessed with flowers, but one has to be obsessed if one is an artist, don't you think?" She scrolled the other way, to make sure she hadn't missed any images, and paused. "Why do you think she took this?" She handed me the phone.

I stared at the screen. Petunia must have taken the image at night. Flares from streetlamps reflected off the windows of a shop, making it impossible to read the shop's name. Dim lights illuminated the shop's interior. "She was searching for a new rental property near the precinct," I said. "Maybe this was the site she had in mind."

"I think you're right. She told me she was hunting for someplace. I don't believe she found anything."

I swiped left and saw a photo of another shop, the name on its window clearly visible—*Garden Delights*. I swiped left a second time and viewed a picture of Lagoon Grill, the restaurant next door to Oliver's shop. Distinctive wood-carved mermaids flanked the door. I spied another photo of the first shop. I examined the date and time Petunia took that one, and my insides snarled. Thursday night at eight-thirty p.m. The night Genevieve had died.

Peony held out her hand for me to return the phone.

"Hold on." I swiped right and stopped on the first image she'd shown me. Something about the exterior plants of the shop looked familiar. It dawned on me that they were fountain grass and coleus, like the ones my father had installed in front of Lyle's General Store. Why would Petunia have taken not one but two pictures of that site?

The space was way too large for a flower shop. I swiped back to the other general store photo, noted the date, and gasped. Petunia had taken that one on Saturday, also at eight-thirty. Not long after, she was dead.

I revisited the first photo, and using two fingers, zoomed in to see if I could determine the reason she might have snapped the photo. The image was fuzzy, but I could make out the back of a person dressed in black, hood raised. That night, Genevieve had been dressed in what I'd presumed was recon clothing. Did she sneak into the general store? Did she hope to take an incriminating photo and post something incendiary online? Whoever was inside seemed to be lingering in the garden tools section of the store. There were bakers' racks of flowerpots to the left and fancy garden ornaments and shepherd's hooks to the right.

A horrid thought struck me. After Petunia moved on, did Scarlet leave the beach, swing by the shop, and catch sight of Genevieve inside? Did she guess what Genevieve was up to? When Genevieve left, did Scarlet hurry inside, grab a shovel, follow her nemesis to the spot outside the festival tents, bash her in the head, and return to the beach?

Another theory came to me. Maybe Scarlet was the person inside the general store, fetching a shovel to kill Genevieve. That had to be what Petunia determined, which would explain why she'd texted Scarlet.

The reality of these photos jarred me. If Petunia had been scouting out new business sites, she might not have realized what she'd photographed at the time, which was why she hadn't mentioned it to the police Friday morning. On Saturday, when she was preparing to send pics of flowers to her sister, she took a closer look at the photo of the general store and realized something was off, so she returned to the site to confirm whatever suspicion she might have had. What had she hoped to hear from Scarlet before contacting the police? An explanation? A denial? A confession?

"What are you looking at?" Peony asked.

I told her my suspicions and turned the phone in her direction.

She said, "Are you sure that's a woman? She looks very tall, comparatively."

I studied the image once more. The figure in black was nearly the same height as the shelving beyond the collection of garden tools. I supposed Scarlet or Genevieve could have been standing on some kind of footstool, like the one on my patio at the shop.

On the other hand, what if the intruder was a man? Say Oliver Killian. Given the nearby location of Garden Delights, he would have been able to sneak in and return to his shop in a matter of seconds. But why would he need to steal a shovel if he'd already purchased one on the outskirts of town? And why would Petunia text Scarlet and not him?

I supposed the person in black could have been Asher but dismissed the theory. He was playing tennis until midnight. Unless he wasn't. He could have ended his game earlier than expected. I came up with two scenarios if that were the case.

One, what if Asher caught Scarlet returning the shovel after killing Genevieve? To protect his beloved wife, after she left, he went in, found the shovel, and cleaned off the blood or disposed of the weapon.

Two, what if Asher was the one initially caught on camera, and Petunia, believing he killed Genevieve, reached out to Scarlet to warn her about him?

How could I confirm whether Asher was really playing tennis with his friend? The guy was in Guatemala saving trees.

"Courtney?" Peony asked, concern lacing her voice.

"I should show these pictures to the police. I'll return the phone when I bring you your fairy garden."

"Yes, of course." She stretched a hand in my direction. "Do you think the photos will help the police solve my sister's murder?"

"Let's hope so."

Fiona, Eveleen, and I hurried home. I wasn't going to contact the police this late at night, and Summers would rebuke me if I sent a text with an unsupportable theory. So I stowed Petunia's cell phone in my purse, got ready for bed, and opened my Agatha Christie book. I started reading, but I couldn't focus, because ideas were cycling through my head.

Genevieve, Scarlet, Oliver, Asher. Who had sneaked into the general store?

Bam!

I jolted upright, heart pounding. I tossed my book aside. Something had hit my front door. A rock? A fist? I listened hard and heard footsteps. Running footsteps.

Fiona whooshed to me. Eveleen, too. Their eyes were wide. Even Pixie, who could sleep through thunderstorms, had awakened. I could feel her erratic chugging by my feet.

I switched on the light, tiptoed to the front door, and grabbed the shovel I kept at the ready to thwart intruders. I shuddered as I flashed on Genevieve and Petunia, both dying from a blow to the back of the head, but I didn't lose my grip. I peeked out the peep-hole. No one was there. The front gate was closed. The street was empty of people. To be certain, I glanced out all the windows in the cottage. I didn't see anyone lurking anywhere.

Cautiously, I opened the front door . . . and screamed.

Chapter 21

All colors of the rainbow
Were in her robe so bright
As she danced away with the sunbeam
And vanished from my sight.
—Laura Ingalls Wilder, "When Sunshine Fairies Rest"

A note was taped to my door. Whoever had stuck it there must have slammed it hard to make sure it stuck. That must have been the *bam* I'd heard. I tore it off, slipped back inside, and closed and bolted the door. I read the note, and my insides turned to ice.

STOP POKING INTO THINGS. IT'S NONE OF YOUR BUSINESS.

I jolted. Those were the words Daphne had said to me when I'd questioned her at her farm. Had she done this? The note was written in generic block letters. I doubted even a handwriting expert could make out who had created it. And I didn't see any fingerprints.

Other than Daphne, who else might think I was *poking into things*? Bentley, perhaps, except Officer Reddick exonerated him after Bentley admitted to tampering with the crime scene and Twyla vouched for his nighttime activities. Scarlet Lyle might think I was meddlesome. Even though Summers had taken the day off, he could have suggested that Reddick question her about the shovel that had been in her festival booth, and inadvertently, Reddick might have divulged that I was the person who'd pointed it out to Summers. If Scarlet was onto me, Asher could be, too. In fact, I could see him leaving a note like this to warn me off investigating his darling wife. I hadn't quizzed Oliver Killian about anything, but that didn't mean he was clueless as to my sleuthing. After pointing out to Summers that Oliver's alibi Thursday night was not truly verifiable, except for the pick-up and drop-off times to the AA meeting, the detective might have invited Oliver back for a chat and disclosed my part in instigating the second visit.

My first instinct was to call my father, but I held off. I needed more than fatherly comfort. I wanted to speak to someone who always respected my opinion. I dialed Brady. He arrived at my house in less than five minutes. Together, he and I and the fairies toured the outside of my cottage, looking for any signs of the author of the note. There was nothing. No footprints. No telltale gum wrappers or other kinds of evidence.

We retreated to the kitchen for tea, and Brady reread the note, turning it over and over, looking for something that might divulge the identity of the culprit, but he came up as empty as I had. I gave him a rundown of the people I thought might have posted the note and their motives.

"I'm staying the night," he said.

I set my teacup on the saucer, and it clattered, exposing my unease. "Stay?" I murmured. We hadn't spent a night together. To be honest, we hadn't done much more than kissing.

"You don't have to," I said. "I'm sure I'm safe."

"I'll sleep on the couch."

Fiona perched on Brady's shoulder and pulled on his ear. It must have tickled. He brushed his ear, nearly batting her.

She giggled. "I like him. He's a good guy."

"Why are you smiling?" he asked me.

"Fiona says you're a good guy."

He grinned. "I agree with her."

Thursday morning, I awakened with a spring in my step. The aroma of bacon and eggs permeated the cottage. Brady insisted I eat before he left. I offered him a savory, rosemary-raisin muffin that my nana used to bake me—I kept them wrapped individually and frozen in the freezer. A guardian angel needed a muffin, I told him. During our meal, he made me promise I'd show the note to Summers, and I said I would. I just didn't say *when* I would do so.

After we did the dishes, he left for work, and I took a quick run through the neighborhood, heading south on Carmelo, east on 13th Avenue, and north on Monte Verde. By the time I veered west on Ocean Avenue, the sun was peeking over the hills. The scent of salty air was sublime. Fiona and Eveleen had joined me. I didn't slow whenever Eveleen veered off to bless flowers. She was a speedy flyer and always caught up. Fiona chatted to me as I ran, saying how wonderful Brady was. I spotted a few regular runners on my tour. Speed-walkers, too. Hedda and Jeremy were strolling hand in hand along Ocean Avenue. I waved, but they didn't notice me.

When I got home, I fed Pixie and the fairies, showered, slipped on a sleeveless print blouse and white capris, tucked the note into my crossbody purse, and sprinted with Pixie and the fairies to Open Your Imagination. Before I entered, Fiona and Eveleen flew off, saying they were headed to the library.

Joss had arrived first and had already opened the register, brewed a pot of coffee, and dusted the showroom.

"Morning, sunshine," I said, plonking Pixie on the floor.

"Morning, boss."

"Aren't you on top of things? How long have you been here?"

"An hour."

I poured myself a cup of coffee and laced it with a teaspoon of sugar. "You're wearing your favorite plaid shirt, and you donned makeup, too. Special day?"

"Buddy wants to take me to see my mother around noon."

"Aw, he's a gem," I said.

She beamed. "Anything new in your investigation?"

"I'm not invest—"

"Uh-uh. Don't lie. I peeked at the whiteboard you draped with a cloth in the office."

I hurried to her. "Take a look at these." I pulled Petunia's cell phone from my purse. As I scrolled through the photos, I told Joss the various ways the events might have played out. "Add in the text Petunia sent to Scarlet," I went on, "and I'm pretty sure the person inside the general store is either the murderer or an accomplice."

"Or Genevieve," she said.

"Right. Or her."

"Have you discussed your theories with Detective Summers?"

I frowned. "I'm afraid of incurring his wrath, even though I wasn't sleuthing, per se. I was comforting a murder victim's sister. Plus, I don't have hard facts, and that's all he wants."

"I know what you can do. You have a pottery lesson with Renee later this afternoon. Why don't you run what you've discovered by her?"

"Great idea. I'll let her tell him what I've found. She can handle his wrath."

Joss laughed. "He could never be mad at her. He dotes on that woman."

Like Asher dotes on Scarlet, I reflected.

I thought of the note left on my door. I'd promised Brady I'd show it to Summers. Would the detective take it seriously, or would he think it was left as a prank? I decided to show it to Renee first, and she could guide me.

"Does this mean Daphne Flores is off the hook?" Joss asked.

Daphne. Had she gone to the police and revealed that she had a second job? Had she asked any of her fortune-telling clients to verify her whereabouts on the evenings of the murders?

"I'm not sure," I said.

Joss went to the entrance to flip the CLOSED sign to OPEN and unlatched the top half of the Dutch door. Meanwhile, I checked the schedule regarding lessons—a pair of women at eleven wanted to make fairy doors—after which I went to the patio with my coffee to get organized.

Hattie and Zinnia ventured into the shop around nine. They planned to have a DIY garden party with the Happy Diggers and wanted everyone to make a fairy garden. Hattie said Zinnia was footing the bill. Zinnia didn't bat an eyelash. A half hour later, they left the shop with over five hundred dollars' worth of merchandise.

"Cha-ching," Joss said when the door closed behind them. "We need more Zinnias."

I laughed but sobered quickly when I thought of Petunia and all the pets she'd given floral names. How she would be missed. "What we need is justice," I murmured, closing the drawer of the register.

Joss rested a hand on my shoulder. "Don't wait to talk to Renee. Call Summers. Suffer his slings and arrows."

"What is the whole quote? It's from *Hamlet*, isn't it?"

"'Whether 'tis nobler in the mind to suffer the slings and arrows of outrageous fortune, or to take arms against a sea of troubles.'"

I sighed. "That's it. This is a sea of troubles, and I'm not quite ready to take an arrow to the heart."

"Summers won't—"

"I'll think about it."

At nine-thirty, the door whipped open, and Scarlet Lyle swooped inside, bypassing two customers who were viewing our array of fairy-themed books.

"Courtney!" Her voice was shrill, her pretty face pinched with anger, and her updo a mess. "Why did you do it?"

"Do what?"

"Why, why, why?" she demanded. The tails of her chiffon scarf fanned behind her as she marched toward me. She wrangled the scarf and tucked the ends beneath the collar of the fitted ice-white jacket she was wearing. "Why did you sic them on me and Asher?"

"Who?" I asked.

Joss drew alongside me. She was pint-sized, but she was formidable.

"The police," Scarlet said. "Why did you tell Detective Summers about the shovel I had for sale at the festival?"

"Because a shovel was the weapon used to kill Genevieve."

She gasped. Apparently, Summers hadn't told her that tidbit. Well, too bad. It wasn't a secret. I hadn't crossed the line.

"Not mine," she stated.

"The one you had for sale wasn't in your festival booth when I passed by on Sunday."

"Because I sold it. To a customer."

"Do you have a receipt?"

"Of course."

"Give it to the police. That should clear you." *Unless a police tech could determine you're the person in the photo that Petunia took,* I thought.

She huffed. "Asher was very upset. He went with me this morning and gave Dylan Summers an earful."

If they'd been questioned this morning and not yesterday, did that prove neither of them could have left the note on my door?

"How could you possibly think I killed her?" Scarlet went on. "We were friends."

"She dissed you on social media."

"I've mocked people, too. They don't want to kill me. It's part of the game."

Some game, I thought grimly, recalling how Genevieve told Tamara Geoffries that what she did was all *in fun.*

"Did the detective ask you about the text message Petunia sent you?" I asked.

She lasered me with a glare that could cow the staunchest of souls. "I told you. I don't look at my cell phone after seven, so I didn't see any message from her. Besides, I was too busy at home—" She stopped abruptly.

"Doing what?"

"None of your business."

I flinched. Her words matched those on the note. Had she guessed I was looking into the murders prior to this morning? "Why can't you tell me?" I asked, recalling how cagily she'd acted at the library. Had she been home having a torrid affair while her husband did inventory?

"Fine." She clicked her tongue. "You might as well know what I was up to, but if you blab a word, I'll skewer you." She screwed her index finger in my direction.

I stepped backward out of reach, noting that her threat didn't sound like she was ready to confess to murder.

An elderly regular customer strolled into the shop, all smiles.

Joss said, "Boss, I'll see to everyone out here. Why don't you two go in the back?"

I clasped Scarlet's elbow and drew her down the hall, but not into the office. Not only didn't I want her to view the whiteboard, even though it was covered, but I didn't want to be in a room alone with her. I released her and said, "Go on."

"I was making Asher a pirate costume," she said. "It's a surprise. He wants to participate in talk-like-a-pirate day. Ever since he was a boy, he's been fascinated with pirates. He's even been watching YouTube videos and practicing how to walk with a limp."

"Can anybody verify that you were sewing?" I asked.

"No. I was *alo-o-one*." She dragged out the word in exaggerated fashion. "If it helps, I bought the fabric on Friday. After the festival closed."

"Did you tell the police any of this?"

"Duh. *No*. My husband was standing right there."

The pirate costume story did sound plausible until something occurred to me. "Your ring," I said. "Where is it?"

She curled her left hand into a fist, her thumb obscuring the ring finger.

"At the library, Asher seemed upset that you weren't wearing it," I continued. "Did you lose it or leave it somewhere?"

Scarlet coughed out a laugh. "Oh, you're too much for words. What an imagination you have! Do you think I was having an affair on Saturday night while Asher was occupied with inventory, and I forgot my ring in my lover's bedroom? Silly girl." She batted the air. "I'm having it resized. A few years ago, I fought my weight. I was yo-yoing, up down, up down. I had the ring resized twice. It fit. It didn't fit. But my weight has been steady for three years now, so I decided to have it resized one last time." She held her hand out as if to admire the nonexistent ring. "Luckily, the previous resizings didn't weaken the structure, the jeweler said, because my husband invested in the best when it came to quality. However, I had to leave the ring with the jeweler this time so he could ensure it was strong enough to withstand one last adjustment." She jutted a hip. "Do I need to tell the police about that, too? Or are you done with me, Detective Kelly?" She nearly spit out the word *Detective*. "Because I'm certainly done with you."

I hated burning bridges, and I had clearly overstepped this time, but I needed two more answers. "Why did you go to the beach Thursday night in memory of your mother's death when, in truth, you hated her?"

"Who told you that?" Her eyes widened as reality hit her. "Daphne." She licked her lips. "She had no right."

"She said you didn't have the right to tell your husband about her past."

Scarlet wheezed, like a balloon losing air. "If you must know, I go to the beach to remember the anniversary of my mother's death because I celebrate the moment of my emancipation."

"What were you wearing Thursday night?"

"A dark blue jogging suit. Why?"

Dark blue could look black in a long-distance photo, I reasoned, thinking of the image Petunia had captured on her camera. "After your meditation time, did you happen to swing by the general store before heading home?"

"Why would I? It's out of my way." She said it with full candor, her gaze direct, her facial muscles calm. I didn't get the feeling she was lying.

At eleven, I guided my students to the patio—they were old pros at fairy garden design—and we started making our fairy doors. I'd set out lots of options. Popsicle sticks, twigs, hollowed-out acorns, tiny pebbles, colorful buttons, a variety of moss, and more. Of course, I'd preheated glue guns, and I'd remembered to include regular glue, too. For the finishing touch, we had a spray can of clear acrylic coating.

We worked side by side, chatting amiably about the fairies they were inviting into their gardens. Neither had seen a fairy yet, but both were hopeful.

At noon, I finished up the class, and Joss left with Buddy to visit her mother. When there was a lull in customer traffic, I clipped my nails short in preparation for my pottery lesson and ate a small lunch of Greek yogurt and grapes. As I was washing my spoon in the kitchen beyond the office, Fiona and Eveleen soared in, super excited about what they'd learned from their aunt.

"My first potion!" Eveleen exclaimed. "My very first. It's a focus potion. Look." She wiggled her wings, and a reddish powder wafted out.

Fiona wagged a finger. "You're not supposed to try it at every turn. Auntie warned you."

I envisioned Merryweather and her stern glare.

"It's meant to help *you* focus," Fiona said. "No one else."

"I only wanted to show Courtney. She understands how excited I am," Eveleen said. "Don't you?"

I held out my palm for her to perch on. "Yes, you're eager, and it's hard to contain yourself, but you must listen to Fiona, for your benefit and hers. You want your mother to approve of everything you learn."

Tears sprang to the young fairy's eyes and leaked down her cheeks. She lowered her chin. Sniffling, she said, "I'm s-sorry."

Fiona perched beside her and drew her into a hug. "It's okay."

At a quarter to four, Joss returned and asked if I'd reached out to Detective Summers. I hadn't, so she clucked like a chicken and waggled her elbows. Before I left for my pottery class, she suggested that I'd better find the gumption to tell Renee everything I knew. I saluted.

Chapter 22

The wayward, white-winged fairies of spray
That ride green lobsters out of the bay
Then float back in on a horseshoe crab,
Scamper and turn and dash for their caves,
Swept by the waves.
—Patricia Hubbell, "Sea Fairies"

Meaghan, Glinda, and Tamara were already in the classroom at Seize the Clay when I arrived. Pinewood shelving lined the walls. One shelf held pick-up items created by other students or potters. Another shelf was filled with restocking items, like take-home clay, paints, and carving tools. A round table, with tea service already prepared, stood to the right. In the center of the room were four potting wheels on a narrow table. Each plaster wheel setup was hooked up to a foot pedal. A huge sink was located at the back of the room near the kiln.

"Welcome," Renee said, handing each of us an apron. "Pick a wheel. Tamara, you'll want to remove your jacket."

I donned my apron. "Any time I've tried throwing a pot before, Renee, I've stunk at it."

"Me, too," Tamara said as she tucked the ties of her linen-blend blouse out of the way.

"I did this in high school," Glinda said. "I've got a warped mug to prove it."

Renee eyed Meaghan. "And how about you, Miss Artist?"

Meaghan pushed the sleeves of her peasant blouse above her elbows. "I've thrown a few over the years. They're not bad. My mother likes them."

"Aww," we all cooed in unison.

I sat at a wheel and touched the clay. It was so clammy, it made me shiver, which surprised me. I'd dug into wet dirt with bare hands for years. I'd touched worms. I'd made polymer clay fairy doors. But I'd never had the same reaction as now. Maybe I was jittery because I knew I had to address the *elephant in my mind*—telling Renee what I'd discovered.

"Let's get started," Renee said, and began guiding us in the art of making a pot. She'd decided a small flowerpot would be the best choice.

First, we kneaded the clay to remove air bubbles from it.

"Now form it into a ball and slam it against the plaster," she said. "Knead it some more. Repeat. Ball, slam, knead."

The whole process would be great for getting rid of aggression, I mused.

After a few minutes, Renee used a wire and cut each of our balls in half to see if there were air bubbles. Confirming that we'd all mastered the air bubble removal technique, she instructed us to mold them into balls and place the ball in the center of the wheel.

Next, she showed us how to use the foot pedal to control the speed of the wheel.

"Okay, position your nose directly over the middle of the wheel." She demonstrated. "The ball should be rotating evenly."

The class lasted forty-five minutes, with Renee showing us how to cone up and cone down, how to create the wall and compress the bottom, and how to draw the clay upward using two fingers on the inside and three fingers on the outside.

"Working slowly is key," she repeated often. She assisted throughout, fixing when we messed up.

When each of us had a piece that somewhat resembled a flowerpot, she helped remove the pieces from the wheel and deposited
them on a rack to dry. In a week, we'd return to paint our master-
pieces.

We washed our hands at the sink, and Renee gestured for us to
join her for a cup of tea at the preset table. "Tea with friends," she
said, "is the best way to celebrate one's success."

I sat between Glinda and Meaghan. Tamara took the chair to
Meaghan's right.

"This class was exactly what I needed," Tamara said. "Like a moment of Zen. I loved every minute of it and can't wait to do it
again."

"I offer a series of six classes, if you're interested," Renee said.

"I'm in."

Stirring honey into my tea, I said, "Renee, I have something to
show you on my cell phone, if now is a good time. It's related to the
murders."

She shook her head. "Courtney, Courtney, Courtney. Don't
you get that the police department is all over this? Dylan and Red are
doing everything they can to bring closure."

"Yes. I—"

"What did you stumble on this time? Show me."

I pulled Petunia's cell phone from my purse, accessed it using the
Lily numerical code, and handed it to her. "This is Petunia's cell
phone. She took pictures last Thursday, the night Genevieve died,
and also on the night she was killed."

"Of?" Renee tapped on the photo app.

I rose, rounded the table, and said, "There. See the photos that
aren't flowers? That's Lyle's General Store."

"And the ones before are Garden Delights and Lagoon Grill. So?"

"Petunia was hunting for property to rent in the area, and I think
while she was searching, she stumbled onto something. Look at the
second photo of the general store. See how it focuses on the garden
tools? A shovel was used to kill Genevieve." I went on to explain my

theory about the person in the black outfit being either Genevieve, Asher, Oliver, or Scarlet.

"Or anyone else, for that matter," Renee said. "Including Daphne Flores."

"No, it can't be her because—" I stopped abruptly. "It can't be. She has a verifiable alibi on both nights." I hoped she'd contacted the police by now.

Renee rotated her hand, signaling me to continue.

I said, "What if the killer stole a shovel from the shop, and the person in the photo is putting the shovel back after cleaning evidence off of it?"

Renee used two fingers to zoom in on the first image.

"Notice the time on the photo," I said. "Thursday at around eight-thirty."

Meaghan whistled.

"Hey"—Glinda tapped the rim of the table—"Cliff and I were having dinner at Lagoon Grill Thursday night. We had a window seat. I recall looking toward the street and seeing a woman with short silver hair focused on the general store."

"Petunia had a silver bob," I said. "Did she seem in a hurry?"

"Nope."

I said to Renee, "I don't think she realized what she'd seen."

"If she saw anything," Renee countered. "This is all conjecture."

Which was exactly why I hadn't wanted to reach out to Summers.

"Glinda, did you catch sight of Scarlet Lyle during dinner?" I said to Renee, "Scarlet is a regular customer at Glitz."

"No," Glinda replied.

"Were the shop's lights on?"

"They were dim. I didn't notice anyone moving about."

"But there was someone inside," I said. "The first photo proves it. I think Petunia went back on Saturday to see if she could piece together what she'd really seen."

"And took another picture," Meaghan said.

"Right. And she texted Scarlet."

"She also called Daphne Flores," Renee said.

I'd hoped she'd forgotten about that.

"You know"—Tamara sipped her tea and replaced the cup on the saucer—"I was at Lagoon Grill Saturday night with a friend of mine. We were leaving around eleven thirty when Asher stepped outside the general store holding a carpet. He began to beat it with a fireplace poker. I remember because my friend covered her mouth so she wouldn't inhale any of the dust."

That verified his claim that he was doing inventory, meaning Scarlet was at home alone with no witnesses. Did she lie about seeing Petunia's message? Guessing what Petunia wanted to talk about, did she go to Daphne's, steal the hoedag, and hurry to Petunia's to kill her?

I turned to Renee. "Will you tell Detective Summers what I've found? Coming from you, he'll take it as solid information."

She propped a hand on one hip. "I'll think about it."

"Do you need Petunia's phone?" I held it out.

She didn't reach for it.

I pocketed it, and we all moved to the showroom to settle our accounts, after which Tamara and Glinda decided to spend time roaming the pottery shop. They had a few gifts to buy. Meaghan and I stepped outside and drank in the late afternoon sunshine.

She hitched her tote bag higher on her shoulder. "Well, throwing a pot was fun, although bending over a wheel was hard on the lower back."

"Do you think Renee will tell Summers about the photographs?"

"She didn't say she would, but she didn't say she wouldn't."

We crossed the street to our courtyard. The lights were out in Open Your Imagination. I was about to unlock the door when Fiona and Eveleen winged to us.

"Why were you gone so long?" Fiona asked. "We were worried. We thought the police found out about the scary note and hauled you to jail."

"What scary note?" Meaghan asked.

"Last night, someone stuck a note on my door warning me to stop poking into things." I pulled the note from my purse and handed it to her.

She perused it, her mouth turning down at the corners. "Why didn't you show this to Renee?"

"I forgot. I was so caught up with the photos."

She scowled at me.

"Don't," I said. "I hate when you look at me like that."

"Why didn't you contact *me* the moment you found this?" She flailed the note.

"I called Brady. He came over."

"Oh?" She raised an eyebrow. "Do tell." She made kissing sounds.

I knuckled her arm. "He took the couch and made me breakfast this morning."

She eyed Fiona, who confirmed with a nod.

Meaghan said, "Why don't you spend tonight at my place?"

"I've got work to do." Actually, I wanted to review what I'd written on the whiteboard, hoping a clearer idea of what had happened would come to me.

"Fine, but I'm sticking by your side. You are not going into the shop or your house alone."

"She's got us," Fiona said, patting her sister's wing.

"Fairies or no fairies, one more human is needed," Meaghan countered. "No argument." She handed me back the sheet of paper and pointed at the building. "Open sesame."

I tucked the note into my purse, unlocked the door, and we all entered. Meaghan bolted the door. I switched on minimal lights. Pixie raced to me as if I'd forgotten about her. Fiona divebombed the cat, who fell backward, paws in the air.

"Ladies!" I said. "Decorum."

"What's decorum?" Eveleen asked.

Fiona explained in their native tongue. "*Féin a iompar.* Behave yourself."

Meaghan strode past me and cut around the sales counter. "I'm going to grab a sparkling water from your office fridge, and I'll lounge in there until you're—"

"No, wait!"

She whirled around and threw me the side-eye. "What don't you want me to see?" She made a U-turn and stomped toward the office.

I nabbed Pixie and hurried after my pal.

"Oho!" Meaghan said the moment she entered the office. "You made a suspect board, didn't you?" She whisked off the cloth covering the whiteboard.

"Yes. But it's not complete. It needs a timeline."

"I'll help." She plopped into the Queen Anne chair and tented her hands in front of her.

"We'll help, too." Fiona flew into the room and alit on the Zen garden. She patted the rim for her sister to join her. Eveleen descended too fast, kicking up sand. Some hit Fiona's face.

I placed Pixie on her cat pillow and strode to the whiteboard. Above the grid, I jotted the events I believed occurred on Thursday in chronological order.

8:25 Petunia takes pictures outside General Store, Garden Delights, & Lagoon Grill.
8:30 Glinda sees Petunia
8 to 12:00 Genevieve killed

"Not a lot to go on," Meaghan said. "Your notes say Genevieve didn't have her phone. Why is that important?"

"I think the killer took it because there was something incriminating on it. I've reviewed her online profile and seen posts she published, but posts for Thursday were nonexistent. Also, I don't have a clue who she might have called or texted after canceling our dinner."

Meaghan hummed.

"The police found Petunia's phone at the crime scene Sunday morning." I explained how Bentley was sweet on Petunia and had gone to her house to check on her. "I believe the killer was startled by Bentley's approach and didn't have time to swipe it."

"So what happened Saturday night?" Meaghan asked.

I wrote:

8:30 Petunia returns to general store, takes a pic of inside shop, specifically tools
8:45 Texts Scarlet—needs to talk
8:55 Leaves brief message for Daphne?

"Why did you add the question mark?" Meaghan asked.

"Because Daphne told the police she didn't understand it, so she erased it. Petunia said, 'Never mind, ask her,' and Daphne presumed she meant she'd ask her sister something. Except she didn't call Peony."

I continued to write.

8 to 12:00 Scarlet alibi—home making pirate costume, no witness, did not see text
9:00 Petunia arrives home, seen by Bentley, me, and Dad

Meaghan said, "Hold on. You saw her? I didn't know that."

"We were walking home from dinner and glimpsed Petunia arriving at that moment. She went inside and slammed her door."

"Slammed, as in she shut it like she was scared or angry?"

"Or the door was heavy."

I added a note at the beginning of Saturday's timeline:

7:00 Saturday Daphne sees hoedag in toolshed. Killer steals it afterward. Why didn't Daphne hear?

Meaghan said, "I thought you said Daphne wasn't home. The lights were out at her house."

I gulped.

Meaghan shot me the stink eye. "You're holding something back. Spill."

Oh, crud. I'd promised Daphne not to reveal her secret. On the other hand, it was Meaghan. She knew all the skeletons in my closet, and as far as I knew, she'd never revealed a thing. I swore her to secrecy, and then I told her about Daphne telling fortunes to make money and having clients on Thursday, Friday, and Saturday.

"The appointments on Saturday were from seven to nearly eleven thirty," I added.

Meaghan said, "She plays music during her sessions. If the killer stole the hoedag during that time, the music could have drowned out the sound of an intruder opening the toolshed."

"Right!"

I faced the board and wrote:

I think Petunia was running out of her house when struck. Killer might have sneaked in and surprised her.

"How would the killer have known where to find the hoedag?" Meaghan interrupted. "Maybe Daphne really is the killer."

I shook my head. "Not if her clients corroborate the appointments. No, I think the killer knows Daphne's habits. Whoever it is might have kept her under surveillance."

"To frame her. That means premeditation."

I continued writing.

9:30 or so Bentley texts asking if she's okay—no response
11:00 Bentley worries about Petunia. Goes to her house.
[Killer hears Bentley and flees without taking Petunia's phone.]
Bentley sees Petunia's body on path. Knows she's dead. Worried police will think he's the killer because of stalking her. He tears off branch from bay tree, sweeps away footprints, and runs off. Tosses branch in neighbor's yard.
Witnesses, Wanda and Twyla, heard him working in his garden on both nights.

As I gazed at the board, a fresh idea came to me. "What if Asher viewed the text from Petunia that night?"

Meaghan squinted, not understanding.

"Asher and Scarlet made a pact not to look at messages after seven," I said. "He had to go to work to do inventory. Maybe he took her phone with him so she wouldn't be tempted."

She blew a raspberry. "Controlling."

"Proprietary," I countered, reflecting how overly protective Twyla said Bentley could be. Asher was the same.

"That makes sense!" Fiona bounded to her feet, splashing sand on her sister. "Hercule Poirot would approve."

Eveleen made a dismissive sound.

Fiona spun around and shook a finger. "Do not make fun of the best detective that ever lived."

"I thought you said Sherlock Holmes was the best," Eveleen taunted.

"Well, yes, I did, but there are two!"

"Three," Eveleen chimed. "Courtney."

Fiona folded her arms and tapped her foot. "Be silent." She turned her back on her sister and refocused on me. "Continue."

"Anyway," I said, "perhaps he heard her phone ping and intercepted Petunia's text message." I paused to let that sink in. "Let's say he knew that Scarlet swiped a shovel and killed Genevieve. He might have thought Petunia had figured things out and believed the only way he could save his wife was to hunt down Petunia. But then . . ." I tapped the dry-erase marker against my jaw. "After killing her, he went back to his shop to cement his alibi. To prove he was where he said he was, he stepped outside with a carpet and made quite a fuss about beating it into submission so anyone in the vicinity would remember seeing him."

"Are you saying that there were two different killers?" Meaghan asked. "Asher and Scarlet?"

"I don't know." Angst swizzled through me. "I don't want Scarlet to be guilty, but her alibis are flimsy, and she admitted to wearing dark jogging clothes Thursday night." I stared at the board as another scenario popped into my mind. "What if the two killers are Asher and Oliver?"

"Go on," Meaghan said.

"What if Asher wasn't protecting his wife but shielding his friend?" I told her about Asher and Oliver sitting at Hideaway Café the day after Genevieve's murder, and they were laughing. "Asher wanted Genevieve gone so she wouldn't continue to be a thorn in his beautiful wife's side, and Oliver wanted vengeance because she was the reason his wife divorced him. What if they collaborated to kill her, and Asher suggested Oliver take a shovel from his shop? However, to throw the police off the scent, he mentioned that Oliver bought a shovel elsewhere."

"So Oliver killed Genevieve, and Asher killed Petunia?" Meaghan asked.

I headed for the door. "I need to talk to him."

"To Asher?"

"To Oliver."

"Why does it have to be you?" Meaghan bounded to her feet. "Why not tell the police? Let's show them the note you received. That should jump-start the investigation."

"No, I've got nothing but conjecture. You heard Renee. Summers expects facts. C'mon. Garden Delights is open late."

I waved for the fairies to accompany us and asked Pixie to be patient until we returned.

Chapter 23

Hear the call!
Fays, be still!
None is deep
On vale and hill.
—William Allingham, "The Noon Call"

A heady aroma wafted to us as we entered Garden Delights. Whereas Bowers of Flowers was a small venue, jam-packed with flower arrangements and containers filled with fresh-cut flowers, Garden Delights was expansive, nearly the size of Lyle's General Store, and the exotic displays stood healthy distances from one another, giving a customer ample space to view each from all angles. There were a number of live plants, like money trees and peace lilies, growing in gorgeous pottery. Heart of the Jungle, which I'd learned at the festival was one of Oliver's most requested presentations, was positioned to the right of the front door. To the left was an arrangement titled Burst of Nature created with cymbidium orchids, birds-of-paradise, ginger flowers, and calla lilies. The price was steep—seven hundred dollars—but many of the wealthy residents in Carmel paid to have fresh flowers delivered daily to their homes.

Fiona and Eveleen scoped out the room, sniffing and admiring. Two female customers who were studying a four-foot glazed vase filled with an exotic fern didn't notice them. Neither did Oliver, who was chatting with a clerk in front of the handcrafted, L-shaped sales counter. The only reason I pegged her for a clerk was because of the nametag pinned to her lacy top. She looked quite trendy in a blouse cinched with a wide woven belt over a mid-calf floral skirt.

A scrappy-looking terrier detected the fairies, however. It limped from behind the desk and peered up at them. Fiona swooped to it and danced on top of its head. The dog yipped with excitement, loving the attention.

"Boris," Oliver said. "Back to your bed and no barking."

Fiona and Eveleen giggled and followed Boris to his spot behind the counter.

Oliver excused himself from his employee and strode to us. "What brings you ladies in?" he asked, his voice as smooth as silk. "Can I interest you in the Japanese magnolia?" He motioned to a minimalist arrangement in a low, wavy bowl.

I glimpsed the price and tamped down a gasp. Three hundred dollars. "Thanks, no," I said.

Fiona and Eveleen reappeared. They hovered directly in front of Oliver, but he didn't blink.

"We didn't come in for flowers," I said. "I'd like to ask you a question."

His mouth turned down at the corners. "Your reputation precedes you, Courtney. People at the festival said when a murder occurs, you like to snoop."

I took umbrage at the accusation. "I'm curious by nature, and when friends wind up dead or are accused of murder, I can be resolute in getting answers, but I assure you, I don't snoop."

"*Resolute* should be her middle name," Meaghan said, trying to lighten the mood.

Oliver dragged his lip between his teeth, resulting in a sucking sound. "Okay. I'll play along. What's on your mind?"

"How well do you know Asher Lyle?" I asked.

"I've bought a number of home goods at his shop. He buys my flowers. We've struck up a friendship. Why?"

"You had lunch with him on Friday at Hideaway Café."

"Ah, yes. We were discussing the ups and downs of being in retail and how to drum up more customers."

"You were laughing."

"Were we?" He thought about that for a moment. "I remember now. He was telling me a funny story about this customer who fumbled in every pocket for his wallet before remembering he'd hidden cash in his sock."

That sounded reasonable. "Yesterday, you two were at odds. Outside my shop. I'm guessing that you discovered he told the police about a shovel you bought out of town, so you accosted him."

"I did no such thing. We exchanged words." Oliver's gaze grew wary. "And, before you ask, yes, I did buy a shovel. I was filling pots the other day using the dirt I keep in the yard behind the store"—he hooked a thumb over his shoulder—"when the handle broke. I make all of the live plant arrangements myself. I couldn't be without a shovel. The police questioned me about my purchase and divulged that a shovel had been used to kill Genevieve Bellerose. But I assure you, it was not my shovel."

"Why did you buy one out of town? Why not pick up one at the general store?"

He guffawed. "I didn't need one as expensive as the ones Asher sells."

This coming from the man who charged exorbitant prices for flowers.

I continued. "On Thursday night last week, did you go into the general store by yourself around eight-thirty?"

He arched an eyebrow. "No. The shop is closed by that time. Besides, I haven't been inside it in months. My house is fully outfitted."

"Someone was inside."

"Whoever said it was me is lying." His gaze turned hard. "Whoa, hold on. Do you think the shovel used to kill Genevieve came from Lyle's?"

I didn't reply.

"Look, I have a solid alibi that night. I was helping out a friend, and he vouched for me. Come to think of it, after I dropped my friend at home—it was around midnight—I spotted Asher walking in his tennis gear. I tooted my horn. He waved to me."

"Where were you Saturday night?" Meaghan asked.

"Why would you care—" He cocked his head. "No, uh-uh." His gaze ping-ponged between the two of us. "You can't think I had anything to do with Petunia's murder. I was . . ." He paused, as if manufacturing an alibi on the spot. "I was walking my dog that night."

Eveleen whizzed to us. "Courtney!" she cried. "I heard what he said, and it's a lie."

Fiona raced after her and signaled for Eveleen to continue.

"While my sister was petting Boris to comfort him," the younger fairy said, "I checked out his injured foot. There's an infected cut on his pad."

"From the zoomies, Boris told me," Fiona said.

I gawked at her. She'd never mentioned she could talk to animals. Had she and Pixie been carrying on lengthy conversations all this time?

"What are the zoomies?" her sister asked.

Fiona explained how dogs might run back and forth crazily to work out their excess energy.

"Well, the poor thing can't take a stroll right now," Eveleen said.

I focused on Oliver. "You walked your dog, Boris? The one with the gimpy foot?"

"It's a small sprain. Dogs can—"

"I hear he's got a torn pad."

"Who told you that, your fairy?" Oliver narrowed his gaze and became acutely aware of the air around him. "I hear you see them."

"I do."

"So do I," Meaghan said.

Oliver sniffed in disbelief.

"What were you really doing Saturday night?" I asked, pulling my cell phone from my purse. "You can tell us or the police."

"The police?"

"You're a suspect," I said, vamping. I didn't think Summers had him on his radar.

"I can't be a suspect. I had no motive to want Petunia dead."

I frowned. "She was planning on relocating her business to this neighborhood. You and she would have been in direct competition."

"Hardly. We had completely different business models."

I glowered at him, waiting.

"Please." Lowering his voice, he said, "I can't tell anyone where I was. It's a secret."

"A secret that could exonerate you of murder? C'mon, you can confide in us."

Fiona dashed Oliver's head with green trusting dust.

"Okay," he said after a long moment, "but you've got to promise not to tell a soul."

"We promise." I motioned to Meaghan.

He exhaled. "My wife . . . I miss her terribly. I'm still madly in love with her. For weeks, I've been sending her apologies in texts, but she didn't respond to any until Saturday morning, when she wrote that I needed to give her more time. That gave me hope, and I felt compelled to speak to her, so that night, I drove to San Francisco around six o'clock, and I hung outside her townhouse. I could see her moving about the place through the window, but I couldn't find the courage to ring her doorbell." His shoulders rose and fell. "Around nine p.m., I gave up, and headed home. Near the Cow Palace, I blew a tire." The Cow Palace, originally the California State Livestock Pavilion, was an indoor arena about six miles south of San Francisco. "I had to wait a half hour for Triple-A to help me. There should be a record of that."

"Did anyone other than your wife see you hanging around?" I asked.

"No one who would recognize me. I was wearing an overcoat, hat, and glasses."

Swell. There were plenty of guys in San Francisco who'd fit that description.

"Please, I can't have my wife learn I was in the area. If she finds out I was watching her—" Oliver drew in a sharp breath. "If she finds out, she'll never give me a second chance. I can't risk that. You understand, don't you? I want her back."

He was so earnest, I believed him. "Oliver, talk to the police. They'll be discreet." I started for the exit and paused. "What time did you get back to town that night?"

"Around eleven-thirty."

"Did you see anyone?"

He heaved a sigh. "No."

Chapter 24

Yet, when I come, the fairies fly
On rainbow-winged rosellas,
And all the treeferns standing by
Put up their green umbrellas.
—Annie R. Rentoul, "In the Gully Green"

On the way out of Garden Delights, I noted Lyle's General Store was closed, as Oliver had stated. The lights were off.

"If it wasn't Oliver Killian in Lyle's on Saturday night, it had to have been Scarlet," I mused as Meaghan, the fairies, and I veered east on Junipero Street toward Open Your Imagination. I had to retrieve Pixie before heading home. "She has an unsubstantiated alibi."

"Or it could have been Genevieve, as you speculated," Meaghan countered, "sneaking in to snap an incriminating photo." She tapped my arm. "By the way, tell me why you were clueless about Genevieve's mean streak?"

"You know how it is with new friends. You skate the surface until you ask probing questions. I suppose that's how my forum friends and I have been all this time, glossing over the issues." I hadn't known about Daphne's fortune telling or that Petunia had a twin sister.

"I have a few friends like that," Meaghan said. "Through work. Artists and the like."

Eveleen said, "I only have true lifelong friends."

Fiona flicked her with a wing. "Do not brag. This is a serious conversation."

Eveleen recoiled. "I didn't mean . . . I know it's been hard for you here. In the human world. Mother wouldn't let you socialize."

"But I can now, and I'm building friendships." Fiona fluttered in front of me. "Go on, Courtney. Let us help you theorize."

I said, "I thought Asher might have been the person in the shop, covering up his wife's transgression, except—"

"Except it couldn't have been him, because he was off playing tennis," Meaghan finished.

"What if he lied about that? Or he ended his game early?"

"You heard Oliver." She thrust a hand in my direction. "He saw him around midnight in his tennis gear."

"Oliver could have been lying, trying to establish his own alibi."

"True, but don't you think Genevieve was killed much earlier?"

Fiona said, "If Scarlet killed Genevieve and went back to the shop to hide the weapon, and if Asher did what you think he did to protect her, like cleaning blood off the shovel, do you think the shovel might still be there?"

I said, "That would be pretty stupid."

Fiona folded her arms. "Hiding something in plain sight seems smart to me."

Eveleen agreed. "Sometimes at home, when we play hide-and-seek, I stand right in front of something blue, like a turquoise flower."

"That's in the pompom family," Fiona explained.

"Or reindeer moss," Eveleen added. "That's blue, too. No one ever catches me. I win every time."

"Okay," I said, "what we need to do is prove Asher wasn't playing tennis or that he ended his game early, but that'll be hard to do, because the guy he plays with is off in Guatemala saving the coffee plantations."

"Let's call him," Meaghan said. "Do you know his name?"

"Yes, it's Fritz . . ." I snapped my fingers until I recalled his last name. "Bommer or Bomer." I couldn't remember how Scarlet had pronounced it. "But I don't have his number."

"Let's do an online search," Meaghan said as we entered Open Your Imagination. "You know how to do that, don't you?" Like me, she was savvy with computers. Often, she had to do searches about an artist's history or about the provenance of artwork displayed at Flair. "PeopleFinders is the site I use."

Pixie was ecstatic to see us and leaped into my arms. I grabbed a tin of tuna from the kitchen and fed her in the bowl beside her cat pillow in the office. Then I sat at the desk and wakened the computer.

Meaghan pulled a bottle of Pellegrino from the refrigerator and cranked off the top. Fiona tiptoed along the desk's edge. Eveleen yawned and tucked herself into a ball to take a nap in the middle of the Zen garden.

I opened the site Meaghan suggested. *"Hmm. I'm not sure if his last name is spelled with one M or two."*

"Try both."

I typed in *Fritz Bommer*, two *M*s. A list of links for persons with a similar name appeared. The first was an Instagram page for Fritz T. Bommer, but the guy was in his eighties. I doubted he was Asher's tennis buddy. There was a Fritz with an umlaut over the *O* in Böm-mer, who lived in Germany, and a Fritz Beumer spelled with *EU*, who hailed from New York. I wasn't open with my social media information and was always surprised when someone didn't mind shar-ing where they lived or had gone to school.

I typed *Fritz Bomer*, with one *M*, and a slew of pictures of the handsome actor Matt Bomer, who'd starred in the popular TV series *White Collar*, came up.

After adding *Guatemala* to the search, a picture of a blond Fritz Bomer, tennis racket in hand, materialized. He was about Asher Lyle's age. I clicked on his Facebook link and hit the *About* tab. Fritz lived in Carmel-by-the-Sea, was forty-two, and had graduated Harvard with an MBA. His *Photos* were abundant. In one photograph, he was wearing tennis clothes and a cap saying ALL I NEED IS COFFEE AND MY RESCUE DOG. In another, he was holding a colorful sign with the slogan, GUATEMALA, EL PAIS DE LA ETERNA PRIMAVERA—the land of eternal spring—and looking fondly at a handsome golden retriever sitting by his side. I scrolled down, realizing the man had posted hundreds of pictures of coffee plants, towering trees, volunteers, tennis matches, and his pup. He was nothing if not enthusiastic about his service to humanity as well as his sport and best friend. His latest post said that he and his dog were having a blast in Guatemala. He'd finally gotten over the cold that had hit him when he'd arrived Thursday night.

I reviewed the post to make sure I'd read it correctly. *Thursday night.*

"Meaghan, get this." I recapped what Fritz had written. "Asher claimed he and Fritz played tennis Thursday until midnight." I paused. "Actually, he didn't say midnight—Scarlet did—which was the time Oliver supposedly saw him. But the time doesn't matter. Asher couldn't have played with Fritz, because it takes at least eight hours to fly to Guatemala." I'd traveled to neighboring Belize once. "Even if Fritz hopped a red-eye, he couldn't have left Thursday and arrived Thursday."

"Maybe he was wrong about his dates," Meaghan suggested.

"Or Asher lied about his alibi."

Perhaps that night, Asher's concern about Scarlet having an affair had turned into an obsession, so he lied to her about his tennis game and followed her. When he trailed her to the festival and witnessed her murdering Genevieve, he took every step to hide her crime.

I gazed at the whiteboard, and one name stood out to me. *Genevieve.* How would Scarlet have known she was outside the festival tents? Had Genevieve texted her to meet? Was that why Scarlet had stolen her phone? Or—

"What are you thinking?" Fiona asked, flitting above the keyboard.

"The other day, I was wondering whether Genevieve might have photographed an image of Scarlet with a lover. That could be the reason she stole Genevieve's cell phone."

"Why take her purse?" Meaghan asked.

"To make it seem like she'd been robbed. Misdirection, if you will, hoping the police wouldn't focus on people in Genevieve's orbit."

I consulted the whiteboard as something Holly said zipped through my mind. Petunia had met Scarlet at Percolate, and in the course of their conversation, Petunia questioned whether Asher might be the one having an affair. I flashed on the posts Genevieve had created and how upset that had made Scarlet, but I couldn't remember seeing any negative reviews of Lyle's General Store. Had Genevieve spared Asher because she'd been in love with him?

I blew out a puff of air.

Eveleen awoke with a start.

Fiona alit on my shoulder. "Are you okay, Courtney?"

"What if Asher had been having an affair with Genevieve?" I suggested.

"And Scarlet caught them," Meaghan whispered, "and killed Genevieve."

I bobbed my head. "And to make things right between them, Asher covered up her crime."

Someone pounded on the shop's front door.

Fiona *eek*ed. Eveleen, too. Meaghan darted to the showroom. I trailed her. At the sales counter, we halted. Two men were peering through the side window.

My father and Gus, his security guy.

"Oh, no," I muttered. Gus didn't intimidate me, not even given his enormous height and build and military buzz cut, but my father showing up at the shop jolted me. I crossed the showroom floor and opened the door. "Hi, Dad," I said breezily. "What are you doing here?"

"I could ask you the same thing, young lady." He strode in.

Young lady, not kitten. Yep. I was in trouble.

"Hi, Gus," I said.

He remained stoic and joined my father by the teacups display table.

My father folded his arms. "Brady pulled me aside this evening when I was dining at the café and told me about the note."

"Note?" I asked casually, though I knew my voice had squeaked. *Rats.*

"Don't pussyfoot. Did you show it to Dylan Summers?"

"Not yet. I didn't think he'd take it seriously."

My father huffed. "Courtney, this is getting to be a regular occurrence for you, putting yourself in harm's way."

"I haven't *put* myself anywhere."

"Let me see it. I presume you have it on you." My father held out his hand.

I reached into my purse and removed the sheet of paper. "Here."

He perused it.

"Dad, why don't you take it to Summers? He'll listen to you."

My father laughed sardonically. "You're not frightened of me or Gus, but you're scared of Dylan?"

Sure I was, especially since he'd chastised me at the cheese shop.

He ticked the note with a fingertip. "Do you have theories of who might have posted this on your door?"

"I've got a few, but Summers doesn't want guesses."

My father regarded Meaghan. "Did you know about this?" He brandished the paper.

"Yes, sir."

"So you're complicit."

"I . . ." She scrunched up her nose. "I'm supportive."

He snorted. "What are you two doing here so late?"

"Finishing up paperwork," I said.

Meaghan shot me a look.

No way was I going to tell my father about the suspect board. Besides, I didn't want to accuse anybody out of hand without cold, hard facts. It wasn't fair to point a finger at Scarlet or Asher or anyone else if I was wrong. In addition, I would not reveal to my father that Meaghan and I had gone to Garden Delights and questioned Oliver Killian. If Oliver went to the police in the morning and told them his alibi, that matter was solved. Unless . . .

Unless, like I'd speculated, he and Asher were in cahoots.

"Work is over as of this minute," my father said. "Gus will be accompanying you home. And Meaghan, I'll walk you to your mother's."

She said, "But Kip—"

"No *buts*. She's expecting your arrival. She's worried about you. She's been calling you since six."

Meaghan glanced toward the office where she'd left her tote bag. "I didn't hear my cell phone ring."

"Get your things," Dad said.

"You can be a bully, you know?" I sniffed.

"Once a cop, always a cop. And once a father, always a father." He offered a wry, unwavering smile. "I love you, and I want you safe."

I thanked Meaghan and said good night. Then I switched off the computer, gathered Pixie, and with Fiona and Eveleen hitching a ride on my shoulders, allowed Gus to escort me home.

Chapter 25

Jingle pockets full of gold,
Marry when they're seven years old.
Every fairy child may keep
Two strong ponies and ten sheep.
—Robert Graves, "I'd Love to Be a Fairy's Child"

Gus announced he was staying the night, and he'd take up his post in a rocker on the porch. Even though the temperature wasn't cool, I gave him a blanket and a bottle of water for his trouble. He would sleep, but he was trained to do so with one eye open. I promised him a good breakfast in the morning and closed the door.

"Stop it!" Eveleen cried the moment we were alone inside the cottage.

Fiona threw her arms wide. "Stop what?"

"Always criticizing me. Always telling me I'm wrong."

I bit back a smile. She was feeling as bossed around as I was. I set Pixie on the floor. She scampered to the kitchen and mewed loudly, apparently ready for a second dinner. I followed her and opened a bottle of lemon-infused sparkling water. I poured myself a glass, took a well-deserved sip, dished up two extra bites of tuna for the cat, and laid out a snack for the fairies.

They were still going at it when I peeked into the foyer. "Ladies."

"Decorum," Eveleen said.

I smiled. "No. What I was going to say is I've prepared some mallow and grapes for dinner."

They joined me in the kitchen, the two perching on opposite sides of the kitchen counter to dine.

"What's going on between you two?" I asked Fiona.

She jutted her arm. "She thinks I'm being too tough on her."

"Are you?"

"Our mother gave me the duty of mentoring her."

I tilted my head. "Is Merryweather Rose of Song as tough on you as you are on Eveleen?"

That caught Fiona up short. "No."

"Hmm." I dragged my fingertip along the back of her hair. "Perhaps you could learn from your aunt. Mentoring doesn't mean browbeating. It means guiding. Counseling. Being a guru."

Eveleen said, "What's a guru?"

"A sage, spiritual leader," I replied.

She whirled on her sister. "You are not that."

"Why, you little—"

Eveleen giggled and sailed out of the room. Fiona zoomed after her. Their laughter resounded through the house. *Sisters.* I wish I'd had a sister. Meaghan was the closest thing to one.

In the morning, I awoke to the sound of merry laughter in the backyard. I peered out the window and saw Eveleen and Fiona flitting among the flowers. Eveleen aimed her hand at a blossom—it opened wide, as if drinking in her love—and Fiona urged her to tackle another.

My heart swelled at the sight of them getting along. Humming, I dressed for my morning exercise and fixed Gus the breakfast I'd promised him. Like me, he happened to like egg-and-cheese sandwiches on English muffins. My mother had made them for me when I was a girl, and to this day, eating one comforted me.

Assured I was safe—the note writer hadn't made another visit—I bid Gus goodbye and took my time walking the strand and dining on my egg sandwich. It wasn't until I got back home that I received a text message.

Dad: **Go see Summers.**

Me: **I will.**

Dad: **Now.**

Me: **[thumb's up emoji]**

As I was pouring myself a cup of coffee, I heard more laughter in the backyard. I peered out and saw Merryweather and Cedric in the garden.

I stepped outside with my mug in hand. "What's going on?"

"We're working on plant manipulation," Eveleen replied.

"Miss Eveleen is a natural," Cedric said in his courtly way.

Fiona's mouth screwed up. She zipped to me and whispered, "I'm not sure the queen fairy will approve, but I can't control Eveleen. She wants what she wants."

Merryweather flew to Fiona and patted her back. "It's all right, dear girl. Breathe."

"But, Auntie—"

"She's a fine student. You've done very well, and your mother will hear about your stellar leadership."

Fiona brightened.

"I will not let Cedric teach her anything unfit for a young fairy. Come along." Merryweather departed to oversee Cedric and Eveleen.

Fiona bussed my cheek. "We'll come to the shop when we're done."

"Be of good cheer," I said. "Merryweather won't steer you wrong." I gave her a confident wink, changed into a cute pair of jeans and a cropped summer sweater, slipped on a pair of Crocs, and headed to work with Pixie.

At Casanova Street, I spied Daphne working in her yard. I was eager to find out if her clients had vouched for her, so Pixie and I made a detour. "Morning," I chimed.

"Morning, Courtney," Daphne said, a shovel in her hand. Not a regular shovel and not a trowel. It was more like a half-length shovel. She brushed her dirty hands off on her overalls and scratched Pixie under the chin. "Hi, you little cutie pie."

Pixie purred her thanks.

"That's an interesting tool," I said.

"It's good for someone my size, because it's not as heavy as a full-length shovel, and it fits easily in my wheelbarrow." She pointed to the three-wheeled green cart to her right. "It's also handier for getting in and under rose branches without damaging them."

"Your roses already look better."

"You were right. Nitrogen." She palm-slapped her forehead, leaving a dusty mark. "And an extra dose of water to get it to the roots. Thanks for the tip."

"Glad I could help." I paused. "Um, did your clients—"

"Chat with the police?" She cut me off. "They did. Officer Reddick took their statements. Even Tish Waterman attested on my behalf." Daphne smiled broadly. "She's a curious woman. I don't usually talk out of school, but she's not very trusting."

"Life has dealt her a few challenges," I said. "I'm glad the police have cleared you."

"Me, too. If not for you . . ." She wedged her shovel into the ground and gave the blade an extra shove with the heel of her boot to anchor it. "Thank you. You can have a free reading any time you like."

"What do you think you're going to do about the farm?"

"I'm hunting for more people like you who want to rent acreage. If that doesn't work out, I'll be in the market for a loan. I'm not willing to give up yet. Something has to gel soon."

"Say, would you look at a photograph? I'd love to get your take on it." I pulled Petunia's phone from my purse and scrolled to the picture taken Thursday night of the front of the general store. "You can see there's a person inside, can't you?"

She took the phone from me and zoomed in on the view. "Yes. Why? Who is it?"

"Not sure."

"It must be Asher or one of his clerks."

"How did you know it was a picture of Lyle's General Store?"

"Asher's taken tons of photos of the shop from all angles. He posts them on Instagram. Scarlet says he prides himself on getting arty photos. He thinks that will entice more clients to drop by." She handed back the phone and tapped the handle of her shovel. "Maybe I should do that. Snap more photos of the farm and do a photo blitz."

"That's a great idea."

"My photos are pretty lame, though. I don't have the eye."

"I could teach you," I said. "My mother was an expert at macrophotography and taught me everything she knew. In fact, I could take some photos for you."

"Would you?"

"It's the least I could do." I didn't add, *for thinking you were a murderer.* I stared at the cell phone as the theory I'd posed to Meaghan last night came to me. "You know, I can't remember Genevieve posting anything negative about Lyle's General Store."

"Let's take a look at her Insta page." She opened her cell phone screen, tapped on the Instagram app icon, and using the magnifying glass device, searched for Genevieve's site. Once there, she swiped repeatedly, not landing on anything. "Nope. Not a one. Why does it matter?"

"I was wondering if they might have had, you know, a fling."

"Genevieve and Asher? Heck, no. He wouldn't step out with anyone. He is truly smitten with his wife." She typed something new into the search bar and turned the camera in my direction. "Here's his page. Like I said, he puts up lots of photos of his store."

"Lots of Scarlet, too."

"Check out this doozy on their anniversary. It's of the two of them holding hands as teens. Ugh. *Hashtag bonded forever.* Who talks like that?"

"Haven't you been in love?" I asked.

"I don't want anyone fawning over me. Ever."

I would bet her aversion to love had something to do with her lashing out at a girl in high school because she thought the girl had seduced her boyfriend. Who needed the drama? I studied the picture of Asher and Scarlet once more, and an idea formed in my mind. *Bonded forever.* Would Asher do whatever it took to protect his wife? To avenge her if someone, say, dissed her online or threatened to expose her?

"Would Asher know where your toolshed is?" I asked.

Daphne flinched. "Huh? Why?"

"Because someone killed Petunia with your hoedag. How many people know about the shed? It's not visible from the street."

"I did a class on transplanting roses a month ago. I taught six students in the backyard. Asher and Scarlet attended."

"They were both there?"

"They're inseparable. They have been ever since Scarlet's mother died." Daphne removed the short shovel from the dirt and started cutting into the earth around the rose she'd been addressing earlier.

"Stop!" I said, not realizing how harsh the word sounded.

"What?" Daphne recoiled, as if expecting a snake.

"That shovel." I pointed to it. "Do you think it might fit into a tennis racket bag?"

She assessed it. "Probably. Why?"

I flashed on something she'd said the other day about Scarlet's mother. What if Asher caused her mother's stroke to free Scarlet from tyranny? What if he killed Genevieve to defend Scarlet against Genevieve's hurtful posts? And what if he murdered Petunia because she could point the finger at him?

I told Daphne what I was thinking and added, "Petunia went back and took another photo of the general store on Saturday. I think she wanted to confirm what she thought she'd seen, that the person on Thursday was touching the tools. She guessed it was Scarlet, and she wrote her a text message. When Scarlet didn't respond, she dialed you, but the call was brief. The police said Petunia said something like, 'Never mind, ask her.'"

"That's right." Daphne's face squinched into a frown. "It's been plaguing me like you can't believe. Why call me if she had someone else, like her sister, to consult?"

I envisioned the items on Petunia's kitchen desk—in addition to gardening books, there was a miniature crystal ball and a book on tarot—and the events of that evening became clear to me. I said, "I know what happened."

"You do?"

"She called you because she was one of your fortune telling clients. She wanted to run her theory past you, hoping you as Madame Flor could divine the truth. However, she blurted out, 'Never mind, ask her,' because by the time she'd figured out that it was Asher inside the store and not Scarlet, Asher had seen the text she'd sent to his wife, stolen the hoedag from your shed, and sneaked into her house to silence her. *Ask her* was actually *Asher.*"

Chapter 26

"Everything you look at can become a fairy tale,
and you can get a story from everything you touch."
—Hans Christian Andersen

I left Daphne, and Pixie and I hurried to Open Your Imagination while fleshing out my theory about Asher. I'd promised my father I would touch base with Detective Summers, but I didn't want to tell him my suspicions unless I was right. I mean, accusing Asher of not only killing two women in the present but one woman in the past—Scarlet's mother—was a big leap. If only Daphne hadn't erased Petunia's message.

Joss was at the shop, turning books right-side up, when I entered. "We had a few eager readers yesterday afternoon," she said. "How are you doing?"

"I'm okay. You?"

She looked beleaguered, like she'd been up all night. Her T-shirt was half tucked into her jeans, which was fashionable for some but not a look she ever sported. "Mom asked for me at nine last night. The nursing staff thought . . ." She rolled the tension out of her neck.

"She wasn't dying. She didn't. She's fine. But she was really discombobulated and talking about death and asking what heaven was like, so I sat up with her until two this morning."

"I'm sorry."

"It's the new norm," she said with a lilt. "Where's Fiona?"

"Minding her sister."

"They seem pretty good together."

"Until they're not," I joked. "Like humans, they have the same older sibling—younger sibling dynamic. 'You're not the boss of me.'" I struck a pose.

Joss laughed. Like me, she was an only child. "Will the way she treats her sister hurt her standing with Aurora?" Joss had never seen the queen fairy, but after I'd caught a glimpse of her at the fairy portal, Joss was eager to get a peek herself.

"I don't think it will. This might even be a test to see if Fiona can rein in her impulsiveness and show her strength as a leader. So far, so good. Deep-breathing exercises have been in order."

I took Pixie to the patio and checked the figurines and gardening supplies. While organizing, an idea came to me. I returned to the main showroom. "Joss, do you think you're good on your own for an hour? I have to . . ." I hesitated. "Pick up a gift for Meaghan's birthday." Her birthday was July eleventh. I couldn't forget the date, because mine was on the eleventh, too, albeit in February.

Joss eyed me skeptically. "You never shop early for her."

"There's something in the general store window I know she would love to have."

"Uh-huh." She wagged a finger. "You're lying. You're doing that thing with your eyes." She blinked rapidly. "Fess up. Why are you really going there?"

I did something with my eyes? Who knew? I'd have to work on my stony-face technique. I told her my suspicion about Asher and my eagerness to peek in the garden tool corral at the general store to see if, on the off chance, he'd slipped a half-length shovel in with the other tools, hoping no one would notice.

"He'd be pretty dumb if he did," she quipped.

"Yes, but hiding things in plain sight is a great way to feign in-nocence." I threw my arms wide. "Gee, officer, I don't have an inkling how that got there."

"You could be onto something. Go." She shooed me out of the shop. "Text me if you need me."

On my route, I messaged Summers that my father had told me to check in with him, and I would after I ran an errand at Lyle's.

The place opened at eight-thirty. I entered, picked up a basket as other shoppers had, and began to tour the labyrinth of rooms. Acting like a customer, I touched kitchen mats and towels in the home goods section and read the labels on jars of jams, virgin olive oil, and sauces in the natural foods space. I checked out the variety of lamps and side tables in the furniture area and inspected the handiwork of an inlaid-tile coffee table, even though it wasn't in my budget.

Next, I ambled into the gardening section, which was easily viewable from the street. There were high-end racks filled with glazed pottery, arrangements of baskets of all sizes, and displays of gardening gloves, trowels, and shears. As seen in Petunia's photo-graph, the garden tool corral held shovels, hoes, rakes, and yes, a hoedag, all premium quality with shiny handles—not something I'd ever splurge on. As Oliver Killian had pointed out, gardening tools got dirty.

Furtively, I searched for a half-length shovel in the mix but came up empty. I sighed. It had been worth a shot. In all probability, if I was right about Asher, that he'd used a small shovel to bash in Genevieve's head, he had disposed of the shovel in the ocean or at a dumpsite.

"Oho, Courtney," a woman said.

I spun around, worried I'd been caught in the act, until I realized it was Zinnia Walker. She was dressed to the nines, as if heading to high tea after her shopping spree. Over her arm, she was carrying a store basket filled with items.

"Checking out the competition?" she asked.

"Looking for a gift," I said, keeping up the ruse.

"Isn't this place something else? A little bit of everything. Don't miss the hardware room. They stock all the items one needs to redo cabinets and such." She nodded to her basket of hinges and knobs. "I come in once a week to browse. It soothes me." She patted my arm and lowered her voice. "Between you and me, the pottery you carry is much better than this."

"Thanks for the compliment."

Zinnia nabbed a pair of blue-handled shears, dropped them into her basket, and continued on to another room.

"Good morning, Courtney." Asher Lyle wandered in, hands clasped behind his back. "What a delight to see you in my fine establishment." Sunlight filtering through the windows highlighted his thick dark hair. His white muslin shirt fit him perfectly. I could see why Scarlet was drawn to him. He had an ease about him that was enticing. "See anything that interests you?" The gleam in his eyes, however, unnerved me. Pixie often gave me the same curious look when she was ready to pounce.

"I'm searching for a present for a girlfriend."

"Is she a gardener?"

"Occasionally. She likes to add ornaments to her garden, like orbs and metallic flowers." I shuffled to the elegant display of wind chimes. The ones we sold at Open Your Imagination were dainty and fairy-themed. These were large, like those you'd find in a Japanese meditation garden. Some were patinated bronze with three-foot-long tubes. Others were silver with tubes nearly five feet long.

"Those you're admiring," Asher said, "have a relaxing, deep sound with a three-quarter-inch, high-density, polyethylene clapper. It simply requires a gentle breeze to hear its melodic tune."

I read the ticket price—four hundred plus dollars—and decided that I loved Meaghan a lot, but the chimes were too expensive. "I think I'll explore the dining room items. She might enjoy a pair of candlesticks."

"Let me know if you need any assistance." Before moving on, he added, "For your information, I didn't appreciate you talking to the police about my wife."

Something snagged at the pit of my stomach. I forced a smile. "I'm sorry. Detective Summers can be quite persuasive."

He tilted his head in a calculated way, like a bird examining a worm. "You should have come to Scarlet first. She's your friend. You could have asked her about the shovel and whether she'd sold it."

"You're right. It was an error on my part."

"*Mm-hmm.*" He left me to greet a customer who was entering the room but glanced over his shoulder at me as he did.

A shiver shimmied down my spine. I was right about him. How could I prove it?

The dining room area was festive, with a bountiful table set with scrolled silverware, white china rimmed in gold, Baccarat crystal flutes, gold napkins, party crackers and party hats, and white porcelain candlesticks fitted with gold candles. Shelves around the perimeter of the room held duplicates of the items displayed on the table. I found the candlesticks and placed a pair in my basket. For fun, I added a package of party crackers, deciding I'd throw a party for Meaghan in my backyard, and we'd make a little noise. She enjoyed raucous celebrations.

Intent on following through with my promise to visit the precinct—with or without hard evidence—I proceeded to the sales counter. Zinnia was standing in line with her basket. The salesclerk, an elderly woman with a cherub face, was tending to the customer in front of Zinnia.

"Hello again," I said to Zinnia.

"What pretty candlesticks," she said. "Your friend will love those."

Something caught my attention to the right, and the hair at the nape of my neck tingled.

Chapter 27

The little sunshine fairies
Are out on sunny days.
They gaily go a-dancing
Along the country ways.
—Laura Ingalls Wilder, "The Fairies in the Sunshine"

The door to the store's office was ajar, and inside the room, on the floor beside the oak executive desk, sat Asher's red-and-black Head tennis bag. Might he have hidden the shovel in it? To keep as a memento? If I could slip in, take a peek, and confirm my suspicions, wouldn't that help the police?

I searched for Asher but didn't see him in the vicinity. Fibbing, knowing my cell phone was safely hidden in my purse, I said to the saleswoman, "Oh, my, I just realized I don't have my mobile, and I have to check in on my father. He's ill. Could I use the phone in the office?"

The clerk deliberated.

"It'll only take a sec. I'm sure Asher would say it's okay." I used his first name to show he and I were familiar.

"All right. But hurry back."

"You can use mine," Zinnia offered.

"That's okay. I'll go in there. More privacy. You understand."

I did one more scan for Asher, and not seeing him, sneaked into the gigantic office. The door hinges creaked, and I flinched. Why hadn't Asher been more diligent about using WD-40? This was a general store, for heaven's sake. I eased the door closed, although leaving it slightly ajar, and hastily rested my basket on a ladderback chair by the door. It teetered. I righted it, letting out a sigh of relief that it hadn't crashed to the floor.

I strode the ten paces to the desk. It held a tulip-adorned Tiffany lamp, an in-and-out box, a gold pen-and-pencil set, and was so cluttered with invoices and file folders it would take a week to organize them all. I crouched to unzip the tennis bag.

At the same time, Fiona flew into the room, startling me. I bumped my head on the underside of the desk and bit back an outburst.

"What're you doing?" she asked. "Did I scare you?"

"You almost gave me a heart attack," I whispered. "Why are you here?" Remaining crouched, I peered beyond the inch of open doorway toward the sales counter. I didn't see anyone looking in our direction.

"Joss sent me to find you. She's worried. You aren't answering your cell phone."

"It's in my purse."

"Didn't you feel it vibrate?"

"No, and I don't have time to explain." Nimbly, I opened the main zipper of the tennis bag.

Fiona peeked over my shoulder. "What's in there?"

"I don't know yet. Back off."

"Don't be testy. I've had enough attitude for the morning."

That didn't sound good, like perhaps she and her sister had another quarrel, but I couldn't focus on that.

I separated the sides of the bag and could see instantly that there wasn't a half-length shovel inside. In fact, as Asher had claimed, there were three rackets. I was about to zip the bag up when I spied something glinting at the foot of the bag, beneath the racket heads. I removed the Wilson Ultra racket to get a better look and gasped. It was a purse, but not just any purse. It was the stylish Michael Kors handbag with the signature *MK* ornament that Genevieve had been carrying the last time I'd seen her.

Blurt-beep-beep-beep! The building's fire alarm resounded. Fiona covered her ears.

"Everybody out! Leave in an orderly fashion!" Asher shouted.

In a matter of seconds, I heard the salesclerk repeating the command and Zinnia and other customers saying they didn't smell smoke as they stampeded to the exit.

Then the door to the office *creaked*.

Fiona yelled, "Courtney, look out!"

I pivoted on my heels. Asher closed the office door and strode toward me. Shoot! He must have seen or heard me slipping into the office after all and triggered the fire alarm. I screamed but was certain I couldn't be heard over the screeching noise.

Wilson Ultra in hand, I popped to my feet, ready to swing. All I had to do was stall Asher until firemen or the police arrived. How long could that take? The general store was two doors down from the precinct, and the fire department was around the corner.

Asher didn't flinch. He kept coming at me. "You couldn't help yourself, could you?" He batted the racket with his hand.

I recovered quickly, scuttled backward, and repositioned the racket in front of me, gripping the handle firmly. I'd never been an ace tennis player, but I'd learned enough to hold my own. "You and your friend who donates his time in Guatemala didn't play tennis last Thursday night. You couldn't have, because he was on a plane."

Asher growled and groped for the racket's rim.

I dodged left and made a backhand stroke. *Whoosh!* I missed him. "You made sure people saw you with your tennis bag, though. In particular, Oliver Killian. You also made certain people observed you Saturday night, so you could claim you were at your shop doing inventory. Beating the carpet outdoors was a clever touch."

"I thought so." He tried to disarm me again.

I cut right and swung forehand. *Whoosh!* "Why did you tape the note to my door? Why risk being discovered?"

"I didn't stick a note on your door."

He didn't? Who had?

He charged me. I raised the racket overhead and swung downward, connecting with his shoulder. He stumbled and gripped the edge of the desk for balance.

"Scarlet warned me about you," he snarled.

"Does she know what you've done?"

"No. She's naïve. Trusting. But she said you wouldn't let this case go. You're persistent."

"Does she have an inkling you killed her mother?"

He arched an eyebrow. "So you figured that out, did you? Smart girl."

I glimpsed Fiona hovering over the basket I'd brought into the room. She looked like she was doing a jig. Now was certainly not the time, I thought, until I remembered her doing a similar dance on Sunday morning to awaken Petunia's phone. What was she up to?

Asher said, "For your edification, Scarlet's mother's stroke was ruled natural causes."

"Poor Scarlet," I said, swiping the air backhanded, even though he was nowhere near me. "She thinks the world of you."

"And I of her. We're a team. Bonded forever."

Hashtag, ugh!

"You've always defended her," I said.

"Yes."

"That's why, when you viewed Genevieve's dismissive post about her, you knew you had to do something. You had to avenge her name. You couldn't let her suffer any longer."

"They were friends." His handsome face turned ugly. "How could Genevieve be so nasty?"

"Scarlet told me she didn't mind."

"But she did. It crushed her. She cried and cried."

Leaving murder as his only option.

I peeked at Fiona, still hopping. I heard a crinkling beneath her feet and realized she was trying to open the party crackers. Even if Asher couldn't see her, he might be able to detect *something* suspiciously removing plastic wrapping, so I edged in that direction, placing myself between the basket and him.

"How did you locate Genevieve that night?" I asked. "Did you text her as Scarlet? Did you ask her to meet?"

"I didn't have to text her. That woman was so full of herself, thinking everything she said and did was worthy of being published. She was doing live posts, trying to elicit sympathy. She was so upset that she hadn't been invited to participate in the festival. Poor baby." He clucked his tongue maliciously. "Everywhere she went, she lodged another complaint. I knew all I had to do was follow her, like a Pokémon GO game. So I came to the shop—"

"And hid the half-length shovel in your tennis bag."

"Ha! You figured that out, too? I'm impressed. You're as good at this investigation thing as everyone says you are." His eyes gleamed as he skirted his desk to the left.

"And you stole Genevieve's phone so you could delete all of the Thursday posts to stymie the police."

"Correct."

"Where did you dispose of the shovel?" I asked.

"We're done." He yanked open the rightmost drawer, withdrew a Beretta, the same gun my father preferred, and aimed it at me.

I recoiled. In my teens, Dad had taught me how to shoot, but I'd never faced the barrel of a gun before. "Tell me what happened that night," I said. "You owe me that."

"I found Genevieve sneaking around the festival tents," he said. "Like she was on a mission. At the end of Section F, I heard her talking. She wasn't with anyone. She was informing her audience that she was going to take pictures of Scarlet's booth. She was uttering horrible things about her, saying Scarlet was all fluff and no substance." He slammed a hand on the desk. Papers wafted into the air and settled down. "Nobody disses my wife like that."

"Genevieve was wrong to do that," I said in a soothing tone. "She had no right."

"Darned straight she had no right. She was vile. She deserved what she got. And now you will, too, for sticking your nose in where it doesn't belong, and for not defending my wife."

Your beautiful wife.

"Move." He wagged the Beretta. "Get in the crate."

I glanced over my shoulder. Next to a stand of file cabinets was a royal blue trunk with brass edging and padlock. Did he plan to suffocate me? "Asher, I texted Detective Summers that I was on my way here. He knows where I am."

"He won't find you before you bleed out."

I winced. He did intend to shoot me. And he'd get away with it. The shot wouldn't be heard over the fire alarm.

"How can I be so certain?" he went on. "Remember when I told you how long it took the police to show up when we were burgled? Well, a year ago, a fire broke out, and the fire department took an hour and a half to arrive. There you have it, ladies and gentlemen. Our tax dollars going to waste. Luckily, most of the sprinklers worked as they were supposed to." He stepped toward me.

I fanned the air with the Wilson Ultra.

He snickered. "Need I remind you that a bullet can go through the face of a tennis racket?"

I swung again, slamming the racket into the Tiffany lamp on the desk. The lampshade shattered.

Asher cursed. "You witch! That cost a fortune."

"Gee, sorry," I said. *Not.* I brandished the racket again, this time kicking up the invoices and folders. Paper billowed everywhere.

He fired the gun. The bullet went wide. I shrieked.

At the same time, something went *pop. Pop-pop-pop.* Fiona had unwrapped the party crackers and was bursting them one by one. Not with her feet but with some kind of magical command. She was

making broad strokes with her arms, like she was conducting an or-
chestra. *Hoo-boy.* I hoped the queen fairy wouldn't be mad at her.
After all, Fiona was supposed to help humans solve problems.

At the moment, I didn't care, because the sound had distracted
Asher, giving me the chance to land a blow on his arm. He yowled.
The gun went flying.

I fetched it off the floor, rounded the desk, and broke the window. I yelled out, "Help!"

Seconds later, the office door whipped open.

I'd never been so happy to see Detective Summers in my life.

Chapter 28

Adieu, adieu—I fly, adieu,
I vanish in the heaven's blue—
Adieu, adieu!
—John Keats, "Fairy Song"

On Saturday, we closed the shop and threw a party on the patio, celebrating being alive. Brady showed up with trays filled with pot stickers, empanadas, and mini spinach quiches. Yoly and Yvanna provided desserts, including my new favorite, Sweet Treats' chocolate mousse pie.

Merryweather Rose of Song, Cedric, Zephyr, and Callie were flitting around the fountain. On the learning-the-craft table, Fiona and Eveleen were entertaining Ulra, who had finally found the courage to join us. They were teaching her a fairy dance. She kept eyeing Brady. I'd bet she was hoping he would acknowledge her. After all, Hideaway Café never wanted for customers. Did her sweet spirit, and not purely Brady's incredible menu, have something to do with that?

Joss approached me with a tray of beverages. I took a flute of champagne and sipped.

"Ambrosia," I said. "It'll go perfectly with the pot stickers Brady brought, followed by a slice of pie when I can entice Yvanna to swing my way."

My father and Wanda were sitting at one of the tables. Wanda was pointing into the air. I was pretty sure she was telling him about the fairies, even though she couldn't see them. Dad kept looking around and shaking his head.

Renee and Hedda circled the patio, both enchanted with the paranormal activity. They reminded me of children at a magic show, eyes wide with delight. Dylan Summers and Jeremy Batcheller, who trailed them, looked as skeptical as my father.

Twyla had offered to play her flute at the event. Her mother and Bentley—yes, Twyla had agreed to go on another date with him—were sitting at a table at the far end of the patio, listening in.

Daphne Flores was sitting at a table with Peony Fujimoto. The two were showing each other pictures on their phones. With the resolution of Petunia's murder, Peony had convinced the owner of the winery she worked for to partner with Daphne. He'd needed more land to grow grapes. Her farm would remain a viable operation.

"Hey, girlfriend." Meaghan sidled to me and bumped me with her hip. She'd dressed like she was prepared to disappear into the fairy realm in a wispy silk top over sparkly leggings.

"Some outfit," I said. "Not your typical attire."

"Callie advised me."

I studied her sweet fairy, who was twirling beneath Cedric's arm. "Since when did she become a fashion guru? I mean, she's always in green."

Meaghan tittered and excused herself when she spotted Redcliff "Red" Reddick loping through the French doors. They kissed fondly, and my insides went gooey with happiness for her.

Brady wandered to me, carrying a small plate of appetizers and a glass of wine. He tapped the rim of his glass against mine. I selected a cheese empanada from the plate and popped it into my mouth.

"I love you," I murmured.

"For feeding you?"

"No. I truly love you."

He smiled. "I love you, too, and I want to spend the rest of my life with you."

I gulped. That wasn't a proposal, was it? I adored him, but I wasn't ready to—

"You did it again," he cut in.

"Did what?" Had I said aloud what I was thinking?

"Solved a case."

I guffawed. "I didn't solve anything. I guessed."

"You're too modest." He sipped his wine. "I heard Asher has secured one of the best lawyers in California for his defense."

"Poor Scarlet. She was devastated when she learned the truth. She had no idea he'd killed her mother."

"Is it true he also killed her best friend in college?"

"Yes."

Summers would have his hands full, reviewing every suspicious death over the past ten-plus years.

"How he got away with so many murders is beyond me," Brady said.

I took a sip of champagne. "I heard Scarlet, thanks to Daphne, has found a highly specialized psychiatric treatment center where she can regroup." Daphne had stepped up to help Scarlet the moment the murders were solved. "By the way, Scarlet was the one who taped the note on my door. She thought I was bearing down on her."

"Mystery solved. Good." He smiled. "Say, I heard Oliver Killian has made amends with his wife. After he revealed his alibi to you, he found the courage to call her."

I smiled. "Aren't you in the know."

"They came to the café last night for dinner and looked as blissful as newlyweds."

"I'm happy for them."

Holly, Hattie, and Zinnia traipsed to the patio. Tamara Geoffries was with them.

Hattie said, "Look who we recruited to the Happy Diggers!"

All of the women were sporting lavender HAPPY DIGGER T-shirts featuring potted flowers on the front and the logo on the back. Each was holding a glass of wine.

Fiona, Eveleen, and Ulra flew to greet them.

Tamara sipped her wine and leaned into Holly. She whispered something, and Holly bobbed her head. An amused grin spread across Tamara's face, and she said directly to the fairies, "Well, hello there."

"Attention, everyone!" Fiona cried.

The other fairies gathered round her. The chatter on the patio softened. The humans who could hear her were listening with bated breath.

"My sister Eveleen has completed her training. She is ready to return to the fairy realm." Fiona's voice snagged as she clasped her sister's hands, their wings flapping in the same rhythm. "I will miss you, Sis, but I trust you will go back with a newfound understanding of humans and why our kind are here."

"To help them blossom and find hope," Eveleen chimed.

"Exactly!"

Eveleen pecked Fiona on the cheek. "I know I gave you a hard time, but I love you, and I will miss you." She released Fiona and spiraled into the air, and suddenly, a circular glow appeared in the ficus as it had the day she arrived.

Joy coursed through me. She didn't have to seek a portal. She took one step inside, glanced over her shoulder at the fairies, waved goodbye, and disappeared.

Fiona winged to me and perched on my shoulder. Tears were trickling down her face.

I whispered, "You'll see her soon."

"I'm not crying for her. I'm crying for me. I was hoping Mother would show up to escort her and . . ."

"And would tell you *job well done*?"

She pressed her lips together.

"Well, my sweet fairy," I said, beaming with pride, "job well done! As an older sister and future queen, you rock!"

RECIPES

Apple Strudel Muffins + Gluten-free Version
Banana Blueberry Scones + Gluten-free Version
Cacao Nib Brownies + Gluten-free Version
Chocolate Mousse Pie
Gingersnap Brownies
Lemon-Raspberry Delights + Gluten-free Version
Monte Cristo Sandwich
Prosciutto-and-Cheddar Drop Scones + Gluten-free Version
Raisin-Rosemary Muffins + Gluten-free Version

From Courtney:

My mother used to make apple strudel muffins before we would take a romp in the fields. She thought something sweet might entice fairies to play with us. There are so many memories I have of her, but baking alongside her and drinking in the aromas are the memories that linger with me. Enjoy these muffins. I hope they stir good memories of your loved ones.

Apple Strudel Muffins

(Yield: 14–18)

Topping:
¼ cup flour
3 tablespoons sugar
2 tablespoons butter, softened
¼ teaspoon ground cinnamon
½ cup chopped walnuts, if desired

Batter:
1½ cups flour
½ cup sugar
2 teaspoons baking powder
1 teaspoon ground cinnamon
½ teaspoon ground allspice
¼ teaspoon baking soda
¼ teaspoon salt
2 large eggs
1 cup sour cream
¼ cup butter, melted (½ stick)
1 cup peeled, diced tart green apple (about 1 apple)

Heat oven to 375 degrees F. Line two muffin tins with 14–18 muffin cups and spray with non-stick spray.

For the topping, in a medium bowl, using a fork, mix the flour, sugar, softened butter, and cinnamon. They should form a fine crumble. If desired, stir in chopped nuts. Set aside.

For the batter, in a large bowl, mix the flour, sugar, baking powder, cinnamon, allspice, baking soda, and salt.

In another bowl, whisk the eggs. Then add the sour cream and melted butter, and whisk again until blended. Stir in the peeled, diced apple. Pour the egg mixture over the flour mixture and stir until just moist.

Using a cupcake scoop or ladle, fill muffin cups ⅔ full. Top each muffin with 2 teaspoons of the strudel topping.

Bake the muffins for 20–25 minutes or until a toothpick inserted in the center comes out clean. Remove from oven and cool at least 20 minutes before serving.

Apple Strudel Muffins

Gluten-free Version

(Yield: 14–18)

Topping:
¼ cup gluten-free flour
3 tablespoons sugar
2 tablespoons butter, softened
¼ teaspoon ground cinnamon
½ cup chopped walnuts, if desired

Batter:
1½ cups gluten-free flour
¼ teaspoon xanthan gum
1 tablespoon whey powder
½ cup sugar
2 teaspoons baking powder
1 teaspoon ground cinnamon
½ teaspoon ground allspice
¼ teaspoon baking soda
¼ teaspoon salt
2 large eggs
1 cup sour cream
¼ cup butter, melted (½ stick)
1 cup peeled, diced tart green apple (about 1 apple)

Heat oven to 375 degrees F. Line two muffin tins with 14–18 muffin cups and spray with non-stick spray

For the topping, in a medium bowl, using a fork, mix the gluten-free flour, sugar, softened butter, and cinnamon. They should form a fine crumble. If desired, stir in chopped nuts. Set aside.

For the batter, in a large bowl, mix the gluten-free flour, xanthan gum, whey powder, sugar, baking powder, cinnamon, allspice, baking soda, and salt.

In another bowl, whisk the eggs. Then add the sour cream and melted butter, and whisk again until blended. Stir in the peeled, diced apple. Pour the egg mixture over the flour mixture and stir until just moist.

Using a cupcake scoop or ladle, fill muffin cups ⅔ full. Top each muffin with 2 teaspoons of the strudel topping.

Bake the muffins for 20–25 minutes or until a toothpick inserted in the center comes out clean. Remove from oven and cool at least 20 minutes before serving.

From Yvanna:

I love scones. They are best if eaten the day they are baked, but these will keep well if you wrap them securely in plastic wrap and freeze in an airtight container. The banana and cinnamon in the recipe give a warmth to the flavor that I adore.

Banana Blueberry Scones

(Yield: 8)

2¼ cups flour, sifted
¼ cup sugar
1 teaspoon baking powder
½ teaspoon baking soda
¼ teaspoon salt
½ teaspoon cinnamon
¼ cup butter, cold and cut into small bits
½ cup sour cream
⅓ cup mashed banana
1 cup blueberries
Confectioner's sugar drizzle, if desired

　　*The confectioner's drizzle recipe follows the gluten-free version of the scones, below.

Preheat the oven to 350 degrees F. Line a baking sheet with parchment paper.

In a food processor, mix sifted flour, sugar, baking powder, baking soda, salt, and cinnamon.

Add the bits of butter into the flour mixture and pulse for about 10–15 seconds until the mixture resembles coarse crumbs.

Add the sour cream and mashed bananas to the mixture and pulse for 10–15 seconds. This will be a very dry batter.

Gently fold in the blueberries.

Turn the dough onto a lightly floured surface and form the dough into a 6-inch circle. With a serrated knife, cut the circle into 8 wedges. You might need to wet the knife. Transfer the triangles to the parchment paper.

Bake the scones in the preheated oven for 20–25 minutes or until the edges of the scones are lightly browned. Remove from the oven and cool on a cooling rack.

May be drizzled with confectioner's sugar drizzle when scones are cool.

Baker's notes: Make sure butter is COLD.

Banana Blueberry Scones

Gluten-free Version

(Yield: 8)

2¼ cups gluten-free flour
2 tablespoons whey powder
½ teaspoon xanthan gum
¼ cup sugar
1 teaspoon baking powder
½ teaspoon baking soda
¼ teaspoon salt
½ teaspoon cinnamon
¼ cup butter, cold and cut into small bits
½ cup sour cream
⅓ cup mashed banana
1 cup blueberries
Confectioner's sugar drizzle, if desired

⋆The confectioner's drizzle recipe follows this version of the recipe, below.

Preheat the oven to 350 degrees F. Line a baking sheet with parchment paper.

In a food processor, mix gluten-free flour, whey powder, xanthan gum, sugar, baking powder, baking soda, salt, and cinnamon.

Add the bits of butter into the flour mixture and pulse for about 10–15 seconds until the mixture resembles coarse crumbs.

Add the sour cream and mashed bananas to the mixture, and pulse for 10-15 seconds.

Gently fold in the blueberries.

Turn the dough onto a surface lightly floured with gluten-free flour, and form the dough into a 6-inch circle. With a serrated knife, cut the circle into 8 wedges. You might need to wet the knife. Transfer the triangles to the parchment paper.

Bake the scones in the preheated oven for 20–25 minutes or until the edges of the scones are lightly browned. Remove from the oven and cool on a cooling rack.

May be drizzled with confectioner's sugar drizzle when scones are cool.

Confectioner's Sugar Drizzle

(Yield: 2 cups)

2 cups powdered sugar
2 tablespoons margarine or butter, softened
1 teaspoon vanilla
3–4 tablespoons half-and-half, more if necessary

In medium bowl, combine all ingredients, mixing until smooth, adding enough half-and-half for the right consistency.

From Meaghan:

I love brownies, and I adore coming up with new recipes. This one is so chocolate-y, it's amazing. The cacao nibs, which are good for your health, add a tasty little crunch. It's like having nuts without having nuts, you know? Enjoy.

Cacao Nib Brownies

(Yield: 9–12 portions)

2½ sticks butter
1½ cups sugar
½ cup plus 2 tablespoons natural cocoa powder
3 large eggs
1½ teaspoons vanilla extract
1⅓ cups flour
¼ teaspoon salt
⅛ teaspoon baking soda
2 tablespoons cacao nibs
4 tablespoons dark chocolate chips

Preheat oven at 350 degrees F. Line a 9-inch square baking pan with parchment paper.

In a medium-sized saucepan, melt the butter and sugar over low heat.

Add the cocoa powder and remove from the burner. Mix well and let cool. When cool, about 5–7 minutes, add the eggs. [I usually clean up the kitchen during this cooling period.]

Add vanilla to the chocolate mixture and stir well.

In a small bowl, combine flour, salt, and soda. Add the flour mixture to the chocolate mixture. Mix well. Stir in the cacao nibs and dark chocolate chips.

Pour the mixture into the prepared baking pan and bake for 40–45 minutes or until a toothpick comes out clean but slightly wet.

Let cool on a rack for 20 minutes before you even think about cutting. Brownies do not cut well when warm.

Cacao Nib Brownies

Gluten-free Version

(Yield: 9–12 portions)

2½ sticks butter
1½ cups sugar
½ cup plus 2 tablespoons natural cocoa powder
3 large eggs
1½ teaspoons vanilla extract
1⅓ cups gluten-free flour
¼ teaspoon salt
⅛ teaspoon baking soda
¼ teaspoon xanthan gum
2 tablespoons cacao nibs
4 tablespoons dark chocolate chips

Preheat oven at 350 degrees F. Line a 9-inch square baking pan with parchment paper.

In a medium-sized saucepan, melt the butter and sugar over low heat.

Add the cocoa powder and remove from the burner. Mix well and let cool. When cool, about 5–7 minutes, add the eggs. [I usually clean up the kitchen during this cooling period.]

Add vanilla to the chocolate mixture and stir well.

In a small bowl, combine gluten-free flour, salt, soda, and xanthan gum. Add the gluten-free flour mixture to the chocolate mixture. Mix well. Stir in the cacao nibs and dark chocolate chips.

Pour the mixture into the prepared baking pan and bake for 40–45 minutes or until a toothpick comes out clean but slightly wet.

Let cool on a rack for 20 minutes before you even think about cutting. Brownies do not cut well when warm.

From Brady:

This pie is so easy to make, even a novice baker should have no problem doing so. It's now a favorite at Sweet Treats, and I cajoled the recipe out of Yvanna. Adding coffee or espresso to a recipe can really enhance the chocolate flavor. It deepens its intensity. Enjoy the smooth, creamy texture. Note: you can find store-bought gluten-free chocolate wafers, so that's an easy substitution.

Chocolate Mousse Pie

(Yield: 6 slices)

One 4-ounce package chocolate wafers, broken into pieces (*they
    do make these gluten-free)
3 tablespoons unsalted butter, melted
4 ounces bittersweet or semisweet chocolate, chopped
¼ cup strong brewed coffee or espresso
¾ cup heavy whipping cream
½ teaspoon vanilla extract
2 tablespoons sugar
Pinch of salt

Preheat the oven to 350 degrees F.

Butter a 6-inch springform pan. Pulse the chocolate wafers in a food processor until finely ground. Add the butter and pulse 3–4 times. Press the mixture into the bottom and up the sides of the prepared pan. Bake the crust for 5 minutes and remove from the oven and let cool.

In the top of a double boiler set over about 2 inches of simmering water, melt the chopped chocolate and the coffee. Remove the mixture from the heat and let cool for 5 minutes.

In a medium mixing bowl, whip the cream, vanilla, sugar, and salt with an electric mixer on medium-high until the cream holds stiff peaks. With a spatula, fold the chocolate mixture into the cream, in 3 batches, until nicely blended. Transfer the mixture to the crust and smooth the top.

Cover and refrigerate for 3 hours and up to 1 day. To serve, remove the sides of the springform pan and cut the mousse into wedges.

*For a 9-inch springform pan, double the ingredients and prepare as above.

From Meaghan:

Well, I've said it before and I'll say it again—I love brownies. This is an easy-peasy recipe using boxed brownie mix and lots of other goodies. If they're too spicy for you, cut back on the cloves and ginger. I have also made this recipe using a gluten-free brownie mix, and they turned out the same. There's something about brownies, maybe because they don't need to rise like a cake, that makes it easy to swap out a regular brownie mix with a gluten-free mix.

Gingersnap Brownies

(Yield: 9–16)

1 package brownie mix (*may use gluten-free)
2 tablespoons unsweetened cocoa powder
1 tablespoon brown sugar
1 tablespoon confectioners' sugar
2 teaspoons ground cinnamon
½ teaspoon ground cloves
½ teaspoon ground nutmeg
1 teaspoon ground ginger
⅓ cup unsalted butter, melted (5⅓ tablespoons)
2 tablespoons brewed espresso coffee
2 tablespoons sour cream
2 tablespoons vanilla extract
1 egg
1 cup dark chocolate chips

Preheat oven to 350 degrees F. Grease a 9-inch pan and line with parchment paper. Set aside.

In a large bowl, mix the brownie mix, cocoa powder, brown sugar, confectioners' sugar, cinnamon, cloves, nutmeg, and ginger.

In another bowl, stir the melted butter and espresso. [You can use strong regular coffee and/or decaffeinated coffee.] Cool for 5 minutes. Stir in sour cream, vanilla extract, and egg. Add the butter mixture to the brownie mix batter. Stir until the batter is smooth. Fold in the chocolate chips and stir again to incorporate.

Pour the batter—it is gooey—into the prepared pan. Bake for 25–30 minutes, until the edges start to pull away from the sides. Do not overbake. A toothpick inserted in the center should come out clean but slightly damp.

Cool brownies at least 20 minutes before cutting.

From Yvanna:

These spread. They're sticky. And if you have to bake in shifts, the second shift might be "redder" because the frozen raspberries will have melted. No matter what, you will really enjoy them. The marriage of lemon and raspberry is sublime. PS they freeze well! Like an icebox cookie.

Lemon Raspberry Delights

(Yield: 24–30)

½ cup butter
1 cup sugar
½ teaspoon vanilla extract
1 large egg
¼ teaspoon salt
Zest of 1 lemon, about 1 tablespoon
Juice of 1 lemon, about 2 tablespoons
1½ cups flour
¼ teaspoon baking powder
¼ teaspoon baking soda
1½ cups raspberries, frozen and crushed

Preheat oven to 350 degrees F. Line two cookie sheets with parchment paper.

In a standing mixer, cream together the butter and sugar on medium for two minutes. Add the vanilla extract, egg, salt, lemon zest, and lemon juice. Mix well. Add in flour, baking powder, and baking soda. Mix on low until just combined.

Add in the frozen crushed raspberries and stir gently. Don't overmix. I like to put the raspberries in a baggie and crush with a mallet. No mess.

Using a spoon, drop the dough onto the prepared cookie sheets, about 1 tablespoon per cookie. The dough is quite moist, so if you have a cookie scooper, use that.

Bake for approximately 15–17 minutes until they are just brown around the edges.

Remove from oven and cool on the cookie sheet for about 5 minutes. Transfer to a cooling rack to cool completely.

Lemon Raspberry Delights

Gluten-free Version

(Yield: 24–30)

½ cup butter
1 cup sugar
½ teaspoon vanilla extract
1 large egg
¼ teaspoon salt
Zest of 1 lemon, about 1 tablespoon
Juice of 1 lemon, about 2 tablespoons
1½ cups gluten-free flour *I like a blend of sweet rice flour and tapi-
   oca starch
¼ teaspoon baking powder
¼ teaspoon baking soda
⅛ teaspoon xanthan gum
1½ cups raspberries, frozen and crushed

Preheat oven to 350 degrees F. Line two cookie sheets with parchment paper.

In a standing mixer, cream together the butter and sugar on medium for two minutes. Add the vanilla extract, egg, salt, lemon zest, and lemon juice. Mix well. Add in gluten-free flour, baking powder, baking soda, and xanthan gum. Mix on low until just combined.

Add in the frozen crushed raspberries and stir gently. Don't over-mix. I like to put the raspberries in a baggie and crush with a mallet. No mess.

Using a spoon, drop the dough onto the prepared cookie sheets, about 1 tablespoon per cookie. The dough is quite moist, so if you have a cookie scooper, use that.

Bake for approximately 15–17 minutes until they are just brown around the edges.

Remove from oven and cool on the cookie sheet for about 5 minutes. Transfer to a cooling rack to cool completely.

From Brady:

This is one of my favorite sandwiches. It's good for breakfast, brunch, lunch, or dinner, and packed with flavor. The trick is to make sure your meats are thinly sliced and that you layer the sandwich so all the flavors meld. I like to serve it with a side of something sweet. That could be jam, syrup, or even cranberry sauce.

Monte Cristo Sandwich

(Yield: 1 sandwich)

For the sandwich:
2 slices thick Challah or egg bread *use gluten-free bread, if necessary*
1 teaspoon cream cheese
1 teaspoon spicy mustard
3 slices cooked ham, thinly sliced
3 slices cooked turkey, thinly sliced
2 slices Swiss cheese

For the batter:
1 egg
½ cup milk
½ cup flour *use gluten-free flour, if necessary*
1 teaspoon baking powder
Pinch of salt

Jam, syrup, or cranberry sauce, if desired

The batter is probably enough for 2–3 sandwiches

Spread cream cheese on one side of one slice of bread. Spread mustard on the other slice of bread and top with alternate slices of

ham, turkey, and Swiss cheese . . . ham, turkey, Swiss . . . ham, turkey. Top sandwich with the other slice of bread, cream cheese side
down.

Beat egg, milk, flour (or gluten-free flour) in a pie tin until well
combined.

Lightly oil a small skillet over medium heat.

Dip sandwich into egg mixture to coat on both sides. Set the
sandwich in the hot skillet and cook until golden brown on both
sides and cheese is melted, approximately 4–5 minutes on each side.
Serve hot.

From Brady:

These prosciutto-and-cheddar drop scones are packed with flavor. Wait until you taste the flaky interior! You can freeze them before baking. You can also make the batter the night before and save to bake for an early morning breakfast. I like to make them as "drop" scones so they don't get too much flour on them by rolling them out. You can use a ¼ cup scooper to form them. Enjoy.

Prosciutto-and-Cheddar Drop Scones

(Yield: 12 scones)

½ cup unsalted butter, frozen
2 cups flour
1 tablespoon sugar
2½ teaspoons baking powder
¾ teaspoon garlic powder
½ teaspoon salt
½ teaspoon ground black pepper
4 tablespoons chopped chives
1 cup shredded sharp cheddar cheese
⅔ cup buttermilk, plus 1 tablespoon for topping
1 large egg, separated (egg white for topping)
3–4 ounces chopped prosciutto

Freeze the stick of butter for at least ten minutes.

In a countertop food processor, whisk flour, sugar, baking powder, garlic powder, salt, and pepper. Add in the chives and shredded cheese.

Grate the frozen butter or shave very thinly—when frozen, it will shave nicely—and add to the flour mixture. Pulse until the mixture looks like cornmeal. Place the container in the refrigerator—you want to keep the butter cold—while you mix the wet ingredients.

In a small bowl, whisk the buttermilk and egg yolk. Save the egg white for the topping. Remove flour mixture from refrigerator and add buttermilk mixture. Add the chopped prosciutto and mix until the dough comes together.

Now preheat oven to 400 degrees F.

To make drop scones, form about ¼ cup dough into patties, about ¾" thick. Set them on a baking sheet.

In a small bowl, mix the 1 tablespoon buttermilk with the reserved egg white. Brush the mixture onto the scones.

Bake the scones for 22–25 minutes or until golden brown. Remove from oven and cool about 5 minutes before serving.

Baker's Note: *Leftover scones keep well at room temp for a couple of days and in the refrigerator for up to 5 days. You may freeze them, wrapped individually, before baking. You may also freeze baked goods and then wrap in foil to reheat at 200 degrees F for about 15 minutes.*

Prosciutto-and-Cheddar Drop Scones

Gluten-free Version

(Yield: 12 drop scones)

½ cup unsalted butter, frozen
2 cups gluten-free flour, less 2 tablespoons
2 tablespoons whey powder
½ teaspoon xanthan gum
1 teaspoon psyllium husk, if you have it
1 tablespoon sugar
2½ teaspoons baking powder
¾ teaspoon garlic powder
½ teaspoon salt
½ teaspoon ground black pepper
4 tablespoons chopped chives
1 cup shredded sharp cheddar cheese
⅔ cup buttermilk, plus 1 tablespoon for topping
1 large egg, separated (egg white for topping)
3–4 ounces chopped prosciutto

Freeze the stick of butter for at least ten minutes.

In a countertop food processor, whisk gluten-free flour, whey powder, xanthan gum, psyllium husk, if you have it (*the husk helps with texture), sugar, baking powder, garlic powder, salt, and pepper. Add in the chives and shredded cheese.

Grate the frozen butter or shave very thinly—when frozen, it will shave nicely—and add to the gluten-free flour mixture. Pulse until the mixture looks like cornmeal. Place the container in the refrigerator—you want to keep the butter cold—while you mix the wet ingredients.

In a small bowl, whisk the buttermilk and egg yolk. Save the egg white for the topping. Remove flour mixture from refrigerator and add buttermilk mixture. Add the chopped prosciutto and mix until the dough comes together.

Now preheat oven to 400 degrees F.

To make drop scones, form about ¼ cup dough into patties, about ¾" thick. Set them on a baking sheet.

In a small bowl, mix the 1 tablespoon buttermilk with the reserved egg white. Brush the mixture onto the scones.

Bake the scones for 22–25 minutes or until golden brown. Remove from oven and cool about 5 minutes before serving.

Baker's note: *Leftover scones keep well at room temp for a couple of days and in the refrigerator for up to 5 days. You may freeze them, wrapped individually, before baking. You may also freeze baked goods and then wrap in foil to reheat at 200 degrees F for about 15 minutes.*

From Courtney:

This is my nana's recipe, one she tweaked from an old baking cookbook. She could never remember the name of the cookbook, since she copied all the recipes that she liked onto 3 x 5 cards and then donated the cookbooks to libraries or church bazaars. It's one of my favorite muffins. Warm, savory, soothing. For Yvanna's family's sake, I made a batch gluten-free, and they turned out just as tasty.

Raisin–Rosemary Muffins

(Yield: 10–12)

¾ cup milk
½ cup golden raisins
1 teaspoon dried rosemary leaves
¼ cup butter, diced
1½ cups flour
½ cup granulated sugar
2 teaspoons baking powder
¼ teaspoon salt
1 large egg
2 tablespoons sugar, for sprinkling

In a small saucepan, simmer the milk, raisins, and rosemary for 2 minutes. Remove from the heat and add the diced butter. Stir until melted. Let the mixture cool. If desired, you can set the saucepan on a bed of ice water in a bowl.

Meanwhile, heat the oven to 350 degrees F and fill muffin pans with cupcake liners. I like to spray the liners with nonstick grease for ease of peeling.

In a large bowl, mix flour, sugar, baking powder, and salt.

Whisk the egg into the cooled milk mixture and then pour over dry ingredients and stir until flour mixture is moist.

Scoop batter into the muffin cups. Sprinkle with extra sugar.

Bake 18–20 minutes or until browned and a toothpick comes out clean in the center. Remove immediately from pan and serve warm. These may be cooled and wrapped in saran and stored. Warm at fifty percent capacity in microwave for 12–15 seconds.

Raisin–Rosemary Muffins

Gluten–free Version

(Yield: 10–12)

¾ cup milk
½ cup golden raisins
1 teaspoon dried rosemary leaves
¼ cup butter, diced
1½ cups gluten-free flour
¼ teaspoon xanthan gum
1 tablespoon whey powder
½ cup granulated sugar
2 teaspoons baking powder
¼ teaspoon salt
1 large egg
2 tablespoons sugar, for sprinkling

In a small saucepan, simmer the milk, raisins, and rosemary for 2 minutes. Remove from the heat and add the diced butter. Stir until melted. Let the mixture cool. If desired, you can set the saucepan on a bed of ice water in a bowl.

Meanwhile, heat the oven to 350 degrees F and fill muffin pans with cupcake liners. I like to spray the liners with nonstick grease for ease of peeling.

In a large bowl, mix gluten-free flour, xanthan gum, whey powder, sugar, baking powder, and salt.

Whisk the egg into the cooled milk mixture and then pour over dry ingredients and stir until flour mixture is moist.

Scoop batter into the muffin cups. Sprinkle with extra sugar.

Bake 18–20 minutes or until browned and a toothpick comes out clean in the center. Remove immediately from pan and serve warm. These may be cooled and wrapped in saran and stored. Warm at fifty percent capacity in microwave for 12–15 seconds.

Visit our website at
KensingtonBooks.com
to sign up for our newsletters, read
more from your favorite authors, see
books by series, view reading group
guides, and more!

BOOK // CLUB
BETWEEN THE CHAPTERS

Become a Part of Our
Between the Chapters Book Club
Community and Join the Conversation

Betweenthechapters.net